undiscovered

ashley anglin

Undiscovered

Published by Shadow Spark Publishing
www.shadowsparkpub.com

Table of Contents

dotter   eva
av

amid the acrid ash of fathers dream
slight footprints eastward flaming sword behind
bearing the embers in a diamond vessel
she lights her way across an obscured threshold
to dominions undiscovered in plain sight

in a land of always day but never dawn
discerning light and shadow fiends and the monsters
who ensnare her with the subtlest smiling spell
how would it be if you came and had tea with me

beasts would tell secrets drawn by your trustful spark
trees bloom and dance for two worlds valiant child
desolate rock be melted new to flesh

by the deep magic in the truest love
as edens breath imbues
your ardent kiss

-   v north, *uncharted*

Chapter 1

Cabo de la Vela

Four little spotted seals shadowed our hovercraft on approach to Aberdeen Beach. When we glided over the mast of a pretty sailboat lying fully submerged on her side, they left us to head down for a closer look. An uprooted kelp stipe passed unhurried as the reflected clouds between us. Amid its fronds a faded umbrella nestled inside-out near a soccer ball that had seen better days; my sight interpreted them as a pale hibiscus blossom and bud amid the clouds. For those few moments, I didn't know which way was up, which side of the water's surface was where I belonged. *Everything flows and nothing stays*, as Dad used to say.

I craned my neck, squinted to try to read the name cheerfully painted in looping white script on the vessel's bright blue hull. I made out *Nimue* as we passed her by.

There was no choice but to land on the beach, one more among many natural and human-made objects to wash up in the last few days. The pier had been too damaged to accommodate our craft or any others.

My brain drifted back to La Guajira, thirty-some hours ago, half a world away. Daydreaming about my own recurring dream.

For weeks before, as I'd slept, the whole world kept going underwater. Often, my alarm would go off before I reached the story's end, but it always started the same.

It began with a sound--like an earthquake slowed down, an eerie deep song possessing both a complex rhythmic structure and its own range of pitches, although I felt no shaking.

The sea came swiftly up to cover the unknown shoreline where I stood: not a wave, but a peaceful steady flooding that engulfed me in a matter of seconds. I didn't panic. Even in my dreams, I was the closest thing I knew to an amphibious human. I didn't ever kick to the surface or fight for breath.

Sharks swayed purposefully down urban streets transformed to seabed canyons, but they and I would always go about our respective business unconcerned. In the dreams, the necessary navigation signals came through without distortion to the communications ring around my wrist.

Down an alley between taller buildings there was a small stone house where I would find the swan queen's clutch of eggs, which I'd been tasked with retrieving. The old doorknob sometimes stuck at first, but I jiggled it and was able to push through. I made my way around the house without my feet ever touching the floor; I still didn't need to take a breath.

In a small white bedroom, bay window open and lace curtains fluttering in the current, I found myself surrounded by floating egg-shell fragments. There was just one intact egg, like pale green marble but much lighter for its size. It shivered as I took it between careful hands. A black cygnet soon emerged.

How long could she hold her breath? She fought with me, jabbing her tiny beak into my thumbs, as I cautiously caught her and flutter-kicked fast out of the little house.

At the surface I scanned the watery horizon, one hand shielding my eyes from the glare. Breaking waves stung against my face. I found my footing on an underwater crag and launched the baby bird with both cold-numbed hands, returning her to the ark before it could lift off.

But in La Guajira, when my dream ring pulsed, I pulled up the message in a language I couldn't understand. Where the hell was the ark that had been scheduled to meet us here?

And on waking, I found myself not in a cold-sweaty bedsheet tangle, but standing waist-deep a few dozen meters out from Cabo de la Vela. I was still in my street uniform and shoes, with no memory of losing normal consciousness or entering the surf.

Nor was this the time to seek an explanation. The increasingly urgent vibration of my real ring linked whatever I'd just experienced to a nightmare that only grew more terrible the longer I kept my eyes open. The day of wrath swept whole coastal suburbs of Edinburgh away, smashed the fishing industry to hell, slammed the River Ness inland at record high levels. Furious waves stormed right over eastern-lying islands in the tiny northern archipelagos of Orkney and Shetland, wrecking ports and runways, laying waste small but vital cities.

"'Because it is so unbelievable, the truth often escapes being known,'" came a voice in my mind's ear as I sat where I'd stumbled from the water, dazed and dripping on the hot sand.

"Ursula Le Guin," I sighed aloud a random guess.

"Heraclitus, Ardencita."

I shook my head and seemed to look up into his shallow-Pacific hazel eyes. "Whoever. And you should have been here for this," I told him.

But he just gave me a hint of smile and one of his little upward nods, and wasn't.

If he was really anywhere he could see me, I hoped he'd like knowing I answered the pulse right away, marking myself available for transfer. They'd need as much help as they could get.

I did stop in for an evaluation first, but neither the medic nor the psych found anything too far out of the ordinary. It had been just over a year, so the grief-coping side of things was still well within the expected range. (I decided not to bring up how reasonable it would be to the Indigenous people who considered this place sacred, a gateway to the afterlife. Perhaps a soul could take a year to swim the whole Caribbean from its final stop in Miami.) Moderate dehydration, common enough in this climate, and sleep deficit. Maybe cut back on the caffeine. I hid a laugh at that suggestion and got on a transport to Edinburgh.

They brought us up the coast to Aberdeen in a land-sea hover-craft to get a more accurate sense of the devastation. Like most others in the developed world, I'd researched and watched since it had happened, all the way here from Colombia, so I knew this wasn't even the worst of it. Further north, the tsunami had reached five meters. The flat wrong media-favorite word *unprecedented* was thrown around a lot. Still, I understood why people reached for such a term. Small fishing villages populated by anonymous brown people, not first-world cities, were expected to be where giant waves might smash people's life work to matchsticks.

"Ahmad," a firmly polite tenor voice behind me interrupted my reverie.

Banh, the site lead, met my startled eyes with his salt-and-pepper head tilted to one side, curiosity ready to turn to irritation on a face younger than I would expect to go with that hair. Then again, few people remained in United Forces Environmental long enough to go really gray.

Everyone else had disembarked from our hovercraft while I was lost in thoughts of high-tech arks, swimming birds and flying eels, the Lady of the Lake having picked a hell of a time to wander this far from home. We were alone on the deck of the craft.

"I said, are you coming?"

"Yep. Sorry, sir," was a lot faster and more effective answer than launching into an explanation of my altered sleeping and waking consciousness since just before the tsunami had struck.

He was your typical emergency site lead, a marine engineer pressed into service as a manager. I might be sleep-deprived, my attention wandering, but that wasn't so unusual for me; Banh, though, was probably stressed as hell right now. No wonder if he forgot the tech available to help him with the people side of his job as well as with the science.

"Been a long couple days already," I agreed with his expression. Then I added, in case he was the rare person nowadays who didn't have a retinal implant, "But--I'm Araujo, sir." I glanced over the assembled group as we approached them, everyone else waiting on the beach like normal people. "Imani Ahmad is over there," I said, softer, indicating the woman whose uniform included the gray-edged white headscarf. We'd met on the ride up.

"Anyway," he said with a slight smile. "Got to hit the ground running here. Araujo. And people won't mess up your name if you don't disable your badge."

"Crap." I'd turned it off en route, not feeling like handling questions from a boatload of raw generalists ten years my junior, many of them without the social finesse gently-smiling Ahmad seemed to have.

They'd done a study a hundred or so years ago, before they went ahead with the Storegga oil and gas projects, but they hadn't taken into account how fast human greed would overcook the glaciers. The seafloor had warped under the rapidly increasing mass of water, destabilizing deposits near the rim of the Norwegian continental shelf (Storegga, the "great edge," to the locals); the massive resulting earthquake took a big new bite out of the continental shelf, sending the tsunami barreling over here. The really big one had come eight thousand years ago, before any of us were listening… and the one scientist who predicted we could cause another one ourselves had taken a lot of shit for it and no credit, until now.

So, no; I hadn't felt like explaining to a fresh bunch of kids in their first few years' service how I hadn't heard the same kind of bedtime stories from my only parent as they all probably remembered. Storegga and Doggerland, the Mid-Ocean Ridge and Cayman Trough, Mariana Trench and Rosalind Bank had been the faraway lands in my dad's fantastic tales; basalt and gabbro and peridotite were the buried treasures; and the Earth's own power to transform its shape, the first magic I'd ever learned to hold in awe.

"Sorry about that, sir." I reactivated my ident. "It's--a weird name to have at the moment."

"I guess." Banh smiled more fully. "Just--in the absence of a badge… Your coloring reminded me of a generalist I worked with last year. Egyptian." He stepped precisely down onto a firm patch of sand, with a light laugh directed at himself. "It made sense at the time. Long couple days, as you said."

"No worries."

As the clear, cold leading edge of the rising tide flowed around and over the toes of my boots, then Banh's, I considered what so often drew people to try to explain my appearance. No one had guessed right so far.

Despite nasty flooding and damage close to shore, the city center was in decent shape compared to footage I'd seen from further up the northeast coast and from Scotland's two scatterings of North Sea islands. People displaced from those disaster areas were sent here. In many cases, those seaside homes not swept away were uninhabitable. Scottish first responders had their hands more than full; that was where United Forces Environmental and Peacekeeping troops came in.

Keeping essentially a big homeless shelter running smoothly wasn't the most adventuresome assignment I'd ever had. My kind of work, even so. Every cup of tea, every freshly folded sheet helped a family or individual into whose eyes I could look as I listened to their delightfully accented questions, fears, and hopes. As bitterly as I'd disappointed my father when I dropped out of college for the last time, wouldn't he still have been proud to see me help UF rise to this occasion?

There was enough personnel to allow for reasonable shift lengths after an intense start, and home visits where it was feasible. So, as I settled into a routine of mostly morning shifts, I had some opportunity to explore the city's remaining western areas in the evenings.

About a week in, I traded with Imani so she could take care of some business over the grid with her family in Kuala Lumpur. It was a gray, misty day: I hardly minded the opportunity to sleep in until it was my turn to brew tea by the urn, stir giant pots of soup, and assemble endless sandwiches.

By this time, I'd learned a bunch of guests' names, especially the kids'. This evening, though, a new hover must have come in: I didn't recognize quite a few faces.

One evacuee in particular drew my concerned eyes, curled up alone at one end of the table with most of a sandwich going stale on her plate, mug of tea cradled in pale hands delicate as a doll's. It was hard to see the rest of her, enveloped in a gray hooded sweatshirt many sizes too large. She didn't look old enough to be here on her own.

I sat lightly opposite her, instead of at her side. She lifted oversized eyes, wide-set like mine and very dark in her breathtaking porcelain face, just for an instant. She wasn't a young child. A petite fourteen or fifteen, maybe.

"Hi," I said quietly. "I'm Arden."

"Hi," she barely more than whispered.

"I can look in the back for something else… We got fresh produce in today. I could do cheese and tomato?"

"Oh…" I glimpsed feathers of black hair at the big hood's edges as she shook her head, offering me the faintest smile.

"You here all by yourself?" I pressed cautiously.

She nodded. "I'll start for home in the morning."

I couldn't place her Scottish accent specifically. She had an unusual voice to match--low for a woman, let alone a young teenager, with a whispery quality even when she spoke aloud.

A hunch fluttered in my chest. Maybe the distinct accent meant English wasn't her first language. She'd hardly be the first off-grid refugee I'd encountered in this line of work.

Undocumented, they'd been called in the days when my great-grandmother had arrived that way in the US from conflict-ravaged Venezuela. Documents had been printed and carried with you and filed, back then. Belonging to society hadn't been as fully electronic, implanted, biometrically connected as it was now. So Amalia Quintana Sandoval melted into big-city life in Miami and captured the hearts of the successfully established Cuban-American family whose surname I bore now, and their oldest son's body and soul as well as his heart. Under their collective wing, she'd satisfied the powers that were and gained her legal citizenship.

In our time, the only way she'd survive in a big city was as a homeless person. So, more often than not, that wasn't where they hid anymore, migrating instead to the fringes of civilization. Barely-populated places like a tiny island way out in the North Sea. She would never have dreamed somewhere like that would betray her. None of us had believed it could.

"Can I help you contact anyone?" I offered, keeping my voice soothing. "Use my ring if you don't have one."

She shook her head again.

I tried one more time. "You can really get home by yourself?"

"Yes. Thanks." One tear splashed into her tea, another hit the tabletop. She sighed and wiped her face with elegant tapered fingertips.

"Well, we can give you a transportation voucher. Anywhere public transport is running, at least."

She nodded, brows like perfect strokes of calligraphy which I read as surprise or relief. "Really? I'd heard...." She shook her head. "Can anyone have one?"

"Anyone who comes through here."

Her soft sigh might have been gratitude or relief; her right hand still caught more tears. I hesitated before laying my own hand over her left, but the clash between hope and weary desperation almost emanated from her invisible pores. It was as if I could feel her heart pounding too fast to accord with her still, small exterior.

I chose my words as carefully as I knew how. "Home is somewhere safe?"

She slid her hand free as her wide liquid eyes finally met mine full-on and held them for a disquietingly long moment.

"No, I don't expect my home is safe," she said at last. "But I have a good place to go, where my sister and my family will be."

"How did you get separated?"

The faint hint of a smile she showed, instead of answering me, caught me further off guard. "You're a lot farther from home than I am. America?"

I nodded in turn.

"But someone in your family came from Scotland?"

I shook my head. "Ireland, back on my dad's dad's side," I said.

"Your hair," she agreed with a fleeting smile, which I returned.

Her eyes were so big, so dark, almost unblinking. I half wondered if they were dilated from some kind of chem. She seemed coherent, though. Just strange, and so full of anxious grief.

"Anyway," I fumbled. "If you're sure you're all right… I'll get that voucher."

"You're very kind," she said, as if that weren't a weirdly formal response for a kid in someone else's hoodie in a refugee shelter.

All I could do was smile and get the help I'd offered.

As the dining area emptied, I wiped down tables, stacked chairs, swiped a mop across the floor, reflected upon my misspent three and a half college semesters, felt grimy, craved a quick shower. I lay awake a long time after that, wondering and worrying about the tiny girl with the big black eyes.

I hadn't seen her reappear by the time the next morning's hot breakfast was done at nine, when the other three came looking for her.

They all resembled each other strongly enough I guessed I'd misheard her: sisters, not just one. These three were older, taller. They shared the same delicate beauty, pale skin, and wide dark eyes, but weren't as inhumanly exquisite as the one whose face had seared into my memory.

"Hi," I said. No; she'd been more formal. "Um. Good morning. How may I help you?"

The one who answered had a similar voice, too, low in volume and in pitch, with the odd accent and the perfect black eyebrows raised my way. "Transport vouchers, please."

So, the first girl had slipped out before dawn to let her friends know to come here.

By the time I came back from the little office area with the three biofiber chipcards, two of them were murmuring to one another; one kept looking over her shoulder at the door. The silent one hugged me in thanks for the chipcard I placed in her waiting palm, anxiety radiating from her small form as she trembled against me for that brief moment.

I had a sudden flash of understanding right before she let me go. "Maybe you'd like a ride somewhere?"

"Ach, could you really?" sighed the talking one, eyes huge with appreciation.

It wasn't a busy time of day, no trouble getting clearance to take them, and what would have been a long and probably scary walk was only a few minutes' drive. They wanted the NorthLink ferry to Kirk-wall, Orkney, the one that had brought them here during the evacuation. North? Yes, their spokesgirl assured me, soft voice a little uneven now; it was for the best, I shouldn't worry.

No one was in sight, and the pier gate was shut. I pressed the buzzer. A woman, late forties or early fifties, came to talk to me through the bars.

"Is that the other three for Kirkwall?"

"Yes. I guess that means the fourth girl is here already?"

She nodded. "I set her up in a cabin. Fast asleep when I looked back in on her, poor dear."

"I couldn't seem to find an updated schedule on-grid, so I didn't know..."

She shrugged and gave me a little smile, sun-rays creasing the freckled skin around her eyes. She looked like the kind of mom who'd send care packages to someone else's kid. "We've had not one passenger northbound since the tsunami. I'll just take them."

"Have you had any more southbound?"

She shook her head. "Half those islanders won't have heeded the evacuation order, if I know them at all."

I found myself smiling. "I guess you do?"

"Dad grew up in Baltasound, about as far north as Scotland goes."

"Anything left up there?" I asked, softer. I'd read that several of the northernmost islands had been all but swept clean of civilization.

She smiled in answer. "Well, he's been here with me and mine for some years now, so I didn't have to worry more than the ordinary. But they're actually the odd village to have got through it all right. Because the sound is sheltered by Balta Isle, he says. Whether he's right or not, I've learned not to argue."

"I guess they grow those dads at all different latitudes."

She laughed briefly. "I've no doubt. Well, speaking of those who don't take no for an answer... I'm told these young ladies are in a bit of a hurry to be off."

"Thanks for going out of your way for them."

"I've got daughters that age," she said softly. "I'd hope someone would do the same for them."

She pushed the gate open just far enough to let them through, then let it click shut again, scanning their vouchers there. I bit my lip instead of asking, but the first girl had pretty clearly told this woman more than she'd felt ready to reveal to me.

"Here," I said instead. "Hold one of those cards back up for me?"

With gate bars between us, I could still bring my ring close enough to share my ident to the chipcard the little spokesgirl offered. "If you need anything else, you can still get in touch with me."

You're very kind, her huge dark eyes seemed to say.

I waited until the white boat was well away from the dock, until the sight and sound of the surf began to calm my inexplicably jangled nerves, until my ring pulsed. Chen, hoping I was on my way. I reluctantly turned my back to the North Sea and headed to work.

Lunch prep, service, and piles of dishes later, with more wiping and mopping in the afternoon forecast, Abdullah's sharp "Ah, son of a--" interrupted my sink-side reverie. It was the closest I'd ever heard him come to swearing.

Ever eager to shed the sanitary gloves that irritated the hell out of me, I'd been on dish duty again. I rubbed the back of my wrist over the bridge of my nose. "What's going on?"

I couldn't see what he was staring at, direct from the grid through his retinal circuit. He blinked, taking in my perplexed face simultaneously.

"Hyenas," he told me.

My heart sank sharply, as if shrinking from my eyes accessing the same bad news as Abdullah. I didn't go on-grid to confirm it.

Chen sighed. "Of course they'd move in here. All up and down this coast, probably."

Imani, still in her first six months with UFE, glanced in consternation from face to face. "Hyenas? In Scotland?"

Abdullah smiled slightly. "Sorry. Not literal ones. The human kind that move in after disasters like this. They were operating a fake shelter… telling evacuees without documentation they could avoid the authorities there. They'd set up camp beds and everything in freaking shipping containers. Ready to go. Like, walking distance from here."

The inexpensive aluminum pan slipped from my hands, splashing dishwater as it dented against the tile floor.

"Damn," Imani said. "But they arrested them, I hope? The – human traffickers?"

"Three men under arrest, this says. But no one with much of a prior history, which means the key players probably weren't there."

"Now? Of course they weren't," Chen said. "And yeah, the ones pulling the strings do it remotely most of the time, right?"

"Who'd choose to be here?" Imani agreed. "Other than us, I mean."

"Hijodeputa," I muttered, picking the pot up and slamming it back into the sink. It wouldn't be on the grid, not that I'd ever had their names anyway, but I knew. Running from an unimaginable flood and its aftermath, this was the kind of sanctuary those beautiful girls had found.

It was probably only good for recycling at this point; I still scrubbed the pan as if in doing so, I could get the stain of my own human race off me. I would have shed my skin entirely if I could. Hopefully, it looked like I'd just splashed soapy water in my eye.

Chapter 2

Nola and Venice

I pushed through, then bundled up and took myself far enough away into the unspoiled nature of my favorite little quiet spot in town, Johnston Gardens, to get these thoughts out of my head for an hour or two.

I didn't see funny old Mr. McKerrow, usually quick to offer a wrapped toffee from his coat pocket whenever I spotted him with his wheelbarrow and tools. He was always busy preparing for the coming season of showy blossoms, as if east of here nothing was wrong at all. I looked forward to flowers, longer and brighter days.

I was standing on my favorite bridge with the bright blue railings, lost in memories of Armstrong Park and the Grand Canal, when my ring pulsed. I watched water flowing from under my feet for a few moments, not eager to be drawn back into work. When I finally activated to look at the caller's ident, though, a much-needed grin lightened my face.

"As I live and breathe. Vega Hazan Chocolate Caliente Ramos, MD."

"Hey, mi cafecito con leche. Thought you were gonna ignore me."

I laughed. "Nah, just standing here with my mind wandering. You know." She laughed too. "So where are you these days?" I asked, though the tech could tell me just as easily.

"Close to you, if your locator is right. Shetland Islands."

"Wow. Like the epicenter. How bad?"

She sighed shortly. "Scary. I mean, besides the obvious. Already shifting staff around like crazy people… Because who'd listen to someone who looks like me, telling them from the start they had too many docs and not enough engineers, plenty of peacekeeping when there's basically zero need for that here, and practically no generalists, why?"

"Because we're here making sandwiches and handing out transport vouchers, regardless of our demonstrated skillset?"

"Of course. And now that I can ask for more generalists... Well, you know I don't do well with your run-of-the-mill kids."

"If that's code for you being picky as hell, then yeah."

She laughed. "Yeah. Así que I thought I'd see if you feel like transferring. They're anticipating your typical four-to-six month, unless they extend, which Lord only knows. I'm at intermediate administrator for this assignment, so I have the actual magical powers to transport you here."

"Wow. Do you get a gray and white wand for that?"

"Nah. Just have to wave my fingers así... Is it working?"

"If generalist up there means more than waitress and housekeeping." Zero need for UFPKs, I didn't add aloud, sounded pretty good, too.

"Putting your name in as we speak, then." I heard the smile warming her melodious low voice. "We'll see what they say. Watch for a notification, hopefully."

"Well, thanks for thinking of me, fairy madrina."

"I think of you a lot," she answered, still smiling.

"Me too. It's been… wow, year and a half? No me digas…"

The way everyone usually moved around, that gap had been longer than the average UF friendship. For Vega and me to have kept up for a decade, let alone shared assignments whenever we could, was a lovely anomaly.

"Overdue for a visit," she agreed. "So yeah, come on up. No power, no trees, I'll show ya a good time." She laughed again. "One thing we do have though, even if it's only going to be about eighty of us here, is some fine scenery. UFE, plus these local fellas with that rrrolled Rrr that'll currrrl your toes…"

"Since when do we need someone to roll our Rs for us?" I laughed.

So did she. "Ah, cafecito, trust me."

"Okay." Not that I was looking to meet anyone, UF or otherwise, if we were honest, but it was always entertaining to watch Vega look. "I hope it works out."

"Me, too, mija. I'll be optimistic and say, see you soon."

Most transfers had come from other assignments, not already in Scotland. Pretty much everyone except me had banded together in Edinburgh on the small plane that picked me up.

It was about an hour hop to the Shetland Islands, with patchy storm clouds that felt like dirt road most of the way. We came through into a sunny break in the weather, though, close to landing. I craned my neck for as much of the view as I could manage. I'd found in myself such a visceral love, over the years, for places like this--where time and human history hadn't so radically changed the landscape.

Before this year they hadn't, at least. I knew the view wasn't so uplifting over on the east coast, but we were approaching the west mainland, close to the UF central base set up in Scalloway. Vega, true to form, had been too concerned with the attractive guys to say how strikingly beautiful the place itself was: windswept landscape and pure seawater rivaling each other for shades of emerald, glittering lochs, waves dashing themselves to foam against incredible cliffs and coves and stacks. We flew over a pod of seals or otters, each dark head leaving a tiny v-shaped wake as they made their way home before the early dusk.

"So you buzzed your entire mane and still look as great as ever," I greeted Vega as we flung our arms around each other on the runway. "Fine."

She smiled as I reached way up to run an admiring finger over the few naturally textured millimeters. "Yeah, no way I was keeping up all that in the darkest Cajun swamplands. Jamie thinks it makes me less intimidating. Although up here in the Arctic tundra, I'll probably let it grow." She laughed. "What was it you said when you did it?"

I had to laugh, too. "Wow, that must've been about two minutes after just-out-of-college me met just-out-of-med-school you. 'I define my own beauty. Eff the patriarchy.'"

"Yeah." She held up her first and fourth fingers in a rockstar salute. "Or words to the effect of those letters. Eff all those guys. Meantime…" She tugged my heavy braid. "Like you're having your dates climb all this to pick you up, these days."

"Yep. Don't tell my mom. You know how weirdly jealous she gets."

She laughed lightly. "So there are dates?"

"I just landed. Even you don't work that fast."

She gave me a little sideways head slide, eyes bright. I laughed, too, glad she hadn't changed much more than her hairstyle.

"Speaking of… for meals here, it's like in Nola and Venice. You can go to our sometimes aptly-named mess or you can trade for credit points to bolster the local economy."

"Nice. I'll remember that one grilled vegetable pizza on my death bed. But can anything here even be open?"

She nodded. "Basically just this one pub right now, here in town anyway. They're running on wind/bio generators and whatever supplies we can get to them, but they're happy to have us. I'm actually meeting some people there in a few, assuming you're hungry…"

She checked me in herself, a few simple gestures of her ring hand. I wouldn't report for work until morning.

"Nice ring," I said, belatedly noticing the stylish device around her wrist. Mine was the type I usually went for: an inexpensive, flexible skin-tone polymer band, easy to replace. The underlying tech and bio-connections were the same, but Vega's was encased in a close-fitting gold bangle with an interesting faceted texture, lovely against her dark complexion.

"Thanks," she said. "Present to myself when I hit ten years, last August."

"Wow, spec admin lady. I recall treating us both to an extra scoop of gelato for mine."

"Moment of silence for that beautiful gelateria." Her smile altered. "Yeah. The other one was for free. Went year to year instead of biting off a whole nother ten, promising I'm doing this until I'm forty-five."

"Of course," I murmured. "Good for you."

She held her elegant ring against the ignition plate, firing up her assigned two-seater amphibious hover. The aging power grid was knocked out of commission for a while, she told me. But wind and waves never really stopped, so it was easy to recharge every night when she brought the craft back to our ad hoc power station in Scalloway. She took me a few kilometers down the road to a little inn where twenty or so of us would stay, tourism being obviously disrupted as hell. I'd room with her, like old times.

"So how's everybody?" I asked. It had been a while, but for years we'd had a good thing going where the abundant Hazan clan were my primary East Coast family; Dad had been Vega's West Coast family as well.

"Good. Joaquín finally got his butt the rest of the way out of school, so Dad's threatening to retire now."

"If I ever get five crazy kids through college, I will not only re-tire on the spot, I'll buy champagne for the neighborhood." I laughed. "That man is an American hero."

So did she. "Not that he would even know how to open it. I doubt he's ever bought a bottle of champagne in his life."

"Unlike some people's dads. Anyway. That's great."

"Sorry," she said, softer. "Arden. Sorry."

I shook my head. "Thanks. It's fine. And sorry I missed raising a cervecita to Nelson Jr and Jamie. Nice capture of you singing 'At Last' during the reception, by the way. So fitting."

She chuckled. "It's okay, half the population of the Caribbean was there. They just told me a few days ago she's having another baby, actually."

"That'll make three, huh? Still no ticking at all, yourself?" I couldn't resist.

"Ye gods, no." She wagged a finger at me. "You're over thirty now, too--Get ready for the patriarchy to expect you to do your part."

"I mean, they can try, but…"

"And FYI. Sometimes the matriarchy's even worse."

I laughed. "Well, then eff them, too."

I quickly stashed my duffel, then we headed down a long gradual hill from where we'd be staying. Too close to the water, although the erosion, building damage, and debris washing up here on the west coast was minimal compared to what I knew I would encounter the next day. The painted sign outside the pub showed a well-fed and sleepy bunch of seals, hauled out on a sunny rock.

"Ooh, jackpot. Caperucita Con Leche," she said in my ear as we settled into our booth and she got a look around. "Meet the Big Bad Wolves of the Shetland Isles. A bunch of 'em already at one table."

"Ugh," I whispered back. "How are there even wolves in a place with basically no trees?"

She chuckled, low in her throat. "Invasive species."

"Well, I'll bring them some cookies another day, ma… Tonight, can we just eat?"

"Fine… Abuelita."

"Oh," the pub server said moments later, pausing in her bustling. Our platter landed with a couple of uneven thumps, jostling a few chips onto the polished tabletop.

I glanced up mid-sip to find her getting a good look at my face, rather than just glimpses from the side. She'd probably expected freckled fair skin to go with the auburn hair, not the color of the milky coffee Vega had nicknamed me for. People looked all kinds of ways where I'd come from. Less so, here on the fringe of Scotland. To compound the challenge, I wasn't sure if she realized she wasn't speaking standard English.

I answered with just a diplomatic smile and drawn-together brows.

She looked upwards of seventy, even shorter than me and quite a bit rounder, her face spattered with freckles liberally enough to make me think her faded hair was once as bright as mine. Her sparkling eyes were wonderful, the same clear blue-green of the Shetland coastline as I'd seen it on landing a few hours earlier. I'd have loved to understand what lit them up with such intensity.

"'Tis nothing," she answered, with a belated smile and one light brow lifting in what could as well have been curiosity as mischief. "An old saying when folk round here would see a lovely lass like you, is all. Do enjoy your tea." And off she bustled.

"Uh. Did you get any of that first part?"

Vega laughed. "Something about silk? Silken?" With a low giggle, she brushed a few fingertips up and down my cheek. I scoffed and bit into the scalding chip.

The blue-eyed lady stepped behind the bar around the same time I came to get the next round. The aproned little old man already busy there didn't pause in his work, but it was sweet the way his glance flickered up to her face. When she came to stand in front of me, I noticed a plain gold wedding band on the hand she'd put lightly on the back of his waist as she passed behind him.

She gave me a conspiratorial wink as she scanned my ring. I gleaned from whatever she said that she knew a bonny single Scottish lad, if I ever wanted to meet him instead of the UFE men surrounding us. Her pretty eyes lifted to something or someone behind me, and her smile turned a hint wry.

I hadn't really paid attention to the table full of boys Vega had indicated, but this tall, stunning guy's highly focused blue-gray eyes with amber centers were lupine enough.

"Your hands are so small," he murmured, so low and so close I could practically feel the individual vibrations of his voice. "Let me get one of these for you."

I turned around on the barstool, hoping he'd back up a step, but as long as his arms were, he could do so keeping his hand where it was.

"Anton Krol." I didn't pay close attention to the virtual badge he highlighted for me, but the blue bar indicating his rank, Specialist Administrator (Engineering), came as little surprise. "Are you even old enough for a man to buy you a drink, at home, Arden?"

I likely had five years on the oldest male colleague I'd noticed here tonight. Generalists, at least. I sighed.

"Okay, okay. But what big eyes you have, Little Red." He smiled down at me. So that little joke wasn't just between Vega and me. Maybe she'd shown him photos.

"The better to spot trouble," I answered under my breath.

"We've gotten off on the wrong foot," he said softly. "Words get in the way sometimes."

I laughed. "The wrong words, especially."

He rewarded me with a practiced little smile. "Little Red, that's the wrong story. You're some kind of *berehynia*..."

I sipped from one of the glasses. "Okay, which is?"

"Like a chimera goddess… Shapeshifter with protective and generative powers…" The smile tilted. (What big teeth you have.) "Though I must say, no statue or monument prepared me for your mythical ass."

"Charming." *Mythical ass* was right. I took Vega's glass back from him, sloshed it down in front of her.

"Luring them was always the part you're good at," she chided. "I see we still gotta teach you the benefits of catch and release. At least say there's been anyone since that little ausshole Samir way back in Perth, Caperucita."

I rolled my eyes away from hers.

Even as she shook her head, her own eyes wandered the menu options on display, sitting and standing around the room; her thick sleek brows lifted elegantly in suggestion. I shrugged. "Eff all those guys" certainly had gotten lost in translation.

Not more than half an hour later, I left her at a different table with Anton and a couple other beautiful men in gray.

"You want to take the hover?" she called.

"Nah, no worries." I kept walking. Even if pulling up a map on the grid weren't as easy as blinking, it was just the one little street.

My feet took me to the water's edge, though, not up the road yet. On an empty little dock, still littered with kelp, wrack, and sand, I slipped my boots and socks off. With my toes in the very cold water, I watched another seal family making their way home for the evening, dark heads bobbing against the last brightness reflecting off the water. It was like a page out of a favorite childhood storybook (definitely not Caperucita Roja). I stayed past nightfall, lulled by the slow music of the waves.

Chapter 3

Finges of Civilization

When my ring pulsed in the morning, displaying my assignment for the day, Vega's eyes opened too--blurry from a much later night than mine.

"Ya tú sabes que I don't want to hear about where you were hasta las 0230…"

She shook her head, half-smiling, as we looked together at the display.

"Wow. I thought I'd snap you up… but your file, or the rest of you, caught someone's eye already. Right into the frying pan. Wait." She laid her head back on the pillow. "Whatever. I'll buy you the cervecita you'll want tonight, mija. See you then."

At the drizzly, cold appointed time, a twenty-seater amphibious craft awaited an assembling group in gray and white. A no-nonsense Shetland police officer whose badge read Fenella Haye directed a mix of generalists, environmental engineers, and a marine bio badge. And the youngest of Vega's friends from last evening, with gorgeous skin like a black calla lily. I hadn't realized Vega was hanging out with a generalist like myself. Her fellow specs were more her usual crowd. Then again, this one was awfully pretty.

"Stéphane Mbala," I read his badge. "Hi. I'm Arden. We--didn't quite meet last night."

"Yeah." His very white smile was genuine. "Or you'd know it's Stefek around here, at least if you ask Anton."

I shrugged, bemused.

"Like, Polish for Steve…"

"Okay. Well, hi, Stefek. As they call you back in the motherland."

"Nah, I guess they mostly just say Steph in Bertoua…"

"Cameroon? Cool. Did Vega tell you my first UFE assignment was up the road in Ivory Coast? We met there."

I looked at my hand on the seat armrest, remembering one of the greatest thrills of my career. In the course of preservation work, our team had identified a previously uncatalogued species of galaxy-eyed brownish tree frogs small enough to perch on a fingertip. A bio spec unofficially named them after me, because of the eyes and how they didn't shy away from my careful touch.

They were later determined to be near critically endangered status, but we'd managed to help the little guys stay on the map. What kept me up at night for years after was the undiscovered places, crea- tures, plants, gone before we ever saw them. Cures meant for us to find, burned to ash in the former rainforest without saving a single life. Marine flora or fauna with something to teach us, but we poisoned it before seeing its face or giving it a name.

"She did mention something. How you feel more at home in fine Scottish weather like this. Some kind of tropical flower you are," he retorted, in a good enough approximation of Vega's Bronx snark to provoke my genuine laugh.

Same crap she'd given my dad. From the earliest days, he'd bonded with my more socially and professionally ambitious, taller, browner, Latina-er friend more easily than with me. She'd never be-lieved a caribeño miamense could feel so drawn to work up here in the cold and dark. But she knew perfectly well that I was a hardy hybrid blossom, more of my DNA originating in this part of the world than anywhere else.

I scrounged for the right words. "So few places around the world feel this way. Untouched? Primal?... How the air tastes here."

"Not so high on the communications composite score, huh?" Stéphane teased, not unkindly.

Ah, the classic new recruit rite of passage. That made me feel old. Still, I projected my file for him. "Nah," I said. "I can mostly han-dle English on a good day, decent Spanish but not like Vega's. I kind of got by in Italy with it, too, though. Ish-talian, she called whatever I was speaking. Oh, and random bits of Norwegian I studied, getting ready for a semester abroad I never ended up doing."

"Coming from a country with over two hundred indigenous lan-guages, you know, I wanted linguist track," he acknowledged without rancor, "but they've started me at generalist, so... What's this?" He zoomed back to a cluster of scores separate from the communications series. "You crushed me here."

"Sensory memory. Whatever that means." I remembered the static-adhering electrodes and the test requirements, which had seemed absurdly easy and led to my extreme outlier ninety-ninth percentile score. Something to do with picking skills up quickly, or creative prob-lem-solving... The med tech had laughingly told me high scorers on this one tended to have outlandish dreams. When I'd said that certain-ly held true for me, he'd managed a sly sleep-study suggestion clever enough I might have taken it if I hadn't believed I'd been spoken for at the time.

Stefek scrolled on. "Ah. You're well ahead on the diplomacy composite, too. Looks like the down spike on introversion throws the rest off for me."

I was glad to encourage such an affable young newcomer. "Prob-ably tick up when you retest at eighteen months. After your short-term skill acquisition and problem solving, that ability to connect is the other hallmark of a generalist who shouldn't end up as just an engineering mech."

Stefek nodded. "So when the aliens land, we'll make first contact."

"Darn right."

"People don't realize it's a serious responsibility."

"You with the serious language skills, most of all." I smiled.

Alien invaders hadn't wrought the destruction of the harbor town where we arrived shortly, though. In retaliation against the abuse our own kind heaped upon her, it was Mother Nature who'd outdone her sometimes brutally bitchy self, smashing dozens of structures along the east Shetland coast to sea-borne splinters, leaving behind broken concrete draped in kelp.

The island capital of Lerwick wasn't even in the worst position, sheltered by Bressay isle just to its east. But the city, built right down to the shoreline, had been home to about a third of the islands' twentyish thousand residents, not all of whom heeded the unheard-of tsunami warnings and made it safely to higher ground. Even without a direct hit from the apocalyptic wall of water that had wrecked places to the north and south, extreme surge and rip tides together had been deadly efficient.

UFE's work here, primarily removing the rubble to waiting barges, had gone on for days before my arrival. We were well past the urgency of search and rescue. North of today's site was an area already cleared down to foundations and broken asphalt.

I recognized the craft anchored up there: UFE marine engineer divers. I'd been rejected as a candidate to train with them the last four years running. I was more than qualified as far as diving, less so regarding college grades or training certifications. It hadn't stopped me from trying this year, too, although I wouldn't likely hear back for another month.

I'd applied for reef preservation and coastal rewilding, aimed at letting places like this go gracefully when we could afford to give them back to the planet. That they'd brought the engineering side in here meant the goal was to rebuild. Both programs trained at the same center in Miami. It looked like they were investigating the remaining structure of a partially demolished ferry terminal. I didn't hold out much hope they'd salvage it.

Stefek got a shift working one of the big movers. I volunteered to join the marine biologist, collecting wildlife in clear seawater pooled shallowly on a raft so she could relocate them later. It meant plenty of walking around to see what the movers had sorted from among the wreckage, and bringing them back to her. Yes, it might be a dumb little bureaucratic task. But this ecosystem, not just the city which relied on it, could use any help we'd give toward healing and rebuilding.

"Wow," she said, taking an orange sea star from my bucket in a gentle gloved hand. "Far from home and wondering what the hell happened to you, huh." Her English was nearly too precise, making me think of other cold countries bordering the North Sea.

Her raft held a few other stars, anemones, a whelk that had managed to survive the crazy journey here, some bivalves, a dark-colored lobster. I was about to make a mildly inappropriate lunch-related remark when her ring pulsed.

"Another seal," she said matter-of-factly. "Poor guys, of course they don't get it. Help me out?"

I nodded, belatedly reading her badge--Engel--as we made our way up the shore. One of the big movers had stopped halfway through a debris layer, out into shallow water.

It was Stefek who had sent up the alert; a juvenile gray seal refusing to get out of the mover's way. He'd shut the motor down, waiting for our assistance.

"Hey, girl," Engel greeted her in a soothing tone. The seal vocalized urgent squeaks and barks as Engel tried to coax her aside. She dipped her snout and one flipper insistently between some smashed planks painted barn red on one side, and what looked like a disembodied sailboat spar. My brain wandered for half a second back to *Nimue*. The sea moved quietly back and forth through the gap.

"Please say it's not mommy down there," I murmured.

Engel reached a gauntleted hand toward the seal, who snapped defensively.

"Scheisse." Engel sighed, reaching into her tool belt to set up a tranquilizer. "I don't like doing this, but when they're so worked up… We won't knock her out. Just take the edge off."

The seal whined higher in agitation. Her wide dark eyes locked onto mine, shiny teardrop shapes with their points at the inner corners. She got quiet as the two of us watched each other. She wriggled cautiously, deliberately away from Engel, close enough for me to touch.

"All right, little miss," I said as I knelt to her level, daring to lay a hand on her panting flank. She snorted softly at me, but didn't fight. "Show us what it is."

She turned back to the gap she'd been guarding, thrusting her nose down into the water.

Engel raised her light brows at me. "Normally I'd say hands off, but… apparently you've logged significant marine bio time yourself, hmm."

I stroked the seal's pelt a few times. She whined and laid her head on one of the red planks.

The truth was, I'd never had the grades for anyone's marine bio program, either. "Where I grew up, there was a great marine aquarium. I volunteered there a lot as a kid," I said instead: addressing Engel, but my gentle coaxing tone was the part the seal would understand.

"Okay, pretty girl," I added, with a little rub of the seal's head.

Some smaller pieces we could lift out of the way: splintered wood, kelp leaves, a disintegrating biofiber cup. Below that was clear water, with dark feathery seagrass waving through. Slight silver lining, if the port's impact was low enough for that to grow here. The fronds swirled away from my fingers as I tried to move them aside.

"Shit," I whispered, starting back a little.

It wasn't finding a person, instead of the sadly expected seal carcass, that caught me off guard. The UF Peacekeepers' forensics team had been alerted a couple times already that morning, although not close to where I was; unfortunately, it came with this kind of work, on whose front lines I'd spent a decade. As soon as I recognized the long black hair--not seagrass--and saw the blindly staring, wide-set black eyes of the drowned kid just below, the worst sick ache gripped the pit of my stomach.

I didn't try to find words, just touched my ring to send another alert. Engel, her angular face newly sober, reluctantly administered her low-level tranquilizer to the seal. We needed to get her out of the way for the smaller mover equipment and a diver who came to assist.

"We'll go for a ride up to a nice quiet beach and let you sleep it off, little one," Engel murmured as we got her onto one of the hover platforms that doubled as stretchers here. "You did a good job for your buddy, okay?"

Stefek, ashen face echoing the dead child's skim-milk pallor, climbed drunkenly down out of the mover once he'd backed it to a safe distance, and just watched us work. No one, least of all me, gave him a hard time. There had been a first one, or a first few, for each of us in our day; and the young ones were always the worst.

I still couldn't help breathing half a sigh of relief when it became clear that at least this wasn't a girl I'd put on the ferry to Kirkwall. The diver got in underneath, freeing the body without further damage: a small, slender young man, without a scrap of clothing or even a ring on him. I could think of no immediate reason why he'd been naked in the North Sea in March... maybe he'd tried to cast off garments weighing him down in the angry water where he suddenly found himself. Or, hell, maybe he'd had the awful luck to step into the shower of his beach cottage right before the alarm went out. It wasn't as though there had been any normal kind of logic to this.

He'd been cocooned in a pocket between enough packed-to-gether debris to keep the fish and crabs away, and the water was cold enough to have kept him almost as beautiful as he had clearly been in life. I laid my jacket over his lower body until the forensics team could finish where they were and come to us.

Since there was no ring, I tried scanning his fingertips to match him to idents on file, but the prints were illegible. They would have more sophisticated tools to use at the morgue. I fought the desire to close his eyes, now reflecting the sky's brightness like glass, before forensics could get here. I contented myself instead with stroking the fine, thick hair off his forehead and down around his wiry shoulders.

"Thanks, generalist," someone said softly at my shoulder. "We'll take care of him."

I hadn't noticed the tears flooding my face until then, but I didn't hide them as I stood up and moved back to let the PKs do their part. One of them handed me up my jacket, after laying a blue drape in its place.

I stayed a few respectful moments, long enough to watch them close his eyes. I didn't know why I so needed to see him more at rest, but the sharp stitch under my breastbone came loose, freeing me to breathe a little easier.

I looked around for Stefek. He still stood by the mover, hand on the ladder for when the all-clear came, though as shaken as before. Without fully wiping my own tears away, I put my arms around him.

"Was that the first…"

"Double digits, by now." I heard his hard swallow. "It doesn't get better, though."

I patted his back. "I think that just makes you a good human being, Stevie."

The forensics team moved past with the drowned boy on another stretcher, signaling Stefek back to work. He gave one more unsteady sigh.

"I could drive if you'd rather." I gestured toward the mover. "Swap jobs. They don't usually mind, as long as everything gets done."

"Thanks."

Engel approved the trade, just giving me a sober wave as I got up into the mover. Stefek didn't want me to buy him dinner after our shift. He sat back in his seat on the hover, arms folded, eyes closed. I touched his hand in solidarity, then left him alone. Time to myself was the last thing I wanted, though. I rang Vega and agreed to join her for the end of her own workday rather than have to sit quiet with my thoughts somewhere.

She met the big hover in her two-seater before we were back to Scalloway, and immediately offered me a cinnamon almond protein bar, which she knew was the only kind I found worth eating. There were cases of them in the back, along with packs of other shelf-stable food, household items, water purifying filters, and similar supplies.

"Since the first few days, it's just this little trickle of people coming to the relief centers," she explained with a shake of her head. "So a few of us started going out on rounds instead."

"Best practices, baby. We did in Aberdeen, too."

"Can't accuse them of not being tenacious, up here. Day before yesterday I had to re-break this old granddaddy's broken arm to set it properly. Lost his footing in floodwater. He knew it was broken, but didn't want to leave his wife, who's ninety-one." She laughed shortly. "Learned some fine new Scottish profanity at that place."

"I bet," I said through a mouthful of nutrition bar.

"Still," she said, softer. "I'll take the messiest life stuff over a beautiful dead kid on your first day."

I raised the remaining piece of the bar. "Hear, hear."

"How was young Esteban with that?"

I took a sip from the water bottle clipped to my belt. "Honestly, he's a nice kid, but… maybe too nice to be a good fit."

She nodded as if she'd expected my answer. "I was thinking I'd talk to Anton and Raj about pulling him more onto straight engineering instead of the field mech thing. Poor kid."

I nodded, too. "Good."

"Hey, you gotta at least do that brujería of yours where you make the specs think it was their idea, though. Switching up assignments like you did for him today."

"Ma." I sighed. "I've been in longer than any of these specs. Long enough to know no one cares who drives the big mover."

"I know, mija, but then you end up with another little squirrel on fire flag in your file."

Ardencita ardilla ardiente, one of Dad's childhood names for me. I didn't mind it so much, coming from her. When he'd said it, the endearment had been a pretty thin veil for his frustration with my tendency to focus best on any tree or cloud or water outside the classroom window; later, my constantly renewed interest in trying the next thing without perfecting the current thing. I'd never fully convinced him I'd made it into an advantage in the end, picking my UFE track.

"Ugh," I answered Vega. "Anyway, I did get a spec to sign off. It was a girl, though."

"Ugh… Okay."

Hover technology had taken over these and many other small islands during the time of Dad's childhood, obviating most car-ferry routes and many regional flights. The transformation was so effective that in places like this--outside the main cities and highways--often there weren't even actual streets anymore. Nature had quickly taken back what were once dirt or gravel roads and lanes. As we delivered water filters, soap, and MREs, we could follow the way indicated on-grid visuals, leaving almost no trace.

The last house on Vega's list was close to the water but set high enough, on a westward-facing little cliff, to have avoided damage. Firelight flickered through the big rear windows. Someone had cleaned off the pier where we moored the hover, carefully raked the ground, and swept the steps carved into the bluff, up to the house. There were no kelp leaves or driftwood or any of the sadder debris objects we'd gotten used to seeing. I wondered at them taking the time and energy already. Not even rich people living this far out of the way would anticipate visitors right now.

"Who knows why folk this well-off aren't at their other house in Glasgow or whatever," Vega said as we made our way around from the top of the steps to the front door. Not that the gray house was unusually large, but its strong angles and solid, cool-hued materials stood out for their elegance in a place where architectural design tended more toward the utilitarian and comfortable.

Before I could knock, a small lithe figure slipped around the door, closing it behind her. When she lifted her eyes to mine, I recognized with a start the first quiet, dark-eyed evacuee kid who had come to us in Aberdeen.

She seemed even smaller than I'd been remembering--maybe only twelve or thirteen and not more than a meter and a half tall, her pale face thinner in the shadows.

"Wow," I blurted out. "Hi. What are you doing here?"

Last I'd heard, she'd headed for the Orkney Islands. I'd worried enough about the four girls making their way even that far in the wrong direction. She'd said she had a safe place to go to; I would never have dreamed she'd come way the hell up here. Then again… maybe not even Shetland felt like far enough away.

Her midnight eyes widened to truly improbable proportions. My memory had somehow underreported her extreme beauty even worse than it overestimated her height. Like the human visual cortex couldn't process her image fully, although I kept trying. She'd traded her borrowed hoodie for a delicately patterned lambswool tunic over slim pants. Her unbound black hair fell, fine and soft, past the hem of the tunic.

"Hi," she said in a murmur. "And what are you doing here? Were you… looking for me?"

"What? No, they just transferred me up, I had no idea... Didn't you say you were going to Kirkwall?"

"Oh. The NorthLink," she barely breathed, nodding her raven head a little.

She was weirder than I remembered, too, if that could be. I decided not to press her further yet. "Uh. This is my friend, Dr. Hazan, doing rounds today because not everyone seems to know about the relief center in Scalloway. So if anyone here needs medical care… We also have supplies for those who've decided not to evacuate to the south. If your parents are here, or…"

She smiled like a sliver of crescent moon, raising the hair on the backs of my arms. "No. But could I see what you have?"

I wasn't sure why I'd perceived her accent as Scottish when we met. Tonight it seemed harder to identify, full of fine sharp edges beneath its softness. Scandinavian, maybe. "Give me just a moment," she murmured.

I strained my eyes to see around her when she opened the door for another fleeting second. I couldn't tell if her three little friends were among the other dark-haired kids in there, sitting around a big stone fireplace.

Vega came up the walk while I was waiting. "Buddy of yours?"

"Uh, no. I gave her a transport voucher from Aberdeen. Kinda thought she was getting away from—You heard about that trafficking situation there?"

"Yeah." Vega's eyes and mouth narrowed. "Man, how many times have we seen that shit moving in after a disaster, like some goddamn opportunistic infection…"

"And now she says her parents aren't here, so I don't know who she's with instead."

Vega's brows pulled together and she shook her head. When the girl came quietly back outside, now wearing her shoes, Vega's firm "I'm sorry. Are there adults here, miss?" greeted her.

I didn't expect her to laugh in response, let alone the way she did. Silky and smoky and nothing like a child's laugh should be. Her eyebrows lowered fractionally everywhere but their inner corners. "Yes."

"Okay. Can we talk to them? Do they have documents we could see?"

The black eyes cooled to obsidian shards. "Is that what you're here for?"

"No." I pointedly caught Vega's gaze. "We're relief. Not law enforcement."

Vega glared back at me, but waited for the girl's reply.

"Here. He has. It's his house."

A figure significantly taller than myself stirred in the shadows over her shoulder, where she hadn't fully closed the door; a young Viking warrior in modern dress emerged to slip a protective left arm around the child.

He released the ident section of his data. Vega quickly interfaced it with her own ring. What I could discern through the door he'd left open behind him was mostly just small silhouettes against the flames. Still, I strongly felt them watching me, too.

"It's in order," Vega admitted, deactivating the link. "So, Mr... Adie, Lachlan K. This says your primary residence is Inverness and you're enrolled in a research program at the University of Edinburgh. What are you doing here in a zone that's been recommended for evacuation, and with all these kids, if you don't mind?"

"I do mind." Unlike the girl, he had the classic Highland accent I'd grown accustomed to. "Edinburgh and Inverness are shut down like the rest of the northeast coast. The house is mine, as you saw. This is our family. You don't need more information from me."

The child laid a tiny hand against his chest in a way I would not wish for a girl her age to touch a grown man. The gesture didn't make me as uneasy as the way their eyes met, though, for a long wordless moment. The guy sighed heatedly and headed down to the hovercraft to see the supplies for himself.

"Miss." Vega found her voice first. "We can take you someplace safe..."

The girl shook her head impatiently. Vega set her jaw and followed the man.

The child's wide black eyes dismissed Vega with a flick of long lashes, then turned upward to scan my face. "Where did you come from?" she murmured, out of nowhere.

"United Forces Environmental," I reminded her.

"No. You."

"Uh. Monterey, California, USA."

Brows lifting higher, she shook her head again. "Of Scottish descent, though." As she'd already guessed, and apparently forgotten; I shook my head, too. "Or Norwegian... Irish?"

Now I fought to keep my mouth from gaping. "Both. I was born in Bergen, where my mom lived. Is that... where you're from, too?"

"Oh, no." She smiled again. "We've been on Shetland forever. Other than Lachlan, as he's said. The easternmost side, though, where the wave hit us far worse. Fortunately, we had this place to come to."

A little connection sparked in my brain. Hadn't the Aberdeen girl mentioned a sister? Maybe this one really hadn't seen me before.

"I think I met your twin in Aberdeen...?" I ventured. "Could she have been displaced that far?"

Staring anew, she shook her head once more.

They looked like twins to me, but I didn't begin to know how to argue. "Okay. Well, I hope she made it here too."

"Not yet. I'm grateful she's on her way."

Footsteps crunched up the path behind us, Vega and the Viking coming back up to the house with an armful of packets each. A second child emerged, fluid and quiet as an eel: a teen-size boy whose pale skin, black hair, and big dark eyes might or might not make him the girl's twin, either. The corner of my eye caught his lingering curious glance my way before he took the things Vega carried, bending his head slightly.

I didn't focus on him, knowing I only had another moment with the girl. Her extra-long sleeves clung semi-sheer enough around her tiny wrists to show she wasn't wearing a ring of her own; no surprise there. I quickly scrounged a chipcard from my pocket and pressed it into her hand.

"I'm Arden. If you need our help for anything at all," I said under my breath, bold enough to glance in the man's direction. "Ring or locate me with that card. Any time."

Her smile wasn't merely reassuring. She was, unfathomably, trying not to laugh. Holding the card between her thumb and index finger, she took my extended hand between her other three fingers and her soft cool palm for a second or two.

In that instant, I saw the man, Lachlan, as she did--with fierce adoration and the tender certainty that he wouldn't hurt anyone in that house. She didn't need me to protect her from him at all, but they needed him to protect them from people like me. And despite the way his temper flared when he was this tired, he meant me no ill, either.

I must have gasped. She released my hand, but I didn't succeed in tearing my gaze away.

"Thank you. My name is Brynja and I'd love to talk to you again, Arden," she whispered, glancing at Vega something like the way I'd looked at Lachlan moments before. "Another time."

Vega was strongly for alerting the peacekeepers as soon as we'd left the beautiful house, to make sure the kids were safe. I agreed enough to be the one to do it while she was driving.

"I wasn't going to say this after the morning you had, but… they've recovered a couple untraceable bodies up here already," she told me after a minute's quiet concentration on my part.

"Yeah… This is their kind of place." I didn't bring up my expectation that one more would be added to the list after they did their best to identify today's drowned kid.

"Yeah. So you have that message in?"

"Almost."

Yet I hesitated. Whatever the hell had just happened, it had none of the surreal vagueness of my dehydrated hallucination the day of the tsunami. I hadn't daydreamed the otherworldly sensation of the small pale fingers still tingling on my skin. Her deeply secretive attitude had absorbed right into my veins; I couldn't shake the need to maintain her

37

privacy, despite having not a clue on earth what enormous secret she was so intent on keeping. Finally, I got the alert perfectly ready to go except for one setting--which was the kind of thing I'd been known to do innocently in the past--then left it hanging. All it would take was a few gestures of my hand and eye to activate it later.

Chapter 4

California, USA

I slept unevenly until my alarm pulsed, too soon. Outside my window, a steady quiet rain fell. Today, Vega mumbled a half-coherent Spanglish greeting or benediction and rolled over.

Back at Lerwick Harbor in the dark gray chill before the March sun could struggle over the horizon, Stefek was missing in action.

So sweet you might melt in this weather? I rang him.

The reply came right back. *Spoke to Anton about helping w power grid We'll see*

Great minds thought alike. I was glad he'd taken this step on his own behalf, no fairy godparents required.

I was assigned one of the smaller movers for the first few hours. I didn't complain about the chance to be under its transparent canopy. As the machine did its work, only requiring a human element to guide it from time to time, I watched raindrops beading down the polycarbonate: becoming smaller rather than slower until a fine mist was all that was falling. The sky grew paler gray, then a weakly radiant white.

My concentration, such as it was, evaporated like one of the low clouds at the roar of a very different engine in counterpoint to the low clunk and throb of my own craft's motor. I turned my head to spot a navy blue custom Icon, gleaming without direct sunlight as it coasted down to stop near the water's edge. Recognition prickled inside my rib cage even before the rider removed his helmet. He turned to look around the site, revealing distinctive honey-blond hair pulled back in a thick braid. My red head was equally easy for him to spot. He raised a hand in unsmiling greeting.

My heartbeat quickened as I sat there a few moments, trying to decide what I wanted to do. My ring pulsed. The ident matched the one he'd given Vega: Lachlan K. Adie.

I'd meant the chipcard, with its short-term access to my locator, for any of the children--anyone but him. I considered correcting the sabotaged alert before exiting the mover. Given personnel distribution in the immediate area, I should get an answer in about ninety seconds.

I brought the mover onto solid ground near his bike, shut it down, and stepped out onto packed wet sand. If nothing else, I could still send the alert while I was with him, or after I got rid of him.

"Mr. Adie," I said, feet apart and voice firm. "Good morning."

The sudden smile brightening his features caught me off guard. He wasn't even old enough for real smile lines around his big storm cloud-blue eyes; last night I'd perceived him as bearded, but it was more like a week's groomed stubble over a boyishly smooth face.

"Mr. Adie's my dad." He shook his head and offered me his hand. I reached out to shake it: his earnestness washed through me like a shot of liquor taking effect. I caught a startled breath and let go immediately.

His smile altered. "Wait, can you actually feel something from me, too?"

"What the hell is it?" I breathed.

He laughed softly, not unkindly but as if in solidarity. "Yet that's never happened to you before you came to Shetland, has it?"

"Definitely not," I started to say, but a flash of memory interrupted. I'd touched the hand of the first girl, in Aberdeen, too. Maybe I'd so deeply comprehended her sadness in the same way that these weird linkages of understanding kept happening now. "At least, not before I started meeting people who look like the ones you live with."

The deep blue eyes scanned my face intently a moment or two. "Well. I'm here because I'd really like to talk about this, but--" He glanced around us at the busy worksite. "For now, we at least wanted to see if you're accepting help from the locals today."

I nodded. "Every day. We?"

He looked up the hill behind him at the small hovercraft following where he'd just driven, its polycarbonate canopy retracted despite the damp. They parked nearby, but all three riders stayed in the craft, watching us. Two were boys with the same pale skin, wide-set dark eyes, and sleek black hair as the one whose body we'd discovered yesterday. Even without knowing which sister the third passenger was, her familiar features made my pulse skip around.

"Uh, absolutely," I said to Lachlan. I pulled up the task pool on my ring, marked my mover as available, noting its current location, and looked for a job the five of us might share out of earshot of my co-workers. There was a new lot of recovered belongings to sort through. I put my name in, then spun the display for him to add theirs. To my pleasure, he didn't have to.

Lovely to have you lot again today Mr Adie, Officer Haye rang us at once via the task interface.

"Okay," I told the six dark waiting eyes and the two blue ones, and I pointed toward the northern end of the harbor. "Just up there. We should be able to talk," I added, softer.

"Cool." Lachlan gestured to the girl in the hovercraft, who wrinkled her nose but climbed down and got on the bike with him. The taller of the two guys moved back to take her spot. With an extended hand and slightly bent head, he offered me the front seat. His velvety hair, as long as Lachlan's and gathered neatly at the nape of his neck, spilled forward over one slim shoulder with the gesture. I'd never seen hair like that: smooth but not shiny, as if it drank up what light there was rather than reflecting it. He didn't exactly smile, but his stunning features were friendly.

"Uh. Thanks," I said without nearly as much grace as he had, and got in the craft.

The one driving the hover wore threadbare jeans, a brownish sweater shapeless with age, and a brown-gray tweed cap pulled carelessly down. He tipped the little hat in my direction as I sat beside him. His eyes, more sleepy than round--maybe thanks to the weight of all those lashes--smiled at me under strong, sleek brows. A charming hint of the smile barely reached his sculpted pale lips enough to register as a curl at one corner.

"Hi," he greeted me, "California, USA."

So he'd been watching us from around their fire the previous evening, although I couldn't have said whether he or the other fellow might have come out to help Vega. His quiet bass-baritone was the farthest thing from a kid's voice. And he might not have been of any more than my height, or near as powerfully built as Lachlan, but the spare lines of him were all sinuous muscle. I found myself wondering if any of the small people in that house had actually been children.

"Hi, uh, Caledonia, UK," I managed in answer as we started up what was left of the seaside street. He handsomely rewarded me with the rest of his smile. "And it's still Arden."

"Sorry. I'm Geir," he said with an engaging soft laugh. "He's called Hano. And we honestly weren't raised by wolves."

I laughed a little, too. "Obviously. No forests here, right?"

"Ponies, then," he said.

"Seals," I said at almost the same moment.

His eyes widened at me, a brown so dark I could hardly distinguish the pupils. I raised my brows in answer, having no earthly idea what I'd said wrong now.

"So you've noticed the seals?" was all he said.

"Well, they're hard to miss…. they're all over the place up here. But yes, I always do, anywhere I travel at the right latitudes. They make me think of home." I looked out over the wreckage, suppressing a little chill up my arms. "I met a very sweet one yesterday, actually. Right over there."

"Yes, she told me," Geir said softly. "She liked you, too."

My uncertain laugh slipped out more like a small voiceless sigh. Words didn't come any easier. His eyes were on the way ahead of us now, not looking up at me, but as I stared at his flawless profile hoping for some sort of answer, there was no hint of his earlier smile.

My ring pulsed as we neared the location. I cleared my throat a little. "Uh. The orange kind of pallet, hover pad, over there."

"Okay," he said, still quiet and serious, and he parked the craft and shut off the motor.

Still finding myself desperately short of words, I led the two guys to the work area we had just claimed. Lachlan and the girl were right behind us.

"So the tech sorts things out for us that might be worth keeping, but we like human eyes to go over it if there's enough personnel. This pallet for what you think is of enough monetary or sentimental value, in good enough shape someone would want it back," I showed them. "The rest..." I picked up a yellow windbreaker-style jacket, still dripping seawater, with a kelp frond sprouting from where one sleeve had torn halfway free. I tossed it into the mixed-waste receptacle. All that stuff would be sorted mechanically again later.

"That wasn't yours, man, was it?" Lachlan said to Geir, who chuckled under his breath. "Arden," he added. "You've met these two troublemakers?"

"Yes." Troublemakers. Surely Geir had been deadpan joking, then, about the conversation with the seal.

"Ah. Not really. You'll find they're both perfect gentlemen." Lachlan glanced over his shoulder at the girl, then back at me, with bright eyes. "A more interesting question would be if you've met this troublemaker as well."

I took one more good look at her. She was as nearly identical to the Aberdeen refugee as to the weird one who'd said they weren't twins. Brynja. If I had to guess, though, this person's wiry slouch, the quirk of her small pale mouth and the skeptically narrowed eyes, didn't belong to either. She seemed even more willowy and narrow if there was such a thing, the straight bridge of her nose finer. She had impossibly long black eyelashes, easy enough to buy in more urban places, but on a face free of any kind of enhancement, I was pretty sure they were her own. I shook my head, earning her grudging little smile.

Lachlan smiled too, pleased. "Arden, meet Ysmay."

"Also not Brynja's sister?"

"No," he laughed. "But the sister of the woman you met in Aberdeen."

"The one who let her sister end up alone in Aberdeen?" I said softly.

Ysmay narrowed her fey eyes at me again, as though I had no business judging her sister or her; I got a sense, too, that she thought both of them could handle themselves just fine.

"Okay," was the best I could really answer. "I'm not that patient with riddles, so."

"Okay." Lachlan's smile altered. "I didn't mean to pose one. We're all family, as we told you. Brynja is Geir's sister. Hano's sister-in-law." He drew a breath. "Also Ysmay's mother."

For the second time, I wanted to laugh but couldn't, managing only to shake my head.

He held a small, dented lockbox in his right hand, but he extended his left, for me to touch him again. Basically like offering for Santa Claus to prove to me that the Easter Bunny was real. I stared long enough at his big palm and long fingers to notice the plain gold band on the fourth one. The hairs on my arms and the back of my neck stood up in warning all over again.

"Also your wife?" I guessed, teeth tight around the uncomfortable words.

He nodded soberly, watching my reaction.

I shook my head again. The half of me that had input the PK alert couldn't possibly keep trusting a grown man who'd stand right there confirming to my face what kind of relationship he had with the girl I'd met at his house--a child, not possibly anyone's mother. The half that had left the alert hanging knew just as surely that in her inexplicable, wordless way, she'd told the truth then the same as he was now.

With an irritated growl in the back of her throat, Ysmay took my hand instead. At her touch, my vision--her vision?--went suddenly, subtly abstract, pixellated, colors saturated beyond normal.

Startled, I grabbed my hand back--but, uncannily strong as she turned out to be, not fast enough to avoid the core-deep understanding that Ysmay herself was much older than anyone I'd ever met. She rolled her eyes Lachlan's way for me to see him as she did: one such as her mother hardly needed a child like me to protect her from a child like him. I stumbled a little, one boot heel splashing into the edge of the water.

I took the biggest breath I could manage. "Say this is somehow true. You're all, like, elves or whatever, out of a kids' book." Ysmay gave me an unnerving moonlight smile like Brynja's, but she didn't contradict me. I met Lachlan's eyes again. "Not you, or at least you don't look like one. So why can you do the thing too, when I touch your hand?"

"My grandfather is one of them," he said, with just the hint of a self-deprecating smile. "And believe it or not, I'm the short and dark one next to my half-brothers who aren't related to him. The question is, why can you do the same thing even though you're not from here and don't even seem to have known the possibility exists... which means you're just doing it, never having learned how." The smile grew, gentle and encouraging. "I'm quite confident it's not your dad's family. Mam, I think you said, is Norwegian..."

I nodded, not because I understood anything, but at least I knew that one concrete detail to be true. "Was. Yeah. Not even part elf, though."

Geir responded with a faint, indulgent smile. "We're not fair folk," he said, appearing totally in earnest. "Finfolk. We thought you might have guessed it, supposing the Norwegian grandparents would have told stories. Or maybe even your mother."

I clenched my teeth before my lower jaw could drop. Finfolk was the Scandinavian name. Selkies, they usually called them on this side of the North Sea. Shapeshifters capable of concealing their human form within a magical sealskin.

I didn't know anyone on the Norwegian side at all, let alone well enough for them to have told me stories--yet the favorite old book of my childhood hadn't had elves, but selkies. There'd been a song, too, that I'd known so long I didn't remember where I'd learned it. *Joan Baez, Ardencita.*

It took quite a few more moments of staring before I was able to formulate any actual words. I looked from Geir's hint of smile back to Lachlan's sober, expectant face. "You're really saying you've hidden her sealskin somewhere in that house, and if she finds it, she'll go back to her kingdom beneath the waves and never return to her human shape?"

Geir gave a light snort of laughter. "Well, sea-level rise, not to mention the undersea landslide that sent your tsunami, have been hell on her kingdom," he said. "But we're working on it. Just like you."

"And no," Lachlan added, "the bit about hiding the skin wasn't ever true. Not only because there's no skin to hide... It seems a restless few end up in the songs and stories. But you do have the right idea."

"Wow. Okay." I started back on foot. "Thanks for the ride. You guys have fun digging for pirate treasure. Or was it the pot of gold at the end of the rainbow? Whatever."

My businesslike walk was no match for legs the length of his. "Hear us out, Arden."

"Heard plenty, thanks."

"Well, so have we, about you. Twice in twenty-four hours, before we met." He paused, watching my face again. "You do know, I expect, who the two people were that said they'd seen a dark and fiery selkie lass, come here to help us rebuild."

I drew a slow breath. Tolerance for ambiguity, ninety-two points. "Assuming any part of that is reality, just for the sake of argument... Geir claims the seal who led me to the body yesterday told him about me. Hypothetically, she..."

He nodded. "She's called Sefa, and you found her grandfather Seoras. We'd counted both of them among the missing."

I shook my spinning head. "Haven't spoken to any other marine mammals that I can recall."

"No. But you ate at the Seals Roost pub one night this week?" he said with an incipient smile.

"Oh crap," I blurted out in a startled whisper. The lady with the beautiful sea-blue eyes hadn't meant I had a *silky* face. It was that way too, *silkie*, in the childhood song. "So does she have a fairytale grandparent too, or what?"

He shook his head. "That's our friend May. She had a selkie husband when she was younger. Hano's son."

It took me a moment to work through someone who looked like Hano having a daughter-in-law who looked like May. Some less-dizzy part of my brain supposed Lachlan's grandfather must appear to be an absurdly attractive college student, too.

"Okay." Lachlan grinned. "I'll also admit I looked you up last night, once you'd given us your name. To see if Oliver Araujo had kids your age. Then... I found all your swimming and freediving wins and records. Horribly jealous, by the way, but maybe that's a different conversation."

I sighed. "I'm still not sure how I could be having *this* conversation with someone interested enough in science to know who my dad was."

He nodded again, seriously. "Unless he knew the folktales were true because he'd seen abundant proof, all his life."

"Beyond the--empathy thing."

"So far beyond it, Arden," he said, softer. "Let them show you, too."

I wrapped my arms around my waist, letting out my breath in another, slower sigh. Behind us, Ysmay and the two guys were back at work. Hano polished a big serving spoon on his sweater sleeve before laying it on the pallet. Ysmay picked up a little crab with delicacy and calm, stood up to find it a safe place to burrow. Then she turned to watch Lachlan and me, her head off to one side, stray black silk ribbon tendrils of hair fluttering in the breeze. Her eyes and mouth narrowed once more: was I going to make her uncles and her do everything?

"Okay," I murmured. If nothing else, it was good to have more volunteers. I was willing to spend a few hours alongside them.

The three selkies, if for the sake of argument that was what they were, proved to be models of quiet efficiency. I did notice Ysmay's eyes drifting in fascination to some of our tech, particularly the big movers. I guessed it wasn't every day you saw things like that here.

As we worked away the continually brightening morning, Lachlan was the talkative one. "You do realize, though, you've come to diving paradise... It's as clear as it looks, and there are as many coastal features underwater as above. Caves. Shipwrecks going back at least to the seventeenth century. As well as, you know, loads of seals."

I smiled, nearly salivating. The cold water here was great for slowing the respiration. Freediving with wild seals would be incredible. If there was really an undersea kingdom, maybe you could get to it that way, depending where it was and how deep. It was so logical for Lachlan that I supposed he'd learned specifically for selkie business purposes: unlike me, who'd lucked into having the right skill for a situation I couldn't have anticipated in a million years.

I shook myself a little. Awfully quick to fall down the rabbit hole. I attempted to steer the conversation back to reality.

"I guess you'd need wetsuits, with these water temperatures." As a rule, I disliked anything that came between the ocean and me, but this far north, there wasn't much way around it.

"Yeah." He chuckled. "All the pricey toys, for those of us who can't just shapeshift like nature intended. I've got a few of these great prototype rebreathers, too. Wee ones like you're in a film or something. No tank; they pull oxygen from the water. They're limited but if you use them in combination with free diving techniques, it's pretty brilliant."

"Prototypes."

"Yeah, we can thank Dad for those. It's all who you know. Sure you've found the same."

I would definitely have to look up his dad. Meantime, I tried to seem nonchalant: as if being my father's daughter had led to designer bikes or recreational tech of the future instead of working out my diplomacy composite muscles with police officers and the occasional colleague, medical professionals, the mortgage company.

"My grandfather taught me, though, not him," Lachlan softly answered my unspoken question. "And where did you learn?... Maybe from your mother?"

"No. I don't actually remember her, and we didn't ever know her family, so."

"Oh. I'm sorry."

I shrugged. Not like I could miss what I'd never had.

"True to the folktale trope, I can't remember mine either," Lachlan said, almost under his breath. "She died when I was four days old. Spontaneous coronary artery dissection. Freak thing."

"Sorry," I murmured too. "So I... guess you've seen Dad's stuff on the grid lately?"

"Among other times." He rang me a link, media files from his research node at Edinburgh. Dozens of titles, paired with my father's name. Lachlan knew far more of his work than what had been in the recent press.

"So you're not studying, like, architecture or botany," I said. "This is..."

"Wild coincidence, right? These are readings toward my thesis topic. Although I was going to go in a different direction before, you know, the whole repeat Storegga slide prediction came true..." The deep blue eyes refocused, finding mine again. "I had it all planned, get a meeting with him and ask his advice."

"Sorry," I said again.

"Me, too," he answered, so appealing in his sincerity that I already found it hard to believe I'd been unwilling to trust him. "I hate that I never got to tell him he wasn't the only one who saw all this coming."

I followed his gaze to Hano, Geir, and Ysmay, who steadily met my eyes and let me look. I tried to imagine it. If they understood one another's emotions by some telepathic energy transfer, how did they perceive the environment surrounding them?

I thought of Everything Bagel, the sweetest of my seal buddies in Monterey Bay, named for her light-colored coat's elaborate pattern of small spots. Though she'd lost the exceptionally keen underwater sight that was normal for seals when she'd been hit by a hovercraft, we didn't have to take her in as a rescue animal. She got by just fine with her highly sensitive vibrissae, great hearing, maybe other senses we didn't yet know how to measure, and a little help from her seal friends. I recalled my aquarium teachers, Zane and Dr. D., arguing about whether pinnipeds like EB could echolocate or not.

Maybe these people had some kind of mental equivalent of vibrissae, of the superior underwater sight, of echolocation. Maybe for them, the subsonic rumblings of wave resonances, of shifts in the plates of the seafloor, were a comprehensible means of communication too. I wondered about one or both of the sisters going to Aberdeen to offer aid, whether they'd arrived after the tsunami or foreseen it.

"Not that any scientist wouldn't want the glory of such a major find, but… You were going to give up these guys' whole secret?" I said.

"Of course I wouldn't." His slight smile slipped away. "Not least because some of their people would quite likely try to kill me. No; we were working out how I might replicate their data and take credit for them, if we're honest. Although… seeing your face and knowing we'd be able to tell you all of it is amazing in a different way."

"Crazy that I just showed up at your house like that…"

He nodded. "But that's how it happens in the old stories."

He wasn't expecting the cold seawater that sprayed in his face, any more than I anticipated the few drops that got me--but while I was still looking around bewildered, he laughed and returned Ysmay's warning splash with interest. She said something to him, quiet but fierce: so she could talk, although I wasn't sure what she said was in even May the pub lady's incomprehensible dialect.

"Ach, lass, please," he muttered with a lingering smile, rubbing salt and wet out of both eyes. "Even if somehow I were so foolish, how do you know Arden's not as married as I am?"

Ysmay's giant eyes challenged mine, flickering with amusement despite her righteously indignant expression.

"Lesson learned." I softened my head shake with a slight smile. "Happily never after."

She gave me a tiny return smile and a prim little "Hmm" sound, and went back to work.

"Where is she today, anyway?" I asked, quieter.

"Oh." Lachlan nodded. "Not only the human Scottish people need help right now, as I'm sure you can imagine."

"Oh," I echoed, just a breath in the shape of the sound. "There are more here than this family..."

Of course. I'd helped pull one from Lerwick harbor while his granddaughter watched.

"Not as many as we once were," Geir spoke up quietly. "Something between the size of a family and the size of a kingdom, we are these days."

I met his teardrop eyes for a moment. "Then I'm surprised they could spare you."

His fond fatherly smile for Lachlan was at once jarring and incredibly natural on his apparently sixteen-year-old face. "Well, there's always the worry that this one won't be charming enough on his own."

"I thought we were worried he'd be too charming," I laughed, with another glance at Ysmay. Hano, the silent one so far, chuckled softly.

Lachlan laughed too, rolling his eyes. "I'm meant to ask you to come with me and see her later if you're free."

I checked my ring. "Looks like I have a briefing when I'm done here," I said with a reluctance I wouldn't have expected.

"Nah, another time." He smiled. "Any time. You know where to find us."

They still stayed the full day, working in near-silent synchrony even after Engel called me away to help with a banged up little otter who couldn't figure out why his usual friendly shoreline looked so different. This time I read the small print, Noemi, on her badge.

I made sure to say good evening to the four alleged finfolk before getting on the transport at the end of my shift. Ysmay surprised me with a quick, forceful hug that seemed to say she'd enjoyed her day out here, though she wanted to be promoted to playing with the movers next time, and that she admired my hair. I didn't know if it worked like that, but I tried thinking about her fantastic eyelashes, and got another odd little smile as she let go.

Only as we started away to the south, putting distance between them and me, did the spell break. Surely, I hadn't spent the workday sorting trash from treasures with three fairytale creatures and the grandson of a fourth. Surely I was not, myself, a descendant of their kind. Dad would surely as hell have laughed aloud at the suggestion.

As much as I'd ever known about my mother, though, she could have been a Martian. And I couldn't deny what seemed to happen whenever these people touched me. I wanted to hop out and head northwest instead, even more urgently than I usually wanted to skip briefings.

"You okay?" Noemi said, in the seat beside mine.

I caught the overwhelmed tears on the fingertips of both hands. "Oh. Yeah. This one is just…. Something else."

I'd stared eagerly out the transport windows everyplace else I'd been on these islands so far, but now seemed a good time to bury my focus in the grid like three-quarters of the other people on board. I searched on the source of the magnificent motorcycle and the tantalizing idea of micro-rebreathers, inputting the only information I really had. *Adie Inverness wealthy.*

Two names, Kenneth Adie and KXA Shipping Industries Ltd., dominated the search results, trending news for the strength of his philanthropic efforts even as the great wave played hell with KXA's massive holdings. Its state-of-the-art minimal impact facility right across Lerwick Harbor from here, on the ground-zero island of Bressay, was shut down until further notice, future status undetermined.

Photos of Kenneth Xavier Adie, CEO, showed a handsome man of fifty-five or sixty. I didn't think Lachlan particularly resembled him, but his staggering net worth sounded right. I recalled Lachlan's middle initial, also a logical match. Adie Senior, assuming I was correct, had brawny shoulders, ruddy skin, piercing light blue eyes. The thinning hair that photographed as white could have been blond once. I flipped past more pictures to one of him visiting a sustainable fuels depot in Copenhagen. Appearing at least as comfortable in work coveralls as in tailored suits, he stood half a head taller than the next-biggest man there. I envisioned both my feet fitting into one of his boots.

Anton's overly frank recent assessment of my own appearance rushed to mind. Although the athletic curves he'd pointed out so bluntly bore no more resemblance to the finfolk women than my coloring, there were the small feet and hands and big eyes, making it hard to judge my age. I'd always thought my eyes were the feminine version of Dad's seashore-hued hazel ones, so striking in his brown face. Mine were just darker, rounder, set wider beneath longer lashes and more delicate arched brows. Now, though, it was pretty clear I didn't get them just from him.

Chimera.

My field of vision blurred; I rubbed at my wet lashlines. I'd never desired to find out about the mother who hadn't wanted to know me, but a little warning what was swimming in her gene pool would have been damn helpful. Dad must not have known she was part fairytale creature. It could be far enough back that she didn't know, herself. Still, I found myself craving the kind of story Lachlan's family must have always been able to tell each other. Even if I already understood it didn't have a happy ending, I ached to know.

Chapter 5

Cape Town

Even so, perhaps I was making a point to myself when I didn't immediately run away with the fairies. Instead of ringing Lachlan, I recruited Stefek and Noemi to tour some local sites of interest when we all happened to have off on the same day. Vega could have swapped herself out to go with us, but didn't feel dead white dudes were worth getting up at a specific time for, or wearing pants on a rainy day off. Noemi took over the organization with Germanic precision; her new Cameroonian and Caribbean Californian buddies were content to go along for the hover ride.

All without leaving the general Scalloway area, we visited an Iron Age castle-tower called a broch, a Viking burial mound uncovered in a family's back yard a few years earlier, the bigger castle right in town, a hill where some women had been burned as supposed witches in the 1700s, an exhibit about Shetland fishermen's involvement with the Norwegian Resistance during World War II. I didn't care that Stefek laughed at me for getting the tingles at historic places, particularly the oldest ones. If we got days off together later, there'd be a wealth of other places to explore on islands farther away.

By the time I admitted to myself the desire for more of the really wild energy interactions my historic tour left me craving, I ended up stuck waiting for days without them. The North Sea had been sulking all along; now it came right out and showed us how mad it still was. A spring storm system moved in and stalled over us, adding insult to injury. Everyone put in extra hours to stabilize what we could along the east coast. Buffeted with sleet and stinging rain driven by winds not much below hurricane force, we ended each of those four days too exhausted to do much more than get hot food and a hot shower before bed. Vega threatened with regularity to walk away earlier than her contract stipulated, leaving a good chunk of the year's salary on the table. We talked her down to promising she'd reject future assignments to places whose weather patterns matched the uniforms this disgustingly well.

Can I pull you into another briefing today, Noemi rang me early the morning after the storm finally moved out. *I like your wildlife whispering + diving skills for this*

Thanks, I rang her back. *What is it*

Decisions to be made regarding whats left of coast level Lerwick

Interested thank you

OK will recommend Watch for notification

Just when I'd felt ready for another shot at quality selkie time. Yet I couldn't think of a more direct way to try to help their kind.

Inspiring new sense of purpose or no, it was still pitch dark. I drowsed, dreaming vaguely of shipwrecks, treasure, seals swimming in and out of filtered underwater sunbeams, until my alarm pulsed.

When my ring pulsed again in the shower, I thought I hadn't disabled the alarm correctly, but it turned out to be Lachlan.

Hey dad is asking me to attend this meeting on his behalf at 1500 re lerwick plans Part of pier complex there is/was KXA holding Know anything about who will be there

Not much, I rang back. *I was just invited too actually*

Would like to check in during day w marine engineer diver staff, have look round first Whats on for you today

Usual, I sent back, with a little sigh.

He didn't ring again right away. I finished my shower, wrapped my hair in a towel, dressed, and braided back the still-wet curls. I was lacing my boots before I heard back.

Exec asst putting me in touch w divers Asked Spec Admin to request you too

I struggled a few moments with my second bootlace, my uncomfortably ambivalent heart rate. Not that I wouldn't go, if the prince and his royal dad's fairy godmother/executive assistant worked it out. Lachlan knew more about my qualifications for this project than Noemi possibly could anyway. I took a couple more minutes to swap my undergarments for UFE swimwear, in case he was successful.

KXA came through for us within two hours. By 1100 or so, the clean-electric Icon coasted down the slope to where I'd been operating a big mover again. What a difference a few days made.

It was logical he'd come alone. I still dared tell him, under my breath, how much I looked forward to diving with his extended family when the time was right.

"Trust me, that's entirely mutual." He laughed. "They're plotting it already."

UFE Spec Admin Rajan Dessai--another of Vega's big bad wolves, if I wasn't mistaken--met the KXA heir and representative in person at the site. His face was about the same warm bronze as my dad's, but his princely features and the shine of his thick black-brown hair made me think of movie stars with origins further east than any of my ancestors.

He was already in his gray wetsuit, but showed Lachlan and me to where we could don ours. He pulled a UFE-issued suit for me, Lachlan of course having brought his own sleek black one. Rajan managed not to stare too openly at me as we were changing; the interloping generalist was there to be seen and not heard, I guessed, as he addressed every single question and remark to KXA Junior.

Lachlan, in the course of polite conversation, asked where Rajan's home was.

"Vasco da Gama," he answered, with a skeptical head tilt. "I'm sure you haven't heard of it."

"Goa is beautiful." I shook my head. "We flew into Vasco da Gama when I was there."

Rajan lit up somewhat. "Business or pleasure?"

"Work, but I wouldn't miss the incredible diving and swimming."

"Oh, wait, Hazan did say--You had some transcendent spiritual experience swimming with dolphins at Baina Beach? I couldn't tell if she was joking when she said that's normal for you..."

Of course she had. "Mystical harmonic convergence, was probably what she told you," I admitted, although the big silly words Vega liked to employ whenever she picked on me for this had certainly never come out of my own mouth. "Anyway, it was giant mantas."

Blue eyes glinting with amusement as he played along, Lachlan smoothly hit a return volley: tossing a zippered pouch too small to hold a decent sandwich, not to Raj but to me. "We haven't got mantas, but all manner of cetaceans if you stick around long enough to spot them. This should help."

What was inside flexed as I grasped it and weighed almost nothing. "Minimalist rebreather," I smiled as I guessed aloud.

I saw white all the way around Rajan's rich brown irises. "Those aren't--the long-awaited Steyns? 2098 release, I thought I'd read."

Lachlan smiled. "Yeah, technically they're prototypes, but it's more a question of working out mass production and appropriate price points for the larger market. Yolandi Steyn gave them to my dad when he was in Cape Town last fall."

Even sweeter was the look on Raj's movie-star face, with the cherry on the top when Lachlan told him there were just the two.

Sadly, the product itself did not yield a result that tasted remotely good. Yes, they were wonderfully intuitive to use, and I loved it that the close-fitting, foldable mask had no traditional snorkel-type tube to hold between the teeth. We'd still be able to talk during the dive. It even had an earpiece for users who couldn't tolerate a cochlear circuit. But the air I got through mine was rainforest-heavy and had an unpleasant tang, like it had been stored in an unwashed empty pickle jar. I found myself taking as few and as shallow breaths as possible.

I only worried about it for the first minute or two in the beautiful-beastly sea. The news below the surface was at least as bad as above. My father would have immediately made me a virtual diagram with elegantly curved arrows to explain how the monstrous tides had eroded the coastline from under itself. In my much less well-informed opinion, it was too dangerous for a worthier heir such as Lachlan Adie even to be down here.

"Gotta hate it that KXA took such care to minimize impact here, and the environment didn't return the favor," I said.

"Yeah." Lachlan shook his head. "I said that to Dad in the early days, but he says it's fair enough for the planet to go on defending itself. The worst damage was done long ago. He just mitigates it however he can, now."

I guessed that was all UFE could do, either.

Not until we'd reemerged to breathe deliciously fresh Shetland air and sip hot tea some kind person offered from a dockside thermos, did I realize the remaining significance of our dive.

"I captured plenty of footage, but I hardly even need send it to know what he'll say," Lachlan said as he ejected the mostly spent scrubber cartridge from his device.

"Rechargeable, right?" Raj said, holding out a hand to ask to examine it.

"Yes. I've got the soaking solution at home. Good as new by morning. Unlike everything else we've just seen."

"Not that it's up to me, but I share your assessment, unfortunately."

I found the right combination of places to press to pop my own used scrubber out from behind the mouthpiece. Lachlan raised his sandy brows at the sight of what I handed him, but didn't comment before slipping it into its pouch. I saw it too, though, as he palmed the slim rectangle. His cartridge was the color and texture of an old tennis ball. Mine was still almost smooth, a brighter green: not nearly as depleted.

Rebreather--Grandfather says mam outgrew actual shapeshifting But in adulthood could do what you can, Lachlan messaged me as we got separate hot showers. I leaned my head against the tile wall a moment, trying to imagine what she'd lost. Lachlan went on with the positives, *Heightened dive reflex high carbon dioxide tolerance but are you that sickening all the time or would you say its a north sea specific thing*

We'd been under for about forty-five minutes, on a scrubber that would last someone like Lachlan about an hour. I was smaller, and diving had always come easily for me... but even so. Breath control on a longer dive usually required the most serious concentration I could manage. This had been so effortless as to escape my notice.

Never like this Has to be this crazy place, I answered.

Still hate you quite a bit, he shot immediately back.

There was time to grab lunch at the Seals' Roost before the meeting. May winked one Caribbean-blue eye when she saw me walk in at Lachlan's side. Both guys ordered fish and chips, Lachlan taunting Raj a bit by having the beer we weren't permitted during the workday. I enjoyed a warming bowl of rich vegetable soup with split peas and lentils, and some of May's lovely fresh bread on the side. It was fun to hear the man who'd first seemed like more of a Viking bodyguard or bouncer sounding quite brainy enough to have been reading a whole list of Dad's stuff.

I figured the fun had ended, or at least my part in it, when we ran into the real bouncer looming in his easy slouching way. Good old Anton Krol stood at the conference room door, in conversation with a sharp fiftyish woman in black whose badge indicated press affiliation, and with a stocky man of similar age--Chief Administrator Gordon

Muir, one of the joint site leads. I had to admit, Anton looked even better in crisp dress grays than in his everyday uniform. The effortless textured upsweep of his hair was straight out of a high-end cologne advertisement.

He stopped chatting, turning his two-tone gaze like a lazy searchlight over us.

"Generalist Araujo, hi. Sorry if you didn't get the update. We can't accommodate Spec Engel's request to have you join her. Unfortunately, there's limited space so we have to give priority to the specialists. I'm sure you understand."

I was pretty sure I did... down to the strong hunch that Noemi had declined a first or subsequent date with this guy at some point, too.

"Generalist Araujo's here at my request as well," Lachlan put in smoothly, holding out his hand. "Lachlan Adie. Attending on behalf of KXA Limited."

There was a little ripple of nearby people standing up straighter, greeting him as *Mr. Adie,* thanking him for coming. In the end, though, Muir himself apologetically pushed the door open to show that there really were just fourteen chairs crowded around the conference table. Noemi pulled a wry little face as she gave me a quick wave. She was sitting next to the Orkney and Shetland MP, who didn't know me from a hole in the wall but smiled recognition at Lachlan.

I sensed, like an electrical storm, him gearing up to disagree. I subtly brushed the back of my hand against his, thinking out loud that it wasn't worth the fight. He met my eyes a moment, questioning.

"Ach, no worries, then," he said with a shrug. "Come over for tea, after. We'll catch up on everything, and I can pick your brain."

I finished out my shift at Lerwick harbor smothering a grin, after all. Damn right. As it turned out, no one in UFE belonged here more than I did.

Chapter 6

Eshanes

Lachlan rang me some mysterious coordinates less than half a kilometer from the house. The spot he'd directed me to find was pretty, a tumble of coastal rocks still glistening wet from the last few days. Other than some sheep up the slope and a couple of seals I spotted swimming into a geo, I seemed to be the first one there.

I didn't get it until I heard their voices echoing softly back out over the water. Not just seals. My pulse quickened. I didn't know if I should wait for them to come out, or look in, or what; curiosity won out, and I ducked in on a narrow little strip of shingle at one corner without having to step into the water.

There was a tiny sea cave at the geo's head. It was best I'd given them those few moments, I realized as my eyes adjusted to the dimmer light. I saw the taller one, first, Hano, magnificent long hair clinging against the sculpted lines of his wet back as he fastened the dark pants he'd just pulled on.

They had an old crate that might have passed for flood debris, mostly hidden between rocks on a ledge at the back of the little cave, and were dressing in clothes they'd stashed there. It figured. Movie werewolves generally ended up naked, too, at the end of their full-moon nights.

Geir, facing more in my direction, buttoned the waist of low-slung old jeans. He pulled his dripping, collarbone-length hair back to wring the water out and secure it with an elastic band from his pocket. Both men displayed exactly the smooth, wiry musculature I would have expected if I'd been thinking about either of them between our first meeting and now, though it was the little guy who caught me looking.

"Arden, hi," he called quietly, half-smiling at me over the subtly sparkling water.

"Hi. Sorry, I… should have knocked, maybe."

He chuckled. "Keep going round that edge, you won't get wet past your knees, and those look like good boots for it. I guess Lachlan said where you'd find us?"

"Yeah. He's on his way, too." Although he would have to hunch over to stand here. My head brushed the multi-colored, wave-sculpted cave ceiling a few times. The whole grotto wasn't bigger than your average family room. It was easy enough to continue the conversation as I made it around and pulled myself onto the ledge with the two men. Geir sat at the edge, smiling eyes offering me the spot next to him; I took a seat, not too close, one boot tucked under me and one dangling.

"And we're just waiting for a couple more of ours," he said. "One you haven't met yet, one you have."

"Both are ladies," Hano assured me, now tucking a t-shirt in at his narrow waist. I tried to think if I'd ever heard his voice, that day in Lerwick Harbor. It was nice, quiet, not as low as his friend's. He didn't have the off-the-beaten-Scottish-path accent that Geir and the Aberdeen girl did. He sounded more like Scandinavian, the same as Brynja.

"Arden's well used to heroes like herself," Geir was saying in a tone more serious than his mischievous eyes, as he zipped up a hooded shirt faded to an indeterminate greenish hue. "Helping coastal folk all round the world. I expect she's no easier to shock than she is to impress. Are you, Arden?"

I couldn't fight my smile all the way, even as I cleared my throat a little.

"Good," he murmured: not teasing when he had been the moment before, and with his eyes now focusing past my shoulder. "Have a look, then."

I turned, following his gaze to the pale blur speeding toward us under the surface. She flickered in color and flexed in shape, like a camouflaging octopus. I wasn't sure if the lightning-like flashes along her shifting skin were reflections from the sea cave's ever-altering light, or her own energy illuminating her from within. She took a few heartbeats to go from a small gray seal with darker spots to her human form, floating face-down as if she were just a snorkeler who'd happened to leave her suit at home.

Then she stood, slightly above waist-deep in the gently moving water. Like the selkie wife in my old book, she waded toward us, long hair floating atop the waves. She didn't seem concerned to find me there, though she'd never met me. I guessed there'd been plenty of time for word to travel.

She was similar enough for the four of them to be quadruplets, but this woman's eyes in the glittering low light were charcoal gray, not espresso-black, and pale freckles adorned her lovely face, chest, and arms. She didn't look like a little girl with her clothes off. She was muscular, fully developed, albeit with childlike satiny skin and hardly any body hair. Her breasts, with all their slight fullness below the tiny dark nipples, had likely nourished a child once; as she waded shallower, I saw a few faint silver stretch marks across her nearly flat lower belly. She was altogether stunning.

I let out my pent-up breath and quickly rubbed a few stray tears dry as she smiled at us but reached her hands to Hano, who helped her onto the ledge. He'd already pulled a dress from the crate for her to slip on.

"You okay?" Geir murmured, gentle and earnest now.

"Yeah, I…"

He nodded and gave me an encouraging little smile.

"So. This one's your other sister?"

"Right. Our half-sister from Orkney. Runa."

"Then none of them are twins?"

He chuckled. "Ysmay and Berenys are, but not Bryn and Runa. They just both favor our father, while the twins entirely take after their mother."

I filed away the name of the Aberdeen girl.

"They don't all like it when I call them the weird sisters," he added, "but it fits so well."

"Right country, but wrong number for the weird sisters..."

He raised his brows at me a bit. "You're a Shakespeare reader, among all your other skills? Lovely."

I shrugged. "Not so much. It was Dad who was a little obsessed. There was a Doré engraving of Caliban in his office..."

"Oh. Good man." Geir nodded thoughtfully.

"You think? I didn't really get it. Him. Whatever."

He watched me with another slight smile. "No job for the faint of heart, being father to someone like you."

Caught off guard, I considered the likelihood he'd know such things firsthand if youthful-faced Hano was old enough to have lost at least the one adult son.

In the lull, the Icon's distinctive bass purr approached.

"He'll follow her along the coast like a puppy chasing its owner's car," Geir said with a different sidelong smile.

I smiled too. "I'm guessing they must be newlyweds?"

He shook his head. "Coming up on seven years together this June."

I didn't pretend not to stare. "What? He's only a kid."

"Well, that's fairly amusing, coming from you... But yes, he is very young, and he surely was then... just shy of eighteen at the time."

"Whoa." I failed to stifle a startled laugh. "How'd the billionaire shipping tycoon handle that one?"

Geir lifted the outer corner of one brow. "Young as he was, Lachlan had been of legal age for almost two years by then, and he was no more a fool than he is now. Then, too… You don't really know my sister yet, but neither Kenneth nor any other man alive could have told her she wouldn't have him once her heart was set."

"Love at first sight, I guess… Isn't that how it works in children's stories?" I murmured, getting yet another little smile in response.

"Near enough. At first sight, she was a grieving widow and he was all of eleven… though already taller than she was. But they both say they were drawn to the spark inside one another from then on, independent of age or circumstance. When next they met, seven years later, she'd had a little time to heal, he was grown, and it was quite another matter."

He glanced down at the water; following his gaze, I caught the flash of gray transforming into the fairest of them all. Runa handed another thrift-store type dress down to her sister, who did not come up onto the ledge with us. She just put it on where she stood; the hem floated around her hips at first, then sank with its own saturated weight.

I couldn't have seen it the night we met, the way her dark eyes--fixed on my face almost immediately--sparkled with as many colors as the cave itself: chestnut and chocolate and glints of greenish amber.

"Arden," she said, her voice and the water composing the tiniest sweet song together. "Darling." She stepped to the side, the way I'd come in, motioning to me with her elegantly bent head to join her. She lifted both small hands to my shoulders.

I couldn't possibly have explained what happened when she kept them there, instead of the fleeting contact I'd had earlier. I still saw, heard, smelled, felt everything I'd experienced the moment before, but now I also shared the startlingly clear, staggering depth of her wild and ancient heart and mind. There weren't any words: just emotions, perceptions, memories she recalled for me. Her thrill of excitement the night she'd first seen my dark and fiery selkie face; how her heart had raced when I handed her my card, asking to be found again. Selkie folk my age, even ones with only a little bit in their blood, were so rare.

It was far more profoundly disorienting than getting the retinal circuitry implant placed in my non-dominant right eye at fifteen. I was still breathing, more or less, but I'd made no attempt to stop the tears I found coursing silently down my face. I realized I'd reached up to grip her wrist where it rested against my shoulder.

"Bryn, go easy on the peerie lass," Geir said.

"I'm okay…"

"Dammit," Brynja whispered with another gentle smile, and she smoothed the tears away with her other hand. "No, it's true. I'm rubbish at this. Ask Lachlan." She caressed the little curls escaping my braid in the sea air, and thought they were beautiful.

"So I thought we'd agreed, tea invitation first, selkie madness after," her husband said with a low laugh. He'd stooped through the low cave opening with perfect timing, while I was so focused on her. "The chef's even arrived. She's at work as we speak."

"No, I mean, for a regular person, I'm pretty well-versed in madness, so. If this is real, then… I do want to know more. I would have wanted to know all along if I could." I summoned a wobbly laugh. "It's a lot to take in, though."

"I know," Brynja murmured. "Coming to live among your kind was a very sudden change for me too, once. Unimaginably sweet as well, but…"

"Exactly," I answered in a tone as soft as hers.

She kissed my face, still not entirely free of tears. She had loved me at first sight: not in the same way, yet as surely as she'd lost her heart to her young fairytale prince. I could only begin to grasp the sort of love of which such a heart was capable. I caught back a full-blown sob, but didn't stop myself from bending my head to her shoulder and putting my arms around her impossibly slender little shape. She held me close and stroked my hair again.

"So we'd be delighted if you'd come to tea with us," she said, and I had to laugh through the tears.

"Not that Bryn will really eat, but anyway."

I just looked up at Lachlan, waiting.

"Not all your selkie folk like people food very much," he smiled. "I learned some time ago, it's not an insult to my cooking. Ysmay's worse. She won't even pretend to eat anything Berenys hasn't made for her."

"But then, what do you… Oh."

"Already had a fine meal," Brynja agreed placidly. "I'm quite ready for a good cup of tea, though."

"Well, your chariot awaits, my lady," Lachlan said, holding out a hand for hers. She caressed my damp cheek one more time; then her sparkling eyes moved to find his, and she stepped lightly away. I watched, with no more consternation, the palpably smitten lowering of his fair lashes as she leaned up to kiss him, the delicacy of his big hands on her tiny shoulders. Actually, I couldn't help loving it, the more I understood how she had the perfect specimen of an alpha male wrapped so inextricably around her smallest selkie finger. The age thing was still wild, even now I knew I'd had it backwards--and off by who knew how many orders of magnitude. But with as much power as each one held in their respective realms, theirs wasn't at all the unequal marriage I'd first supposed.

I brought Hano, Runa, and Geir home in the hovercraft. On the way, I peppered my passengers--mostly Geir, Runa being another of the extremely quiet ones--with shapeshifting questions.

"Is it something mental that you're doing? Physical?"

His mouth went quizzical a moment, his eyes distant. "It's like--whispering or shouting instead of talking, maybe? Or singing. I think that's closest to the feeling."

"I'll take your word for it. No one wants to hear me sing."

"You're in good company among this family, then." It was sort of fun, figuring out which of my words might provoke his full smile. "I said feels right, not sounds right…"

I smiled too as I explored the idea. "So you... have to learn how?"

"Usually. Though once in a while, a baby works out how to shift while they're still in the womb, and they're born within the seal shape. It's kind of... a good omen. A lucky thing. Those ones never have to learn."

"Whoa..."

He laughed softly.

"What age does everyone else learn?"

He shrugged. "Depends on the child. Around when they're learning to walk and talk, usually."

I shivered a little bit. "So they're--stuck in the underwater wherever it is, till then?"

"Well, I liked that you said undersea kingdom... how the Orkney finfolk legends have it... but there's not, really. More like underground, with an underwater way in. During the last few centuries, that's how most families kept their children safe, what you're saying. What children there were. Before, it worked well enough to choose a remote place and just keep away from prying eyes."

"Which one were you?"

"Oh. I'm a bit different, but I was born and raised above the surface, north of here. Eshaness."

Maybe he was some kind of hybrid, then, like Lachlan's mom. "Different, how?"

"Well. Once a lovely selkie lass called Arinví loved a troublesome finman by the name of Brunn. Together they brought into the world a son who's no longer here, and a beautiful daughter called Brynja. Then Dad did a not very selkie thing, sad to say, left for Orkney and had another wife and daughter there, one of whom you've just met. World and tides keep turning, when the second wife was no more, our troublesome finman made his way back home thinking maybe to win back his first love... only to find she'd gone to live with a fair-haired, kind-hearted fisherman, name of Calum Craig. My mother was tempted enough by her old husband's return that I ended up making an appearance, but not enough to leave her fisherman. He was a lovely soul. Best laugh you've ever heard."

"And you're in the 'shouldn't really be here' club, same as me," I murmured before I could think better of it.

He gave me a different, bemused laugh in answer, brows drawing together. "How no? If we weren't meant for some purpose, we wouldn't be here, would we?"

"Huh." That was the fairytale creature perspective on it, I guessed. "Okay."

"Okay." He shook his head at me, smiling. "Anyway, you're right, I lived in his house as a child and learnt his trade… and so I'd always rather have the sky above me."

Dad said something indistinct in my head, some quote about the sky that my daydreamy mother had liked, but Hano surprised me back into the present moment by answering, too.

"And where he got his taste for whisky, and for the other fishermen's daughters."

I laughed. "As beautiful as your kind are? What could possibly be the draw of humans?"

Hano chuckled, with an expression that made me think they'd batted this argument back and forth for years.

But Geir just raised ink-stroke brows at me. "Och," he murmured. "What sort of mirrors have they got there in California, USA?"

His bright gaze held mine with gentle intensity and no hint of self-consciousness. I floundered for words a moment, a blush climbing to my cheeks as I realized my mistake and managed to get my eyes back on the way ahead of us.

So that part of the legends was true. Shapeshifting wasn't the only mystical energy manipulation these guys could pull. There were no old stories about a dutiful selkie husband who eventually found his sealskin in the rafters and returned to the sea wearing it. Finmen were the mythological explanation for babies of unknown paternity: the ones unsatisfied wives would summon in the dark, who ruined unsuspecting maidens forever for ordinary boys. A sudden, different understanding about Lachlan's origins tingled through me.

"Déjame, cabrón," I breathed as soon as I could. I wasn't sure why it slipped out in Spanish, except that the last guy I'd asked to back off (as opposed to just walking the hell away myself) would have been one of numerous pushy Colombians on my previous assignment.

Geir answered me with another easy laugh, shook his head, and didn't request a translation. "Oh, I don't doubt you'll have heard it from too many men before me. Sorry, but it's no less true for that."

His wicked hint of smile when I glanced back, those bright eyes and expressive brows, gave the lie to at least the one word he'd spoken. He might be a far cry from a blunt instrument like Anton Krol, or your average fellow in greater metropolitan La Guajira for that matter, but still. At least Anton dressed appropriately for the current decade; he wasn't extremely short or way too old for me, either.

By the time I could come up with anything else to say, we'd reached the house and curiosity overtook my other emotions. I'd seen my share of rich people's homes before, usually connections of Dad at his most successful. Lachlan Adie's house was the kind I'd always liked: not sprawling or ostentatious, just quietly opulent in the extreme quality of every last stone, fixture, dish, and drapery.

Through the front door was a great room. Off to the right, the big fireplace divided the lofty space from a glimpsed birch and steel kitchen. Ahead was a wall of big windowpanes, French doors in the center leading out onto a sweep of rear deck, Vaila Sound beckoning beyond.

Despite the stunning view, I gravitated to a graceful structure filling the one solid wide wall to my left. Equal parts history, sculpture, and furniture, the massive bookshelf was crafted from the shapely skeleton of an antique vessel, its dimensions and proportions something between those of a canoe and a rowboat.

"That's from your hometown," Lachlan said.

"Really?"

"You said Bergen, right? Eela boats came from there. Well, the pieces did, at any rate. Short on lumber here…"

"Was it your grandfather's?"

I didn't see whose eyes Lachlan met, glancing over my shoulder; he shook his head. "Quite a bit older."

My father would have ignored the boat, as well as the promised meal, and just gotten lost in the gorgeously bound physical copies of this library. I glimpsed not only Shakespeare but many others from the bewildering stacks of stuff I'd donated when I got his place ready to sell. Homer, Ovid, Gilgamesh, Beowulf, Joseph Campbell, Lewis, Tolkien, Calvino, García Márquez, Allende, L'Engle, Le Guin. All that was missing was some treasury of the obscure Celtic tales he'd heard from his grandmother, and maybe a mind-bending philosophy section. At the far corner stood a fabulous harp, inlaid with an intricate knot pattern in several colors of wood.

I turned to find the actual twins sitting at opposite ends of the smaller of two couches, each one's legs stretched with her feet near the other's hips. One wore a cloud-soft pale lavender sweater, draping with effortless elegance off her little sculpted shoulder. Her chic loose raven braid spilled over the other shoulder, in among the edges of the pages of a little notebook. The second twin didn't seem to be doing anything in particular, although her ribbed tank top and athletic pants with grease streaks on the thighs made me imagine she'd been tinkering with something mechanical earlier. Her surreal eyelashes drifted up in my direction, and she gave me the hint of an unnerving smile that made me pretty sure she'd never worn a borrowed oversized hoodie to match those pants.

Brynja whispered a few syllables to the first girl, who got reluctantly to her delicate bare feet. *My heart* something, I understood; the way you'd say "my love" in Norwegian. Though the daughter's feet were much prettier, I noticed her fine-boned second and third toes were webbed together like mine.

At first, I thought I didn't have to touch anyone to read the situation. I'd been a kid who'd displeased my parent by staying out longer than we'd agreed, too. I didn't recall my breaking curfew ever being greeted with wide liquid eyes and a fervent hug like the one that left Berenys damp with seawater for what must have been the second time that day. Then again, I kept forgetting Berenys was much older than she appeared; I couldn't have said, either, what other communication passed unspoken between them.

Before I got a chance to say hello, the daughter heaved a quiet sigh and rounded the corner to join Geir in the kitchen.

Lachlan turned around. "Ys."

Ysmay pulled up her pearly fused toes and hugged her stained knees to her slight chest, watching me coolly. The subtle blue medallion-patterned cushion where I took a seat was firmer than it looked. My fingertips recognized indoor-outdoor fabric, which made perfect sense.

"So," Lachlan said with a smile, seating himself next to Brynja. "You missed nothing at the meeting, beyond confirmation of what we'd seen already. And I'm sure Hano and Runa answered all your questions on more important matters."

"Almost." I laughed.

"Okay. So what else?"

"Okay… So. Loch Ness Monster, also real?"

He grinned. "I've never doubted.'

I smiled too, but pressed it. "Fair folk?"

He raised his sandy brows, catching the shift in my tone. "No real woods here and I wouldn't think they'd hang about in the bigger cities, so. I do expect they'd exist somewhere, given the overwhelming evidence of our finfolk…"

"Cock up the forests as badly as we have the oceans, and make refugees of them as well, then we'll have our answer," Berenys said, reemerging with a square platter of cookies arrayed in a curious grid with miniature sandwiches and some kind of canapés, which she set in front of me. Her exquisite downturned face was slightly rounder now that I had them all to compare to one another, with broader cheekbones, fuller lips.

"As long as no one lies and offers them an eastbound shipping container for a shelter," I greeted her softly.

Unlike Brynja's, the eyes my sad girl from Aberdeen finally lifted did not sparkle with other colors even in this light; they were uniformly the darkest velvet brown. They still didn't meet mine for long.

"There'll always be that sort," she breathed. "But... as long as the hero rides in soon enough to keep them safe, so... Thanks."

"Seemed to me we both did our part."

The teakettle whistled in the quiet that followed.

"Here," I said. "I took your spot."

"Oh, no." She settled her small self on the lovely antique wool rug instead, close to the hearth. Ysmay sighed and joined her, legs folded yoga-style, their knees touching. I imagined the whole conversation they might have without talking.

"Anyway. Geir's meant to bring the tea, but you needn't wait. There's plenty. Bryn and Runa and Hano won't eat anything, and Ys might just have one or two, so."

I picked a canapé to please her, and was rewarded as it hit my tongue. "This is gorgeous. You made this? What's in it?" I demanded before I was done chewing, screening my mouth with my fingertips. "No wonder you didn't think much of my sandwiches."

Her smile faded. For a few seconds, the darkness of her eyes seemed something far beyond their natural pigmentation. I half wished I hadn't said anything about Aberdeen, half ached for her to tell me how else to right whatever wrong she'd seen there. For a moment I wondered, too, whether the criminals she'd encountered had been targeting every pretty refugee kid they met, or the quiet ones with wide-set black eyes in particular.

In any case, she shied away from telling me anything more about it now. "Oh, the food there was fine. Anyway..." She brightened her expression for me again. "It was you who brought us flour, and oil and vinegar, right? I begged the crofter widow up the way for a couple of eggs too, so we could have mayonnaise. She gave me the biscuits, as well. Technically those were for Geir, which we all know is because he makes her feel pretty…" I appreciated the slight roll of her beautiful eyes. "I found the oysters and watercress. And the sandwiches, that's only a bit of smoked fish from tins that were already here."

I laughed. "Fairytale homemade mayonnaise. Just the usual."

"And now you know why we like it when Berenys is in town with us," Lachlan said.

"Town," she sniffed, with a tolerant smile.

Hano and Runa didn't join us. As predicted, it was mostly us four demolishing the platter of delicacies, though Ysmay daintily nibbled her share of cookies before drifting away. Brynja too, after the tea she'd wanted: maybe her acknowledgment that she'd overwhelmed me enough for one day. A little later, someone rang Lachlan; he headed off down a hallway with his second or third cup.

Out of reflex, I started stacking empty plates, cups, and saucers on one side of the tray.

"Hey," Geir stopped me with one of his partial smiles. "I've been a great supporter of UFE since the days before its founding, but--Since when is it your policy to take away a job from a local who's already got it sorted?"

"Never." I raised my hands away from the dishes, laughing a little. "Sorry. Force of services generalist habit."

Still smiling, he shook his sleek head. A shorter strand of hair fell forward with the gesture, framing his jawline. "Well. I'm the services generalist here," he answered with a very low-pitched laugh under his breath, as he took the cup and saucer I'd just set down and put them on the tray.

UFE had gotten its start when Dad was a small child. I'd seen some of the founders honored for the branch's fiftieth anniversary, during my first few years in the organization. One of them was dimly in my mind's eye as I sat back: a petite white-haired marine biologist with a soft voice and big shining eyes. In my competitive diving teen days, I'd unsuccessfully striven to beat records she'd held for decades.

My gaze focused for the first time on another pair of noble older faces, a framed photograph on the end table near my elbow. Lachlan so resembled the old man in the photo--his broad forehead and strong brow, the slight upturn to the end of the nose, the attractively angular jaw--that I would have said it could be his father. But even if I hadn't already seen Kenneth Adie's photo, I knew Lachlan's mother would never reach the age of the lovely white-haired woman at this man's side. I looked closer at him, handsome well beyond his years. The newly familiar wide-set eyes didn't appear as dark as those of anyone else of his kind I'd met so far.

"This must be--the lady who owned the house?" I said to Geir as he came back from the kitchen.

He nodded. "Isla Russell Maclachlan and her true love, Elis."

I drew a breath. "I figured he'd look the way you do."

"Oh. He does again, now she's gone."

The question of Elis' actual age, any of their ages, the expected selkie lifespan, stuck in my larynx and would have to wait for another time. Geir smiled at the look that must be on my face.

I swallowed and tried again. "How is that? Shapeshifting, too?"

He paused. "It's so weird to get to say this to anyone who hasn't always known it... And you'd have to get himself to explain it to you if you want the actual science, but--The energies that make us who we are, we seem to draw them from the North Sea."

"Even if it's really the Atlantic on this coast, isn't it?" Wow, had my inner Dad seriously needed to point that out right now?

Geir had the grace just to laugh at me quietly. "So it is, though in all my years, I've never yet swum through any border crossing."

"Yeah. Anyway."

"Anyway. Limit our time there enough, and we become much closer to human. So if there's someone to grow old with.... We can choose that, as he did with her."

And the effect was obviously reversible: if they spent more time than normal beneath the waves, wearing their sealskins, I imagined.

"I guess your mom did that for your dad? Step-dad. Her fisherman."

He shook his head. "Different times. There were people who still believed the tales, in those days. Calum knew us for who we were, and she didn't have to hide it. We lived a bit off by ourselves, so there weren't ever many questions. He didn't really live to a great age, either, unfortunately."

"Well, what about you?" I heard myself asking, again before I could think better of it. "With your… other fishermen's daughters? Have you ever chosen to look like an old man before?"

My boldness earned me more than the usual fraction of his warm smile. He nodded again. "Like the old man I am, you mean? Och, every chance I've ever been given."

I kept pondering it after I said good afternoon to everyone and headed south. Excessive flirting aside, he seemed like a pretty good guy. It was hard to think of him setting himself up for what sounded like the repeated loss of his own true loves. It was harder to think how soon, from their perspective, the same thing would happen for Brynja. No wonder none of them seemed to consider Lachlan too young for her. If I was right, there was no human alive old enough; she would have so little time with him, as it was. I found myself siding more with Hano, supposing selkie lovers would be the less painful way to go. Well, then again, not that anyone—let alone such an apparently accomplished ladies' man--should be taking relationship advice from me.

Chapter 7

Little Havia

The next four days, between that first real visit and the dive my selkie folk had been plotting, felt like as much of a gray blur as their seal forms glimpsed under the water. Once, accompanying Vega on her evening rounds, we came close enough I could see their beautiful house across the sound from us.

A woman something like Vega's age answered our knock.

"Hi, good afternoon," Vega said. "UFE. Just seeing if you need anything."

Her tired, freckled face lit with relief. "Have you got biodegradable nappies? Newborn size ones. We can't launder properly, without our power or water back yet..."

Vega chewed her lip a second. "If I don't, I'll have some sent up. How old is your baby?"

"Nineteen and at uni in Glasgow now, where his dad is." She smiled. "My sister's is about eighteen hours old."

"What?" Vega stood to her full height. "And you didn't bring her to the hospital, why?"

I didn't remind her plenty of babies around the world weren't born in hospitals, and we'd turned out just fine. Her preference, with the newest tech and the sterile gloves, was hardly the only way.

The woman straightened her shoulders, and her smile altered as she shook her curly brown head. "No, I'm a nurse-midwife. We'd always planned on having her here. Just… with the power on. Turns out everything was beautiful without it, though. Textbook. Perfect baby girl at thirty-eight weeks. I'd have gone to see about supplies in the morning, but… here you are."

"Wow," Vega said, somewhat more gentle. She highlighted her badge. "Well, I'm a doctor, so if there's anything else I can do for your sister… I'd like to look in on the baby and her."

"Come in." The woman shrugged, stepping back from the door. "I'm Mairi Ross. Emer is my sister. The baby's called Finley."

Mairi might have a slight chip on her shoulder, but Emer, the younger blonde version of her, was grateful to see us. Once she'd passed her own part of the check-up with high marks, I held the surprisingly wiggly little Finley. She watched me with the tiniest disapproving old lady face while Vega took care of her mom and Mairi looked through what we had in the hover.

"Well, your sister's right. You superwomen didn't need anybody's help," Vega concluded, tucking Emer back in.

"Thanks," Emer said with a tired laugh.

"Last thing; this is a medical statement, not me getting in your business, okay? Because some ladies do like to play roulette."

I rolled my eyes back to Finley's cute scrunchy expression. Again with this. Not much point trading side effects most people never noticed, but I certainly didn't enjoy, for some benefits I hadn't needed in a long time. Not to mention the others which, by all credible medical accounts, nature had probably provided for me free of charge.

"But you're fine to restart treatments whenever you want," Vega went on. "I have a first dose here if you like. A few mamas tell us it doesn't help with their milk production, though. So if it's… just you three here, how it looks, you'd be okay to wait a little while. Then come see us when you're ready."

Emer smiled, not exactly meeting Vega's eyes, either. "For now it's just Finley and Mair and me, but you know these things change…"

Vega answered with a low-pitched, conspiratorial laugh and one more pointed look in my general direction. "Yeah, girl."

She scanned Emer's ring data first, to track the treatment for her medical file. Then she retrieved a laser injector from her kit, fitted a little vial of chartreuse fluid into the chamber. She placed the injection among the golden freckles on Emer's soft shoulder.

"So, even though she's very good at this, no little brother or sister until mama's ready again, Miss Finley," Vega said to the baby, who wrinkled up her face in a disdainful yawn. "You're right. No icky bugs or boy cooties, either. Unless mama does something super crazy in the next seventy-two hours."

"God, no worries there," Emer giggled.

Mairi brought us fresh strong tea, and we passed the baby around so everyone could enjoy a cup with oatcakes she'd toasted in a skillet over her match-lit gas stove and drizzled with honey. Before we moved on, we exchanged information in case she were to need our help. Superwomen that they both were, I doubted it.

All Lachlan had said in the ring that set my heartbeat on edge was *About time you check out the undersea kingdom*

"Hey," he greeted me at his door, but he tapped his wrist. "I'm just on for a sec…"

He paused, listening to a voice in his cochlear circuit.

"Believe it or not, Oliver Araujo's daughter, who's some manner of selkie folk herself."

He listened for a moment, rolling his eyes at me. "Yeah. Amazing coincidence. I'll tell you another time." Another pause. "Ach, Elis. Yeah, if I had eyes for anyone but my queen, I'd surely think so, okay?… Stop… Yes, she's really well. You know how Edinburgh wears on her, so she's glad to be home, and having both the twins here too... Oh yeah, and you can let her know how it's been going. Hold on."

He called inside the house, not in English--and sounding even more Viking-like than usual. I remembered Ysmay speaking briefly that first day in Lerwick Harbor, Brynja greeting Berenys. Of course, Lachlan would have learned the selkiese language too.

Brynja appeared in the doorway. He slipped the ring off his wrist, a plain sport one like mine, and gave it to her.

She patted her pockets one at a time. Looking for an earbud to connect. For that instant, she was exactly like Doña Maite, my grand-mother in Florida, who wasn't suited to receive implants, like many older human people. Obviously, implants couldn't work for a shape-shifter's two quite distinct species of ears, and I could only imagine how much older than Maite Brynja might be.

Lachlan touched a command on the ring where it rested in her upturned white palm. "Here, my heart. Right? Just project it."

I would have bet her smoke-soft words meant *Thanks, my love.* She stepped back inside.

He smiled at the look I didn't doubt was on my face. "Have a go at me and my older woman. I can take it."

"Nah." I laughed. "You just took all the fun out of it, offering like that."

"Ach, well." He shrugged, laughing too.

"I can't be the only one who ever thought the opposite, anyway."

"You're not." He glanced where she'd gone. "It's hard for me to remember how she looks to other people. She never seemed that way to me."

"Your mates at university," I guessed.

He nodded.

"I can't really imagine them giving you too hard a time about it, though..."

"Well. The teenage wedding thing, a fair bit. But otherwise... I mean, of the lads I know there, I'm the only one who's never spent a night alone in our block of flats except when she has to be up here without me, so."

As if a guy like him needed more respect than life afforded him already. I laughed. Still smiling too, he gave another easy shrug.

"Speaking of the old folks... that was your finman granddad? Or--is it selkie-level security clearance stuff you can't tell me?"

He raised his blond brows, with a different smile. "You know she's granted you the full security clearance, Arden. When the university suspended instruction, he took off for some of the other islands to send word about how our people are doing there. Ordinarily, there's no easy way for all of them to stay connected, you know? So Orkney, first, and soon he'll likely go on to the Hebrides."

"Oh. He studies in Edinburgh too?"

Lachlan shook his head. Of course not; he'd need extensive documentation, enrollments and exams, medical and tax records, and I still doubted whether any of these guys were even legitimately on the grid.

"He's worked as a caretaker at different universities for years, before and after Gran."

"Like an actual job," I stopped him. "With a paycheck."

His "Yeah" sounded as much like a question as an answer. "But he'll sneak into the libraries and lectures... finman his way into labs and supply cabinets... Anyway, he likes the travel, same as Berenys and Ysmay. In time she might send them and maybe Geir along as well, although so far they've been kept busy here."

"Will anyone check in on Norway?"

"I don't know." His tone softened, although his words didn't spare me. "To be honest, we're not sure who, if anyone, is left on that side. In the past they've found ways to send each other the big news... updating population numbers, leadership passing from one to another. But no one's heard anything from them in this century, if I'm remembering right. Bryn has sent people east looking before, same as she's having Elis do now. And Johan the Fair, the last leader's name was? Something like that. Anyway--when Kjaran died, Bryn's husband then, and she took his place here, I know she sent someone to Johan--assuming it was still him--but they didn't find him or anybody else to tell. Not that that proves anything. Bit tricky researching a fairytale, even with modern tech, isn't it."

"Oh." I sighed.

"Sorry if I shouldn't have just said it like that," he murmured, watching my face.

I shook my head. "It's okay. I just… would have liked the chance to know them."

He nodded.

We were still quiet when Brynja reappeared. A quick, compassionate glance, a gently revealing caress of my hair and my cheek caught her up on the conversation.

She answered in words, though. "We're not in the same place but we're one people, Arden. It's the same sea. We're all your family."

"Okay," I whispered.

"Your mother lived in Bergen? What was her name?"

"Rea Strand." I shrugged. "I don't even know she lived there. Just that I was born there. When she and Dad used to see each other, it was in Kristiansand."

"Have you got a photo?"

I shook my head. "He didn't keep any."

She looked thoughtful for a few moments, but ultimately shook her head too. "Still, surprises can come at any time. We do make ourselves hard to find. Elis was just saying he met a young couple in Whitehall. Living on their boat for the last forty-five years, not attached to anywhere. Who knows how many more there could be, or in what little corners of the earth they're keeping away from the wrong eyes."

"Okay," was all I could whisper again.

She smiled, much closer to a real person's mom than a full-force Galadriel. "And I'm doing that thing again where I push you too close to crying, though I swear I mean the opposite."

I quickly rubbed my eyes as I shook my head. "No, you're--like listening, this time. Before, you were showing me things."

Her smile shifted, provoking a quick chill after all.

"You'll learn to manage it, too."

"Uh. Really? How do I…"

She drew a slow, audible breath. Then she breathed out a controlled stream of air, like dive team practice.

Only not with your actual lungs, I thought I understood.

Brynja's hand was still on my arm. I visualized breathing out to her my pleasure and curiosity. Probably I was physically breathing out, as well, but she didn't comment.

Then I tried to concentrate on drawing her consciousness in, like oxygen. She was focusing very specifically on me: the color and texture of my skin, how unusual for there to be any blue in hazel eyes as dark as mine, the sun hitting the tight waves of my hair, the standard laundry detergent and shampoo bar scents in lieu of anything more stylish.

For fun, just to see, as I breathed out I pictured my dresser top at home. My appearance seemed to provoke enough curiosity that I'd never bothered much with makeup, but perfumes were a different story. Dad had brought them home from his travels from when I was about fifteen on, divine things from the duty-free that no one else at school or work had. I'd kept them on a cut-crystal tray that had belonged to his adored Irish grandmother, once upon a time. I remembered each bottle, the varied colors and fragrances. I didn't choose with my mind's eye the one I'd pick up right now if I were there. I thought about the lush scent itself: citrus blossoms, sandalwood, and pink pepper sparkling in the lightest vanilla musk.

"Sirenetta di Bulgari?" she murmured, wide-eyed with delight. "I wouldn't expect someone your age to like something so old-fashioned, but yes, it's always beautiful."

"Holy crap," I said, once my mouth would form words.

She nodded, brows lifting further with her slight eloquent smile. "There's a full bottle on Isla's dressing table. I think maybe someone gave it to her, but she just liked her Chanel. It's yours if you want it."

"Ach." Lachlan laughed. "I'll get it if you like, Arden, but don't take that to mean I don't hate you right now."

Again. For ending up with so much more than him. I managed not to laugh aloud at the irony, because at the same time, I understood. All I got from him were emotions, not full-on sensory overload like I did from her. He'd listened in on our exchange, his hand lightly on the back of her shoulder. Given the depth of their connection, I had a hunch he'd perceive more from her than from someone he'd only known a few days, but I guessed he must not get to share this kind of impressions and perceptions.

"At least you know where the hell yours came from."

"So will you," Brynja assured me. "Only give us some time to work it out."

Lachlan cut quite the long, lean selkie-Viking hybrid figure when he met the rest of us at the pier, wearing only incongruously hibiscus-patterned blue board shorts. Even when he'd put on the wetsuit he kept on board, he left the top half and sleeves hanging loose around his hips. Tolerance to their cold environment was a logical enough selkie trait, though one he'd managed to carry down the family tree with him a lot better than I had. When we met, I'd pretty much gone straight from thinking of him as my adversary to considering him sort of a younger brother--but right now, I took a moment to concede that Brynja was a seriously fortunate woman. (The family's big skimmer hover was a hell of a lot more luxurious than the typical UFE models, to boot.)

I didn't want to make too big a point of his exposed skin, once we were on our way west, but still gestured with my glance toward his right upper arm. "Wouldn't really have taken you for a tattoo guy."

He chuckled as he looked down at the Norse world serpent, fierce head biting the tail in the sculpted hollow where deltoid met bicep. He held up his left hand in front of his chest, displaying the narrower band of artwork halfway up that forearm. Viking style, too: a warrior's arm ring.

"There may have been a bit of a phase, my first years at uni, reminding my dad I was my own man." Another short laugh. "Possibly aided and abetted by a particular troublesome finman you've not met yet, who enjoyed flexing his rare ability to piss Dad off."

The sight of his actual ring, below the tattooed one, reminded him of something. "Hey. We've got to disable our locators here, obviously."

I caught back a breath and shook my head. "UF overrides that for all of us."

"Shut it off entirely?" Ysmay suggested.

I guessed that was the best I could do. Even so, I risked raising an alert by powering it down. Maybe, in the unlikely event anyone was tracking a second-string generalist on her day off, I could say it malfunctioned. I'd had this one at least two years.

Closer to the site, I got into my suit too, shucking off my uniform pants and pulling the limestone neoprene up over my gooseflesh as fast as I could, then repeating the process for my top half. Berenys eyed my UF-issue bathing suit avidly enough that I might have wondered if she was ogling me, had the garments not been too utilitarian for her or anyone else to bother: basically one unisex style, fitted rash guard and shorts in plain charcoal gray.

"I thought maybe you'd have--ach, the pretty ones, like Bryn's underthings?"

By this point, most of the selkies were stripped down as well, in preparation for our impending dive. I hadn't looked directly at Brynja while she undressed--not that she or any of them seemed to mind-- but I'd glimpsed the matching delicate pale green lingerie before she slipped out of it. Now I got a better look than I'd bargained for, as Berenys lifted the miniature brassiere lightly between her white thumbs and forefingers for my perusal. It was nicer than I'd ordinarily bother investing in, richly detailed lace embellished with satiny embroidery. Exactly what I guessed I'd picture a faerie queen wearing beneath her airy lambswool sweater tunics.

Lachlan made a sound somewhere between an Ach, a chuckle, and clearing his throat.

Like him, I was learning to roll with such talk, though, and its implications. "These are work clothes." I laughed too. "I have a drawer full of bikinis in storage. Don't you?"

She giggled sweetly, like the adolescent girl she appeared to be. "Whatever for?"

There wasn't much to do but smile. "You could still have one just because it's pretty, couldn't you? Maybe from wherever Bryn gets her underthings."

"Nothing in the shops here fits her. He orders them from Asia," she told me under her breath, loud enough for Lachlan to hear too. Then she held the dainty straps against her shoulders, draping the filmy garment over her still fully-clothed chest with a curious downward glance. She arched her back a bit, one shoulder forward, then the other; then, with an expert flick of her ridiculous lashes, she quirked a saucy little glance up at us as if to ask someone's opinion.

"Yep," Lachlan laughed, out loud this time. There wasn't any awkward tension in the way he stood and dusted his hands on his thighs before heading across the deck to where the rest of the selkie folk had gone. Dressed as he was, there was also no hiding the blush creeping from beneath his beard, down toward his chest as well as up his cheeks. Brynja's pretty blond boy toy must be accustomed by now to taking his fair share of teasing from the family he'd married into.

I considered that none of the weird sisters might have been as stylish as Berenys and Brynja were now, before Lachlan Adie's bank account entered the picture. Though I failed when I tried to imagine Berenys in the thrift-store finds Geir still seemed to favor. All I knew for sure was that she would manage the same understated allure, whatever clothes she had.

Whatever Lachlan muttered when he walked over to the other two men made all three burst into companionable laughter, surprisingly loud for selkie folk. Without thinking it through, I looked over to see what was so funny and caught an eyeful of two mythical boyish asses. Thankfully, the one guy facing in my direction was still tastefully clad in blue hibiscus print.

"Hey," he teased. "Eyes up here."

Berenys giggled aloud, too. Lachlan gave Hano a light prompting slap behind the shoulder. Amid more laughter, both selkie men slipped into the water, then their seal shapes; Geir cast a quick, unrepentantly smiling glance back at me first. Beside me, his niece muttered something fond and disparaging, punctuated with more soft giggling.

Still laughing too, Lachlan reminded me, "Naturist set of the North Sea, these ones. It doesn't mean much to them."

"You know quite well it means as much for us as for you." Brynja's tone provoked the full-on blush Berenys' antics had warmed him up for. I supposed I could be forgiven for not noticing her sooner, sitting beside where her brothers' feet had been, her own feet dangling toward the water.

"Just that for us it means more than that one thing it seems to for your kind, Arden. So yes, popping off a boat, for example... I don't see why anyone should care."

"Right," I said with another laugh, although I couldn't help thinking just the one of them certainly did continue appearing to care.

Lachlan smiled. "They'll have you skinny dipping with them in no time."

We anchored south of Little Havra, took ourselves off the grid, fitted ourselves with Steyn rebreather prototypes, and hit the water a minute or two behind the others. They'd hung back to wait for us, though I didn't imagine Lachlan needed a guide to where we were going.

The clear, chilly water felt more delicious than a well-earned scoop of ice cream after a grungy day in the field. I found myself fighting the ill-advised urge to ditch my wetsuit like the full selkie folk.

I couldn't tell the girls apart in seal form, even less than I'd been able to distinguish their human faces from one another at first. Hano was still the slightly larger of the two darker males. All six were so effortless in their strength, speed, and grace, I battled envy again toward whoever had been born far enough up my family line to share that much of the magic.

I imagined we were following Brynja, nearly straight down for a little more than twenty meters, coming to a vent between undersea boulders overgrown with wrack. I could have passed right by it, if not for the selkies, then Lachlan vanishing from my view between two sandstone surfaces. I was grateful to know I could have gasped nasty-tasting rebreather air, though I didn't take advantage of it, in the few sharp heartbeats before I followed them.

Just inside the vent, Lachlan turned to look in my direction, blue eyes selkie dark in the otherworldly green half-light.

"Okay?" he said in my rebreather mask earpiece, startling me. I hadn't realized they would stay connected even with my ring powered off. Nice safety feature.

I didn't want to give up on my held breath and talk yet. I nodded and gave the standard diver's thumbs-up.

"Right. Show-off." He laughed, switched his headlamp on, and went ahead. He had to turn kind of sideways and maneuver his cautious way through, but after a few seconds, his fins disappeared after the seal flippers. Taking a deep mental breath, even if my physical lungs were still waiting for one, I turned my lamp on and followed. I was small enough to fit through pretty well, though I did feel my glutes brushing against the rock face above me as I gingerly pulled myself through with my hands.

The narrow space was only a few meters long. Beyond that, it opened into a somewhat wider tunnel. I could use my fins here, a tight flutter kick like Lachlan was doing. There were maybe ten meters of nearly horizontal before we started angling sharply upward.

The reduction of pressure was telling me we were just about at the surface when I ran into a rush-hour tangle of seal forms. It felt like Runa I bumped into. I couldn't understand her anxiety, but it was contagious: I activated my rebreather to catch a sour, clammy breath.

"What's going on?" I asked Lachlan, though I couldn't see him amid the knot of seals.

His voice was serious enough to sound commanding, though not panicked. "Touch them and ask them to let you get up here. She could use your light."

Making my way through a changeable tunnel of sleek pinniped shapes as everyone transmitted simultaneous concern and support, to one another and right on to me as they nudged me higher up the passage, I truly understood the reason for their wordless skin-to-skin communication for the first time.

The bottleneck was a kind of valve, crafted by who knew what hands, how long ago or how recently. I gathered it had malfunctioned by the way Lachlan was tugging at a mechanism I couldn't see very well. I willed my heart not to race. We were underground, underwater, and off-grid, but I'd barely tapped the capacity of my rebreather, and we belonged to one hell of a team.

One of the selkie women was near us, in her human form, tiny hands emerging from the black cloud of her hair to work at something else. I moved carefully alongside, aiming my headlamp at what she was attempting.

Shoulder to shoulder, though I couldn't see her face, I knew it was Ysmay. She didn't share anyone else's worry. I breathed easier, knowing she wasn't panicked for breath at all. She'd had to jury-rig this thing together in the first place, as the tides had risen ever higher: long enough ago that sometimes it would stick, these days. She'd never been unable to get it moving before.

Chapter 8

Hudson Canyon

Not more than a minute later, I felt the current as water started to flow through the widening opening. Ysmay, mermaid hair aswirl in the headlamp beam, flashed me her brightest weird sister smile in triumph before she swam on up, leaving a glittering trail of bubbles. Lachlan smiled too, and motioned me after her.

The second valve, at the top of the tunnel, opened without difficulty and we emerged into a little pool. I pulled my rebreather mask awkwardly off and looked around a grotto a lot like the sea cave where I'd seen them shift their shapes for the first time. Except that here, there were more wide dark eyes, more pale faces than the six I knew. Maybe twenty more. My heart fluttered sharply.

No one said anything I'd be able to hear, all of them shoulder to shoulder staring at me. Their uneasy silence felt pretty loud, to the weirdly-colored finfolk-like stranger my friends had brought into their midst. They weren't doing the selkie naturist thing here at home, which answered one question I hadn't figured out how to pose. What they wore mostly looked old, scavenged, thrift-store style, without much regard for the season outside.

Brynja spoke with calm authority, her low voice carrying over the pool's surface. A few answered her aloud, selkiese syllables like *Rø*something*meen* (with the weird ø sound I remembered from starting to learn Norwegian, between English "rook" and French *rue*). I didn't recall learning a word for *queen* in NOR 101. But I had a pretty strong sense it hadn't just been me, and wasn't just a term of endearment either, when Lachlan referred to her as such.

One man countered her--with ringing sharpness that surprised me both because it was a quality most finfolk voices lacked, and because he was the only person I'd ever heard take such a tone with her.

She tossed her regal head and gave me an encouraging hint of a smile. She'd apparently said all she planned to say.

When the man went on challenging--me, her, whichever--Lachlan answered. His selkiese was fluent enough to spur an envious pang in my chest; full of heartfelt conviction, certainly less quiet than anyone else's, with a touch of Highland accent still noticeable around its slightly rough edges. Whatever this guy's argument was, Lachlan wasn't having it. He'd been so amiable after our first meeting, I'd forgotten how quickly his temper had amped on the night we'd met.

I thought I caught a word like *hvalp* on the finman's barbed tongue, "puppy" in Norwegian. I got a pretty clear sense he tolerated the leader's young husband only because Brynja hadn't given anyone another option. I would have bet that even so, these two had clashed once or twice before. The image of a territorial battle between two bull seals flickered briefly through my awareness.

Lachlan pulled himself easily out of the pool to stand face to face with the other guy, both of them still talking. The selkie man was taller than Geir or Hano, but like them, all wiry muscle. Still, I was fairly confident he was no match for our burly Viking defender if their mutually aggressive vibes were to take physical form.

Brynja watched them coolly from the water. Then again, I wouldn't put it past her to end a guy like this with nothing more than her thoughts, if she'd decided to. Between the two factors--for now, at least--no one moved any further.

Lachlan's bright eyes scanned the small assembly. I didn't catch the sounds he uttered next, but I understood they'd been a person's name when a young woman edged forward.

Dark hair falling past the fringed hem of cutoff shorts worn with what might have been a local school kid's football jersey, she appeared maybe college age, several centimeters taller than Berenys or Ysmay. She seemed more like an exceptionally pretty human, not so much an impossibly perfect fae creature. Her eyes, a warm lighter brown rather than espresso-black, were round and free from malice as a child's at the sight of my foreign face.

Ysmay greeted her as well. The girl came to sit on the lip of the pool, feet dangling, as Ysmay led me over to her.

"Sefa," Ysmay repeated her name for me. "You remember."

I didn't, until I touched the tapered hand she held out. Her impression was harder to grasp, clouded, distant, but I saw myself--bending toward her, talking in soothing nonsense syllables. I recognized a pale sketch of Noemi Engel behind me.

"Sefa," I agreed. "Wow. I'm glad to see you again."

She hugged me lightly and said something else, close to my ear. The only sound I understood for sure was "thanks": softer than Norwegian, more like *dakk* instead of *takk*, but recognizable.

"Thank you for helping her Seoras to be at peace," Ysmay translated. "A lot of these ones don't know English... but you're clever. You'll learn our words."

Raising her head at a familiar, lofty angle, she arched one brow at my challenger while her slight pleased smile lingered.

His eyes, stubbornly fixed on me a moment or two more, remained dark and cold as the Hudson Canyon. He didn't say anything else, though. Eventually, he bent his head a degree or two in Brynja's direction and shifted his gaze away.

He wasn't the only one who slipped away into the recesses of the caves without waiting around to greet their leader, however, let alone the unlikely visitor she'd brought. I finally heard one or two of them muttering to each other as they went. Repeating a series of sounds I'd heard from his mouth more than once. *Ut land isk*, or close to that. Doing a little verbal math, I guessed *out land... Foreigner.*

"Thanks for having my back," I said to Ysmay.

Her eyebrows danced like the reflection off the water. "Huh?"

I put my hand on her slippery little shoulder and said it again, allowing her selkie sense to fill in the meaning. She nodded, although as I breathed in, I found I hadn't needed any visual signal.

I waited there as she wanted, treading clear water while she slipped beneath its surface without any splash. I watched our selkies climb out of the pool. A woman held a dress out for Brynja, a bias-cut chambray maxi with spaghetti straps, a popular style when I was in high school. What the woman herself wore brushed the floor, and was faded to no color I could name. A lot older than the vintage collection I'd seen Geir sporting, if I had to guess. Lachlan kept his wetsuit on, which I quickly decided would be great for me as well.

Ysmay swam back up in front of me and offered a pale sea urchin on her palm, spines still wriggling.

I smiled. "Pretty."

Startling me with a smoky low laugh like Brynja's, she delicately reached both thumbs into the creature's central opening and tore it in half with one decisive, practiced outward motion. She fished out a little golden sac of roe, dipped it cradled between her fingers in the pristine water, and offered it to me.

My own laugh transmuted to a stifled groan of pleasure as she retrieved a bite for herself as well.

Ysmay's big eyes flashed amusement, darting to her sister--standing very close to one stunning young man, who seemed glad she'd come to visit--as if to invite my agreement that Berenys' cooking had nothing on hers. I just laughed again. Ysmay wiped a stray drop of juices from the corner of my mouth. The treat had been a reward for putting up with those of her people who weren't ready to trust me yet, as well as thanks for trusting she wouldn't fail to open the valve.

"They just met me, though; I have no reason to doubt you." I honestly wasn't trying to earn another piece, but I didn't refuse it, either.

Sefa was on her way back to offer us thrift-store finds to put on. I touched Ysmay's hand and shared how different Sefa's impression had felt. Ysmay answered with a slightly abstract, but sharp and saturated image of her own: herself, the same as yesterday or today, holding a baby whom I understood to be Sefa.

"She's our youngest, not counting Lachlan," Ysmay added. "Hardly older than you."

That was the reason for the dramatic lessening of the communicative ability? "Okay," I said, moving my hand away as if that settled it; actually, I didn't want Ysmay to sense my keen disappointment. Something between the size of a family and the size of a kingdom, Geir had told me their people were, when we'd met. With all my heart, I didn't want their most astonishing species ever to devolve or dwindle.

Lifting herself weightlessly to the edge of the pool, Ysmay traded the last piece of uni for an old dress. Sefa ate it with an endearing little grin. I declined the other dress, and together we made our way into her home.

I didn't realize I'd expected a real kingdom underwater--spires, stairs, rooms with human furnishings. Not until I saw what was really here, and remembered I'd been the one to suggest it in the first place. What they actually had reminded me of places I'd been, but certainly nowhere in Disneyland.

We walked through a surprisingly big cavern where I never had to duck my head, though Lachlan frequently did. Small groups I imagined to be families seemed to have their own areas set up. Some people were returning from the entry pool to their places in nature's refugee shelter as we passed among them.

Our headlamps weren't the sole illumination here. Others had artificial lights at their little campsite homes--headlamps, flashlights, or battery lanterns, no flames. You wouldn't need fires for cooking, I guessed, if you preferred the North Sea sushi buffet right outside. And although it was cave-cool here if not as stubbornly wintry as above ground, you didn't need a fire for warmth either, likely as you were to be close to the heat of another person's body.

Where Ysmay drifted away from us to curl up knee to knee and not chat with her little buddy Sefa, I noticed they sat on a soft surface of dark furs. Others had them as well, neatly rolled or folded against the cavern wall if no one was wrapped up in them. The familiar pattern of slightly darker spots lifted the tiny hairs that were as close as I got to a pelt of my own.

"Are those..." I tried to ask.

Lachlan nodded. "Not how you might be thinking. Halichoerus grypus or phoca vitulina. Not--you know, beloved ancestors."

Not laughing at myself, because he hadn't, I shook off the moment. I, of all new *ut land isk* visitors to this kingdom, should have remembered--had seen behind my closed eyelids a hundred times--that selkie dead came to rest in their human form.

Brynja ran a warm hand down my arm, smoothing the goose-flesh. "We'd never hunt the seals. But they were widely hunted in the North Sea at one time.... Many of these were gifts from the seals to us, in those days."

Robbing the seal hunters of part of the value of their kills, at the same time. I didn't mind the poetic justice there. Particularly when it occurred to me that in the history of seal hunting, selkies must have suffered collateral damage. Brynja, her hand still on my arm, felt gravely serious and didn't correct my suppositions.

In my childhood selkie storybook, I'd read the legend that fin-folk would stir up storms and wild seas to wreck the ships of those who hunted their little seal friends. But Brynja did a mental equivalent of shaking her head as I considered that. Anyway, if anyone hadn't figured it out before this year, we all knew now that the North Sea was perfectly capable of defending itself from human atrocities.

I didn't fully realize what other memories were bleeding through my thoughts until Brynja reached up to stroke a salt-infused curl back from my temple.

"She doesn't talk to me about it," she murmured. "In time, I hope she'll feel safer telling you."

It wasn't so much the visual of Berenys' bent head in the gray hoodie that I'd been remembering, tears falling into a steaming teacup, although a consciousness such as Brynja's could lift that thread to the forefront of my own. My link between that moment and this wasn't an image, but the sick sinking sensation, the human atrocities from which Berenys had helped defend her little seal friends there.

Brynja shivered slightly, as if the unclear dark emotions I recalled were already more than Berenys had chosen to share. She breathed bruised longing for the wayward child who didn't seem to wish to be understood. Before I could find a way to tell her I got it--although the willfully distant one in my own family hadn't been the child--Brynja reluctantly broke the contact between her silken skin and mine.

I looked around for the real Berenys, but she seemed fittingly enough to have slipped away. With her scorchingly handsome friend, maybe. Wherever they were, I hoped he was making her smile.

Hano and Runa soon drifted off, as well, shrinking our party to just Lachlan, Brynja, Geir, and me.

"Didn't you say--these caves are a newer thing?" I asked Geir as we walked. "Not like in the last few decades, but selkie new. That once upon a time people didn't hide down here."

He gave me a hint of smile. "Well, we've always had them in case we needed... It's just more likely nowadays, for our folk to want such a place at least some of the time."

He glanced at his sister, who nodded.

"Someone's been there as long as I can remember," she said.

I heard a kind of tense crackle in my swallow, biting back the question I still couldn't figure out how to ask.

"I mean." My laugh came out middle-school awkward. "I was just thinking... How many other places in the world people have lived in caves, or used them... you know, much earlier in history."

Brynja nodded again, without any trace of awkwardness herself. "That's what Lachlan thinks. That our people have been here for millennia."

"No evidence of past rituals or anything, I guess could make sense if they've been continuously in use, right?" I asked him. "But I've never seen a cave like that without any kind of pictographs or markings…"

"Can't have evidence of past anything," he countered.

I entertained the half-formed notion that although they couldn't leave visual traces, artwork of their own, they still sensed in the world a music the rest of us could never share. Participated somehow in the ocean's song, if I could believe Geir's explanation that shapeshifting felt akin to singing instead of speech. Maybe that was their artistic expression.

"Well, no, I lied. There are--kind of decorations under Out Skerries and Papa Stour. They aren't cave people's handprints or anything, though. I always thought one sort of--graffiti artist must've done them," Lachlan said, brows lifting.

"Whoever made those, they were already there when I was a girl," Brynja put in. "In Orkney, too. We'll show you, Arden. Another time. You'll come back, won't you?"

"Oh." I smiled wide enough to crack my salt-chapped lower lip. "Hell yes."

Chapter 9

Isle of Wight

Back at the pier after a damp and salty goodbye, my craft made a hair-raising grinding noise, then an ominous series of thunks, without starting.

Runa opened at my sheepish knock.

"Sorry to bother you guys right away."

"No bother," she answered, hardly more than whispering. "What's the matter?"

"My hover won't start, I hoped Ysmay…"

She smiled and called softly over her shoulder in their language. I didn't hear a name; the answering voice could have belonged to Ysmay, or her mother or sister. But it was Geir who came to the door in a moment, pulling the usual worn sweater over his wet head.

"Back already," he greeted me with that little one-corner smile.

"Never left." I glanced back at the idle craft.

"Ah, okay. Battery charge? That's tricky at the moment, but I'll see…"

I shook my head. "No, the battery was full this morning. Is someone chucking a handful of rocks into the motor while I wasn't looking an option?"

"I guess, if they wanted to keep you here badly enough…"

I ignored him. "Well, that's what it sounds like."

"No problems getting here earlier?"

"It's never sounded great, but it was running. Now it won't even turn over."

He walked out with me, barefoot, to where I had parked the craft. As much as various areas of these people's skin had been on display, I hadn't noticed before that he had the webbed toes, too.

"Staring at my weird feet, Generalist?" he teased, as if he hadn't made it abundantly clear he was comfortable with me looking at whatever part of him I liked.

I couldn't help smiling. "Nah. Same as mine. Selkie thing, right?"

"You could have compared everyone's feet today," he said with another smile. Or smirk.

"So could you. Anyway." I popped open the access panel over the motor. "I'm no mech, but it's pretty obviously this fan."

Still smiling to himself, he opened the housing.

"Handful of rocks," he agreed, holding up two treacherous shards of what should have been the fan blade.

"Hijodeputa."

"Not properly modified for saltwater, is my guess."

"Typical half-ass short-on-time UF job," was my own guess. "I don't suppose you have a spare lying around, that you feel like letting me have."

"We might do. Come on, we'll have a look."

I followed him to a little shed under the deck. It wasn't locked. He rummaged through bins and shelves.

"You're not just here because you got evicted from someplace else by the tsunami, huh," I realized aloud.

He looked around, his eyes meeting mine. "You're right that where I lived before is gone. It was at the south end of Lerwick Harbor, so. But no, I've been here since Isla died.

"The Maclachlans lived in Nairn; this was a second home, and Elis came with it. He was her caretaker, soon her choice of revenge against her contemptible brute of a husband over the next fifty years. They lived up here together the last ten, after Blaine was gone. She left the place to Elis, but understandably he didn't have it in him to stay here without her… so he gave Lachlan the house, and asked me to take over his job and keep that in the family, too."

"Really?"

He quirked his head to the side. "Of course. And Ysmay helps part-time when I need her. Just because my sister found a rich lad to keep her, doesn't mean the rest of us sponge off him."

"No, I just thought…"

"Mythical beasties don't require money?" he said, his hint of smile teasing but not mean.

I rolled my eyes away. "No. I get it, if you're going to live up here…"

He nodded. "The half-life, Elis calls the secretive hunter-gathering thing. It's never been for either of us."

"Yeah, I don't blame you." Especially not now I'd seen that alternative first-hand. "But I meant… just taking care of someone's boats and grounds and stuff? I thought you were joking when you said services generalist."

"How no? Invisible man, a job like this. Elis always thought it was perfect."

"But you…" It was unexpectedly weird to put it into words. "I mean. With the Shakespeare, and… Today they greeted you all like… Leaders," I said instead of *royalty*.

"Oh." He went back to work, unfazed. "Not how you're probably thinking. Our people have always deferred to the oldest ones among us. The oldest mother, particularly. In the past that didn't mean one family, the way it does these days.

"And this is nice work for an older fellow." He was teasing again. "Not as rough as

fishing."

"Or sheep or pony herding, I guess?"

He moved things around in another bin, shook his head. "Yeah, can't say I never tried those, but we're always most drawn to the salt-water creatures, aren't we."

"Yep, I guess we are."

"Elis was better at this stuff than I am, though. As far as your newer tech goes, he and Ysmay have always been the clever ones in our peerie tribe."

"Yeah, how come I get you for this when I asked for her?"

With a triumphant little smile, he held up a blade, of comparable size though it didn't look brand new. At least it was in one sturdy-looking piece, and presumably modified for saltwater.

"Because Runa has always had a soft spot for her fisher boy baby brother," he said, the smile going charmingly crooked.

I sighed, biting back my own smile. "Walked right into that," I said, more to myself than to him.

From a different shelf, he picked up a clean rag and what looked like a little bottle of motor oil. "With sparkly bits on both your wee selkie feet," he agreed, and closed the shed. I followed him back to the pier.

During one of my unsuccessful stints in college, I'd decided to have the webbing pierced; since then I'd sported little crystals, like for a lip piercing, where normal girls could wear toe rings if they wanted. I'd been in a phase of learning to celebrate my differences. The short laugh I didn't keep back was as much for that irony as for the flirtiest little bastard on Shetland, of course, being the only one to notice my silly body modification.

Wrong again. "Berenys wants to know how much that hurt," he said with a glance down at my boots as they crunched over the path.

I shrugged. "You know. Things hurt. I guess they took longer to heal than some. Less time than others."

The eyes he lifted to my face were like hers, velvety brown-black unadulterated by any fleck of lighter color. He didn't make any more smart remarks. He just watched me for a few seconds and nodded his head. For that moment, he didn't look like a kid to me at all.

We'd made it back down to my craft. Still without comment, he bent to his task.

"You've seen fashion trends come and go," I said, watching his small deft hands managing to remove the mangled shards without injuring himself. I slipped the pieces into a gather bag I'd found on board. "What's a couple weird selkie feet piercings to you. Did you have any favorites over the years?"

He smiled without looking up. "Well, it's Shetland, not Paris. But yeah, we have seen things change. Especially once there were the pictures, and telly… internet… and now the grid."

I attempted to push a stray salt-sticky curl off my forehead with the back of my wrist without getting grease on my face. "You remember before movies," I challenged.

He glanced up with another hint of smile. "You're sure you're ready for this line of questioning? I can remember before there was any kind of photography."

My eyebrows ran for my hairline, but I made myself nod. "So that one long kind of gray gown someone had on today, with the embroidery? Is that before your time?"

Geir smiled. "Still no photography for the half-life ones... No fashion trends to speak of. For sure I can remember when all the ladies wore their skirts that long..."

"I mean. Were there pants yet?"

He laughed, low but aloud. "Yes."

"Trousers," I said, and had to laugh too. "And kilts? Were they invented?"

"Oh, I'm not sure... that's not a Shetland thing. We did have them for my sister's wedding in Inverness. She said I don't wear one as well as Lachlan does."

Still chuckling at that memory, he picked up the rag and rubbed the inside of the cylinder clean. "How about this. I remember years that started with seventeen."

"Okay," I whispered. "Seventeen what?"

"Best estimation, I was born in 1767." He offered me the little curly smile-corner. "Still okay?"

I took a deep breath, let it out. "I've just… needed some frame of reference."

"Fair enough. Bryn can only guess about her timeline, and her girls may prefer to maintain their ladylike air of mystery, but you're well within your rights to ask. You might have, sooner."

He paused to fish something else out of the bottom of the housing, then oil the threaded ring in the center of the replacement blade.

"The beautiful boat up in the house…" I tried to ask.

"Belonged to Calum Craig once, and then to me," he said in a disarmingly gentle tone. "Back before the ladies wore pants."

Then, with patient little motions, he maneuvered the motor blade into position and replaced the nut and cap he'd scrounged from underneath. He nodded, with a fleeting smile, and pushed the housing shut.

"Okay. Try it now."

I let him take a step back before re-trying the ignition. It protested, but started and ran as smoothly as it ever had. He smiled at me, already cleaning his fingers off with a corner of the rag.

"Thanks."

"Sure." He helped me lower the hood, and I hopped into the craft.

"They still teach about hippies in your history classes?" he asked, eyes bright, before I could shift it out of neutral.

"Of course. California, USA was the epicenter…"

"You asked my favorite fashion trends," he said, half-smiling again.

"Peace and love and generosity. That does sound like you," I admitted.

The smile became a surprisingly sweet grin, at once boyish and not at all. "Bold barefoot lasses with flowers in their long hair. No corsets or girdles or such nonsense," he said, quiet enough I had to work to hear him over the motor but clear enough I caught every word.

I watched his eyes again. "And... what was her name?"

His brows lifted a little in pleasure that I'd figured it out, yet he hesitated a second or two.

"Beryl. Beautiful English rose who came here on holiday one year. The kind of free spirit to stay longer, when she liked what she found. She used to sing me this sad old Orkney folk song about us, even though she thought she was just pretending I was her selkie lover... Joni Mitchell, I think, had recorded a version back then."

"'I am a man upon the land, I am a silkie in the sea, and when I'm far and far frae land, my home it is in Sule Skerry,'" I found myself singing, although very softly and only until I saw the startled tilt of his black brows. The "Oh" sound never made its way to his slightly open mouth.

"Sorry," I filled the lengthening quiet. "You, uh, made it sound like the crappy singing voices were a selkie thing."

He nodded and went on watching me.

"Anyway... it's Joan Baez," I said.

He found his smile, nodded again. "And wherever did you learn a thing so much older than yourself?"

I could only shake my head. "I don't remember."

He nodded one more time, focus lowering with the gesture, his memory concentrated on his own 1960s folk singer.

I didn't like making him sad. "Hopefully you didn't die tragically at the side of your kidnapped mystery baby, like in the song," I suggested in as light a tone as I could manage. Obviously, the old folk tune wasn't research-based: among other inconsistencies, the finman character was ugly.

As he shook his head, his quiet laugh faded into a wistful smile that wasn't aimed in my direction. "Though you might enjoy knowing that she and Elis and I took the mystery baby to the Isle of Wight Festival with us, to hear the real Joan. Joni as well, actually. And that the baby went on to live a truly great, long life. Most of it far and far from here, yes, but that was of her choosing."

"...Oh," I breathed.

His focus barely flicked up toward my face; as if to ease my awkward quiet, he touched the cuff of his sweater sleeve. "She made this for me. Beryl did, not our girl."

"You come from a family like yours, and work for a family like his, and you're still wearing a hundred-and-thirty-year-old sweater because it was a gift from someone you loved?"

He looked thoughtfully at the brown-gray garment. "More like a hundred years." His eyes found mine once more. "As I've said, I gave her every reason I could to stay."

A guy like him must have developed a pretty robust skill set for that. I bit my lip from the inside, and let his gaze hold mine. He might be ten times my age, but I found myself wondering whether he would really have had any more lovers than I had. Just that for him, such relationships would have been far from the fleeting kind that had been regrettably normal in my life.

"Which you'd better not. At least, not at the moment, right?" he added with a different, friendly kind of smile.

"Huh?"

"Stay."

I attempted to shake off the spell. "Right. Seriously, thanks so much for your help."

"Thanks for all of yours," he answered in a silken murmur, his eyes warm and steady on my face until I was the one to look away.

By the time I made it back to Scalloway, my stomach was strongly reminding me how long ago our sandwiches on the boat had been. Very different lovely brown eyes smiled at me from our customary table at May's.

"Hey." I smiled, sliding into a spot across from his. "You're the language person. You don't know any Norwegian, do you?"

Stefek laughed. "Not yet. Should I?"

I tried to tell just enough of the truth. "I've been spending time with this family. Really proud Shetlanders, you know? There's an old, basically Norse dialect that was spoken here once, and they've sort of studied it and were showing some of it off to me… I took that little bit of Norwegian in college, but I only know enough to know they sound a lot alike. I'm just trying to put together some of what they said."

"Cool. What language is it? Was? Is?"

"Uh, I don't know if it has a name…"

He gestured a few purposeful flicks with the fingers of his ring hand. "Norn, it's called. Not just a dialect, its own language. Have you tried matrixing it yet?"

"What?"

He tapped his ear, shot me an Ysmay look.

"Oh yeah. I didn't think to."

Any more than I liked rebreathers or food prep gloves, I considered as I reactivated the appropriate ring connection. Although these days, my not wanting a layer of anything between me and the world made more sense than it once had.

We accessed the language matrix that had nevertheless been valuable during a recent UFE assignment among the Amazonian Mashco-Piro. The logging industry hadn't respected their wish to remain uncontacted--though they'd expressed it clearly enough, through crossed spears placed at the edges of their territory. A small UFE group had stepped in, really just far enough to mitigate the threat to their immune systems, while a few UFPKs helped them maintain their boundaries safely. Right in the middle of Peru, my Spanish had been useless, but this tool had helped me translate and acquire high-frequency words.

"I guess it wouldn't make sense to have an extinct language," he said after a quick search and a shake of his head.

Critically endangered, I didn't correct him aloud.

"Individual words, though, if they're close enough, they'd probably come up in the related languages. Hence your asking if I knew Norwegian, right?"

As he guided me, I cherished the most concrete realization yet that my quietly brilliant friend was unlikely to be stuck at generalist for long. I voice-input some common selkiese words that had stuck in my head, to see what source the matrix detected. Sounds like *Ya* for "yes" and *Nay* for "no." *Du* for "you." *Ut land isk*, foreigner, was right. *Brun*, brown, also directed toward me in the selkie bouncer's sharp tones. The matrix suggested Danish, Norwegian, Swedish, Icelandic, Faroese. I wished I could remember what everyone had said to Brynja, but I couldn't recall enough of the sounds for the matrix to count that as a word.

I searched her name: used in Iceland, mainly, it meant "armor" in Old Norse. There turned out to be guys named Geir all over the nations the North Sea touched, even if it wasn't pronounced the same everywhere. It meant "spear," funnier the more I thought about it for someone whose mission in life was pretty clearly to make love, not war. Offensive or defensive armaments, I wondered. Either way, Ysmay and Berenys made fairly good shieldmaidens. Their names weren't Norse, though. Neither was Hano's.

Runa's was, having to do with secrets. I thought of her whispery little voice. She'd been the first to transform where I could see, the biggest secret anyone had ever revealed to me. I guessed that answered what the armor and spear were there to protect.

I was too engrossed to notice when Vega sat down next to Stefek, or to catch what she said to me.

"What?" I answered, dragging my focus outward from the display inside my eye in time to see Vega roll hers.

"I said Qué onda, cafecito."

"We're just researching Old Norse for fun…"

She glanced from me to Stefek and back, with a knowing glint like my grandmother's. "Uh-huh."

I smiled and shook my head. Stefek got it easily enough, too, and laughed as he stood up. "Refill?" he said to me.

"*Dakk*," I answered.

"Vega?"

"Sure. Gracias."

"Sooo," she said to me, her supple voice low in tone and pitch.

"Not really, ma. Sorry. He's like, the age of everyone I ever used to babysit."

"Fine, you little weirdo." She shrugged and reached out to touch the hair I'd pulled back still wet. "This is what you do with your day off, though? Wash your hair, and discuss the mysterious tongues of exotic lands with a beautiful man even though you're not interested in… Ah, I mean, the pun makes itself."

"There are more things in heaven and earth, Dr. Hazan, than are dreamt of in your philosophy," I said lightly.

"Don't you go quoting Oliver Araujo to me at a time like this, young lady. You know he'd agree with me, not you."

"Well, I can't help noticing you haven't been seeing the beautiful boy in question, either."

"Hmph. Really, though, where were you?"

I caught a quick breath. "I've gone back a few times to see the people in that nice gray house in Walls. I was with them today."

Her brows echoed the widening curve of her eyes. "Odd little hillfolk with the big bouncer dude? Seriously?"

I nodded. "He's a diver too. Lachlan Adie. They're all. They invited me out there with them."

Suddenly she laughed aloud. "You're finally ready to try tall and blond again? And you're okay with him being a complete tool, as long as…"

"Writes itself," I preempted quickly.

"Okay," she said with a sly little grin, "we'll call that progress."

"Ha. Not quite, ma."

"Hmm. Why not? Unless… maybe not all the boys up here are brave enough for the interracial thing."

I didn't keep back my chuckle. "Nah. He's a man of the world. Also, unlike him who shall remain tall, blond, and nameless, a decent husband. I think pretty highly of his wife, too, so."

"Really. Was she there that night? Kinda thought he was babysitting or whatever by himself."

"Yeah." I hesitated. "The one who came out and talked to us."

Vega's features wrinkled around for a moment as she tried to decide whether I was serious. "He's married to a kindergartener?"

I shook my head. "Some of us are just small."

"Apparently you still like to let tall blond boys lie to you…"

"Nothing ever came back on the report to the PKs, right?"

She cocked a skeptical brow. "Well, now you're assuming there's a branch of UF that ever gets it right." She sighed. "Gotta say, I've had a day that would suggest otherwise."

"Hmm. Do I maybe smell big bad wolves here?"

"Little pigs, is more like," she said with a slight snort.

"Like I said, eff 'em," I murmured, laughing. Too bad Vega would never get to see Brynja as she truly was. She'd admire the hell out of our matriarchy's *Røsomethingmeen.*

Chapter 10

Ravenna

My days at work, purposeful as they were, began fading to something like dreams; I was fully awake and alive whenever I managed some time with my selkie folk. Between their full dance card and my own packed schedule, it didn't happen as often as I'd wish. I caught meals at May's with a few of them, now relying on the tech to help me pick up any Norn words I noticed them using. (Dad had hated when I'd answer his Spanish with English, but my new adopted family didn't seem to mind.) We didn't get another chance to dive together for almost a week.

This time, we planned to see the Out Skerries islands to the northwest. After they showed me their kingdom's hiding place there, which they said was smaller than the Scalloway Islands one, we hoped to check out one or more nearby shipwrecks.

It was farther-flung than anywhere I'd visited yet, fifty kilometers or so from where they picked me up in town right after breakfast. We spent much of the beautiful morning ride in companionable quiet, watching waves, birds, a few leaping fish, and one pod of killer whales we spotted in the distance. They'd placed an offshore wind farm out here a decade or so ago. Zooming in for a better look, I appreciated the turbines' design: pleasing curved shapes, silvery surfaces subtly faceted to reflect sea and sky, a kinetic sculpture despite its practical purpose.

Just past the rows of spinning turbines, close enough to our destination that I could see a lighthouse on one of the tiny low islands, Geir trailed a hand through the water, catching something in his palm. He held it out to me: a kelp frond with translucent plum-brown leaves and a little central spike of air sacs, like orchids about to bloom.

"Uh, thanks?" I laughed as I accepted it.

"Early spring blossom from the Forest of Arden," he said in a sparkling-eyed murmur, precisely loud enough to be heard over the quiet hover motor.

Berenys' giggle was accompanied by a mighty roll of her own beautiful eyes, but her sweet smile took a while to fade.

And damn if she wasn't right: he had me with that one. As I turned to look where he'd been looking, down shafts of sunlight filtering far enough through the glass-green water to illuminate the canopy of waving kelp just below us, my throat constricted. If anyone wanted to name any part of their faerie kingdom after me, even as a flirty little joke, I wasn't about to turn down the honor.

"Ever since you said your dad liked Shakespeare, I've wondered if that was how he'd chosen your name," Geir said, maybe even softer.

I cleared my throat, pulled one bare foot up under me on the seat to give myself a reason to look away briefly. "Yeah, he was more a fan of the ones with monsters and magic. The Tempest was his favorite, so I was almost Ariel. But only the one with the Forest of Arden has an Oliver, so."

"Your element isn't air," he agreed in a pleased low tone. "Courage and transformation and discovery suit you better."

I didn't fight my smile very hard. It was nice to think Dad had gotten that much right.

"Though the Disney Ariel's quite watery," Berenys said without irony. "And with the hair, as well."

She leaned forward to pick up the kelp stem, which she tucked behind my ear as if it really had been orchids. With Brynja's approving low chuckle wafting down from the upper deck, I didn't remove it until we reached the dive site.

The entrance to this cave was closer to the coastline and deeper, past thirty meters. The vent or tunnel shot almost straight upward. Maybe the fairytale airlock here was newer than the Scalloway one, because it opened without slowing our ascent.

Above the water's dancing surface there was illumination, surprisingly bright after the pitch black of the tunnel. I caught one good breath, hadn't managed to focus my eyes yet when everything went gray and I was slipping below the surface again.

Only for a few seconds, it seemed. Next thing I knew, there was a strong arm behind my shoulders, a hand I didn't recognize by touch cradling my head. The rebreather would have been enough to keep me safe, but I was grateful that whoever had grabbed me back up had already pulled my mask off for me to breathe real, cool salt air.

"I'm okay," I mumbled, forcing my eyes open.

"Better be," Geir said, low and gentle.

I gave him the usual thumbs up that meant a diver was all right.

He answered with a soft laugh. "Okay. Bone white isn't really your color, though, Generalist."

I shook my head and forced coherent words to come out. "Shallow water blackout. It's cold here. Maybe I didn't hydrate enough earlier. No worries as long as someone's there to catch you, so… Thanks."

"My pleasure."

He was steady enough he had to be standing on something, which meant I could, too. We were the same height. I lowered my feet to find the rock ledge. Unfortunately, I didn't have his advance knowledge of where was safest to put my feet, picked a spot slick with some kind of algae, and went splashing right back down.

He caught me against his chest easily, as if I'd been the size of a selkie girl instead of a regular person. I'd knocked his feet out from under him, too, but he regained his footing in half a second and held both our heads above the surface. Entirely at odds with his strength, his wet skin under my palms was fine as a child's.

"Hey," he insisted, still whisper-soft, but the sound carried easily across the water. "We're already impressed, I promise."

Flushing with indignation, I raised my eyes--only to find myself fighting tears of stress, sudden fatigue, and the unexpected insistence of what I felt from him. He still had a supportive arm around me, so I knew he wasn't mocking me, and for once he wasn't flirting, either. His kind eyes were wide as they reflected the rippling light. I was the only human he'd ever known to do what I'd just done. I bent my head with my face turned away from his, closed my eyes, and took a slower breath.

It wasn't as if I blacked out again, but it still felt like a dream overcame my awareness for a second. Behind my eyelids, it was the same as here and now: except our limbs and hands and mouths tangled blissfully together, for neither help nor comfort, and very much without the wetsuit or anything else between his velvet skin and mine.

My gasp echoed off the water. My head lifted reflexively, both for my eyes to seek his again--new moons, suddenly round and as bright as they were dark--and to keep them as far from his own real state of undress as possible. It didn't end up mattering where I looked; we could both still feel everywhere he'd never touched me.

"What the carajo?" I was frustrated in the certainty that he could sense my racing heart.

Rather than blush too, or turn his gaze away, he favored me with a slow finman smile. "Sorry," he murmured, in not at all an apologetic tone. "I can explain…"

I thought a string of other Spanglish expletives as loudly as I could, in the moment before I pushed off with both feet and swam over to the lip where everyone else was climbing out.

"Arden, wait," his soft voice carried over the water. I kept swimming.

Lachlan gave me a hand up. "Everything okay?" He glanced behind me, to where I guessed Geir still was.

"Yeah. Actually, I... blacked out for a second, but he caught me. It's fine."

"Blacked out. Why?"

"I'm fine," I said again.

His brows drew down and together. "I don't know what you keep trying to prove by not using the damn tech, but there's no need to be a hero."

I sighed. "Probably not."

Our headlamps revealed a cavern barely half the size of the Scalloway one. Most of the open space was taken up by the pool, with just a little crescent of real estate along the wall where people could stand.

For this once, maybe due to my parallel-universe mental state, I failed to distinguish one twin from another where they stood already dressed, greeting some friends. Maybe it was Berenys eye to mahogany eye with the man, and Ysmay forehead to forehead with the woman, touching her distinctive wavy hair.

Other than those two, there wasn't even a selkie-kingdom-sized crowd waiting poolside to greet Brynja with *Røsomethingmeen* or me with *Ut land isk*. So much for my plans to matrix more of their language today. She seemed to have said her hellos to the few who were here. Smiling, she held out a small pale hand for mine.

I caught a quick breath. I knew I couldn't hide my unsettled energy from her; the best I could hope was that she'd think it was my response to the blackout she'd just heard me describe to Lachlan. She looked at my face a moment but didn't comment.

"Let's show you the cave art," was all she said.

We wound our way down a passage where even Brynja had to stoop a bit. At the far end of the cavern where we emerged, our headlamps illuminated layers of sedimentary rock wave-sculpted into a breathtaking diagonal upsweep, striped ivory, gray, beige, iron, and brown. At first, that was more than enough to take in.

"Closer," Brynja said near my ear, after a moment.

A few meters away, I saw a slight glitter in the shadowed hollows separating the layers. At arm's length, I discerned subtle green and blue and violet, pixies' wings dancing at twilight, in the spaces between. Closer, I realized the artist had enhanced the gorgeous natural formation with tens of thousands of tiny bits of broken bottles or plates, shells, and stones, carefully sorted by hue, with some iridescent glass tiles mixed in.

The choice of medium didn't tell me much about the artist. When I'd liked the mosaics we'd seen in Venice and Ravenna, I'd read on-grid that the oldest ones in Greece dated to the fourth century BCE. They'd commissioned and unveiled a pretty one in the Lighthouse District at home, not quite four years ago. So this could be ancient, recent, or anything in between.

I stooped, then stood, running a careful hand over a bluish vein of tiles stretching diagonally upward from the sandy cave floor and artfully fading to bare rock, at perhaps the height Brynja would be able to reach. My empty palm could extend higher than the creator's hand had gone. There were at least a dozen mosaic lines, arrayed there in the dark and quiet.

I fought passionate tears I couldn't explain. Not that there was any pressure to do so from my queen; she watched me thoughtfully, without expressing any questions aloud or by touch.

"This must have taken such a long time," I managed. "Doesn't anyone know who did it? Why?"

"We don't know who. But of everyone that ever wondered why, my brother's got my favorite answer," Brynja murmured. She laid a cool hand on my shoulder. Together, we saw the stunning sculpted and enhanced wall, then the slight reflection off the tiles seemed to brighten: aurora borealis, underground.

"The mirrie dancers, we call them here," she said.

I glanced at Geir, my eyes still streaming, despite whatever the hell had happened between us earlier. He wore no fraction of a smile now; he almost looked tender, like he didn't want to see me crying. Maybe like he'd stood here with tears in his midnight eyes before, too.

I'd always rather have the sky above me, I remembered him saying when we'd first met. I guessed he must not be the only one.

But why had this, possibly the only selkie artist who'd ever lived, needed to bring the clear northern sky underground with her? Had she had to stay longer than she wanted? Or not really been trapped, but still felt that way?

"You said there are others like this?" was all I asked aloud.

Brynja nodded. "There's one more, up to the other end of this network of caverns. As well as my favorite lovely warm springs for bathing."

"Lovely if you're not too particular about the mineral smell," Lachlan said.

Looking at the assembled group, I hesitated. Selkie style, I came up with one truth and one lie. "Is it sulfur? Because that does kind of turn my stomach. And never washes out of your suit all the way."

"Yeah, this is one place I tend to embrace the selkie naturist thing," he admitted.

I shrugged. It had been weeks since I'd felt so awkward around them. "I think I'll check out the cave art. You go ahead."

Geir managed to catch my eye, challenging as I made it, while the others started up the passage. "I'll sit this one out, if it's because of me you're not going," he offered just above a whisper, no hint of mischief in his slight smile. So we were back to peace and generosity, I guessed.

I shook my head, already turning away. "You guys enjoy it."

He could have sighed quietly, or it might have been just the soles of my feet brushing the cavern floor. I didn't look back to find out--I would have had to show him the confused blush I couldn't keep from lighting up my face, as I failed to suppress the thought of sitting with everyone in a finfolk hot tub where he could compare what I looked like to his more tactile, less visual daydream version.

We passed through an inhabited cavern similar to the Scalloway one. I didn't glimpse either twin among the handful of people there. At the far end we slipped into a narrow passage; a few twists and turns in and upward, the air grew noticeably humid, sharply tinged with more minerals than just sulfur.

Brynja showed me the turning to find the next cave art installation, advising that it would be a few more minutes' walk. It was quite close to the other way in, she smiled conspiratorially; a fissure half-hidden at the back of an innocuous geo, just big enough for most finfolk to use.

Close enough, it turned out, for a hint of sunlight and plenty of fresh salt air. I followed them to find the tiny entry she'd described, and peered through at a little slice of the quiet sparkling ripples on the other side. Maybe I could have squeezed through there, but I wasn't keen on getting my Caribbean butt stuck attempting to reach the North Sea.

I reactivated my headlamp as I slowly retraced my steps in search of the artwork I must have passed. Brynja had been evasive as to what to look for, saying she didn't want to spoil the pleasure of finding it in my own way. Even she'd only discovered this one in our current century.

My eyes would have missed it coming back this direction, too, had my ears not caught a slight sound, enough to make me turn my head. A single, sweetly high-pitched drop of water falling somewhere to my right. I aimed my headlamp beam into a sort of drapery fold of the cave wall, a slight shadowy alcove only wide enough to hide a young child.

The clear water, dripping there since before the time of anyone I knew, created a depression in the cave floor where it pooled not more than four or five centimeters deep. What I took at first for delicately hued mineral deposits revealed a telltale glitter when I focused my light there.

I caught another breath in poignant admiration. She would have had to stop or re-route the water temporarily, for the tiles to adhere to this undreamed-of surface. Tiny ones here, each square maybe three millimeters, more uniform than the pieces making up the big aurora borealis downstairs. In my estimation, these would be newer, as might be whatever waterproof mortar or glue she'd used.

I found myself drawn to kneel and touch the water's cool surface with cautious fingertips then lift them to my face, flushed with hiking around in a wetsuit. Like nothing so much as Doña Maite's gesture upon entering and leaving her church. At least there was no one to see me being this weird. I tasted it--a fresh spring, not salt--then let a few more drops fall on the crown of my head and trickle down my scalp, as I watched the miniature pool grow completely still in anticipation of the next droplet.

Before it could fall, the mirror-clear surface blurred with some slight vibration. A passing hover or boat, I considered, although I heard no motor.

The standing waves grew more pronounced at the same instant my ears detected the first low-frequency rumbling. Before the rest of my body felt any shaking, I recognized it, as any Californian would.

Aftershock.

Chapter 11

Under

Fortunately, it seemed like a minor one. It was still enough to set my heart racing, raise every hair on my body, and get me on my feet. I took a couple steadying breaths and decided to find my selkie folk. Caves were not my first choice of place for any of us to be while the adjacent seafloor tried to flex back into a shape it liked.

The next, stronger tremor came thirty seconds down the passage. I pressed my back against the cave wall, arms folded above my head, pulse pounding. I was still so close to the nearest exit, but I couldn't dream of abandoning my new family. When the shaking stilled again, I sprinted to find them.

I caught half a sigh of relief at the sound of footsteps pelting toward me. It was Berenys, wearing only a man's t-shirt, and her friends, the lighter-eyed man and the wavy-haired girl. Berenys didn't say anything, just kept running toward the hot springs. That must be where Ysmay had gone.

With wide wet eyes, the girl tried to tell me something in rapid Norn. I shook my head and held out a hand.

She bit her lip for an instant; I understood the hesitation as soon as her trembling fingers touched mine. Her fear and stress didn't mask the honeyed afterglow they hadn't fully driven from her body yet. I just met her gaze long enough to reassure her I wasn't about to pry into Berenys' business, or hers or her man's. She looked away; I was flooded with anxious insistence that we needed to go back the way I'd just come and get safely out of here, assuming the tunnel remained passable.

"You go," I said, shaking my head. The words wouldn't reach her, but I knew the thought behind them had, when she looked more scared and shook her head too. "I have to help anyone I can."

The guy said something to her under his breath. Understanding me better than she could and translating, maybe. Or encouraging her to do as I suggested.

Her breath shook as she squeezed my hand bruisingly tight, wishing for my safety before the two of them hurried up the tunnel. I rushed in the other direction, following Berenys toward the last place I'd seen her family. I'd been preoccupied with such different things on the way to the secret selkie holy water font, I hadn't realized how far it was from where I needed to be now.

I made it close enough to smell the spring water before the big shock made me stumble onto one knee and two hands, bruising my left shoulder against the rough passage wall. The horrifying bass drum-beat of a rockfall echoed toward me and died away. I heard no voices, just my rapid breath loud in my ears. I regained my balance and pressed ahead.

My heart lurched into my throat, forcing out an inarticulate cry of dismay when around a bend I found two small dark forms kneeling over the tall, fair body supine on the passage floor.

Berenys turned her tear-streaked face to me and drew in a sharp breath. Geir spoke to her, a few words in their language that sent her running again. I understood: she'd wanted to get to Ysmay, but our queen's injured husband had been the priority. Now Geir would have me to help him.

"Let me look," I said. His pitch dark eyes were full of saltwater too as he lifted them to my face. He put a hand on my shoulder as I examined Lachlan's sickeningly pale gray face so that as I felt for a pulse I couldn't find, I saw the stone splitting apart around them, the hot spring draining away into a sudden fissure. The head-sized boulder tumbling down the shifting wall to knock Lachlan in the back of the skull with a nightmarish deep sound.

I put my hand there, finding far more blood than I ever wanted to see, but no obvious crushed area. He wasn't breathing, though.

"Was he knocked unconscious right away?"

"No." Geir showed me flashes of himself, in pain I didn't comprehend for the moment, Lachlan's arm heavy around his shoulders as they stumbled to the passage. Lachlan had abruptly collapsed to the floor just as Berenys reached them. I shook my head, knowing that probably meant brain swelling.

Maybe he understood, too, how short of time we were: he was leaving out a lot of information between those flashes. "Geir," I whispered. "Where's everyone else?"

"Him first, okay?"

I sucked in a sharp breath. "Okay."

I had no medical experience, just basic first aid. I moved to the step I should have started with. My hands remembered what to do. Lachlan's heart didn't seem to have received the same instructions.

I began compressions, moving oxygenated blood through a body too young and strong to be lifeless. My breath hurt in my tight throat. I didn't find the mental energy to ask why Geir knelt by Lachlan's feet as I worked, his hand small around Lachlan's ankle and head bent to rest on his calf.

"Look," I said. "This is what you do until the medics get there, but his heart won't re-start without…"

He let out a short rough sigh as he straightened up and looked at me. "The electric shock," he answered softly.

"I know I can't--tell them how to get in here. But--"

I glanced at the tiny sealed pocket on the waistband of the shorts Lachlan had kept on in the hot spring, after all. Geir as well, though at the moment I could barely register gratified surprise. Perhaps they'd thought I might still join them there. My rash guard, too, like virtually all athletic wear produced these days, carried the same precious bit of tech you hoped you'd never need.

"There are discs in there--to deliver the shock. The only thing is--I'd have to reactivate my ring to do it."

Geir looked extra pale but nodded. "You can leave the locator off, no?"

"His is off. But I don't control mine," I muttered, frustrated. "It's a safety feature. I don't see why anyone would be looking for me right now, but the defibrillator pulse will send an alert with our location."

"We can get out before the hover gets here. We're pretty close to the geo."

"I saw that gap. There's no way he'd fit through there even if he were able to pull himself right now, Geir."

"Damn," he agreed, shaking his head.

"Can we… I don't know. How fast can we get him down to the far end? Shock him down there, then jump in and run him up to the surface? I'll show you how to take over for me while I set it up."

I heard his breath catch. "Yes, that's the best we can do. But you'll need more help than just me."

My mind spun in too many directions--wondering whether the twins would be heading straight up for the sea cave exit, thinking how strong he was and that between us we could do this--but stopped short as I finally got a better look, and understood the strain in his voice.

I hadn't focused anywhere below his eyes until now. As soon as I did, I knew why his left arm hung too far below the sharply protruding bones of his shoulder, with an unnatural hollow between. He wouldn't be able to make the climb by himself, or tow Lachlan either.

"Oh, shit. Did you dislocate it helping him, or before?"

"Before," he said, new tears seeping through his thick lashes as he squeezed his eyes shut for a second.

Without touching him, I had a pretty strong sense they were unrelated to his physical pain. I wasn't trained to reset the shoulder, even if I'd been able to stop CPR on Lachlan.

He shook his head. "Don't think about me right now."

He hurried to find the twins before they could slip out the back door. Between the four of us, we carried Lachlan's dead weight to the entry pool, stopping every few hundred meters to keep compressions going. The twins pulled his dive suit back on, leaving it unzipped to the waist. I explained to Ysmay how to take over CPR while I hastily geared myself up.

Berenys dried Lachlan's exposed skin with someone's thrift-store shirt. I removed the two small, clear circular discs from their sealed pocket and placed them low on his left rib cage, high on the right. The enhanced negative charge enabled them to cling to his skin. The tech glinted inside, a faint silvery geometric web of micro-circuitry absurdly reminding me of the mosaic pool upstairs. I shook my head. Focus.

"Okay, where's the--" I looked around for the bag with the re-breathers.

"Oh, dammit. No."

Smaller rocks had tumbled from their places here, as well. The bag was half-covered in dust and the fragments of a delicate smashed stalactite.

Trembling now, I uncovered and opened the bag. One of the masks was cracked all the way across.

"You've already done this dive without one." Geir's good hand brushed the back of mine. I had no idea how he could be so full of faith in me despite the relentless waves of horrible luck that kept knocking us under right now.

I took over for Ysmay; she slipped the mask over Lachlan's head. We didn't cover his mouth yet, in case. I had Berenys take his ring off and place it on the dry stone next to his right shoulder. Then, biting my lower lip, I powered my ring on as I laid it near his left side. I set it up for the charge. We all moved clear.

Berenys gave a startled cry. Ysmay's eyes glowed in fascination. Geir didn't visibly react, just waited as I checked for the heartbeat.

"Stubborn selkie-Viking hybrid bastard," I muttered, with a slap to Lachlan's still upper left chest. "Vámonos ya, cabrón."

With one more shock, he finally took a choking breath and started to get color back. He still didn't open his eyes, and couldn't answer when I tried to speak to him.

"It's okay. Rebreather," Geir said. "Then just a quick swim to the doctor's office. Yeah?"

Ysmay got the mask correctly on, Berenys pulling the ring back onto Lachlan's arm at the same time. As I replaced my own, it was already pulsing.

"Shite," I whispered. "Gotta go."

Chapter 12

Danger Zone

As soon as we cleared the vent, me gingerly pulling Lachlan through from outside while my three seal buddies pushed from inside, we went hard for the surface, following the anchor chain.

It had taken under three minutes to make our way down, then up through the vent earlier. Calm and content in my sun-dappled forest, it had seemed easy until that last-moment gray-out. Now, however, we needed to move fast, and Lachlan's dead weight might as well have been in full Viking battle gear. I couldn't slow my heart rate worth half a damn.

Already fighting the instinct to take just one more deep breath, I came agonizingly close to a lung-flooding gasp of shock and dread when the first orca vocalizations vibrated through my body.

I pressed my palm hard over my mouth and nose for a few seconds as I turned to see a pod of seven or eight approaching. On a better day, it should have been a moment of fantastic wonder, but not when Lachlan's battered head was the most overqualified chunk of bait in the world.

Geir's teardrop eyes met mine, dark through the dark water. He'd sensed them sooner than I could.

There wasn't time for him to do it, but he left the girls to support Lachlan just long enough to come close to my side, sleek sealskin caressing my arm in nothing but encouragement. His own pulse remained steady. Unable to breathe in physically the oxygen my body craved, my spirit took in his calm and strength instead.

We continued upward, one sleek black dorsal fin passing less than a meter under my artificial fins and their seal flippers as we ascended. The pod couldn't have cared less for us. Selkies must speak orca well enough to know when they were prey and when they were just another evacuee from the danger zone.

I shouldn't have needed further reminding that killer whales weren't the deadliest animal in this or any other marine ecosystem.

Upward, brighter and brighter, my heart hammering for air. Close to the surface, they let me sprint ahead and gulp a few precious aching lungfuls. I turned right back around, though, to help get Lachlan the rest of the way up. The twins, by some unspoken agreement, took off as soon as we reached the boat. I thought that was more than justified.

Geir stayed, already in his human shape by the time we broke the sun-dazzled surface. Big bad selkie or not, I heard him gasping in air as roughly as I did. He gave me a poor imitation of his usual smile, a diver's okay signal with the thumb on the end of the normally-working arm.

"You were swimming well enough I hoped shapeshifting might have fixed your shoulder," I said.

He shook his head, the smile ebbing. "I wish it worked like that. Just that I don't need it the same, in the other form." His good hand sketched the right motion, elbow close to his torso and most of the work happening between elbow and fingers.

"Well, hang on," I reassured him, helping him float Lachlan on his back and ignoring the stress and exhaustion seeping from my eyes.

He coughed as I went for the ladder, still reacclimating to the air. "Hey. If we'll be telling them we were on a cave dive together, I need a suit. We've got one or two more under the bulkhead, aft of where everyone put their clothes. Maybe even some shorts of Elis', if we're lucky."

"Not sure today's our day," I said as I pulled myself onto the deck. Both the suit and swim trunks were where he'd said they'd be, though: right below the little spray of North Sea orchids, undisturbed on my seat.

I disregarded emergency rescue protocol and rang Vega directly.

"Mija, Jesus, why have you taken this long to pick up? You were diving out there in aftershock surge? Without your goddamn ring on? At least tell me you weren't swinging from the turbine when it fell."

"What?"

"Who's hurt?"

"It's Lachlan Adie," I whispered. "We got his heartbeat back but he hasn't regained consciousness. Please get me some help, doc, then you can fire my ass or break up with me or whatever you need to do…"

"On our way." She rang off immediately.

I couldn't see the turbines clearly from here, with the glare on the water. I pulled a quick image off the grid, the neat rows now set askew. I found the missing one that must have fallen underwater, as well as several surrounding ones listing at wrong angles. Had the impact of the collapsing structure sent the sudden rockfall our way, or had the seafloor flexed first? Chicken, egg, and no mad scientist here to explain it.

Kenneth Adie was right. It was fair enough for the planet to go on defending itself. I just hated for my selkie folk to keep getting caught in the crossfire.

There wasn't time for emotion. I quickly deployed the life raft, safer by far for Lachlan than trying to get him up onto the deck. I tossed Geir's suits into it, then went back down into the cold salt swells. We hauled Lachlan out onto the raft first. He was still breathing well on his own when I pulled his mask off.

Geir was having less success putting on the shorts one-handed. I got in one more time to help him.

"Ach, selkie lass, trying to get in my pants at a time like this." He chuckled roughly.

I smiled for him. "Who knew not getting eaten by a killer whale would be such a huge turn-on."

He couldn't pull the wetsuit up over his arms either. We put the bad side on first, which involved him grabbing my arm in a bruising grip, turning ghostly gray (it really wasn't his color, either), and gritting out a few words it was probably better I didn't know. Then I tugged the right sleeve and the zipper into place.

He breathed hard for a moment, looked up at me, and reached out his good hand to smooth saltwater off my face. I didn't know how he could tell tears from North Sea, but he wasn't wrong.

"Did I hurt you?" he asked, his voice ragged.

"Doesn't matter." I didn't let go of his good hand once I'd helped him up into the raft. "They'll be here soon." I turned my palm up under his, so I could grip his fingers. I needed him to tell me one more critical thing. Was there anyone for us to go back for?

He gently pulled his hand free. "Bryn will be okay. Runa, I don't know…" He shook his head. "And it's not worth the risk of going back for Hano when he's where he'll never need anyone's help now."

"Oh, Geir. Shit. I'm so sorry."

He hesitated before taking my hand once more and closing his black eyes. A bloodcurdling scream echoed in his mind, the loudest sound I'd ever heard torn from a selkie throat. My fingers went slack around his, but I didn't let go.

I knew it was Runa's voice because, in the impression, Geir hadn't lost hold of his oldest sister's spark of life. He felt her unhurt, facing down her worst fear with deliberate calm. More rocks pounded down. He didn't hear the anguished voice again.

I held him, his breath ragged against my shoulder as he wrestled with his tears. I didn't want him to control them for my sake. He thought of the approaching hover, of not wanting to have to explain his grief--or supporting details--to the UFPKs piloting and manning it. As far as they could know, it had just been us three on the dive gone wrong.

I hoped Runa was all right. Geir clenched his teeth and couldn't agree. I gasped in comprehension.

He controlled his breathing. "I don't know if you'll ever have reason to understand this, but for our kind, unless... For two like Hano and Runa never to spend a day without one another... It would be more comfort to me, more merciful for her, if she doesn't look forward to decades or centuries without the man who's loved her as long as I've been alive. You can't know how nearly it crushed her to lose their son."

The scream he remembered had expressed not physical pain but joined spirits suddenly rent apart. All my life I'd known loss, but never like that.

Chapter 13

Iverness

The rear door of the big UFPK hover lowered, revealing the best thing I'd ever seen: Vega Hazan Ramos, M.D., among our rescuers. Geir's smile might be weak, but his eyes sparkled with amusement as she tore into me in rapid-fire Spanglish.

"Not like I could predict an aftershock, Vega…"

"Ajo," she muttered, shaking her head. "Tell us what happened to your friend."

I cringed. "I don't know if it was the quake itself or that turbine falling… There was a--partial collapse. Uh. We were in a sea cave."

"Por Dios." She shook her head again, then turned her attention to Lachlan. Her face quickly set in a sober expression of deep concentration as she scanned around his head, starting where the injury was visible on the outside. She blew out a slow breath. Then, without explaining anything to me, she started giving orders to the PK medic. They were cutting open the top half of his wetsuit, putting chem-ice packs behind his neck and around his head, speaking medicalese as fast as Vega's Spanish to each other.

"This is a triphibious craft. Why bring him back to the boat rather than let us come to you?" she asked over her shoulder, not looking up.

I gasped for words.

"We were in a restricted area. Too close to the wind farm," Geir said. "I was--trying not to get Arden in any more trouble."

Vega shook her head once more, dismissively now.

His good hand found mine. I thought as loudly as I could that it wasn't worth it, keeping their secret--enormous as it was--in exchange for such a life.

He agreed. But it wasn't his call.

Shaking took hold of my entire body, soon more violent than fever chills. I hated not having done more. Geir pulled me close, my head on his good shoulder, his strong arm firmly around me. The gentle kiss he pressed to the top of my head had nothing to do with before. He was only grateful to his exhausted bones that I'd been nowhere near that rockfall.

"Jespersen," Vega said aloud, still without looking at us. "Take a second and get a point-five for Araujo's distracting crazy squirrel shit, please."

I sighed. "Lo siento, ma."

The young peacekeeper medic, a guy almost Lachlan's size, stripped his gloves for fresh ones and came over with his kit and a laser injector. I didn't argue; I unzipped the neck of both suit layers far enough to expose my shoulder, rather than let him burn a little hole in the sleeve of each garment as he injected the mild sedative.

"Anything else?" he said under his breath. "The call said one of you had also been hurt?"

"He is," I said, feeling the chem's instant effect: all the heavy calm of a couple glasses of wine in quick succession, though none of the silliness. The shaking stilled within seconds, anxiety receding past arm's reach. My eyelids fell shut a moment.

"Don't worry about me," Geir said.

"At least something for the pain," I insisted. "Until they can get to you."

"Agreed," Jespersen said.

"Half dose, then, if you can manage it," Geir asked softly. "I have a chem sensitivity."

I sat up, allowing Jespersen to access his right shoulder rather than mess with the left side.

"If I could get your ident," he said, and I held my breath.

"I don't wear my ring diving. But here." I bit back a startled smile as Geir held up his hand for a fingerprint scan.

"Geir Craig," Jespersen said a moment later, pronouncing the vowel in his first name as something other than its Norn sound. "Good enough... So everyone here is connected to KXA, huh. My dad's with their Copenhagen branch. Well, you're all set."

"Thanks. Good man."

With just a nod, Jespersen quickly returned to the real task at hand. Geir and I leaned against each other again, his head drooping to my shoulder this time. Even the half dose was dizzyingly strong for his different physiology.

Only then, as the pain started to fade, did I realize how carefully he'd kept me from sharing his suffering. I reached up to rub the good side of his back a few times, acknowledging his strength and generosity. He didn't want me to think he'd done anything special.

"I guess I was wrong in thinking fairytale creatures wouldn't have last names and idents?" I whispered, instead.

I felt, rather than saw, his little smile. "No. Most haven't got idents, and names maybe fifty-fifty. What if I tell you about that some other time, though."

"Okay..."

His breathing slowed. He inhaled the warm skin scent from where I hadn't zipped my suit back up. I wasn't sure anymore whether he was having such deliciously specific thoughts about that zipper that they raised my skin temperature a few degrees further, or whether I was daydreaming it, or both of us together, or just the good drugs. Whichever; I couldn't quite grasp whether my bending my head to kiss his silken, utterly willing lips was dream or reality either, until I'd really done it.

"Okay," I breathed again, staring into his newly glowing eyes. "You're quite the confusing fellow, Geir Craig."

What I did understand with clarity was that--as much as he'd been comfortable flirting at any opportunity--his never having touched or come this close to me once, until I needed his help earlier today, had been no coincidence.

He whispered the sweetest laugh. "No, I've been as straightforward as I dared. You're the one making it more complicated than it is."

"Only a fairytale creature could say this isn't complicated...."

Still sweetly, he lost his smile. "Try me."

I lowered my eyes out of reflex. "Is that what we're calling this morning? Straightforward?"

Another faint laugh. "It's true I slipped up then; whatever you do to make your hair smell like that. But... this kind of mischief takes two selkie folk who both want the same thing even if they've never said as much, so it's as new to me as it is to you. And if we're honest, you... met me more than halfway," he added in the most disarming whisper. "Caught me quite off guard."

Skin to skin and breath to breath for a few long, quiet seconds, it wasn't as if I could tell him anything but the truth now. Not much point in continuing to lie to myself, either.

Instead of pushing it, although he certainly could have, he gestured past me with a flash of his dark eyes. "Ask this boy here, when he wakes up, about how he and my sister all but burned down the church during Isla Russell's funeral."

A pretty good rendition of the whispery selkie giggle escaped my lips.

"Nah. She'd have found it as fitting a tribute as Elis did." He glanced pointedly at my zipper pull, before looking back up into my eyes. "You mixed ones, though, who don't get to learn how to manage the spark in you from childhood... you lot are nothing but trouble."

I couldn't pull my gaze away. "Wasn't I here to stop trouble, not start it?" I whispered eventually.

He gave me a slow, beautiful smile I hadn't seen from him before, and shook his head.

I kissed him one more time, or he kissed me; whichever. Just one more small kiss, lingering but not leading us anywhere we couldn't go together here or now, on such an awful day. Still, it was enough to raise many more tantalizing shared questions than could be answered yet. At this moment, all I could do was sink back down alongside his strength, my head leaning against his, and close my eyes.

I wasn't really aware when they stabilized Lachlan enough for us to take off, but it was only a few minutes' flight from any part of Shetland to any other. The engine vibration shifted as we descended toward Scalloway. Before my eyes could struggle back open, I felt a few gentle taps on the side of my calf.

Vega was kneeling beside me. "He's as stable as he's gonna be for now, but we have to send him on to the mainland. Am I remembering right, Inverness is home for him?"

I nodded.

"Good. Closest place that has what he needs. And your boyfriend? Mazel tov, by the way. He's not any kind of next of kin, is he?"

I glanced down at Geir, dozing with his head on my shoulder. "He's not anyone's boyfriend," I whispered. "But yes, he's family. Lachlan's brother-in-law."

"Oh yeah." She chewed her lip for a second, putting that together. "Any idea where the child bride is?"

"Out of town," I breathed.

"Okay. Well, there's not a lot of time. Should I send you with them?"

"Please. Yeah, if I can."

"Since, as much as you and I are still not okay, you are the one who saved his life."

I just met her eyes and nodded.

"Okay, then just me hopping off at this stop. Kuo and Jespersen will get you to Inverness. And you'll connect with the rest of his family?"

"Okay. Gracias, doc."

"Not your boyfriend," she said, with finally a hint of smile. "I mean, what the hell, girl, no to UFE's finest but yes to this little fella? Has it been him this whole time?"

"Well... no one has exactly said yes to anything yet," I answered with a rusty laugh.

"Didn't look like a no, a few minutes east of here." She turned around for something. "And it is kinda cute. You're like a little set of salt and pepper shakers."

The small vial she shook where I could see it contained not a seasoning, but a distinctively chartreuse-colored fluid. She lifted her eyebrows in a question she didn't need to ask aloud.

"Yes, ma." I was too warm from the sedative to guess whether I was blushing enough for her to see, past caring much anyway.

"Nice to know there's some unnecessary BS you're willing to prevent with a little normal planning." She snapped the vial into her injector, lasered a pinhole in the arm of my suit. "Okay. We both know you were out of date enough we might as well be starting from scratch, so... seventy-two hours for full effect."

"Unofficial diagnosis, dislocated and probably separated left shoulder," I answered with another rueful laugh. "We're plenty safe there."

"You can always follow up with the Inverness medics, por si las moscas." She patted my leg once more. "Jespersen. Think you can keep an eye on Mr. Adie here while you help out Mr.--" She glanced at me.

"Craig," I supplied as if I'd always known it.

"Who's been sitting patiently in our comfy waiting room with a probable glenohumeral luxation. At least get a scan, let Inverness know what they're dealing with."

"Tough guy," Jespersen said, brows lifted and voice lowered in admiration. "Yes, ma'am. I'll be right there."

"Araujo's useful, just don't let her operate the heavy machinery right now. And if anything, Kuo can even put it on autopilot for a few. Just give her a yell."

"Yes, ma'am."

Vega drew a quick, deep breath and let it out. "Diosito, tough chick, we didn't even really ask. You're not hurt?"

"No, I'm okay."

She nodded. "Good. You know I don't tend to handle that so well."

The southern-accented American voice of Kuo, the pilot, came through our rings. "We're at exit altitude now, doc. Unless you want me to touch all the way down."

"Negative, negative. You know we got a brain trauma and now there's a busted shoulder back here too."

Kuo laughed. "Okay. Holding at present altitude, deploying the fancy hammock thingy for your descent."

"Thank you. All right, mija. You and your hillfolk take care of each other," Vega said with a quick maternal caress of my salt-stained cheek. "Ooh, silky," she teased. "See you in a day or two, okay?"

Back at altitude, Jespersen turned his attention to Geir, who slept uneasily in the curve of my arm.

"Any way you can do it while he's asleep?"

He shook his head with a regretful smile. "That would be the most rotten wake-up call I can think of. But here. We'll get a look."

He had to cut away the dive suit as he had with Lachlan's, carefully removing the pieces to reveal the disconcerting hollow area.

"Yep. Wow," Jespersen murmured. "Fortunately for him, the poor guy is really out, just from half a dose." He scanned the shoulder with his ring. "Damn. If this was me I'd want total anesthesia."

I bit my lip. "You can't do that without his consent, right?"

"Not when he's competent to give it, no. We'll have to wake him either way. Or wait till Inverness, but they'll just tell him the same thing there."

"Yeah. I have a feeling he'd rather not bother them if we can get it done now."

Jespersen nodded.

I touched Geir's damp, salt-crusted hair. "Hey. What do you say we try to put your arm back?"

"Great," he said, slurring only a little. He picked up his head. "Tell me what to do."

"First off," Jespersen told him. "By some miracle, nothing's torn, but you're stretched to the very limit, including the ligament between your shoulder and your collarbone. Plenty of swelling, thanks to the lag time between injury and treatment. So the reduction is going to be a raging bitch. Be okay once you're settled, probably much better than now, but…"

Geir caught a quick breath. "Okay."

"I can put you under if you'd rather."

"No. Thanks."

Jespersen tilted his head a little to one side. "Well, it's not as though we're taking the arm off, which I've done without real anesthesia available, so between us, we're in fine shape." He glanced up at me. "Generalist. Grab that green bottle by your other buddy's head, some unused chem ice packs, and an empty basin?"

He helped Geir lie down, a blanket folded up under his head, while I gathered the supplies. The green bottle contained supercoolant, which he spread with a gloved hand over the whole shoulder and upper arm. I didn't know the real medical term for the clear gel Vega had used to ice a spectacularly sprained ankle I'd sustained long ago on the wrong end of a bad mudflow. It was faster than real ice or the chemical packs; Geir sighed sharply, eyes closed with the immediate relief.

Jespersen shed the gel-covered glove into the empty basin, put a clean one on.

"All right, Mr. Craig. You're not going to like me anymore after this."

"Ach." Geir chuckled in spite of it all. "You'll have to call me Geir unless you really want to sound like a movie villain."

"Okay." Jespersen laughed, too. "And I'm Jens. All right, man." Smile fading, he gave Geir a nod and took his left wrist, keeping the elbow close to his waist and bending it so his hand pointed up toward the roof of the craft. I held his other hand as Jespersen slowly rotated the left arm downward and out, pointing the hand away toward the cockpit. Geir squirmed, spit out a few expletives I couldn't translate yet, but apparently for nothing.

Jespersen was laughing again, though, as he released Geir's hand. "You learned how to curse a man out in Danish, in case you'd ever need it? That's some dedication to the fine craft of swearing."

"Spent enough time on fishing vessels around the North Sea, is all." Geir's right hand rubbed sweat off his forehead.

"True enough about how sailors talk, I guess." Jespersen picked up a spare blanket and started forming it into a tight roll. "Your accent could use some work, though. You sound like my grandfather."

"Fisherman?"

"Yes, actually."

"Well, there you are."

Jespersen placed the rolled blanket under the injured arm. "Okay. This is my distant second choice, man. Sorry." Bracing his feet against the floor, he leaned slowly backward, keeping a steady pull on the arm. Geir groaned from behind gritted teeth. I lifted his hand to my lips and closed my eyes, spiritually inhaling as big a breath as I could. Just hoping to share enough to take the edge off for him.

Instead, I had to choose to cling to his hand as the wave of it knocked me under and pounded my head into the sand. I held on long enough for the sharp thud of the bone's end settling back into its socket, the equally sharp relief flooding over Geir. Then I grabbed the basin with Jespersen's used supercoolant glove, so I could retch into it.

"Whoops. Haven't assisted at many medical procedures yet?" Jens said lightly.

"Yeah… not, you know, combat theater style." I wiped my mouth on my sleeve. "Sexy, huh?" I said to Geir under my breath.

But his eyes were wide, brows lifted as he looked up at me with more admiration than ever. He put his good hand on the outside of my knee; not a romantic gesture, more that it was the easiest place to reach with the limited strength he could muster. As clearly as I'd felt his suffering, he'd sensed me diverting some of it into myself.

"Aw. You two kids are so precious I'm going to have to borrow that basin back in a second." Jespersen chuckled as he got to his feet. "I don't care how sexy she is, don't move before I can get you a sling."

Laughing along with both men, I slightly stumbled aft to empty the basin and rinse my mouth, wash my face and hands. By the time I got back, Geir was sitting up, sling in place, sipping from a cup of water. The impressively efficient Jens Jespersen had already returned to Lachlan's side, not with any seeming urgency.

"So… what age does your ident say you are, Mr. Craig?" I breathed in Geir's ear as I sat back down next to him.

He gave me a guilty smile. "Lachlan's clever uni friend taught him to rig it so it stays at twenty-two," he barely whispered back. "It's not as if anyone who happens to see it would ever check back."

Then he brushed a kiss, more fiery than it had any right to be, just below my ear. "What about yours? Are we entirely sure you're a thirty-one-year-old human woman?"

Looking into his eyes, I could only agree: we weren't entirely sure of much at this point. "I mean. That's all the info I've ever had to go on."

The signature tiny smile touched his beautiful lips. "I'll work it out for you. Maybe... not today, though."

"Okay. Tomorrow." I laid my head on his good shoulder again. Hard to say who felt more worn out. "Yeah, let's get some rest. I doubt we're even halfway there."

"We can give each other nice dreams," he agreed, his tone as sweet as his intent was wicked.

I giggled, remembering when Lachlan had told me Geir was a perfect gentleman.

"Didn't seem in my best interest to stop the lad misrepresenting me as such..." His voice died away into a sleepy chuckle.

They were nice dreams, though, free from the pain that had dominated our waking day. I dreamed of my own Inverness: a full-moon night on McClures Beach in Point Reyes. The dream Geir didn't walk beside me or hold my hand. He wanted to check out the beautiful clear water, while I relaxed on the sand and watched him swimming amid mirror-bright ripples. In the dream, I could still feel him just as if he were by my side.

Chapter 14

Raigmore

Much too soon, the real Scottish Inverness broke through the dream California one. I didn't have it in me to look at the flood damage, but the hospital was on high enough ground to have been spared. Kuo set the craft down, light as a fairy coming to rest on a leaf, with a combination of perfect technique and extreme concentration. Jespersen helped Geir down the ramp, then went back for Lachlan.

I knew the man who walked briskly out to meet the hovercraft, dark trench coat waving back in its wake, because I'd looked up his photos not long ago. He really was even bigger than Lachlan. In person, he exuded a younger, more vital energy than I'd supposed.

"Mr. Adie."

He nodded. "This is my son?" His controlled voice was a slightly lower and more gravelly version of the younger one I'd grown to love.

"Yes, sir. He--"

"He's here with us thanks to Generalist Araujo's quick thinking," Jens said, having guided the hover pad down the ramp with Lachlan on it. I took half a step back and let him be the one to speak the fluent medicalese. Adie nodded at a couple points but didn't seem shaken. He only held out an authoritative right hand for a moment to the orderlies who came to bring Lachlan inside, long enough for Jespersen to finish his quick explanation and for Adie to lay the same hand firmly on his son's still jaw for a heartbeat. Then the team whisked Lachlan inside, Jespersen still talking fast as he accompanied them to the door.

I was almost too worn out to hold up under Adie's piercing gaze, now he knew who I was. "Right. Lachlan did mention you'd been stationed there, and had met them…. Didn't know he would have dragged you into one of his mad schemes already, though."

I couldn't help smiling at the magnitude of his understatement.

"For quite a while there, a majority of the Raigmore staff knew him by name, but it's been a few years since he gave us a scare this good. The little wife's influence, I expect."

I was pretty sure it was Adie, Senior they knew by name, but I chose to agree. "I can't think of much he wouldn't do for her."

He glanced around us. "She's not with you, then?"

"No, she's been…" I didn't know what I was supposed to say. "With other family, sir. Dr. Hazan in Scalloway plans to notify her as soon as possible."

His eyes bored into mine again, two sharp-pointed blue icicles. "Not the first time we've run into something like this. If she'd wear a ring, like a normal person," he said under his breath.

"Well, sir, now she'll have both of us working on her."

A faint smile softened his expression. "Thank you for that. And for the rest of your work here with UFE."

"Small piece of the puzzle compared to yours, sir."

His keen gaze shifted, focused behind me as if he'd learned as much about me as he needed for now. True, this wasn't the time for an extended conversation about environmental planning strategies.

"Oh," he said: addressing Geir, waiting on the bench with Jespersen, who must have looped back around to sit with him until he was squared away, too. "Out of the corner of my eye, I took you for the other one."

Wow, I managed not to say aloud.

Geir shook his head. "We'll get word to Elis from here," he said in a cool tone that reminded me why neither Adie's age nor his status would provoke a *sir* from him, even if the man's greeting hadn't been startlingly rude. "I didn't see a need to worry him while we were still in the air."

Adie nodded. "Let's hope there never is."

"Aye."

He looked closer at Geir. "You're injured, too?"

Geir shook his head slightly. "Taken care of."

Jespersen shot him a skeptical glance but didn't put himself in the way of the palpable dynamic between the two men.

"Well, whenever we get to that point, you're welcome to stay with us."

Geir answered with just a princely little selkie head bend.

I hadn't noticed the doctor waiting to one side, until she took advantage of the chilly pause in the conversation. "Mr. Adie," she said, sober but businesslike, and he turned to speak to her.

"You're not really refusing follow-up care?" Jespersen pressed Geir quietly.

He sighed a little. "I really just want a place near Lachlan where we can rest until there's some news."

Adie went off somewhere with the doctor. Jespersen wrangled us a quiet dim room where no one immediately showed up to pester Geir, who fell asleep within minutes. I lay on his good side and rang Vega a quick update. Between her authorization to view the data from our in-flight medical procedures, and the fact that Jespersen was getting ready to return to Shetland with Kuo, my communication was probably unnecessary, anyway.

I closed my eyes, more than weary enough to rejoin Geir in Point Reyes or wherever we might find one another, but my stomach kept grumbling loud enough to wake him. I crept into the hall in my borrowed scrubs and found a gregarious, freckled nurse who showed me where to get a packaged sandwich and brought us a pitcher of water with two cups. Fergus (according to his badge) scanned Geir's shoulder while he was in the room, commenting that Jespersen J had done an amazing job considering how little chemical assistance there had been for the patient's muscles to relax. I just nodded in grateful agreement.

Once Fergus had gone out, I inhaled the sandwich and a cup and a half of water. Then I curled up at Geir's side again, pulling a slightly scratchy blanket around us both. It wasn't a romantic gesture. I couldn't even have said if we were there yet, or what; I just found myself craving the interrupted energy. I thought about drawing his usual restfulness into my spirit, in exchange for as much of my strength as he could use to bolster his own right now.

No time seemed to pass before I woke with bright sunlight coming in around the blinds. We'd slept from early evening straight through to the next day. We hadn't dreamed together as far as I could remember; we'd hardly moved, except that his arm had come up around me. His perfect features were peaceful as a child's, although this morning, for the first time since I'd met him, there was the hint of dark stubble on his upper lip and under his chin.

I cautiously extricated myself so I could sneak over to the bathroom, feeling every moment of the last twenty-four hours in all my muscles and joints. Feeling temporarily twenty-four years older, not just hours.

I heard the quiet knock outside, soft footsteps before I was done washing my hands.

"Ach, Fergus, you daft bugger," came the voice of a different nurse.

I awkwardly emerged. "What's the matter?"

The nurse shook her head. "He's put in here that this shoulder was dislocated yesterday? And some... J Jespersen said the same?"

I nodded. "I was there when he got hurt. Jens Jespersen was the UFPK medic who reduced the dislocation."

Her blue eyes popped at me. "I don't know what you lot are trying to pull--"

"Ladies fighting over me before I'm even awake," Geir murmured, lush eyelashes struggling open. "What can I have done to deserve all this?"

"Sure, you'll only lie as well." The nurse scoffed and stomped out of the room.

He opened his eyes wider, if still not all the way, questioning.

"She's saying we faked your file. That it's not a new injury."

He laughed. "Who wouldn't rather have a hospital bed than Celeste Cameron Adie's luxurious guest cottage overlooking the firth..."

The shrug that accompanied his words stole his smile, and his eyes finally opened the rest of the way. I watched him gingerly lift and lower his shoulders, shrug them forward and back. He shouldn't have been able to do it without cursing out Jespersen's grandfather at least a bit.

"Okay?"

He nodded. "Too bad Jens didn't listen to me last night," he murmured.

"Magical creatures don't belong in regular hospitals?" I whispered.

He gave me a different smile. "I guess that's the short version," he got out before covering a huge yawn.

"Uh oh." I laughed. "Well, get some more beauty sleep before she kicks you out of here."

"Okay." He smiled, dark eyes beckoning to me from under half-lowered lids. Ach, now he was just showing off.

"I'll check in with Lachlan," I breathed, leaning in to kiss him first. With his lips lightly pressed to mine, his hand coming up to rest on my back, I had a sudden sense of the energies that had woven themselves between us while we slept. As though he was the power source, but I was the specific implement needed for the task: drawing his energy, shaping or reconfiguring it to be of help when I returned it to him.

"Really?" I whispered.

He gave me one more soft kiss, eyes already shut. "No. Really that shoulder thing is just my party trick."

I overlaid the hospital's info on my bleary vision. First I found some coffee, thin and bitter but effective enough; then I tracked down Lachlan's room. He wasn't conscious yet, but now it was by deliberate medical induction. If not for the big blue-black bruise on his jaw, he would have looked just peacefully asleep. Silly as it was in the grand scheme, I wished they hadn't had to buzz his Viking hair, but he should have a good long future for it to grow back.

They told me the surgery had gone by the book. The swelling had already decreased below the most dangerous level and continued to ebb steadily. I still couldn't help wishing Brynja could have come with us and done for him what it seemed I'd helped do for Geir.

"If all keeps going this well, he'll be back learning the ropes of Dad's empire before we know it," a nurse was saying. I enjoyed the mental picture of Lachlan, biker boots on the polished boardroom table, tattooed right bicep and left forearm displayed as he leaned back in a cushy ecoleather chair, hands behind his head and the intact braid trailing forward over one shoulder.

An elegant laugh interrupted my daydream. "Oh, it's Cam who'll take over for his father one day. Lachlan is our--" She said "scientist." I heard *black sheep.*

I had to lift my head appreciably to the speaker's face. She looked younger than her husband, maybe fifty. The immaculately smooth creamy blonde hair brushing her shoulders was as perfect as her understated makeup, diamond solitaire earrings totaling at least three carats, cashmere sweater and the pale silk paisley scarf knotted effortlessly around her slim straight shoulders. The air around her smelled as amazing as she looked.

"Good morning, Mrs. Adie," one of the nurses greeted her with a deferential head bob that might as well have been a proper curtsey.

"And to you. What's this, then… impromptu nurses' meeting in the room of the most handsome boy in the ward?"

"Of course not." The second nurse stood up to her just a little. "Generalist Araujo came to ask after Mr. Adie, at the moment we happened to be attending to him."

"And I'm sure they know as well as I do that Mr. Adie is a happily married man." It startled me how much my nicest diplomatic voice sounded like Dad--just the kind of polite jab he'd made during our joint dealings with the Araujo matriarch this one reminded me of.

Her cucumber-green eyes focused unsmilingly, seeing past my borrowed scrubs now. "Generalist Araujo. Kenneth mentioned you were here. Out of uniform, evidently."

"It was either this or the wetsuit I had on when we got here, so, yes, ma'am, I was grateful for the loan."

"Oh." Another short laugh. "We'll have Siobhan send something round for you. You're, what, one sixty or so tall?"

I nodded reflexively, startled.

"Maybe fifty kilos?"

"Not since freshman year of high school." I glanced at the nurses waiting for my fashion consultation to finish up. "And you really don't have to…" I began. Although they seemed more entertained than bothered, I wasn't sure I agreed.

"Nonsense. She enjoys a challenge. Shoe size?"

"Here? Uh, three."

"Another little fairy maiden," she murmured, gesturing a message with her ring hand (a brushed platinum ring, sparkling with tiny diamonds). Let her interpret my quiet laugh however she liked. "Mind if I send an image, too? A bit more to go on."

I shrugged. "Thanks."

"Please, after all you did for Lachlan yesterday, think nothing of it." She snapped a few shots as she spoke. I supposed she could be generous, as well as not wanting a grubby creature in borrowed scrubs and clogs potentially showing up at her perfect house later. "We'll send round some things Elis keeps at the guest house as well, for…"

"Geir," I supplied, lifting a brow at her.

"Of course. Geir. I imagine he'd prefer that, don't you?" I did, actually. "Lovely. And if--well, when, I'm sure--you're both free to leave, do have them ring us at home and we'll have a car here for you."

I knew just fine when I was being dismissed. "You're very kind, Mrs. Adie."

Geir was grudgingly awake when I got back, sitting up shirtless in the bed, talking to a doctor. Bruises had bloomed across the whole troublesome left shoulder and clavicle. He looked comfortable, though, and gave me an easy smile.

"Turns out Dr. Fraser is a sport fisherman. We've just been comparing notes."

"As there's nothing much wrong with Mr. Craig," the sandy-haired doctor agreed with a nice smile of his own. "Fastest stabilization I've ever seen for this sort of injury. Like he's made of polymer bands. Ah, to be twenty-two again."

"Great news." I hoped my amusement passed as pleased surprise.

"Yes." The doctor gave the mattress a couple sharp pats as he stood up. "It takes a while for the bureaucracy to set its hindquarters in motion, but sometime in the next few hours I'll expect you to free up my bed space, Mr. Craig."

Geir chuckled. "Fair enough."

That was near 1100. I sat on the bed and updated him about Lachlan's progress, the slightly-evil stepmother's visit. He messaged Elis on my ring. We looked for news about the aftershock, which seemed to have had miraculously few consequences beyond where we'd happened to be, and what was wrong with the region already. The collapsed Out Skerries Wind Farm turbine was set to be towed away by barge as soon as seafloor stability could be reasonably ensured. We didn't talk yet about the members of his family who, as far as we knew, might still be somewhere along the unstable seafloor. We shared the lunch they brought, supplemented with another sandwich and a little packet of chocolate ginger biscuits.

Close to 1300, a nurses' assistant stopped by with a glossy paper shopping bag. There was a nice set of clothes and shoes for Geir. And I felt wrong to have ever doubted Siobhan. She'd chosen a loose, pale blush sweater knit finely enough to float like gauze, a matching support-stretch camisole, dark stretch jeans, elasticized flats. She'd included a simpler second top in plain black, two pairs of underwear I left in the bag rather than show them to Geir at the moment, and assorted toiletries we could both use, even a perfume sample from a brand she couldn't have known I loved. All that was missing was a mouse-drawn pumpkin coach.

I tried not to dawdle, knowing he would enjoy his turn in a fully-functioning first-world bathroom. I came out in the camisole and jeans and a towel around my head.

"I can't believe Penhaligon's re-released this scent," I chattered at him. "Rosalind. My dad got it for my fifteenth birthday, right before they stopped making it…."

I held up my wrist for him to sniff the wonderful scent of woods, spicy moss, and cool greenery with the hint of a hidden rose. He came close enough to catch a breath of it near my throat, instead.

"Someone brave and clever who went through part of her life far from where she belonged, looking like something she really wasn't," he murmured.

I had to catch my own breath. "You could tell I was a girl, couldn't you?"

His quiet laugh grazed the side of my neck. His hands moved to the back of my waist, savoring each curve. I tasted my perfume on his lips, reached for the sleek channel of muscles at the small of his back. He enjoyed my pulse-quickening realization of how many chances he'd had to perfect the art of the first real kisses with someone who mattered this much to him. The hint of what might come after couldn't help but make me a bit dizzy.

"I forget sometimes how young you are," he barely whispered in reply. "We needn't keep up the pace of what we've come through together in the last few days."

I did my best to kiss him slower.

Of course, when Mrs. Adie said a car, she hadn't meant the kind of self-driving pod I was used to. Within the hour, we were presentable and behaving ourselves, companionably quiet in the back of the Adies' fairytale gorgeous clean-electric gunmetal Jaguar as it sped through Inverness, a distinguished fellow named James at the wheel. We'd tried to see Lachlan again on the way, but his room was dark; we decided not to disturb him, just in case.

Geir held my hand lightly, pleased by my pleasure at seeing the beautiful town recovering as well as Lachlan, in the glow of late afternoon gilding the river that had long since returned to its accustomed level. I wished it wouldn't be such a quick trip. I'd love to see the castle, nearby Loch Ness and everything.

The sizeable family estate, of sandy-hued stone and surrounded by a garden perfect in its curated near-wildness, was tucked out of sight down a tree-shaded lane, evoking the same understated opulence as Isla's house on Shetland. Someone took our luggage (just the shopping bag, one wetsuit and two bathing suits now tucked inside) back to the guesthouse Geir had mentioned. Kenneth had stayed late at the office to make up for his time at the hospital; Celeste would go back to see her stepson later in the evening. Meantime, she offered us cocktails on a brick and stone terrace under the sunset. She seemed to mellow somewhat as she sipped her Hilton Fling. Maybe her earlier chill had been simple anxiety. I couldn't imagine a child of mine in such danger.

Lachlan's handsome blond brothers joined us for an early dinner inside as twilight fell: poached salmon, new potatoes, fresh spring vegetables, a Pinot Grigio that coordinated flawlessly with Celeste's hair, a candied orange peel shortbread of such perfection I expected to dream about it for weeks. Lachlan hadn't exaggerated that at nineteen and sixteen, Cameron and Kennan were taller than he was; it would take them both a few more years to fill in as he had, let alone reach their father's size. Iain, just fourteen, was the quietest but the burliest of the three even now. I could only guess what a soft-spoken giant he might turn out to be.

The boys didn't pretend for a second not to remember Geir. He smiled at their stories of fishing and football and school crushes. It wouldn't look to them like the bittersweet expression of a dad who missed his child, but it did to me. I just hadn't seen him around kids before, let alone the day after he'd lost other dearly loved ones.

Celeste laid a surprisingly tender hand on his shoulder as the boys trooped off to studying and the grid and other pursuits.

"I ought to get back. You're more than welcome to join me, or stay up here, as you like," she said. "Or the guest house is ready."

Geir raised his brows in my direction, ready to abide by my answer.

"As long as these few days have been, some quiet here sounds amazing, unless there's any change in his condition," I said. "Mrs. Adie, I can't imagine how you're such a perfect hostess at a time like this. Thanks, more than we can say."

"Of course." I noticed the tired edges of her smile. "We'll notify one another of any news, yes?"

"Definitely."

We exchanged ring signals; she gave me her husband's as well, just in case. Geir assured her we wouldn't need an escort back to the guest house; we certainly didn't require James to drive us there. We walked down the brick path through the garden below the terrace where we'd started our evening, across a tiny bridge over the brook that wound its charming way through the property, to the little stone cottage.

Chapter 15

Big Sur

The door was unlocked, a fire burning in the hearth. Geir sighed and kicked off the shoes that had been too big for him all evening. While he went into a bathroom to change into more comfortable clothes he'd known where to find, too, I explored: two cozy bedrooms, with the firelit room where we'd entered in between and a kitchenette or breakfast area at the back. Everything was lovely, from the vaulted ceiling and deliciously plush wool carpet to the branches clipped from a white-flowering tree in a vase on the coffee table, and the series of framed photos on the mantel.

"Could I pour you one of these?" Geir said from behind me, standing by an open cabinet. He'd left just his t-shirt on with a pair of Elis' jeans, which required him to roll cuffs like the dress pants Siobhan had sent over for him, but at least he could feel more like himself.

"You didn't think we had enough to drink up there?" I kept my tone neutral.

He met my eyes, his chest moving in the slightest sigh, and he poured anyway.

I managed to shut off my internal warning light for now. He didn't need some kid from out of town to preach temperance at him tonight, after the hell of a way he'd spent the last forty-eight hours.

"Is it nice?" I relented.

"Twenty-five-year-old Islay single malt," he said, sipping from his glass. "Too fine for the likes of me, for sure."

"Then I should obviously have one too."

I turned back to the pictures. The best one was of Lachlan and Brynja's wedding: the bride in a dress delicate as moonbeams, tiny pearls looped over her shoulders where a mortal woman might wear cap sleeves, a big blue stone glinting on her ring finger. Her groom grinned radiantly, no older than Cameron was now, the lamented Viking-biker hair not yet realized. His brothers in their smaller matching kilts, at various stages of funny little kid teeth and awkward limbs. Kenneth and Celeste, in solemn highland regalia, hadn't changed so much. There was Geir, the only time he'd worn a kilt himself.

"You made a bonny highlands and islands laddie," I said, taking my glass.

"What a beautiful day it was, entirely." He smiled as he clinked his against it. "To Brynja and Lachlan. And to lovely Mrs. Morgan who laid this fire, and changes out the pictures and the bar according to our preferences, when she's notified we're coming."

"Really?"

Geir nodded soberly. "There are no pictures of her shown in this home when we're not here to want them."

He indicated a smaller frame: the loveliest brown-haired young woman, long lashes blissfully lowered toward the newborn she held with his fuzzy blond head close to her cheek.

"Elisabeth Maclachlan, Ph.D. Pioneering marine engineer, adored wife, lamented mother," he said very quietly. I didn't find it in me to ask if he was quoting her epitaph.

With a pang in my chest, I went back to the wedding photo. "She looks so much like her father. I'm guessing it's him they have a problem with, not you," I said, fingertip hovering near the one dark selkie head with the crisp short haircut. In his renewed youthful form, he was a disconcertingly handsome little devil.

Geir smiled for me, finally. "It's the lot of us. Our existence. But Elis and Brynja most of all, yes."

"I wasn't sure what to say to him when he asked where Brynja was. Kenneth. I didn't know how much he knew…"

Geir nodded, too. "You did well. Elisabeth grew up in Nairn with Isla and Blaine. Obviously, she didn't look like their other children. But despite the resemblance, not to mention Isla coming right out and naming the child after him, Blaine never worked it out, arrogant as he was… To protect Elis, she said she'd had enough wine to make one poor decision on holiday in Italy that year, and he believed her."

"Whoa."

"Leaving her free to spend time on Shetland with the man who loved her, and bringing Elisabeth with her. He confided the truth to Isla, knowing it affected their girl; he insisted she know, too, soon as she was old enough to understand it. Elisabeth never brought it up with Kenneth, though, until she thought she might die. Both that she wasn't truly Blaine's daughter, and who her father actually was."

"Ho boy."

"Yes. As Elis says, it'd be one thing to hear from Wendy that she'd been to Neverland as a girl. Quite another thing for Peter Pan himself to show up on your doorstep later on."

"Fair enough," I said. Personally, though, I would have appreciated a heads-up from Wendy before starting to meet Lost Boys everywhere.

"So we don't speak of it, as a rule. The thing is, Bryn's fine continuing to be mysterious, but even if he understands the need, Elis hates hiding. Ever since Isla died, we've said he's the grandson of the man Isla loved because that's easiest… Kenneth is only fooled as far as he wants to fool himself about it, of course. So. Elis has been here any number of times to see Lachlan, but mostly they just stay out of one another's way."

"Too bad."

He nodded again. "You'll think so even more if you ever meet him." He raised his glass slightly. "To Elis Kyles, the best of rogues and the selkie son I never had."

I drank with him. He'd been right about the heady and really smoky Scotch. While I sipped from my glass, a first exploratory taste, he soon drained his.

"This is hard for you," I whispered.

"Sorry." He shook his head as if to free himself from a spell. "Not my ideal first date venue, no."

I dragged my eyes away from the photos. "You smiled at dinner."

"Sure." He smiled now, too. Wistfully, as he had then.

"You haven't had a selkie son," I breathed. "But you had someone like Elisabeth."

His gaze didn't falter as he nodded once.

I hesitated. "What was her name?"

He exhaled a soft sigh. "I had Owen, Clairy, Jane, Tamsin and Robbie, Beatrix, Alasdair, and Lucy, the one you're thinking of."

I bit back a groan. That would be selkie hell, pure and simple, to love so fully and lose so many times. I took a bigger sip, but could summon nothing like the nerve to ask yet if he'd told them their heritage too; whether he'd had to fade from their lives like a favorite childhood storybook character; let alone about the wives and mothers.

"Maybe you can show me your pictures too, some time. Kids. Weddings. Your beautiful families."

With his forehead against mine, he remembered a young woman with ringlets, voluptuous and innocent in her pale gown, holding flowers as blue as the lovely eyes she raised to his. Someone long before hippie Beryl and her beautiful voice. The baby toothlessly laughing in her arms, next, had his father's wide dark eyes, not hers. I understood he'd kept back most of the emotion surrounding his bride's memory when he shared some part of the immense love he still felt for their son.

His voice remained steady. This was just what he lived with, all the time. "Even for the ones who could be photographed, I really only have this kind of pictures. And the odd antique jumpers and things. Where I could say it belonged to my great-great-grandfather if anyone asked."

Of course, it wouldn't be worth risking the next beautiful family finding too strong proof of the inexplicable previous ones; and maybe that wasn't all.

"My dad couldn't stand to keep any of my mother, either. I guess you and he and Kenneth have that in common." I leaned close for a soft Scotch-flavored kiss and felt his grateful agreement with my understanding.

More beautiful faces flickered with poignant brevity in his memories, but most of what I sensed was like the cold, dark weight of isolation on a deep dive. He'd told me, once, that he'd grown old with his loves every chance he'd been given. For one reason or another, though, few had stayed so long. He was no more one to bounce back quickly after a loss than I was. In my century, wives were very rarely lost to childbirth or sudden fevers. But his way was hardly more than a fairytale now, to women who didn't even realize they broke his steadfast heart by wanting only one night. The day had come when he'd stopped trying.

"I know the feeling," I murmured.

His soft laugh stirred my hair. That day had been long enough ago that I wouldn't have been old enough to be next. Maybe, like Lachlan and Brynja, I would have at least been grown enough to match his height.

"No rush, though," I teased him in a whisper.

"Ach," he answered, a tiny soft groan of appreciative laughter. What radiated from his skin to mine was as intense as the best kiss, but instead of lips touching, it was just his eyes holding mine for as long as I could bear it.

I leaned my head down to his firm shoulder and we were still for a while longer, listening to the soft snapping of the fire. In this clear but wavering light, it was hard to tell how far down we were. We'd come to know each other well enough to find ourselves just below the surface of such things, but there was the sense of pulse-pounding depth here already. Then again, I'd always had the worst trouble orienting myself at such moments.

Not Geir, though. His feet were perfectly familiar with this ledge. He caught me before I could flounder, and quietly held us both steady. Perceiving my awareness of my uneven heartbeat, he laid a respectful hand on my upper chest, fingertips light against my collarbone. "This is normal for us."

He didn't blame me for all the means I'd developed to protect the heart he felt beating beneath that gentle touch, but he wanted me to believe I wouldn't need them here.

Whatever reaction he felt from me made him laugh again, whispery, sweet, and insistently reassuring. "Okay? Please don't black out on me again."

"Okay," I agreed in a shaky murmur.

He stroked my hair and the side of my neck, wondering if there were any photos of me as a bride.

I let out a startled, rueful laugh. "Uh. I guess."

It took a little digging around the grid; in my case, I hadn't kept my pictures anywhere obvious because I wasn't very proud of the whole story. My former sister-in-law still had some on a node of hers. She'd attended the wedding with her tiny firstborn, and had four kids in middle school and younger now; she'd probably never had time to take the old photos down.

"Here." I picked one where they'd particularly captured the beauty of late afternoon on the Big Sur coastline, pulled it up in projection and was rewarded with another changeable, wistful smile.

"That's Dad's and my favorite place in California, USA."

I felt his immediate admiration for my father, tall and slim and distinguished in his linen suit. He had only cool distaste for the gorgeous blond boy with rolled-up sleeves showing off the tanned arms wrapped around my shoulders from behind, meaningless wedding band glinting in the angled sunlight. I chose not to point out to Geir just then how similar the two handsome men in the photo had been, as far as the ladies were concerned. It felt too nice to have someone think uncomplicatedly well of Dad.

I hadn't cried looking at pictures of that day in years. But Geir's surge of wonder, longing, regret, and desire for my protection as he took his time over the hopefully glowing image of me--barefoot in my creamy silk slip dress, with flowers in my hair--sent helpless tears spilling fast down both cheeks.

"How old were you?" he breathed, caressing them away.

"Not quite twenty." I sighed. Only a baby, myself. Everyone, including my bridegroom, had thought I was crazy to insist on it so young, if ever. But there'd been nothing in the world I'd wanted half so much. At least now, here in the warmth of such a different man's affection, I understood maybe my selkie heart hadn't been as childish as the whole affair had made me think all this time. Perhaps I'd just needed the right sea to dive in.

He slipped a finger under my chin, turning my face up to his, and held my eyes a moment before kissing me gently. "Forgive me," he whispered.

"What?"

"How could you do that to your beautiful hair?"

I smiled. It had been expensive and I still thought it had looked great, styled into big smooth curls, colored a rich chestnut brown full of highlights closer to the shade of my skin and lighter ones that brought out the gold in my eyes.

With some flicks of my ring hand, I went backwards in time through other days gone by, from now until not so long after the wedding: the naturally curly phase before I'd given up on coloring it, all over caramel blonde to match my skin; spunky sea-hued A-line waves, about the length of his own hair; the pixie crop with wine-red lowlights was his reluctant favorite, for the way it showed off my eyes. He loved the carefree grin of the Arden looking up at the camera with a tiny frog on her thumb, even if he could hardly believe her olive-iridescent buzz cut had been real.

"Unmodified photo taken by our own Vega Hazan, if I'm not mistaken."

"Sacrilege." He laughed softly. "For the sake of what? Artistic expression?"

"Eh. Maybe finding myself? It's taking me a while, I guess."

His hands were so delicate, his continued impression of never wanting to hurt me so sweetly vivid, as he removed the few pins and elastics holding my braided chignon in place, then carefully spread the tamed waves down around my shoulders. I gave my head a little shake for him, heard his breath catch and sigh free faintly in turn. He'd waited a long time to run both hands through all the silky curls still fragrant and damp from washing, to set my hairline alight with kisses from temple to nape.

"I hope you'll keep it just like this," he breathed without lifting his head. "As long as I'm around."

My throat tightened abruptly. I'd never been contracted for more than a six-month mission anywhere. I would be the one who wasn't around sooner or later, or both. Here I'd worried about self-preservation when it was all but guaranteed I would be the one to break his selkie heart, the same way his old loves had.

"No. Your own way." It wasn't a new realization for him, of course. He hadn't been so quick to pour another drink only because of everyone he'd lost in the past. "It's okay." He tried to kiss the tears away while they were still falling. I guessed he had no reason to fear a little more saltwater.

It wasn't okay at all. I downed the Scotch I'd only sipped, then laid my head against his good shoulder again.

He sighed, stroked my hair a few more times. "Finman joking aside, I hope it's gone without saying I wouldn't ask for anything you're not ready to give, now or ever. You pick a bedroom and I'll have the other one."

"Well, maybe let's not be that hasty," I whispered, earning a tender quiet laugh.

We chose the larger room on the left, decorated in subtle jade tones. He asked if we could leave the drapes open; there wouldn't be anyone back there, where the property dropped away down a hill and the big northeast-facing window offered a beautiful view of sunrise over the Moray Firth. I gingerly laid my filmy sweater over a chair; otherwise, we curled up together with our clothes on.

For a time, we just slept, both of us still needing rest as badly as we did. But some hours into the night we dreamed together again: not only walking on the beach in the other Inverness now. Exquisite dreams, so vivid I couldn't have ever said later exactly when we woke each other to continue them in the glow of the rare spring aurora borealis over the dark water.

We awoke breathless for the blissful shock of one newly-joined reality, too drawn in to waste the few moments it would have taken to get most of our clothes off. Later, we took our time undressing one another the rest of the way. I'd never been half so naked with anyone before. From his perfect surface, pearlescent against mine in the otherworldly light, all the way to the unexplored depths he was willing for me to swim, he was absolutely the most beautiful place I had ever come to rest.

Chapter 16

Uncharted Waters

I started awake after what felt like a few minutes when my ring pulsed softly, on the floor on top of my discarded camisole. The skyglow had faded to early daylight before we'd reluctantly slept again, but we'd missed the sunrise he'd hoped for; now I blinked at the full sun shining in. Stretching carefully, so I wouldn't wake him, I activated the retinal controls as I slipped the device onto my wrist.

Morning

Araujo

IS THIS THING ON, Vega had been ringing me over the last several minutes.

Sorry im here doc What do you need

Why are you not at the hospital

G and i invited to stay at lachlans

Ooh Rrromantic?

I hesitated.

Mystical harrrmonic converrrgence, I sent back.

There was just enough of a quiet moment for my brilliant friend to do the simple math.

Waittttt someone done said YES?

I ran a hand over his beautiful hair and tried to remember if any words had been spoken at all.

YES, I still had to answer, even though I thought there hadn't.

Pick up

I hesitated long enough to pull my own hair quickly back with the elastic around my wrist. Lifting my hands, I noticed the now-familiar, faint clean scent clinging to the band, seawater and skin musk. I remembered taking his hair down to match mine, hours before; I left my hair and the band exactly where they were.

ARDEN.

On a hunch, I inched the wardrobe door open and found two fluffy spa robes. Sized for guests of Adie stature: slipping one on, I felt like a kid dressing up in an adult's opulent coat. I made my careful way into the central room.

I hadn't heard our ally Mrs. Morgan come in to tidy the fireplace and leave us a clear thermal carafe of steamy tea with a smaller one of milk, a basket of fresh soft bread rolls, and a jar of marmalade.

I curled my feet up under me in last night's spot on the sofa and activated voice on my ring.

"Hi, doc," I said softly.

"Hi, told-ya-so," she answered with a big smile in her voice. "So, I'm picturing something like those diver boys from once upon a time in a land before your vow of celibacy?"

"Uh. Okay…"

"And thinking about all that bass I wasn't expecting when he opened his mouth, perhaps the little dude turns out to be… disproportionate?" I could imagine the accompanying brow waggle.

I groaned with laughter, covering my eyes though she couldn't see them. "His proportions are dreamy, okay?"

"First fella deemed worthy of you since Perth? No, girl, after that long you don't get to be so vague."

I drew a deep breath. Sorry, Dr. Hazan, I couldn't come up with an exact figure as to how lavishly far he'd gone toward erasing that three-year pleasure deficit in a single night. I had no way at all of explaining the as-yet unmeasured underwater topography, mass, depth, or movement of the iceberg where I seemed to have awakened. But that wasn't what Vega wanted to hear anyway, so I tried to describe the little peak above the surface where I found myself floating now.

"Then how about, reading my mind isn't even the best skill he has," I told her finally.

I relished her brief pause.

"Geez, mija. How about, your bar is set low enough for some pretty kid with a ripped-up shoulder to make you wax all poetic."

"Maybe." I laughed, rather than say this was the one area of life where I thought she'd always set her bar much too low.

"And after turning down my perfectly good Stevie for being too young? Por Dios."

Enamored though he was, more than once during the night Geir's sweet generosity alone had saved me from feeling like an unschooled child. I smothered a laugh successfully enough that only a noncommittal sound came out. Fortunately, she didn't push it, the next pause reminding her there was a real reason for her ring beyond the girl talk.

"Well, I wish I wasn't calling to cut the honeymoon short, but."

"Okay." I sighed. "Tell me the plan."

"So, Mrs. Lachlan K showed up early this morning, and I'm told she was understandably unhappy not to find him here."

"Yep."

"So she's on her way there; actually, she should be leaving in a few minutes to get there around noon, so… And we also need to get the powers that be off your back and have you on the return transport, once she's settled."

I closed my eyes against the overflow of every emotion I had.

"Bring Gary too, obviously. Just, if you can't stay within protocol in the helo, keep it out of Kuo's line of sight."

I leaned my head back against the sofa cushions. "Let's wait and see if the family needs him here."

"True. You'll just communicate that to Kuo, either way." She paused. "If he's what you want then I'm happy for you."

"I know. Thanks, ma," I murmured.

"All right. See your wild little self in a few hours."

I wasn't sure of Celeste's agenda for the morning, but as promised, I rang her a quick update. She didn't answer right away. As I made a quick check for any other messages, which I certainly might have missed, the bedroom door whispered open.

We could only watch each other speechlessly for several seconds. His reluctantly heavy eyelids lent him an even more dreamy expression. His hair still fell softly forward around his jawline. He'd known where to find the other robe; it was too big on him, too.

"How's the shoulder today, Mr. Craig?"

He smiled impishly, the spell broken, and came and sat at my side. "I want to say, 'never better,' but that'll be other bits of me trying to do the talking…"

My one giggly little kiss in greeting turned out to have a similarly fierce mind of its own. With a quiet laugh, he moved a few deliberate centimeters away before he entirely lost the question he'd wanted to ask me.

"Rookie selkie mistake," I whispered, wide-eyed, and reached to pour two cups of tea.

"Yep." He shook his head. "Who did I hear you talking to? Was that the hospital?"

"Not this one. Vega." I took a quick breath. "Brynja's on her way, and I'll need to be on the transport when they turn it around. Obviously, it's up to you and her if you stay here or come with me."

"Okay," he murmured, stirring milk into my tea, sugar into his. "What time do they need you?"

"She'll get in around noon, so... It's 9:45... Breakfast, quick shower, and we go up and ring James, right? Easy."

"No rush," he agreed with a seriously untrustworthy half-smile.

As competent and accommodating as James was, even he couldn't bend the laws of physics to get us there by twelve. At least by 1215 we were clean and dressed, moving in the right direction, and I was in a fit state of mind to answer the rings that had started requesting our ETA.

Meantime, I'd missed Celeste's reply to my earlier message. "Oh, wow," I said. "They're getting ready to wake him up."

Geir just smiled and nodded. It was weird not to touch him and know more specifically what he meant, but I'd learned better than to try that again yet.

The elevator doors opened on Lachlan's floor, revealing our queen on a waiting area sofa. Her eyes, bright as the night sky, were already turned in our direction. Her faint knowing smile brought a blush roaring into my cheeks. Geir laughed quietly at my side and bent his head.

"I didn't think we'd find you hanging out in the hallway," I stammered slightly.

"Oh," she said, airily shaking her imperiously erect head. "Kenneth and Celeste can muscle me out into the corridor for the big moment. I've already been in to see him. I know he's fine, and he knows I'm here."

There were no times when I didn't love her, but I most adored her when she scared me a little.

She held out a tiny hand to Geir, who sat beside her. I perched further down the couch, giving him space.

She'd made smart adjustments, for UFE personnel and hospital staff to perceive her as a wife's age: bun at the nape of her neck, simple pearl clip earrings, lab-created ecosuede blazer (ordered from Asia, I imagined), a sea-toned silk scarf gorgeous enough to have been a gift from Celeste. And her wedding ring, a rough-cut oval sapphire set lengthwise in a delicate gold bezel. Our queen knew a few things about shapeshifting. I'd have put her at twenty-two, anyway.

She didn't keep back a smoky giggle of pleasure at what she found when she first touched her troublesome younger brother. Presumably, he wasn't kissing and telling everything.

She lifted startled smiling eyes to mine. "Dreaming together already?" she asked us both. "Even before?"

I could only shrug and nod. How the hell was I to know which impossible thing that happened right now was normal and which was unusual?

"Lovely," she breathed, turning the smile on her brother a little longer. The moment grew sober, though, as they sat twined close together. Geir's back was to me, but his grief and regret radiated like body heat.

Within moments, she was shaking her head; he pushed away far enough to make her look him in the eyes. The communication shifted into words: their language, but I could understand *No no no.*

She got to her feet, slight shoulders straight, and dashed away her tears on the backs of her fingers as she looked down at him. Several sharp heartbeats passed before he lowered his eyes first, bent his head to her again.

She turned her eyes my way and didn't smile now so much as soften, bending to stroke the overwhelmed tears from my face as well. She didn't want to explain this to me herself. She did want me to know how grateful she was that I'd chosen him, just as she wished. Her people, in time, would share that gratitude--if, as she hoped, the next in Geir's impressive string of progeny could be as much like a full selkie as the cream-complected, hazel-eyed, and curly-headed toddler in her longing imagination.

It was so obviously what she would want, what all of them need-ed. My heart staggered back a step realizing she hadn't even tried to hide it, this whole time.

I reeled away, banged on the elevator button. The door chime sounded immediately.

Geir slipped into the elevator with me before it could close.

I let him take my hand because I needed him to tell me if we'd been more than an item on the faerie queen's conservation agenda. Had that been why he'd kept offering me ways out?

Dark eyes shining with saltwater, he shook his head and pressed me gently back against the elevator wall with the whole length of his body, his hands outside my shoulders and elbows close to my waist.

Defiant if shaky, I felt as loudly as I could that we were way ahead of ourselves here, even for us. I recalled as well the general doubtful sense that had come of the numerous but inconclusive tests they'd done on my weird little chimera reproductive system when I'd been younger.

He kissed away a tear that slipped down the side of my neck. "I won't speak for Brynja, but you're already more than I could ask for," he breathed. "Just this. Now or ever."

He remembered the night I'd shown up at their house with Vega—how he'd instantly liked the sound of my voice, loved the idea of a young American woman brave enough to offer herself in aid to his devastated little part of the world. And that had been before he'd come outside to find the undreamed-of sight of a selkie lass like me, inspiring far more than his respect in the UFE uniform. He'd hardly needed Brynja to suggest--after I was gone, as the cluster of raven heads bent close poring over my card by firelight--that he give me as many reasons as he could to stay.

I sagged against the elevator wall, the bittersweet intensity of the inevitable embrace washing over us. Echoes and impressions swirled amid the crashing tide. He must have received from Brynja the an-guishing image of Runa's lifeless marble profile, submerged in shallow clear water. I supposed they'd found her there. I did understand clearly that our queen was sending him back to Shetland, to help her daugh-ters lead in her stead while she was here.

"Okay," I sobbed against his neck.

The elevator shifted awake. I laughed through all the emotions. I hadn't pushed the button for any other floor. At least it looked within expectations for a girl to be crying in a hospital elevator. The lab-coat-clad person who'd called it stood respectfully aside and let us exit.

I didn't even know what floor we'd come out on, but we found another sofa, clung together as on another life raft for a minute or two. Finally, I broke free enough of the mystical hormonal convergence to locate tissues on a side table. He took a few as well.

"Eventually things have to, like, settle down between us, right?" I asked with an unsteady laugh-cry, the best I could muster. "I'll still be a productive member of society, and not, you know, end up institutionalized?"

His tearful smile was achingly sweet. "I like how you ask as though I had any more idea about it than you do. But yes, I have to think so."

"So this isn't how it works with someone who's just an earth girl or just a selkie…"

"Well, I can only tell you about the earth girls." He chuckled at my choice of phrase. "But you're right, anyway you're something else."

"Uncharted waters," I murmured.

There was an inopportune pulse at my wrist before he could reply. Kuo, ringing to say the helo had been checked over and refueled and she was just waiting for me.

On my way with G Craig Few minutes pls?

No worries, she answered. *Gonna grab sammies for road Meet at helipad soonish*

"That's the all-aboard?" Geir guessed.

I nodded. "But we've got a second to see Lachlan and Brynja first."

On Lachlan's floor, Mr. and Mrs. Adie were outside the elevator doors.

"All right, Arden?" Celeste greeted me, unexpectedly gentle.

"Uh. Sorry… hell of a few days. But yes. With thanks to you, for letting us stay at your wonderful home."

She smiled, but he answered. "That's nothing, compared to what you did for Lachlan. If there's anything we can do in return, anything, you've only to name it."

Kenneth Adie offered a heartfelt firm handshake, first to me, then to Geir, who didn't say anything but laid his other hand pale atop Kenneth's massive ruddy one.

Adie cleared his throat lightly, letting go. He tilted his head toward the room. "You're in plenty of time to see him still awake. And we'll be in touch, right."

"Yes, sir. Thanks."

I was grateful to find the patient quite alert, Brynja now contentedly on the bed by his feet. His undimmed storm-blue eyes focused on us with perfect clarity. His wry smile meant he was caught up on our news.

"Hey. Thanks for my cracked rib," was all he said.

I managed a more laugh-like sound than earlier. "You're welcome. How are you feeling?"

"Like they should let me go home with you," he answered unhesitatingly. Brynja rubbed his ankle, comforting, admonishing or both.

"Well, this is your brain we're talking about, so take your time," I reminded him. "We'll hold down the fort."

"Thank you." Brynja slipped down off the bed and put her arms around Geir again. There weren't any more pyrotechnics.

I took advantage of the quiet moment to give Lachlan a careful hug, too. The hospital bracelet's fastener caught in my hair as he let me go. Disentangling it, I happened to read his full name for the first time: *Adie, Lachlan Kyles.*

"You know once you've spent the night with one of them, you never find your way back to the human realm," he teased.

"That's fair folk, not finfolk, my darling," Brynja laughed.

"To-may-to, to-mah-to," he retorted, with a mischievous little smile. Not that I guessed he'd know first-hand, but the human realm was overrated anyway.

"And it was done well before then." My lover smiled faintly. "You can't so much as eat or drink anything they offer and hope to go home again."

Forever ensorcelled by fairytale mayonnaise. Who knew what Dad would make of the rest, but I couldn't help thinking he'd laugh at that much.

Chapter 17

Oslo

I'd hoped the ride home would be easier on Geir, now he wasn't in such uncertainty and pain. Those had been distractions, though, against the vertigo of flying so far above his green highlands and islands and his sea. The helo rotors, harsher than a triphibious hover engine, wore him down even with ear protection, and we knew better than to resort to touch for comfort. He kept his eyes closed except when I nudged him to look at something beautiful. I imagined Brynja toughing it out alone on the trip down, and felt grateful she was with Lachlan now.

In between sights, we talked on the headset Kuo had linked into our coms for him. I asked anything to keep him occupied. He didn't want to talk yet about the unaccustomed animosity between Brynja and him, back at the hospital. I didn't want to ask more about where he was going than I already knew. I went with a lighter-hearted one instead, the last names.

He laughed quietly and told me of a time before idents or any digital information, when they'd only needed them to give to employers, maybe share with families. Cowan meant seal; Geir and some of the fellows considered that too obvious. May's love had styled himself

Eoin Black, for the handsome hair he'd inherited from his father; other guys they'd known used Dunn or Duncan, which meant about the same. Kyles referred to the straits between an island and the mainland.

Geir, like the rest, had taken on various names at different places and times. But, thanks to his human stepfather, he was one of very few who'd always had a real last name. Craig was perfect for a finman, though, derived from the same word as *crag* in modern English. A rock where seals and selkie folk alike could take a break and sun themselves. A place to rest: that was him.

We paused to watch the Orkney Islands, almost as beautiful as their northern sisters, passing serenely below. They didn't draw me at first sight like Shetland, but I'd still love a couple days off to visit. Leaving them behind, there was nothing under us but glistening water.

"Your mother was Rea Strand?" Geir asked me, eyes closed again.

"Yeah. He called her Rei. Some Greek philosopher said that, *Panta rei.* 'Everything flows, nothing stays.' They both thought it was perfect for her. Who knows if either one knew just how perfect."

"'Strand' too, like a beach," he murmured.

A little chill went up and down my arms.

"Tell me what else we know about her…"

I sighed. "Almost nothing. I guess they worked together. They were very off-and-on, for something like fifteen years while he was traveling back and forth between Kristiansand and UCLA. He never knew she was pregnant, and he was in California when I was born. She just dropped me off at the hospital. They scanned for a basic DNA match and contacted him. I didn't have a name other than Norwegian for Baby Girl Doe, then Baby Girl Araujo, until he came to get me when I was five weeks old."

It was harder for him to hear than for me to tell the truth I'd been used to for a long time. "He tried to find her, but never heard anything again," I said, then risked letting my fingers twine between his.

"Until I was three. She washed up someplace near Oslo, so full of party drugs the cause of death on the certificate was inconclusive. Drowning, overdose, accidental or intentional. They'd been unable to locate any next of kin but me."

"God. I'm sorry," he murmured.

I shrugged. "He didn't tell me then, not until I was old enough to ask. Not much reason to. Bipolar, under the layer of hard chem she liked on top sometimes, was his guess as to what happened. She'd tell him pretty mind-bending things, apparently, when she was in her element. He never met anyone who saw the world like she did."

I took a breath. Geir could know more than I usually told people. "I was born addicted to some of her shit... During my five weeks of fun there, they tested me for side effects and everything, but I seemed okay. They didn't believe the syndactyly was caused by any of what she'd been using. And there weren't any other birth defects they could diagnose at the time, so they thought I was pretty lucky."

"Syndactyly?" he repeated carefully. "That's... the medical term for selkie toes?"

I laughed a little, nodding.

He laughed for real. "Hey. They're not defective."

"No, as my dad told them when they went over all the results. And although when I got older, I thought my lack of focus was related to the chem somehow... that's still the official diagnosis... it's occurred to me, maybe I just get it from her."

"And the rest of you? Didn't he ever say if you favor her?"

"You don't think I look like a mini him? Except for the toes... and the eyes and the hair?"

He stroked a curl near my temple. "Hers was red?"

"No, that was his Irish grandmother. I don't even know what color my mom's hair was. Just that he said it was different every time he saw her, so I guess that's where I got that phase, too..."

"Finding herself, do you think? Or more like artistic expression?"

My brows drew up at the accuracy of his guess. "Maybe. She left their hotel rooms before him a lot, leaving pictures instead of notes. Once he woke up and she'd drawn all over the bathroom mirror with eye makeup. He didn't keep anything she'd made, though. Or I've wondered sometimes... maybe he did at first, but it would have hurt to see it every day, after... Same as photos. Same as talking about her without a few glasses of anesthesia first."

Because it was Geir, I found myself saying even things Dad should never have told his teenage kid, but *in vino veritas*. I closed my eyes a moment. How had he put it? "Not that they never used anything together, either, but he said there was no need for chem when it was just the two of them. How often she didn't need words to know his deepest wish."

I felt his eyes on me; I dared a glance too quick for his darkly glowing gaze to pull me under. "Which I always thought was BS. That unrealistic way you remember people you loved. Until..."

I'd already looked away, but still felt the sweetness of his smile.

"Anyway. It wasn't enough for them to stay together or even be exclusive, so."

Geir wondered, nonetheless, whether Dad hadn't ever allowed me too close to him because I was a more vivid reminder than any artwork or photo could ever be.

I sighed. "I don't even think I knew him well enough to answer that."

Geir did something that was far more than lifting and kissing my hand--imagining the artist who had brought the Northern Lights into the sea caves, at work on one of her underground installations. If I'd been remotely ready to talk to him when we were there, maybe he would have said he'd suspected it was a person he'd met. He was trying to remember her for me now.

Neither he nor anyone else had seen her do it, which meant the bits of images were disconcertingly joined into a shifting sensory collage. But... there was something intimately familiar about the way she bent her head as she reached for the next tile, the angles and gestures of her capable small hands. The wrist cocked to keep her messy fingertips away from her face as she pushed back an errant strand of hair. For a heartbeat, Geir widened his focus to the hand and wrist he held now, with the mental equivalent of a ringing echo.

A chill shot up that arm, down my back.

"Arden. Did they ever say what your mother was wearing when they found her?"

"What? How should I..." I trailed off, then whispered, "No."

He drew a patient breath, pulled me close, and held me there like a parent calming a tantrum, my face pressing his neck and shoulder, skin to skin. The crashing breakers were me protesting I wasn't ready to know. He guided me deeper, into the stillness of my own strength, flexibility, tenacity: he could see so much in me, now, that I'd never expressed in words to him or anyone.

I made myself look her in the face he remembered maddeningly vaguely. Only the wide-set midnight hazel eyes were so clear they seemed to meet mine, the curve of the brows achingly familiar. He showed me, on her long-ago features, what my downcast bright eyes and appealingly pursed lips looked like trying to hide a smile. He recalled her sitting as I often did, one boot tucked under her, in a studded black jacket, short hair spiked up and sprayed crimson. 1970s or 80s, I guessed. The last time she'd set foot or fin on Shetland, as far as Geir knew. The last they'd heard of her for sure.

She'd always wandered--gone for months or years at a time, back and forth between the selkie folk and humankind of Hebrides, Northern Isles, and Norway. He remembered she'd come from a place that looked much like Shetland but wasn't anywhere I'd seen yet.

"Westray, Orkney," Geir agreed in a slight murmur.

I shook my head with renewed vehemence. "Well, she could've had kids in Orkney, Norway, wherever. She could be my great-great-grandmother or something. Wouldn't that fit better with what we know about the Norwegian side dying out?"

He didn't need to say *no* aloud. "The birth of a child is as close as selkie folk ever come to shouting from the rooftops. I can't imagine why she'd keep you a secret... but whether she meant it or not, she did, leaving you like that."

Nothing else explained my role in everything, these last days and weeks. And from the second I'd met her haunted eyes in his mind's own eye, there'd been no more doubt. She was the mystical half I hadn't known I had. But I had no desire to carry any fraction of this desperate grief: never knowing someone so amazing, because the moment she'd uncovered her sealskin stashed behind sloppily-folded sweaters in the hall closet of Dad's little student apartment, she'd bolted back to the sea.

He shook his head. "My love, clearly she knew she wasn't in a fit state to take care of you, but I'm grateful she did want you here."

I wrenched away, too late to stop the first sobs tearing free. Or the pathetic question, "You really think the mosaics could have been hers?"

He pursued, one gentle but firm hand cupping my stinging cheek. At least, he thought, she'd been able to leave that much of herself for me to find.

No. This was not one of their damn fairytales with the happy ending. I slapped his hand away, stumbled to my feet half-blind, and slumped into the seat next to Kuo.

"Whoops," she said, audio linking into my cochlear. "Trouble in paradise already?"

"Ugh. No, more like he's--too nice for the real world. The backwards of trouble in paradise, I guess. You know?"

"No, hon, I sure don't." Her laugh conveyed bewilderment and solidarity together. "Even the keepers can be a major pain in the ass, though, can't they? In an ideal world, I'd offer you your own pint of ice cream, but…" She reached to her other side and produced the bag of snacks she'd brought from Raigmore. "If you want anything in there, help yourself."

I'd been spoiled enough by the Adies' hospitality that the remaining packaged sandwich didn't have much appeal. I took the salt and vinegar potato chips, melodramatically deciding they'd replenish the sodium I'd lost through tear overproduction lately. No point trying to tease out how much was actual post-traumatic response, what was selkie mind-meld overload, and what was the stupid treatment injection hitting me.

"There's Fair Isle," she said after a few minutes of companionable quiet, indicating the green jewel floating slightly west of our flight path. "Getting close to home. You want to go tell him, or should I patch in back there?"

I sighed. "No, I'll go."

I was home. That was what ripped my heart right out of my chest. This should have been my life. Like Elisabeth, like Geir's children. Instead, she'd made me roam the world all these years, getting my selkie heart smashed up again and again, never finding my place or even understanding who the hell I was meant to be.

At first, I just leaned against him, sharing not only our current location. He sighed, and put gentle arms around me again.

"Okay, tell me her real name," I asked eventually.

"Nereiður," he whispered.

"Panta bloody Rei" grated free from my tight throat and teeth, both clenched anew against the tears I still didn't want her to get from me.

"Even closer to the truth than Rea," he agreed. "How I wish you could have known sooner, or that she could have done other than she did, love... I know it's felt like a lot of time to you."

I drew a few deep, steadying breaths, body and spirit.

"But if you'd known all along, surely now some Norwegian lad would have you," he nudged me into a smile. "How can I wish for that?"

"Okay, so I guess I wouldn't trade," I whispered. "If you really still want someone who throws two tantrums in one day... Sorry."

He laughed softly. He wouldn't trade, either. "The thing is... there's never been anyone in the world more beautiful to me than a fiery half earth girl, half selkie. I thought for most of my life, that was because all the ones I ever knew were my kids. Biased, right? But then... though the timing was wrong for us... I met Elisabeth Maclachlan." He laughed quietly again. "Well. Everyone who ever breathed the same air as Elisabeth fell in love a little."

"But if that had worked out, you'd be homeless and Brynja would be missing out right now," I teased.

He shook his head, still chuckling. "No worries, dream girl."

I quickly lost my smile. "Geir… Lachlan told me Elisabeth could shapeshift as a child. Your kids… How much like selkies were they?"

Newly sober, he stroked my cheek and chose words, maybe hoping to make it less of a shock than shared memories would be.

"Some of them could too, as children. Owen. Tamsin and Robbie. None of them into adulthood, the ones who lived that long. Perhaps because so few stayed in Neverland."

I groaned with longing. His gentle touch urged me to seek contentment with all I'd been given instead. I gritted my teeth but didn't push him away this time.

"You said Beryl only thought you were her selkie lover, but Elis told Isla the truth. I understand maybe you couldn't tell the moms, but did your kids get to know who they were? Even if they never shapeshifted?"

"Always," he sighed. "I can only believe Nereiður would have told you too, if she could have stayed." He stroked my hair. "The more fool me, not realizing sooner that in all other ways you're just like them. Impossibly brilliant divers. The shared senses and dreams. Supernatural powers of seduction."

"Ach." I sighed with reluctant laughter. "For the last time, that was really you, cabrón."

"The extreme stubbornness, we'll assume comes from your father." He laughed softly too. "Along with Spanish insults, and the willingness to put everything you are on the line to help our little corner of the world."

Kuo gave a wave and a wink as she lifted the helo right back off. I offered Geir a ride wherever he needed to go next. In my mind's eye were the Scalloway Islands, a logical first guess, but he answered with the image of their house and a flicker of lovely faces. One twin or both might be waiting for him. He felt something else that wasn't hunger or thirst, fatigue, or his scarcely-abated need for me. A different sort of drive. Except for our race to get Lachlan to the surface, he hadn't gone within since before the aftershock.

His beautiful face stayed downcast as he nodded in answer to what I hadn't said. With a gentle hand on his hair and shoulder, I also felt the abject emptiness the house held for him right now, sharp as an electrical connection touched by accident.

I thought of how I could help raise the vibrations in their beautiful home for him, if he wasn't in too much of a hurry to invite me in.

"Selkie lass," he chuckled under his breath, leaning his head down to brush a kiss warm with more than sweet gratitude to the back of my hand.

"Career generalist," I smiled with more than friendly professionalism, and tilted my head in question toward the pool of waiting hovers.

"Okay," he agreed, eyes boyishly brighter than a moment before. I got authorization for the hovercraft and we were on our way in minutes, curled together on half the seat. As we crossed the water he showed me how Brynja had gathered everyone safely in the Scalloway caves. He'd head there after checking in at home.

"Please," I breathed. "If you can... stay the hell away from the eastern side."

He caressed the back of my neck and the little curls escaping under my braid. It was a long time since he'd had this compelling a reason to keep himself from harm. He didn't want me to worry.

I leaned my head down to his strong shoulder, remembering the wordless argument between Brynja and him hours earlier.

"She was right," he murmured. "It's okay."

"About what? I've never seen anyone argue with her like that."

He drew in a slow breath, stroked my hair again. "The way my shoulder has been healing," he said, and paused a moment without impressing anything my way. "If that much of the North Sea runs through you... think what my queen could do for someone in need of her." He thought fleetingly of sitting at Lachlan's feet while I did CPR, out of my way yet lending whatever energy he could. "What I probably might, though I'm not altogether like her."

I nodded; I'd already begun to consider it yesterday.

He pictured Hano's face for a reverent moment. I sucked in a sudden, aching breath.

"But think of what it cost you, as well," he said. "For a relatively small injury."

Rarely had anyone made such a sacrifice in Geir's lifetime. He remembered it happening once, when he'd been little more than a child. It had been a father, still a young man, who'd managed to bring his daughter back. He'd lived a fraction of his expected years with her by his side. Her reinstated life, too, had been shortened, her former strength diminished.

I knew enough about father-daughter relationships cut short to understand. And I knew to my bones that Geir was just as much the kind to give himself away for someone else. He'd likely yearned to do the same for his children if it were possible to rescue a half-selkie that way. I found I couldn't want any good deed to cost him so much.

He kissed my temple. Brynja wasn't only protecting herself. Far from it. That had been the fight.

"And. It would have been one thing, as soon as we lost them. Now... it's too late even to try, probably. She's twice right." He sighed.

I imagined how far their unique and beloved energies could have traveled, or dissipated back to the source if it worked like that, in the days since the aftershock.

"Then no way." I rubbed my salty cheek with the back of my hand. "Definitely not worth it. Especially if... like you said, they never had to be without each other."

He knew. He wasn't fighting it anymore. He'd just wished so desperately for the world to have his sister and his dear friend back.

The little pier below the house was in range. I set the controls to reach it automatically and turned in my seat to pull him closer. What began as comfort, sincerely given and gladly received, shifted its shape by the time the craft lightly kissed the dock. We went up hand in hand to the cold, silent, unlocked house, where we made bittersweet good on my earlier offer.

Neither of us could stay long. He dressed in some of his old clothes for the fifteen or twenty minutes it took to walk down to the little sea cave. Then I stood on the shingle and kissed him goodbye like he was getting on a plane for another continent, instead of swimming to a place I could find in local range on my ring. I took the garments he shed, to place them in the crate for his return.

He waded in and submerged himself, but didn't flicker into the seal shape at once. Sleek hair shedding saltwater down onto his bruised but whole shoulders, he stayed there long enough to aim a devastating little finman smile up at me instead. So he caught me shedding a few salt drops too, but I found a return smile for him.

"Hey," he said, soft voice carrying along the clear water's surface. "When I'm back, I owe you a lower-stress second date."

The little sound that escaped my throat wasn't exactly the light laugh I'd attempted. "Okay." I held up the bundle of clothes and caught a breath of his scent. "Now, excuse me while I go hide your human skin so you'll have no choice but to come back to it."

His sweet smile deepened. "Before you know it, my darling."

I just smiled as best I could again too, for as long as he was watching.

Chapter 18

Kansas

Heading from there to work felt like returning from Oz, in more ways than just the colorless uniform. I spent my half shift awash in memories and daydreams, letting the tech pick up my slack for once. I went for a quiet late dinner with Noemi and Stefek. Vega didn't push me after I told her KXA needed Geir tonight despite his exhaustion. When she stopped by the room to freshen up in between her workday and evening plans, she brought me a little airline-size bottle of wine and a couple of dark chocolates she'd procured somewhere. I went to bed early but lay awake for hours.

The next day I had off, but no one else did. I took myself on a tour of Geir's native place, overlaying grid information as I looked around. I saved the biggest sea cave in the UK for another time when I would have my selkie folk with me, but there was still more to see than I could pack into a single day. Eshaness had an area of stunning red granite cliffs and a fjord carved swordlike deep into the island, where the sea crashed up in a blowhole. One beach was astonishingly split by a fault line, lava rocks on one side and granite on the other; on another one, volcanic agate fragments hid like Nereiður's mosaic bits among the pebbles. The wildlife sanctuary staff let me meet some convalescing otters.

Vega's ring found me in the last light outside the medieval church, not fighting the tingles very hard, and considering whether to see Papa Stour, the Big Isle of Priests, next time, or Unst, in all the Viking glory it had left. From what I'd read and heard, the tsunami had ravaged some historic sites, but had uncovered a new one where a dig was set to begin; and those further inland still stood.

"Hey," Vega said with a smile in her voice. "Just heard from Raigmore. They'll release your buddy sometime in the next forty-eight. We need someone with a nice high diplomacy composite to escort the party home. I'll put in your name if you want."

"If you think you can trust me with that, doc," I answered with a lightness she knew perfectly well to be fake.

"You know I still do." Her tone altered. "We're not, you know, in over our cabezas already, though… right, mija?"

I didn't want to lie, even if I wasn't sorry I didn't have to meet her eyes, either. "Ma, ya sabes que we're freedivers. In over our heads es diferente."

She sighed. "This is really not the week for you to be saying that to me, but whatever. It's good to see you living your life. If you're not too underdressed in the next couple hours, I'm going for drinks in the big downtown, and you're both welcome to join."

The door of the gray house opened before I could knock. Ysmay, wearing her grungy work clothes and a wondering variation of her usual wry expression, tilted her head, considering me.

"Hi," I said. "Just… seeing if anyone was back yet. If everyone's okay."

She nodded without elaborating and put a hand up to my arm. I saw myself through her eyes, abstract like an Impressionist portrait:

not so much my physical features as the way she perceived my energies. Why they'd almost led her to expect someone else.

"Ach, he's still all over you," she confirmed, under her breath, and she went into the house, leaving the door open behind her for me to follow.

She'd taken Isla's lovely harp, which normally sat elegant and dustless in its corner of the library, out on the deck with the French doors open. Nothing I imagined she could get away with when the homeowner was around. She walked out to stand beside it, hair flowing around her, but didn't sit to play it. She just turned it a degree or so at a time until she found the perfect angle where the wind made the sensitive strings vibrate a complicated sustained chord on their own.

She stayed outside, listening, the breeze catching her hair. All around her delicate faerie feet, arranged on a clean bath towel, were the disassembled parts of some kitchen appliance--the housing looked like it belonged to a small, sleek food processor.

"He's not, is the problem, I think," I admitted, quietly too, in answer to her remark.

She tossed her head as she turned her back to me, and sat back down to work.

Berenys' low voice greeted me from the kitchen doorway. I turned to look at her. "He sends all his love, of course, cousin." She kept half a giggle inside a demure close-lipped smile. "Having first reassured me he still remembered what to do about it... And yes, the only ones we lost you know about already. We're making room for everyone out west. We tried inviting people up here, but they're wary."

I couldn't do much better than a slight flush and an uncertain smile: although I liked most of her reply, I didn't know how to answer that greeting.

She lifted her brows. "Oh. He did say he hadn't got to tell you that much. There are even fewer of us in Orkney than here. Half the people there are related..."

"What?" I breathed.

"And Kjaran was the son of Nereiður's half-sister, so."

"Uh. That's your dad?"

"Oh," she said with a slight giggle and a nod. "Sorry."

She accepted my startled, delighted hug hesitantly, and only for long enough to answer my unspoken question. They might be kin, but Berenys hadn't known my mother any more than Geir had. She'd only ever made rare appearances in the Northern Isles by the twins' lifetime; it was even more rare that they coincided with Berenys' similarly sporadic presence.

"Come on, I'll open some of Isla's wine for you and we'll drink to our shared DNA."

She showed me the cellar, still abundant since, for most of the seven years since Isla's death, the only person living permanently in the house had been more of a whisky guy. We chose a Bordeaux only a few years younger than I was, dusted it off, and sat on the breezy rear deck to sample it. Ysmay wasn't having any. She continued playing Isla's harp in her unorthodox fae way, ignoring us.

"Elis figures the first big change to happen to our folk was around the end of the Industrial Revolution, when he was born," Berenys said after the first few sensuous, earthy sips. I wasn't sure what had prompted the history lecture, but I was definitely interested. "Do you know what I mean? There were never many selkie children, but almost none now, most of the ones we have are girls, and... You met some. You saw how they're not the same as those few who are left from the time before."

I considered my own century's attempts to undo the mistakes of the one before--too little, too late. There weren't dead zones or overfishing or gyres of plastic waste in the North Sea, but Earth's waters had no borders: all of it connected and flowed together. I wondered if who'd done this to her kind was as clear to Berenys as it was to me.

"Yes," was all I said soberly aloud.

She nodded.

"Would you tell me?" I murmured, suddenly daring. Maybe it was the heady Bordeaux. "What year you two were born? It's so hard to imagine you in the 1800s. Or are you like Geir, and you don't know for sure?"

Ysmay raised her brows coolly. "It's because of him we do know. 1918."

I shook my head. "But that's long after…"

"Are we so like the older ones, to you?" Berenys asked, softer.

"Yeah. You're just like them."

"Well, that was the hope, I suppose." She nodded thoughtfully. "It would seem the older the parents, the better the energies are preserved as they're passed on to the children. My father was quite a bit older than my mother, and you know that's saying rather a lot."

I nodded too, slowly, thinking more of Nereiður than anyone else.

"Yes. So--now we've lost both Seoras and Hano in the space of a single shitty spring--there are really only two men left in Orkney or Shetland with the older, stronger blood in their veins. The same two that have vexed Bryn forever with their stubborn refusal to choose a selkie bride and make old-blooded finbabies instead of lovely hybrid creatures like you."

"Yeah... I've, uh, gotten that pitch from Brynja already," I admitted.

"Ach, haven't we all." Berenys laughed, unfazed. "Sure, there's not even one for my queen herself anymore, do you see?"

I guessed I did.

Ysmay rolled her eyes and stalked silently away down the back stairs, toward the water.

"To be fair, she did her bit. She went looking for him, I mean. Kjaran. She'd been widowed fairly young and still childless before Geir was even born. She went to Orkney with her own dad, to find the right sort and have another go… They did care a great deal for one another, you understand, but nothing like the mad spark that's between her and Lachlan now."

So the twins belonged to the opposite of the shouldn't-really-be-here club. That did sound like Brynja.

"She'd been hoping for Geir and my friend Gyða, for years and years," Berenys added. "That was what I thought I should tell you."

I didn't think I'd met anyone named Gyða yet. I did suppose Brynja would press for them to be together again one day, after our brief time was done, but I pushed the thought away as fast as I could.

"Seoras' daughter," Berenys clarified, her eyes far away for the moment. "And Sefa's mother."

"Oh. Right... Have I met the other man yet?"

Another silvery giggle; she shook her silken head, and topped up her glass. "That would be the aforementioned Elis Kyles."

"And who does she have in mind for him?"

"She'd be equally pleased to see him with either of us." Berenys rolled her eyes in the direction her sister had just gone. "Never mind that Ys... well, perhaps you've gathered how keen she is. Or that he's like nothing so much as a vulgar older brother to me; or that he says selkie women are so barely different to the men for him, it would be like marrying a boy. Which isn't to his taste, so..."

"Wow..." I took a good sip. "You'd kind of think having given her Lachlan would let him off the hook."

Still smiling, she added to my half-full glass as well. "He's not wrong that we're boring here, all looking and sounding and tasting so alike. Certainly, that's been part of your charm from the beginning."

Elis' escapades (and Berenys' own) aside, it occurred to me that just because Geir had only ever gone for earth girls before, that didn't mean Gyða wouldn't have wanted everything that was mine right now. Sefa's father must be much younger; I could imagine he wasn't always enough for her. And how much more perpetually unsatisfying it all must be for the wild siren type that ran in our family. Not as if I'd never yielded to temptation and picked up the crumbs of the deeper connection selkie hearts were wired for, when there was no chance at a whole slice of cake.

Berenys' cool fingertips drew a little pattern on the back of my hand, listening in on my thought process. She seemed grateful that it made sense to me.

"At least I don't have to feel bad for stealing him from you," I said with an awkward half-smile. "Unless... close family members can hook up in your world."

"No." She smiled, too. "And you shouldn't feel bad. It's beautiful to see him really happy."

When I wholeheartedly wished the same for her, she allowed me a glimpse of the roller-coaster loops she'd ridden in her young two centuries, alternately pursuing and avoiding it. I admitted to myself, to her, this sudden depth of intimacy could have been pretty damn scary with someone who wasn't Geir's embodiment of safety. Or, she seemed to think, for someone with more to hide than she perceived I had. There was an instant's nightmare sensation of the car flying off the wildly contorting track, into dark empty space.

By the time I caught a startled breath, the sickening void filled in with calm deep water. Berenys shrugged and lifted her hand from mine, elegant as any choreography.

"There's really no such a thing as what I'd want to find, anyway. Can I make you something to eat?"

I guessed that was the end of that conversation. "Thanks, but I have plans to go out."

With a sudden amused challenge flashing in her eyes, she'd never looked so entirely like her mercurial sister.

"With one of my oldest girlfriends," I laughed. "Chaperone if you like, though."

She sighed lightly. "We're meant to stay here in case anyone comes home, or go back under if there's any news."

"Oh. You--started in with your stuff before I could say. Sorry. They'll be home sometime in the next day or two, the hospital told us."

Her bright eyes grew newly wide. "Take me with you, and we'll go tell them before it gets late enough for the hover to turn back into a pumpkin."

"Ysmay too?"

"You're surely kidding. She'd never."

I rang Vega a quick message. Berenys knew the place, called Hildr's Horn. They'd just reopened, with a new wind-bio generator installed, for drinks and pub food and live music. Gary had to work tonight, but I could bring a cousin along instead, no?

Tall handsome cousin with the pretty eyes?

1 for 3 sorry

Berenys took a few minutes to get dressed. Then we made the quick hovercraft trip down to Scalloway.

Chapter 19

San Miguelito, Humaco, or The Bronx

We dodged a few questions upon arrival about why the cousin looked so much like she'd be Mrs. Lachlan K's slightly older sister. I changed into my nice Inverness outfit, which Berenys admired with greedy eyes; I didn't leave out a few dabs of the delicious perfume. Borrowing from Vega's makeup bag, I even dusted a little color onto my face and put on some mascara.

Vega gave me an appraising look. "No Gary, and you're gonna be this pretty?"

"Don't worry. In the unlikely event, you two can defend my honor."

"As if there's any left, after all your recent shenanigans. Or, wait, is it only shenanigans if he's Irish?"

Berenys giggled softly.

"Oops," Vega said, wide-eyed. "Pardon me, little miss. If you're even old enough to be in a bar."

"They're not picky here." Berenys' arch murmur brought the quiet chiming of Ysmay's harp to mind.

Vega raised both perfect brows, assessing her. Even in her fierce little sharkskin-print stiletto boots, she barely reached Vega's chin, but she coolly held her ground.

"And I guess, if your mama lets you out the house like that…" Vega said, hardly more than under her breath. Now her eyes were on Berenys' fitted jeans and her draping top, its unlined lace back and shoulders making her selkie disregard for underthings clearer than the clinging opaque fabric in front did already.

Berenys, without more comment than a subtle eye-roll, turned back to the mirror. She'd swiped a rose-copper gloss from Vega's bag, making herself appear more of a porcelain doll than ever. Her face, at least. She touched it up, then lifted her gaze from her reflection to find mine in the mirror.

"Help me do my eyes," she said, still quiet.

"Sweetie. You ever heard of gilding the lily?" Vega tried to protest.

"Yes," Berenys answered, head as regally high as Brynja ever held hers, small voice edged with frost. "Arden."

I laughed and did as my lady desired. Just a touch of brown-sugar shimmer and a sweep of mascara that made her lashes lusher than fake ones. She smiled with satisfaction in the mirror at herself and at me; I wondered what I'd wrought.

Vega had boldly gone even more gorgeous than usual, with dark metallic gold on her eyes and lips. Long, tasseled matching earrings shimmered the way toward her relaxed-dress protocol hint of cleavage. Speaking of gilding the lily.

"And you, big miss… Who's all this for? Prince not-really-ly-charming of the fair kingdom of Katowice?"

She applied a small roller bottle of her own incense-spicy perfume oil to her décolletage and up her neck, working her signature sassy head slide into the motion. "Well. I'm told Anton isn't a fan of this establishment, but we'll see."

Hildr's Horn was in what was left of south Lerwick, on high enough ground to have been spared. It wasn't really a club: more like a roomy cafe, tables pulled to the sides for the night, under some creative lighting. In one corner, a trio of serious dreadlocked white kids played surprisingly cool electro Gaelic fusion.

Word had traveled well about the reopening. The tables in the shadows were nicely crowded, but on the dance floor, it was mainly UF people enjoying the chance to dress up for each other, meeting the few locals who were (or looked) young and bold enough to join us. Jespersen, the PK medic, waved from a corner table where he sat chatting with a cute and interested dark-haired Scot of his own. I thought I glimpsed Emer Ross' blonde curls a few tables away.

Berenys pulled me onto the dance floor without letting me look around for any other friends. I didn't mind. It had been too long since I got to dance, let alone with my girl, who joined us after a minute or two with three flutes in her hands.

"Mama's okay with this too, I guess?" she said, glancing at me as she allowed Berenys to take the first glass.

"Who says we've got to tell her," Berenys smiled over the rim of her drink. She sipped it, wide-eyed. "What do you call this?"

"Not La Vega," I said, tasting mine as well.

"Yeah. I guess we forgive him for not having passionfruit. I said just make us something good enough for three ladies as fabulous as us who don't want it too sweet. He got quite a look in his eye, so. He said it's a... Charlie something."

"I love Champagne cocktails," Berenys enthused.

"Course you do." Vega chuckled, with a shake of her head that made her earrings flutter like flames against the darkness of her long neck. "I'm sorry, what did you say your name is again?"

The name itself got sort of lost against the music, making Vega shake her head again. "I like it when people call me B for short," Berenys surprised me by saying.

"Queen B it is."

I'd never seen such a delighted grin on Berenys' face. The glow in her eyes elevated her beauty to a newly impossible level.

We just moved to the beat for as long as it took to finish our drinks. When the worldbeat girl on percussion threw in a lovely *son clave* rhythm, though--maybe having spotted Vega in the small crowd--we got serious. Berenys didn't know our Latin moves at first, but she learned fast. Caribbean energy shone as effortlessly beautiful on her as the North Sea ever had. The two of them drew glances like flies to a Cosmo left unattended. We didn't have to order our own refills, that was for sure. There was one entertaining, burly guy in a kilt, who I thought might give our Polish buddy a run for his money (if Anton ever showed up).

Moving back toward the bar, giving them some space, I caught sight of none other than Stéphane Mbala. He clinked his nearly-empty glass against my empty one and offered me his seat. I watched with amusement as he made his way over for Vega to introduce her alluring little friend. He wasn't a bad dancer either.

Raj had arrived with him, although my second-favorite spec didn't trouble himself to talk to me. Stéphane pulled him over to make introductions there as well, catching Berenys in mid-sway; before he could finish speaking, she stumbled a few startled steps back, and would have spilled her drink had the glass not been mostly empty. She shot me a panicked glance, asked for Vega's glass as well, and skittered over to the bar quick as a crab.

"You okay?" I murmured when she shrugged away my attempt to lay a reassuring hand on her shoulder.

"That man with Stéphane," she hissed. "He worked with you in Aberdeen?"

"No. I never met him before this assignment. And he would have already been up here when we were there."

She drew a visibly fluttery breath. "Then Vega would know for sure that he was here."

I nodded, skin prickling. "Who did you think he was, B?"

But she only shook her head. The next big breath was steadier. She picked up the two glasses and marched back across the dance floor to stand on tiptoe and say something in Vega's ear. Vega's answer seemed to reassure Berenys: she looked up into Raj's movie-star eyes, and smiled belatedly.

I bit my lip in frustration—of course she wasn't going to tell me more about Aberdeen on a night this exciting for her, when she never wanted to on ordinary ones—but at least I knew she was safe at home now, and that I'd helped get her here.

I turned around. The tall guy behind the bar was attractive, fortyish, with salt-and-pepper hair. He dragged his clear hazel eyes away from the dance floor. "Are you ready for another one as well?"

"I'd love a soda water. Not crazy enough to try to keep up with Vega."

The bartender nodded, smiling faintly. As he quickly filled a fresh glass, I studied the artwork taking up most of the wall behind him. It looked like a collage, mixed media, not too abstract for me to enjoy the depiction of an imposing Viking woman. Her right hand raised a drinking horn, brimming with foaming ale and inscribed with runes that looked like an I in the middle and an R on the end--surely her name.

"So Hildr, was she some kind of historic figure?" I asked as I took my drink and held up my ring for him to scan.

He nodded again but waved the payment away with one muscled arm. "Valkyrie," he answered me, eyes wandering over my shoulder again for a moment. "What the Vikings had before our era brought forth the likes of your friends and you, right?"

"Right. Thanks," I laughed again.

He had a lovely, even white smile. "Skol, honored servant of the all-father."

"Skol."

The unsmiling glint of Hildr's amber eyes continued to draw mine long enough for them to remind me of Nereiður's glass mosaic tiles. The wavy folds of her tunic, too, tingled with a familiar energy.

"I really like her." I managed to keep my voice light. "Who's the artist?"

He shook his head. "My best guess, it's a collaboration. I've tried finding out whose. It's was, though, not is. This wall behind me is all that's left of a much older building. Based on the style, I'd say she's been here since the 1910s, 1920s or so, but no one's been able to tell me more than that. I've always loved her too, though. Named the place for her and all."

I was still lost in thoughts of Viking-selkie collaborations when small, warm arms snaked around my waist from behind. Two guesses who'd distracted the nice bartender. Berenys radiated delight. She breathed in the perfume blooming off my sweat-damp skin, associating it at once with the limited Inverness memories Geir had been willing to share: too vividly for me to keep back a startled giggle.

At her back, Vega chuckled lower. "Learn well from this little mama, grasshopper."

Berenys turned, indignant on my behalf. "Which bit?"

Vega shrugged, still laughing. "Just finally figure it out in general."

Berenys' echo of the shrug looked a hundred times more elegant. "That's not at all what I've heard."

Vega slid backwards onto the stool next to mine, as the smiling bartender brought drinks they still hadn't needed to order.

"Of course," she was saying, "not from little babyface with his fake ident... Araujo must've been his first rodeo."

Berenys conjured the most perfect understated expression to go with her tiny scoff of amusement. I just laughed again.

"Okay, then. How old is he really? I don't know who he got to hack his stuff, but that kid is definitely not twenty-two."

Berenys shrugged, looking unconcerned. "Are you mocking our height? That doesn't seem particularly sporting."

Vega's earrings swayed as she shook her head, ready to go on arguing.

Berenys leaned in, admittedly to better effect than if they'd both been standing, and laid a bold hand on the outside of Vega's knee. I stifled another giggle, knowing what energies were at play there even though I didn't know what it felt like for a normal human. "Then what's wrong with our faces?" she murmured.

Of the surviving weird sisters, there was little doubt this one scared me most: so unwilling or unable to shield anyone from her constant radiation. She didn't frighten the big bad Vega Hazan, though. Vega took her time trying to stare her down, eventually biting her lower lip and smiling the slow delighted smile that meant she'd met a rare worthy opponent.

Vega picked up her glass without looking away, clinked it against the one in Berenys' hand. Berenys gave her a hair-raising half-smile in return and took another sip.

"Okay. But you're not gonna tell me you're also twenty-two, now, right?" Vega shook her head slightly, then sipped her drink.

"No. I'm a little younger than he is." Berenys giggled.

"But old enough to be here and starting trouble." Vega glanced back at the dance floor to find a couple transfixed guys still watching them both. One must have been a local. Stefek, may he rest in peace, was the other.

We finished our drinks and were about to head back out there when the band announced they'd be taking a break.

"Nooo," Berenys responded with an absurdly cute pout.

"Hey," I said. "Get them to set you up for karaoke, doc. William Wallace over there would fall at your feet if you sang for him."

"You must." Berenys smiled, eager all over again.

Vega flashed a different smile: challenge accepted. She caught the bartender's eye, made some quick arrangements.

"Fine lad," Berenys murmured to me as they conferred behind her. "I remember him crawling round under the pub table, once upon a time. Different pub. He's got a degree in… anthropology? Archaeology? Only he decided he'd rather be on Shetland than anywhere on the mainland where he'd be able to earn much with it." She smiled into the distance of her memory. "Long before that, I used to play chess with his great-grandfather… There were prizes to the winner, but the kind that made the loser just as happy."

"We just won't mention that to Vega…"

"Not the only thing she doesn't know that won't hurt her. She's quite a girl herself, though. She's really a doctor?"

"Yep. Dad said she was the daughter he should have had..."

She nodded. "And I've thought all this time, you're the daughter my mother never had. Though at least she's had the tact not to say so to my face."

I could only chuckle. It didn't really hurt. That was just Dad and Vega.

"I wish I knew where that left me," Berenys said, softer.

"Either San Miguelito, Panama, Humacao, PR, or the Bronx, depending on the timeline. Her mom's an amazing cook too, and a great dancer. She'd love you."

The open longing written in her every feature caught me off guard. I'd felt the same pangs plenty of times in the last decade. But how had I never considered that Berenys, or any of my selkie family, might also desire to be like my wildly successful and glamorous unofficial stepsister? Of course, they might yearn for more than their existence on the edge of folklore.

Geir struck me as so content with his work, with their island home. Ysmay seemed fulfilled too, in her weird little way. Brynja, in my estimation, must have always been above anything like gainful employment. It was true that if any of them had hoped for one, they'd have had a hard time pursuing a real education.

"Would you want to become a doctor?"

She shook her head. "Just the chance to get good at something. Develop your voice, and know how to use it." Her daydreamy eyes focused, meeting mine. "Don't you think you'll ever pick something, and go back and study it?"

I shrugged. "Too bad we can't pretend you're me and send you."

"Or Ys." She took a delicate sip from her free refill. "Or let Elis do it properly." A fond laugh sweetly cracked her pensive expression. "You know, he'll be mad for Vega if they ever meet." Her smile quirked into a different shape. "Unless she's got her heart set on Will already."

"Will?"

Though I wondered if we'd somehow correctly guessed the kilt-clad guy's name, Berenys' shining eyes indicated the well-read bartender.

The polished, showy version of Vega's voice came over the sound system, now connected to her ring.

"Helloooo, Lerwick and Scalloway. It's me, the songstress Vega Hazan, getting ready to speak the international language of karaoke and hoping some more folks will join me." She winked down at us. "Not you, baby girl. Please."

Berenys giggled as Vega took a few steps out onto the dance floor.

"Okay," Vega purred, and she started the music track. "This one is without doubt for you, though, mi cafecito."

I remembered this song. Off and on during her previous assignment, New Orleans, she'd been seeing someone in an eclectic jazz band. He'd transposed things for her rich, dark alto voice, and given it all a funky lounge-sounding twist or two. I'd gotten to visit once and go to a gig with them. Early days there, when relaxed dress protocol still included her glorious halo of tiny kinky curls, as well as a crushed velvet skirt she probably shouldn't have gotten away with.

This evening, she'd chosen a Gershwin classic from that set, not just because she sounded great singing it. The one about the girl who was so anti-love until she finally kissed the right guy.

"Funny," I muttered. But Berenys had always liked George and Ira's songs, popular when she actually was the age she appeared; she enjoyed Vega appropriating their humor just as much. Plus, she'd never witnessed Vega's magnificence like this before. Letting her fall under the siren's spell seemed only fair.

Everyone, Berenys especially, yelled for an encore. With a low laugh of pleasure, Vega obliged her newly adoring audience.

"Hmm." She scrolled through titles on her ring, pausing to sip her free Champagne cocktail. "Okay. One from the same set for you, Princess Charming. Then it's someone else's turn."

Berenys raised her glass in Vega's direction. Her arm lightly around me as we listened, she wondered whether I'd said anything about Geir and me dreaming together, like in the old Sleeping Beauty song Vega picked for her.

"You're surely kidding, B. I'd never."

As soon as she was sure, she slipped down from her chair, lightly as the referenced ballerina, to ask Stefek for this dance. He accepted with a boyish grin. Though too dark to show a blush, I would have bet the cheek he rested against her hair with gentlemanly delicacy, as they made the first few slow turns together under the faerie lights, was warmer than usual.

Past the pumpkining hour, I left both my dates still reveling with Hildr and laughing at me for being the tired old lady of the bunch. It was silly, but I couldn't go home to my empty bed again. I knew he would have found a way to get in touch if he'd made it back yet; I was drawn there all the same, just in case there was any kind of news at all.

Ysmay came to the door again, now dressed in nothing but a fluttering silky kimono printed with abstract blue and violet butterfly-wing patterns. She answered my sheepish inquiry with a whispery laugh and tilted her head toward the stairs to the lower level, rather than the side where Geir's room was. "Sleep here anyway."

When I hesitated, she grabbed my hand. Here was the thing. She hadn't been sleeping, either. I sensed her softer, sweet-skinned young childhood self, peacefully entwined with her sister's identical small limbs. From before birth, she'd almost always slept that way: except when Berenys wasn't around to share the bed. Then she resorted to cat naps alternating with wandering the house at odd hours, borrowing her sister's robe like this evening, or whatever else Berenys' subtly different scent clung to.

I thought about it a moment; then, as a question, I pictured the tall boy greeting Berenys at the end of our first dive, his fingertips on the back of her slender neck and his eyes eager to drink in the rest of her.

Ysmay gave a little shrug of distaste. It might not be him, but too often it was someone, messing up her twin's energies. I considered that maybe Ysmay just didn't care for boy energy. I'd only ever noticed her greeting women. The one she would have seen in my memory was the wavy-haired girl.

"Oh. Gyða's safe. And Ruadh too, her man."

So that was the Gyða whom Berenys had mentioned. As Ysmay passed the clarified image back to me with a dismissive little shake of her head, Berenys had been the one affectionately greeting her. And as Berenys herself had told me earlier, she wasn't a girl, but one of the oldest people here.

"It was her and my sister first, of course," Ysmay startled me by adding aloud. She pulled a wry face, maybe at whatever expression must have shown on mine; then her eyes widened. "What--was that not what she was telling you yesterday?"

Sure, there's not even one for my queen herself anymore, do you see? Even as I heard Berenys in my head, I saw her—her tiny hand so amusingly at home on Vega's knee, her eyes all over my boring bathing suit. She had, indeed, meant to tell me how little Brynja appreciated her hard-won offspring's struggle to fit into the neat plan she'd laid out for everyone.

I smiled at Ysmay. All I knew was, few people on Earth would say no if Queen B invited them to dance.

"Ach, of course Gyða wanted Ruadh, though, to give her Sefa. He's a nice lad, as well. Sure, and he likes Berenys… doesn't everyone? So the three of them get on… You see."

"Sure. Yeah."

As she radiated shieldmaidenly protection of her twin, I saw, too, that there very obviously wasn't any form of that undignified urgency, intrusion of the foreign, messy mingling of life forces, that woke the slightest desire in Ysmay. An awfully specific impression, for one who so adamantly wanted no part of it herself. Then again, it wasn't hard to figure out how she'd come by sensations that weren't her own and didn't suit her, like a song she hated but couldn't drown out or get too far away to hear.

The harp's eerie unsong was more Ysmay's style. With that as our softly shimmering background music, I thought about Brynja the day before, smiling down a tiled corridor at her beloved baby brother before the elevator doors even opened to reveal him. She and Geir were separated in age by decades, if not longer, and hadn't even lived near each other during many of those years; how exponentially more intense it must be for identical twins.

"You don't have to touch her to share her stuff, do you?"

Not ever, but enough physical distance at least helped fade it. Then there was mainly the problem of sleeping by herself, which Ysmay didn't like either.

The harp hummed louder, decrescendoed as the breeze swelled and calmed. Ysmay reached up to pet my hair a couple times as if I'd been a cat. She'd found it hard to tell whether I might be a member of her no boys, no girls club; she'd been happy to have Geir there, for as long as that had lasted. But it was all right if I showed up infused with his energy now, a member of the Berenys club after all. She thought the whole world of him, even when he was up to shenanigans. I guessed if he'd chosen me, that meant I must be okay, too.

"I'll make us chamomile," she said, as if that settled it.

Orca vocalizations and seafloor groans tried to surface in my sleeping subconscious, but in Ysmay's dreams, she was her lithe, playful and energetic seal self all night, and I got to come along for the safe and sunlit ride. It might not have been as renewing as a night resting close to Geir. Nonetheless, I woke wistfully amazed to have been so immersed in a shapeshifter's perspective at last.

She batted at the offending wrist where my alarm pulsed in the morning, once again closer to an aggrieved feline than to a seal. She rewarded my whispered giggle and retreating kiss on her cheek with a little irritated grunt and settled sighing back into her beautiful dreams before I'd even left the bedroom.

Chapter 20

Maimi, 2067

I hadn't expected to find two UF hovers at the dock. But if I'd considered the possibility, a bleary-eyed Stefek at the helm dropping off still fresh-as-a-daisy Berenys would indeed have seemed the most likely explanation.

"See you later, cousin," she whispered, sashaying past me barefoot with the unzipped backs of her boots dangling from two fingers.

"Hey," Stefek greeted me without quite meeting my eyes. "Link the hovers and ride with me, if you want. Think we'll have time to grab a coffee?"

"Didn't get much sleep? Maybe I'd better drive," I couldn't resist saying as I input the right commands for his onboard computer to control my craft too.

"Oh. We didn't--No sleeping. Nothing to do with beds. We never left the bar."

He shifted aside to give me access to the controls, and we started south over the brightening water.

"She tried to teach me some useful Norn tourist phrases. Though I'm not very quick to pick up the accent, I guess. Even with locally distilled spirits to help me capture the nuances of the terroir," he said with a rusty chuckle. "Will eventually kicked us stragglers out, and we sat on the step under that incredible new moon sky, Milky Way and everything, and compared notes on her constellations and the ones I'm used to… I couldn't believe it was that late when my alarm went off."

He was much too nice for me to tease. "I'm glad you had fun."

His tired eyes were far away, and he didn't answer in words.

"Although maybe I don't need to tell you," I felt compelled to add, "she can be a bit of a wild child, even if she was on her best behavior for someone like you."

He shook his head slightly, still not raising his gaze all the way to mine. "Here we see rare footage of the wild Berenys, prowling her natural habitat. Forty kilos with her boots on, but capable of taking down predators three times her size… No, if best behavior is even an option for her, she wasn't on it until I told her… how much she made me look forward to stargazing again with another brown-eyed girl. In Yaoundé."

"Oh," I blurted, my own eyes pretty big just then. "You, uh, never said."

"We left things open-ended when I took this job." He lifted a sheepish smile my way. "Her name is Oriel. Eh, soon to be Dr. Oriel Oben." The smile widened. "Linguist. And I… would've told you about her, if you'd ever taken Vega up on her endless suggestions…"

I smiled too. "Stevie, at this point I pretty much know a liar and a cheat when I meet one, and you're far from it."

"Thanks," he said with a slight laugh.

"So. Power grid again today?" I asked, instead of pushing.

"Yep. You?"

I checked my assignment for the first time that morning. My "Oh" came out as a startled laugh of pleasure. "Someone's asked me to a meeting about the future of the Bressay site, in lieu of Lachlan. Crap, though… Barely time to read up on what's been said in the other meetings."

"Say hi to Anton." Another sleepy laugh that almost got eaten by a yawn. "I wonder if Vega's told him any of what she told me about your recent adventures..."

"Oh yeah." I sighed. "You're right. I hope there's time for coffee first."

As I took a seat near one end of the table quickly filling up with specialists, I reminded myself I was anything but the *ut land isk* one here.

Rajan Dessai came in a few minutes before the hour. At his side strode a fit Asian woman of probably not quite my height, with dramatic black streaks remaining in her sleek gray bob. Her UF gray jacket with white accents was unlike any uniform I was used to. Raj presented Dr. Noa Shimizu, Marine Geosciences Chair at the United Forces Academy in Brussels, to each person in the room in roughly their order of importance. He got to me last.

She had quite a grip, shaking my hand with a selkie-like head bend I instinctively echoed. "Arden Araujo," she repeated, her sharp eyes unnervingly intent on my face. "Yes. We've met."

I smiled. I hated to risk disagreeing with anyone at her level, let alone spoil the startled tilt of Anton's Hollywood smirk, but I was pretty sure I wouldn't have forgotten it if we had. "Could you--please remind me when, Dr. Shimizu?"

I'd almost taken her for American or Canadian at first; now that she said more than a few syllables, I caught the elegant hint of her native Japanese accent. Like me, she probably hadn't really been home in a long time.

"Christmas Eve party on Jamar Grant's yacht. 2067, I believe," she said, cracking the first bit of a smile she'd shown.

That had been about two months before my second birthday. "Yes, ma'am, I'm sort of vague on that time period." I laughed. "It's nice to see you again."

She smiled fully. "Yes, quite a nice surprise."

Raj, Anton, and Chief Admin Muir started off the meeting by informing Dr. Shimizu that I was there to be seen, not heard: my role was to observe and report back to KXA, rather than having any vote myself. They took twenty minutes to bring her up to speed on the existing research, proposed plans for shoring up and revamping the site. And speed was the right term: it was challenging to follow their fluent engineerese. I resisted the temptation to daydream about the Scalloway Islands I could have seen from the window if it had been a clearer day.

"So this is all proposals," Shimizu was clarifying. "Nothing purchased or set in motion as yet."

"Well, no," Muir agreed. "And now I understand there's been some sort of family emergency, one of Mr. Adie's sons on the mend in Inverness at the moment. No going forward without his full attention and approval, of course. But it should be a formality."

She gave a sharp little upward nod. "I suppose that's why it's taken this long to get anyone from my organization on the agenda here. If it's already a done deal."

Muir's diplomatic smile betrayed some rigidity. "Would you care to elaborate?"

"I understand Adie's got his hands full, but I'd like to get on record here that he needs representation in the broader meetings that have been going on in Edinburgh. There's building consensus that not everything up here ought to be shored up and revamped."

"You mean rewilding the site," Anton put in with a dismissive shake of his head.

"And my signature is already on the recommendation to do the same with the lowest-lying areas of south Lerwick, yes. Just as the former residents have rightly decided they'll be doing with Whalsay, Fetlar, most of Unst. I don't know how much louder the sea could tell us that's what needs to happen."

Shimizu saw the eager nod I couldn't keep back, much as I was supposed to remain neutral. Anton either missed or ignored it.

"With all due respect, Dr. Shimizu, how is rewilding within our mission here?"

She gave Anton a dry little smile. "I appreciate your clarifying your respect, as well as UFE's mission. That perhaps no one has entrusted you with rewilding before, doesn't make it less foundational to our efforts."

While I bit the inside of my lower lip to keep from laughing, Muir took Anton's side. "It's hardly just a question of engineering. This area hasn't got the economic flexibility of Amsterdam, New York, places that can afford to let some things slide. You'd get rid of a hundred jobs at the shipping site alone..."

Shimizu nodded. "The latest estimate I read this morning was that we're likely to end up with forty to forty-five percent of the pre-tsunami population deciding to stay in Orkney and Shetland, with the sharper decline coming from up this way, so the economic picture will shift around no matter what. Almost twenty percent of those who initially relocated have already begun putting down roots in other places like Thurso and Aberdeen... where I'm confident the existing KXA facilities could easily absorb those hundred workers on a more permanent basis."

"More permanent?" Muir asked.

"Since he's taken the majority on in short-term positions already," she said with no hint of the smugness she'd be right to feel.

The chief administrator huffed out a little sigh, and invited Dr. Shimizu to present documents and graphics in support of her argument, although it was as clear to her as it was to me that they had no intention of being swayed. I kept my smile inside, and as the meeting broke up, offered her Kenneth Adie's private contact link, the one Celeste had given me in Inverness. I hoped he wouldn't think I was abusing the privilege. After all, he'd assured me, anything he could do. And my selkie heart was set on any part of their homeland returning to the state in which they'd known it before modern industry, sea-level rise, even the fairly benevolent influence of KXA Limited.

Dr. Shimizu smiled, nodded, and in a most *drøttenmín* way, appeared to decide the subject was closed for now.

"I suppose if I'd stayed in closer touch with your father, I'd have known you'd joined UFE," she said instead. "Generalist--so you're relatively new to the Forces? Working toward anything in particular? Engineering?"

"Uh, no. Mr. Adie is actually a--friend, not a work contact. Well. His son, Lachlan, is my friend. He's--the family emergency in Inverness."

"Oh. I hope he's all right."

"Thank you." It took an effort for my mind not to drift to Lachlan, maybe already getting on a transport.

"And your time in UFE?" she pursued.

"Right. Just passed eleven years." Damn, her dark eyes were like surgical steel. I cleared my throat softly. "It's been good, the generalist track. I like having my boots on the ground where they're needed, and I... also tend to get bored easily."

Or, I guessed, samurai steel. "Forgive me if that doesn't sound like Oli's kid."

I smiled to soften my words. "I turn out to be only half his kid, so."

She laughed. "Fair enough. Anyway, I don't mind seeing someone not hit spec too early. It seems to me you're capable of broader and more divergent thinking when you multitask for a while first."

Shaking my head would have been rude. "I imagine it was-- through your work with UFE that you knew him, Dr. Shimizu? And Mr. Grant?"

"Jamar, yes. I was based out of the Miami center at the time, and later on, especially in the eighties, we worked together pretty closely making the hard decisions about what to demolish and what to keep. Then getting his investments in that revised coastline to last. But Oliver I'd met years before, at MaGI. I was lingering in postdoc limbo when he arrived... Before I'd had the urban conservation epiphany yet, and before he got obsessed with the Norwegian continental shelf. It was a small department and we were encouraged to cross-pollinate the disciplines whenever we could."

Small because the Marine Geosciences Institute of the Pacific Northwest boasted one of the most ferociously selective and innovative programs in the United States, she didn't need to mention; Dad had made sure I was well aware. He'd also liked to remind me how he'd torn through his work there in just over half the time of a normal degree candidate.

"Anyway, even if he didn't tell many graduate school stories... I doubt you'll be shocked to hear Hurricane Oliver was well-known among the women."

"Wait." I didn't dare ask the obvious question but still had to laugh. "Was that his actual nickname? Even before he... actually upgraded to a Cat Five."

She nodded, watching my face again, intense as any selkie I'd ever met.

"Good old Jamar Grant," she smiled, though, instead of continuing with the topic. "When's the last time you got to Miami to see them?"

"Oh. Not since the funeral. I mean... Between both of us always traveling for work, and... You probably know, he never had the closest relationship with his family."

"Cat Five," Shimizu agreed. "You know what? I'm thinking I'll look them up, though, when I'm down there in a few weeks guesting at the summer seminar."

I smiled. "Please eat some Cuban food for me."

"It's a deal."

Not that I expected her to remember me at all, if we were honest, but it was nice of her to say. Meantime, I'd grown to love tea, fish and chips, and fairytale sandwiches.

My Dearest Generalist: I have arrived safe at Home in time to collect Lachlan. I pray you Forgive me if I have taken an Assignment you hoped to complete yourself. He is still doing quite well after his Journey and Brynja is Content. My Family and I thank you again for Everything. You are Most Welcome here any Time at all, I read just before noon the following day.

My heartbeat thumped around like all of Vega's nieces and nephews together on a day as gray and wet as this one, sending an overeager flush up into my face.

Great i think i can be there by about 1730, I rang back, and immediately saved his contact ident.

Lovely. We shall look forward to your Visit.

I smothered a tender laugh. *OK so shall i*

When I got close enough for my locator signal to alert him, he let me know to come in through the French doors at the back. I found he wouldn't have had to specify. Better than any locator, every hair on my skin stood up at the nearness of him by the time I killed the hover motor.

I saw neither Ysmay nor Isla's harp on the deck this evening. Though I'd imagined them all at home, like the night we'd first met, the house was pretty quiet. The twins had split up for the time being, Ysmay on undersea kingdom business with Brynja while Berenys and Geir were here with the doors and windows open, chopping onions and potatoes, foraged greens and herbs. Lachlan, they told me, was resting while they prepared dinner.

"Can I help? What are we making?"

Berenys shook her head. "A bit of soup. For which we won't need the fish for at least half an hour," she said to no one in particular, in an airy murmur. Geir smiled at me in particular, put his chef's knife in the sink, and rinsed his hands.

"I'll have it up here for you," he answered, matching her light tone. As soon as he took my hand, we were swept right back into the delicious tide of shared energy that had surged further, rather than subsiding since our return from Inverness. We slipped away to his room together. Half an hour, or a little more, was just enough to take the edge off.

"Admittedly I'm rusty, but as I recall… you buy her a nice meal first, is the usual expectation." He laughed softly.

I lifted my head, hair clinging to his salt-misted skin, and kissed the little hollow of his breastbone. "Modern girl," I said. "No worries."

He chuckled. "Next you'll try to convince me you're really meant to be a generalist."

I raised one eyebrow at him.

He shook his head. "Even if it's true I can remember a time when the lasses weren't so daring."

Those adoring, effortlessly seductive eyes. It would have been nothing for him to make me forget an argument that mattered, which this one didn't.

He smiled and drew me down for one more intoxicating kiss. "Stay for tea with me, half-ancient modern girl?"

"Love to."

When I caught sight of him in the mirror behind me as we dressed, he had on the slim black pullover sweater Hano had worn the day I met them. He'd just had to fold the sleeve hems up a bit. "Oh. This looks nice on you," I said softly, turning to run a hand across his chest and shoulder.

"Thanks," he breathed.

I looked around his tidy little bedroom. He had no family photos, that was true. But a hand-stitched quilt hung carefully folded on a frame at the foot of the bed, small faded sea-hued squares reminding me of my mother's mosaic graffiti. And on the wall, there was an embroidery sampler that looked even older than the quilt, preserved in a vacuum frame behind slightly gray light-protective glass, with the scrolled initials CC neatly stitched in the lower right corner.

I made a reasonable guess, given what I knew of his unstoppable heart. "So… Whose was the little hat?"

He smiled faintly, more touched than his face showed. "That was my Alasdair's, before he went to serve as a frogman and engineer diver in World War Two."

"Not the… what did you call it?" My memory hunted for one of the little museums I'd visited with Stefek and Noemi. "Shetland Bus. Fishermen helping the Norwegian Resistance."

Geir smiled. "His old man was the fisherman. Alasdair was an officer." The smile grew sweeter, his son's remembered heroism mattering so much more to him than his own. "Ah, how all the lasses loved that cap on him."

From my mind to his, there faintly flickered a handsome youth in military uniform. I thought Geir had dreamed about him.

The smile shining brighter in his eyes, he brought the mental picture into fuller focus and color for me. Alasdair Craig standing taller than I might have expected in a doorway, sunlit water behind him and a familiar one-cornered smile softening his sleepy hazel eyes and beautiful lips. I sighed with the quick understanding that he'd never come home from the war, to make a life with any of his admirers.

Mingling and overlaid with the bittersweet old images came a more recent memory of me glancing down at Geir's bare feet. The day he'd replaced the blade in my hover motor. He pictured my toe piercings, asking about them on Berenys' behalf. I'd said something like *Things hurt. I guess they took longer to heal than some things do. Less time than others.*

I squeezed his hand and didn't need to nod to show I understood. I breathed out how much I loved his way of remembering those who had been dear to him. The smile fading back down to just a hint, he wound a curl of my hair loosely around one index finger; he didn't succeed completely in holding back the thought of keeping a reminder of me, too, someday.

"Geir," I sighed. "Damn."

"Ach. Sorry, my darling. Forget it." He kissed me lightly, then less so. "I'm rusty with that as well. How sharp you young hybrid ones can be."

I kissed him too, my own memory flashing involuntarily back to the first time I'd seen him getting dressed.

He smiled, adding to the impression his little pang of gladness when I hadn't torn my eyes away from his perfection quite fast enough to fool him. Love at first sight, or near enough. "That one has only ever been mine. Here."

Turning, he pulled the clean and folded old hoodie from a drawer, draped it around my shoulders. I hadn't realized I was asking for it until I inhaled his scent from the age-soft fabric and knew he'd never get it back.

Berenys joined us without any audible comment as we left the house. Together we walked down the hill to where they had a woven trap or basket full of beautiful fat silver fish they must have caught earlier, but left swimming in the little submerged cage.

It was close to twenty years since I'd fished with my father, but my hands remembered how to clean and fillet them. Geir and Berenys flung the parts we wouldn't use far out into the water for some other fish to take, then rinsed the good pieces in the clear seawater before slipping them into the clean bucket he'd brought down with the knives in it. I followed their example.

"You're sure you didn't grow up here?" Geir asked in an approving tone, tacking on a few more syllables I wasn't sure how to parse, although they sounded sweet.

"Did you just call me Joe?"

He tilted his head a little as he watched my face. "Do they not say that in California USA?"

"No one even says that here anymore, old man," Berenys answered with a gentle smile. She ruffled his hair with a wet hand. "Don't ever change."

To me, eyes bright with amusement and pleasure on our behalf, she explained. "My jo. It's a darling old-fashioned word for dearest friend or sweetheart. If it was good enough for Rabbie Burns, you still can't really go wrong there."

Geir chuckled. "Okay. All I know is, that was your name already." He met my quizzical glance with a nod. "The night we met. We all had a look at your card. It was the first thing I noticed."

Still puzzled, I shook my head.

"I know that isn't how you say it, but how you spell it. A-r-a-u-jo." His eyes kindled, in that way that could effortlessly make me forget there was anyone else around. "I dared to take it as a hopeful sign."

I breathed out something like a tiny laugh, or a voiceless "oh," but otherwise I was deliciously lost for words.

Berenys' laugh was soft too, but clear. "You really old ones," she murmured. "Good Lord. I'd beg you to teach me, but I don't even think you're doing it on purpose enough to tell anyone else how." She stood weightlessly, taking the bucket with her back up the stairs.

"When you say tesoro sometimes," he leaned closer to breathe in my ear, pretty decently mimicking the pronunciation. "It means about the same thing, yeah?"

A Berenys-worthy whispered giggle escaped my lips. "Do I really call you that?"

I did. But from long before that, he'd always found my rare uses of Spanish sexy as hell.

Of all the humans who'd ever explored his islands and his sea, from Viking tombs to wrecked merchant vessels, I doubted any had discovered a treasure like the one I'd found here.

Chapter 21

Monterey

We slipped into a lovely routine over the next few weeks: work myself to the bone all day, then head northwest to get my energy back. I received the fifth annual rejection letter from UFE Coastal Rewilding and Marine Engineer Diving program with near-relief. Why would I want to go to Miami, or anywhere but here? I spent almost all my time off diving anyway, out in the lengthening daylight among shipwrecks, stacks, and geos, not counting a few more tourist days with my UFE friends and a few bad weather days spent memorably indoors.

Brynja and her daughters weren't always with us; even when they were, we didn't all return together to the undersea kingdom. For one thing--although he was healing and regaining strength as prodigiously fast as his hair was growing back--Lachlan still had no business on any kind of deep dive. Now that they knew me a little better, a few finfolk would come up to see us. Most of them, though, I didn't run into again.

"So," Vega said one evening over fish and chips and sandwiches at May's. It was usually just her, Stefek, and me these days. Noemi was vegan and didn't care for fried foods, so she wasn't such a regular, other than grabbing an occasional beer. I'd caught meals with her at other times and places when we could.

"You hear about the CRewMEn shakeup?"

"What? No. Just that I'm still not worth their time, five years running."

"Oh. Shouting match on the floor of the House of Representatives. What's his name, the program head…"

"Uh… Sincerest Regards, Thierry Farrah, Ph.D."

"That's it. So Dr. Sincerest Regards went three or four rounds with this rep who didn't want to continue funding the program at the same level. Somebody Velázquez."

"Right now?" I shook my head.

"I know. Hard to say who sounded like a bigger dick, him or her…"

"Smaller dick?" mused the resident linguist.

"Long story short," Vega stuck a finger in his poker face, "never argue with a powerful Latina. Funding continues uninterrupted, now he's tendered his resignation. Acting program head TBA."

Stefek laughed obligingly. I shrugged. No dog in that fight.

"Speaking of Latina power… when are we gonna meet this junior division supermodel trophy boy of yours?"

"You have," I reminded her. "Twice."

"Better circumstances would be nice, mija."

The way her smile straightened out, as if too heavy to support its own shape, raised the hairs on the backs of my arms.

"And I was thinking, I'd like to see… whatever it is you see in this place, before I head south."

I thudded down my glass. "What?"

She nodded. "Uh. Speaking of shakeups. I told you before you got here, the staffing was always off. And with projections now that a lot of residents just aren't coming back… They told us this morning, they're drawing down the numbers over the next month or so."

"By how much?" I remembered to breathe.

She shook her head. "Not sure yet. Half, maybe. Anyway--I'm volunteering. I'm ready for trees. Pods. Dining options. There's two twelve-month openings with Barts NHS in London, so I'm throwing my hat in. Teaching and mentoring the innocent babes who might end up out here in the wilds."

"I thought you swore no more gray and rainy," I said, my voice uneven.

"They have twelve-month ones?" Stefek seemed unruffled as ever.

I bit my lip to steady it, nothing to do with Vega taking a new assignment and everything to do with too many flaming squirrel flags for wandering around changing tasks on assignments, openly daydreaming during briefings, forgetting to use the tech as expected. Questionable rapport with certain spec admins. Batshite deep-water rescue requests.

She didn't need selkie skills to understand what must have been my perfectly obvious facial expression.

"I recommended for you to stay as long as this crazy thing gets extended," she murmured. "And I put Bergen or Aberdeen as your next choices. For whatever that's worth."

With one foot out the door as it was already, she arranged for the three of us to take half the next day for a follow-up visit to Lachlan. While she and I were in the house asking the usual questions and looking at some wonderfully unusual scans of his brain, Geir and Stefek set up our transportation for the afternoon. Lachlan and I managed some likely story about how Queen B and the child bride were visiting neighbors affected by the tsunami. It didn't hurt that Ysmay was with them, rather than hanging about getting mistaken for one or the other, and possibly not playing along.

Within an hour, we were in the boss' big skimmer hover, facing one another with a delightful old-fashioned picnic basket between us. Vega put her arm around Stefek's shoulders.

"Well, young man," she said to Geir, as he turned from the controls. "It's about time we hear your intentions for our little Ardelaide."

He lifted thick black lashes, then serious eyes, before the rest of his face.

"Oh, I don't think you're ready," he said, not loudly, but at a pitch low enough to carry beneath the whine and hum of the hover starting up. I'd never seen him setting his finman powers to stun for anyone but me, and wasn't sure how I felt about it.

"Right on." Vega grinned; Stefek muffled a startled laugh.

Holy family resemblance batman, she rang me, cocking a newly appreciative brow my way. Geir kept his poker face, with just the usual one corner of his lips raising a millimeter or two, but on the inside, he was laughing plenty.

We cruised around for about an hour, enjoying the nice afternoon and our picnic lunch, but we didn't see any of the seals we'd hoped to drop in on.

"Why don't you summon them, Arden," Geir suggested lightly, after a while.

"Oh yeah. With my, uh, seal mating call? I'd have to work on that."

I'd never heard such a belly laugh from him, uninhibited and boyish despite the low pitch and volume of his voice. This seal didn't think my mating call needed any work whatsoever. Vega cracked up too, because of how hard I'd made him laugh.

"No, you've got to… send them the right vibes," he said after a while, still chuckling although his dark eyes met mine with seeming purpose. "You know. Underwater."

"Sure," I giggled. "Okay."

I wiggled my fingers in pretend preparation. Then—not convinced he'd been serious—

I leaned over the edge of the craft, trailing my splayed hand in the stinging cold water, and thought about playing with seals like in Ysmay's dreams.

Vega bent over the other side and stuck her hand underwater too.

"Holy shite," she laughed, pulling her chilled fingers back out for a moment. "Ah. Do we recite any magic words or anything?"

"Nah, what use would seals have for words?" Stefek guessed.

Geir smiled.

After maybe sixty more seconds, his sparkling gaze gestured somewhere behind me. I turned to see several spotted heads bobbing up a short distance off. They watched us impassively, with eyes like his, but whatever part of me understood this stuff knew that unlike him, they were no more than they appeared to be.

"Check it out, fairy godmother. We did it."

Vega answered me with another easy laugh, raising her cold wet hand in a victory sign.

"Impeccable timing there, fellows," Stefek greeted our visitors.

My own palm, still trailing overboard, was abruptly full of more than just cold seawater. One of the seals had come right up to butt its head under my hand, like an affectionate puppy.

"Hi, buddy," I said, more delighted than startled.

These were entirely wild seals, not like my little pals in Monterey who were more used to humans. I had no clue if you were really supposed to scratch a seal's head like a dog's, but this one seemed to like it as much as his worldly California siblings, half-closing his eyes and pressing his head against my touch. I laughed out loud.

Though the seals scattered when we jumped in, they came back to Geir immediately, knowing they were safe to touch his outstretched hands. I might have called them if he said so, but they already knew him--even in this unaccustomed neoprene sealskin. Though it was nice of them to accept the rest of us, I still thought they did so because we were friends of his.

The intrepid Vega Hazan, with her prototype minimalist re-breather, went right out to meet them. Stefek followed with more caution, getting acclimated to cold water snorkeling. I hung back a second, hanging off the hover with the same one hand. Coming back to face me, Geir held the same edge with just his palm, fingers lightly covering mine.

"Was that really me?" I breathed.

He nodded, eyes bright with pride and pleasure. He'd done no more than sense them somewhere nearby. The rest had been my ener-gy, drawing theirs. Mystical convergence. But nothing this intentional had happened anywhere else I'd dived with animals, that I could recall. "Okay. So what have you been doing to me?"

He withheld memory impressions that could have gotten us both in big trouble just then. Nonetheless, his brows spoke full sentences, different than the one that came from his faintly smiling mouth.

"No, this is you. Maybe what's between you and me has awak-ened things that were already in you, but if anything, I'd say it's your time in the sea itself."

Suddenly I did remember something: a beach trip when I'd been very small, maybe kindergarten age. I had no idea what beach or even what continent, who the other kids were with me. I'd been the one to find all the best shells, living starfish, crabs that didn't hurt me. I knew there'd still been travel back and forth to Kristiansand, the first few years of my life.

After a few wistful seconds, a big sigh, and a deliberate shake of my head, I decided to enjoy where we were now instead of wasting time wondering where I'd been then. Geir kissed my salty cheek in agreement. And at least I'd gotten brilliant experiences out of it, swim-ming with not only seals, but dolphins and mantas all over the world.

It wasn't more than ten or twelve meters deep right here, and the late sunlight penetrated surprisingly far down toward the rocky seafloor. A silvery tarp, shredded to ribbons on one side, had settled itself in my forest after the tsunami snatched it. Aggrieved, I chucked it into the hover to dispose of later.

I wished that, like Geir, I didn't need the snorkel mask or fins he wore today for Vega and Stefek's benefit. It was nothing to him, echoing the seals' ups, downs, and barrel rolls through the clear water, seaweed waving like grass in their bubble-spangled wake. It honestly looked like they, in turn, copied his pleased little smile. Eventually, I found myself just hanging out below the surface, close to Vega, enjoying the unimaginable view. We really could have sold tickets.

It was probably our relative stillness that brought the little gray mother seal to my side; her baby came too, so close by her flank that I almost didn't notice him. Her flirty long-lashed eyes distracted me too much at first.

I knew she wasn't a selkie, but I couldn't keep from mentally greeting her, *Hey gorgeous*, as I stretched out a hand for her to approve and allow my touch. She arched her neck, at once pressing against my hand and turning her lovely spotted head to indicate her little one to me with a sweet glance.

The baby let me pet him, too. He was old enough to have lost his fluffy newborn coat and grown a sleek gray one like hers, though still young enough to be a lot smaller, and for his beautiful shiny eyes to look huge in his inquisitive face. Once it seemed Mom had decided Vega and I were safe, he came right up to snuggle himself in between her and us. I was tempted to laugh my delight out loud, but it wasn't worth having to surface and catch a breath.

Like a lot of toddler hugs I'd experienced, especially with the numerous and wildly energetic Hazan nieces and nephews, this one only lasted a few heart-melting moments. He pushed his face against my collarbone, allowed me to stroke his head and back. Then he was off again, his mother following with one last lash-batting gaze over her shoulder. He didn't rejoin the crowd. He was content exploring, just the two of them, with Mom tranquilly letting him do his own thing. Vega, eyes sparkling through her mask, followed the adorable pair at a short distance.

Treading water slowly, I continued to watch them. Baby and his pals had given us quite a workout already; I'd be feeling it in several different muscle groups.

Geir's black-clad form came back into my field of vision, as if across the dance floor. He wasn't swimming with anyone at the moment, either, just hanging there watching me. I was pretty sure no one in thirty-one years had ever looked at me like that.

It was more his kind of move than mine, but once the thought crossed my mind, I couldn't resist. I removed my snorkel, pressed my wrinkly fingertips to my lips and blew him a kiss accompanied by a stream of sparkling bubbles. He flashed a wide-eyed grin like I'd just agreed to go to prom with him. Then he dove effortlessly beneath the seal party to catch me around my ribs and pull me to the surface for a return kiss.

"Uh uh," he teased in answer to what he inevitably made me wish for, after a few sweet-salty moments. "What would Dr. Hazan say?"

"She'd cheer me on." I glanced back at Vega, who'd surfaced too in the interim, and seemed to be staring off into the horizon, most likely answering a message on her ring. "If she even noticed."

He still shook his head, laughing. "As if I don't know a boat-tipper when I meet her, anyway. You're still too new in town to have learned the art of keeping her steady. And the water's awfully cold without your suit, remember."

I just laughed again and tried one more persuasive kiss.

It wasn't at all that I hadn't persuaded him. "Come home with me and I'll keep you warm."

"I might be new in town, but you know I am home." I sighed contentedly in answer.

"Hey," Vega called across the water. "You guys need me to get my own ride to school?"

"No." I laughed, moving a little away from Geir.

"Okay, good." She swam closer, her smile fading. "I gotta talk to you, anyway. Stevie too."

Stefek hadn't lasted in the cold water as long as we had. He gave us a contented wave from the hover, just enjoying the sunlit scenery.

"What's wrong?" I asked quietly.

"Not to panic, no more downed wind turbines."

I didn't panic, but the news she shared, after we'd said goodbye to the pod and started back east, did wind my stomach into an uncomfortable knot. Neither of us had made the cut--lack of seniority in his case, last-in-first-out rule in mine, and no one new was being assigned to Aberdeen at this point either. Within about a week, the closest I'd be to here was my first hometown of Bergen.

Chapter 22

Big Old Blue and Green Rock

Two days later, Stefek heard back. Vega and Raj had pulled strings to get him a stint at the Academy in Brussels. Turned out, quite a few of us didn't want to see him stuck at entry level for long. May produced some Cava for us to toast his future success, and the UF family that had helped put him on a faster track there. He promised to tell Dr. Shimizu hello from me.

The day after that, I was off, which seemed stupid but hard to argue with. My jo and I made plans as we fell asleep the night before, some of the farthest-flung places I still hadn't seen. But we awoke to eleven degrees and knifing gusts of cold rain.

Around what I might have guessed was one or two, as we lazily considered lunch, someone knocked on the door, lightly with the softer outside of the palm, not the knuckles. "You two thinking of coming up for air before morning?" Lachlan said.

I reached for my ring. 1740. Damn.

Geir laughed. "If anyone can give us a good enough reason, maybe we'll entertain it."

"Well, there's some kind of five-star pop-up restaurant going up out here in about half an hour." He paused, listening to a feminine voice I could barely hear. "Forty minutes. I can probably still get you a table but you'll have to let me know fast."

Geir raised his eyebrows at me questioningly. I had to admit, I was getting hungry enough he'd be able to hear it even if he couldn't feel it.

"Let me take you to dinner?" I murmured. "I heard about a nice place near here."

He smiled. "Okay," he said aloud. "We're in."

"Excellent. I shall inform the chef."

"How's traffic looking?"

"No worse than usual." Lachlan chuckled, and we heard his footsteps going back down the hallway.

Geir kissed me one more time, as amazed as I was that the whole day could have gone by already. Then he slipped away to get a shower before the fancy restaurant.

I lay back and reactivated my ring the rest of the way. Vega had left a bunch of pulses. With a sigh, I rang her back.

"So you're not dead by the side of the road."

"Nah. Indoors and quite alive, thanks."

She laughed softly. "Good for you. Hey... I've been trying to ring you for hours, wild woman."

"Sorry. What's going on?"

"Ahh... You need to check your messages." She was serious when she should have been making raunchy jokes at my expense.

My heartbeat went jazzy for a few moments. "What am I looking for?"

"Miami," Vega said quietly.

"The "we'll call you" one? I told you, that was like two weeks ago."

"Not that one. Early this morning."

I managed to find the message she meant, through the blur of the tears I was already fighting.

"Hada madrina," I whispered. "How did you do this?"

"I didn't. There's a new acting head there who saw our staffing shift come up in her feed and asked for you. Says she met you at a briefing up here, and knew your dad? They just started a cohort this week, but it looks like a spot is opening up unexpectedly and she'd like to let you in on a trial basis. You'll be amazing, as I assured her probably an annoying number of times."

Miami. I swallowed a sob while the tears seeped as steadily as the spring my mother had once transformed into a mosaic water feature.

My dream job, except.

Before I could speak, Geir came back to find me still wearing nothing but the ring and a lot of saltwater that hadn't been there when he left. He wrapped the quilt and his warm arm around me, kissed my dripping cheek but couldn't understand the clouded impression he gained.

"Vera," he said, close enough for my tech to pick up his voice. "What are you doing to my Ardelaide?"

I projected her sigh for him. "Hey. It's, well, good news and bad news, big guy."

"Give us a few minutes?" I whispered to him.

He kissed my trembling mouth to steady me. "Okay," he said, more to reassure me than in response to her.

"Is he out of the room?" Vega said.

"Yes."

"I'll only take another minute of your time, then."

I felt my stomach drop, like on a badly turbulent flight.

"Do not be a stupid little girl and turn this down for him."

I let out my breath. "I didn't say I was."

"And don't go there and then throw it away because all you can think about is him," she pressed. "You can't keep acting like you have been here, the last few weeks."

I bit a bruise into the inside of my lip to keep from telling her the truth, all of it. "There's a lot I haven't said," was the best I could do.

"Yeah, no crap. You're like sucked into a cult or something. Just because you finally remembered sex is fun. Congratulations, by the way."

"Vega."

"Here's your standard step two after you figure that out. I've seen an awful lot of places on this big old blue and green rock, and there were beautiful men in every single one. Miami? Piece of mango tres leches, mija. Trust me."

"I do not want someone in Miami, unless I can somehow bring him there."

She sighed again, hotly. "You've been here two months and you think he's your soulmate? That's not how it works."

I swallowed a big, jagged sob. "Okay. Thanks a lot for the recommendation, Dr. Hazan. For the record, you could not possibly have any damn idea how it works for me."

I rang off and powered down my ring before I could say everything I meant. After all, maybe somehow what she believed she wanted really was enough for her.

Emerging clean and dressed a few minutes later, I accepted a glass of really delicious wine from the unsmiling, wide-eyed chef. They'd waited for me to share the little platter of glistening oysters I was sure had still been in the sea when the fateful message reached my ring unheeded. Berenys' hair wasn't even completely dry.

"What's all this for?" I murmured, slipping into the empty seat next to Geir's.

"This would have been Isla Russell Maclachlan's ninety-eighth birthday." The honoree's grandson managed a cautious smile as he raised his glass. "To the ever witty, strong, and beautiful Isla. Thanks for getting into the best kind of trouble with your wee selkie love. We owe you all this, and I'd love it if you were here to see what we're getting up to now."

"To Isla," we echoed, and sipped the perfect Sauvignon Blanc in her honor.

Lachlan caught my stinging eyes, then. "She won't mind sharing the glory with you, Arden. Geir said there's good news. Your next assignment, we're assuming."

I took another little gulp of wine. "Um, yeah. I just got invited to do what's been my dream for as long as I've been in UFE. Reef preservation and coastal rewilding."

"Brilliant," Lachlan said, albeit warily.

"But," Geir breathed. He didn't touch me, or really look at me, as I told them.

"It's in Miami."

"Okay," Lachlan said. "For, what, three months? Six?"

"No, it's not like a normal assignment, this is a major training phase." It ached to swallow one more sip of wine. "Two years."

I hadn't seen that hard glint in Brynja's eyes since the night we'd met, when Vega demanded the documents some of her family didn't have.

"You can turn it down, can't you?"

I opened my mouth but no words would come out.

"After everything, you'd really go back to the other side of the world?" she asked, steady and low.

"Bryn," Lachlan murmured, shaking his head. She laid her hand deliberately over his. He sighed, and with apparent effort, met her gaze and shook his head again. "Either way we knew she'd be going away for now. And it's a damn worthy reason."

"No, you're making a mistake," she told me with a slight toss of her hair and a defiant set to her delicate jaw as she broke eye contact with him. "But you're welcome here whenever you realize that, my heart."

She picked up her glass and took a sip, lashes lowered like a spiked castle portcullis against whatever answer I might have made; not that I could find one.

Under the table, Ysmay pressed her knee to my thigh. If she ever got a chance like this, she'd gladly suffer her mother's wrath and take it too. I dared to smile at her and wish that might one day be possible.

Berenys slipped into the kitchen before we were done talking, with no touch or glance to allow me to gauge her reaction. Lachlan, not smiling entirely convincingly this time, took charge of the conversation again. He refilled everyone's glasses and proposed a second toast to my success. I still couldn't stand to touch Geir, to demand a response before he was ready; he continued not to have anything to say.

For the main course, the family chef had also caught lobsters. I tried to focus and taste them. She'd paired them with bitter wild greens in a rich tangy sauce, with scented rice piled delicately to one side of the plate: all without electricity or even a regular place to buy most of her ingredients. She was a true artist. Another time, I would beg her forgiveness for dampening what should have been a wonderful evening and a celebration of her special talent for sensuousness.

It seemed I could at least offer to wash the dishes, some kind of down payment on the penance I'd understood I owed everyone--but Lachlan kicked Geir and me out of the kitchen, going so far as to open the glass door, shoo us through and shut it behind us.

His eyes were very dark, finally meeting mine; his continued silence was getting louder.

"Trust me, I know exactly what it looks like when I disappoint the hell out of someone." I sighed. "God. Just say you're mad at me too."

"Arden," he murmured.

I bit my lip and held out my hands for his. He caught and kissed them, fingers tightening around mine. He overflowed with aching, wistful pride.

"Ah, mi tesoro," I breathed. "There's no way you could come with me, right?"

It meant everything to him that I wished he could. "Oh, love. Not if Bryn can't stay more than a few weeks at a time in Edinburgh, I don't think…"

"Yeah. Still," I said, kissing his hands in turn. "I noticed early on, you're a hell of a lot stronger than even she is. In however many hundred years, she's only done this twice? You eat that for breakfast…"

"Maybe, but you shouldn't blame her. That means she hasn't had as much practice, setting people free. And it's not as though her children can really go off and leave her, even if they did decide to grow up."

Or maybe they hadn't felt it worthwhile to grow up, in part because they knew they could never really leave anyway. Geir didn't disagree. He did always have it in mind how soon the much more final version of this time would come for his beloved sister.

He shook his head, frustrated at the tears starting to fill his eyes and his voice. It felt utterly rotten to be making him sad.

"Ach… No. Sorry. No one usually has to see how bad I am at this."

He had something to show me. We went around the deck to climb in easily through his low, wide bedroom window.

He slipped his hand under a neat stack of sweaters in his bottom dresser drawer to retrieve a tattered cardboard shirt box, which he offered to me. Still no wedding pictures, but there were a few mementos he dared keep. A Victorian-style valentine with a child's signature, J a N E, on it. Alasdair's medal of honor. A dark-haired china doll smaller than my hand.

"I've never kept anyone here a day longer than was right for them," he murmured steadily, although he waited to say it until our hands weren't touching. "Never will."

I picked up a yellowed clipping, from the days when printed newspapers still lingered: the photo of a beautiful young woman, close-cropped hair showing off her wide bright eyes. When I'd seen her in real life, she'd been much older, but they'd shown this picture of the record-breaking freediver and marine bio rockstar. I knew her hair had once been brown, her limpid eyes a striking bottle-green.

"Why do you have a picture of Elsie Fiala in here?"

He smiled. "You know her?"

"Never beat her diving records when I was in high school, hard as I tried. And later I saw her accept an award on behalf of her late husband... in Vilnius for the fiftieth anniversary of the founding of UFE." I recalled being surprised, at that ceremony, by the soft British voice that hadn't matched her Eastern European name. "She died a couple years later. Over a hundred years old... right?"

He smiled faintly. "What a treasure to me, my love, that you'd know who she was. And yes. She lived to right before her hundred and twenty-third birthday, though I think her ident said a hundred and two."

I studied her eyes a second more. They were the right size, if not the familiar shape: so big they couldn't be wide-set and still fit in her face. My own eyes moved to the photo caption. Elsie hadn't been the original spelling. This read L.C. Fiala.

I could think of only one reason the photo of someone with the initial C would have a place in this little treasure trove. It took me a moment to think back to that night in Inverness when he'd told me her name along with those of all her lost brothers and sisters.

"Elsie Fiala, born Lucy Craig?" I breathed.

He nodded. "My mystery baby, you called her once."

"Oh, Geir."

"She did all she could with what she had, as we do. Same agenda with all her lovers. Dr. Evžen Fiala was the one wise enough to take it to heart." His sweet smile faded quickly. "Good man. How could I not want her to go to Prague with him? Or hold it against them if they were too busy with their good work to come back very often?"

"Talk about your fairy godmother," I whispered. "I've never wanted you to think you shouldn't talk about her. Any of them."

With effort, he found a new smile. "I don't think that. Just…
This time is yours."

"My two years to spend halfway across the planet. When we've
only had a few weeks together." I sighed.

"Well, is it anything like uni, this training? Breaks a few times a
year? You'll come home then."

Home. I nodded readily.

He surprised me again with a soft, though not cheerful laugh.
"We waited a lot longer than that for each other."

He had, especially. I sighed again.

"And if… ones like Owen and Beatrix and Lucy are any indication, maybe you've got more time coming to you overall than you've
probably thought… particularly if you can live here."

"Then with my luck, I'll complete the training and they'll station
me in Namibia or Tierra del Fuego…"

He shook his sleek head, and I didn't have to be touching him
to know how sincerely he believed in his fairytale version of events.

"How can you be such a rock?"

He smiled at the pun, eyes welling again because mine were, and
he shook his head. "Rock can't move even if it chose to, eh."

He drew me gently closer to sense something of the turbulent
cold currents threatening to erode him from beneath his brave surface.

I gasped. "Or I could resign."

He held me lightly by the nape of the neck for one more kiss,
hope and even defiant satisfaction surging back against the savage tide.

"It's unfair enough your parents aren't here for it. I hope you
won't deny me the pleasure of seeing what you make of your magnificent life."

I rubbed at the streaky mess all over my face. "I never did one
magnificent thing, before I came here."

He shook his head again. "Didn't know it yet. That's just you
taking the steps of your quest in the right order."

"Okay." I swallowed, as best I could, and tried to smile. "What if this is one of those quests where it takes them a lot longer to get home than anyone thought, though?"

"I promise never to become another man's wife, no matter how long you're away," he smiled in reply.

"Okay. And I'll watch out for those sirens."

"Ach. No siren's a match for the likes of my fierce selkie lass."

I still couldn't help thinking it was my fault we'd had so little time together. We'd both known what we wanted weeks sooner than we'd done anything about it, if only I'd had the courage to admit it. Or if he'd done more with his considerable powers to compel me.

"No," he said with a new smile in his voice. "I wouldn't trade for a moment of the way this happened when it did."

Chapter 23

Crush Depth

By some magic, Geir kept his tears at bay all the morning our flight departed, but they spilled over when we stood on the runway and he smiled at me, releasing my hands. Without touching, I still felt the bittersweet confidence of his longing for me to come home the moment I could. I gave him a shaky return smile and a small nod he didn't need to see, and turned to get aboard. When I took one last look back, he nodded once too in encouragement and tipped his cap my way.

Vega and Stefek had the common courtesy to let me cry myself quietly to sleep on the plane, even though that meant missing the last few hours I'd have with them until who knew when. It wasn't as if I'd even closed my eyes the night before. I dreamed of a little mermaid girl out on a rock in Scalloway Bay, her kelp-orchid crowned head and solemn hazel eyes lifted as she watched the skies for my eventual return. Everything flowed, nothing stayed.

I woke a bit at a time, confused at first why I couldn't reach out to console her, during light turbulence on our descent into Heathrow. One heartfelt embrace with my two friends was the closest I could get. Hopefully, it wouldn't be another year and a half before our next meeting.

We'd landed later than expected there, Vega's destination but our narrowly-timed first connection. Stefek had missed his flight for Brussels entirely and would have to rebook. My near-run over brilliantly-lit, mirror-shiny floors to the gate for La Guardia felt as wildly overstimulating as a night at a club, or the speedy VR games I'd never liked.

It was probably better that there was no time to browse the sensory excesses of the duty-free shops I normally enjoyed, although I'd devoutly wished to grab a bottle of Rosalind for the road. Anyway, as a consolation for my sudden trans-Atlantic move, I'd already arranged for a drone shipment from Monterey to meet me in Miami. Now that I'd be a student for a season, rather than assigned to a humanitarian or environmental mission, I'd have more opportunities to wear the beloved perfumes, beach dresses, sandals, and bikinis I'd had in storage. While we were still in the air, I ordered what turned out to be a limited-edition re-release from Penhaligon's to add to my collection, hardly flinching at the absurd price. On a spec admin salary, I might have stockpiled several bottles.

I landed in big, bright Miami International, at least as jarringly modern as London, about 1400 local time. I collected my bag and my drone delivery box and went through customs. More in than out of a fog of fatigue and emotion, I headed for the rampway where I could catch a pod to the housing address I'd been sent. It took me a moment to understand the brisk footsteps I half-heard were probably following me. I turned around.

"Dr. Shimizu." I hadn't dreamed anyone would meet me here, let alone the acting program head. "Sorry, I didn't know to look for you, but thank you for coming..."

She smiled. "Well. Your cohort arrived together a few weeks ago; I didn't like the idea of you slinking into town on your own. I hope you don't mind."

"Of course not." I glanced down at my travel-creased pants, ran a futile hand over my headful of frizz. "I'd like not to be such a mess, but."

"Oh, please. You're as irritatingly good-looking as your father."

I laughed along with her. "Okay. Thanks, still."

"I thought, unless you ate on the plane, I could get you something. Late lunch here, dinner for you, true? I'll show you where I go when I fairly regularly fulfill my agreement with you."

From onshore, she gave me the quick visual tour of our housing and classroom training space, an adorable floating village like I'd seen in Amsterdam and Perth. I'd have my own little furnished studio, a welcome perk of the entry-level specialist life. Maybe the green roofs and a glimpsed floating garden plot, plus three-sixty oceanfront views, would even help quell the inevitable homesickness.

We parked the pod nearby, leaving my stuff locked inside for now, and headed on foot to the restaurant.

"Also an easy walk to or from the dive center," Dr. Shimizu told me. "It's just two blocks further in this direction."

I didn't expect, or appreciate, the sudden tears sharp as shards of shattered glass when I breathed sofrito, roast pork and strong coffee richly mingling in the air the moment we entered.

Aftershock.

"Some other time," she said in a suddenly gentler tone that didn't do much for my composure in the short term, "let's remember him, and... compare notes. Yes?"

I glanced up in startled gratitude.

"The same thing happened to me once in a random ramen place in San Francisco," she murmured. "Years after my father was gone."

"Yeah." I barely sighed. "Thank you."

Tough memories notwithstanding, from the first mouthwatering forkful of ropa vieja and rice, I was sure I'd be a regular customer too. Given how much time I'd spent with my selkie family, I couldn't even recall the last occasion I'd indulged in this good old American guilty pleasure, red meat. Shimizu, on the other hand, ate like finfolk: she said she was mostly vegetarian although she liked seafood sometimes, today ordering a half portion of black beans and rice with Dad's weakness, sweet plantains.

"I've debated telling you this," she said after a few minutes. "Technically, the Cohort 2099 spot that had opened up is no longer free."

I put two fingers of my left hand over my lips to keep them shut, the fork lightly clattering from my right hand against the edge of my plate.

She smiled belatedly. "Don't worry, I wouldn't bring you all this way for nothing. This is more my way of saying that even after the powers that be had granted the person in question a second chance-- no, let's be honest, a fourth or fifth chance--I still found myself convincing them to admit you. Call it a very strong hunch."

It wasn't easy to swallow the bite of food that had been hanging in my mouth.

"Um. Thank you… I hope I'll prove to deserve that."

The lingering hint of her smile did nothing to settle my sudden nerves. "I hope so, too."

I got a few little gulps of water down my uncooperative throat. At least I brought plenty of previous experience in the shouldn't-really-be-here club to this assignment.

We finished our dishes of ambivalent comfort food and rounded out the spaces with a café cubano--divine, after months of mostly tea. She showed me the walk to the dive center herself. Once a highly desirable neighborhood, it wasn't an ideal area now. We were close to the revised coastline, right in the thick of the work of renovating and shoring up some places while micro-rewilding others. Like other beautiful saltwater shapeshifters of my acquaintance, Miami just needed a little help from humankind so it could live to charm another day.

"Here," she told me, pausing to look out over Biscayne Bay. "These condos were demolished a couple of weeks ago."

We watched for a moment as a crew worked to remove the last traces of the resulting rubble from the shallow water, onto a waiting hover barge.

"How do you keep the contaminants under control?" I wondered aloud. "Demolishing a building with its foundations already underwater?"

She nodded. "There's extensive cleanup even after we get the big pieces, filtration and pH balancing and so on. And still, some collateral damage is inevitable. You know. We never truly leave it as good as we found it. But if all goes well, by next spring--"

She stopped and gave me a prompting look. "We can establish a micro reef or a sandbar. Which would you recommend for this location?"

I cleared my throat. "I mean. I don't know anything yet about who lives down there, the tides or current patterns, typical boat traffic."

She nodded. "All true. But if you had to choose?"

"Reef," I said without overthinking. "Seems more protective for an urban area. I'd expect you'd want a sandbar further out on the edges of things, like in the Keys."

"Well, let's get some seminars and dive tank training under your belt, and this will be your classroom, Arden. We'll see how trustworthy your instincts are."

I didn't know if it was part of the test, my pressing for the answer now or not, but I chose to respond with just a selkie-sized appreciative smile. Far more than needing that specific answer, I already itched to learn enough to get back to East Shetland and help with the same process there.

The piercingly clear new thrill of purpose didn't last long. As soon as I could escape from the first full seminar day onto the nearest lovely green roof, I rang Vega in a cold sweat.

"Ma, me van a botar de aquí inside of a week."

"What are you talking about?" she laughed. "After the special invitation and everything?"

"Yeah, that's what I mean. She practically introduced me to everyone as Oliver Junior, even though she knows otherwise."

"Well, you're good under some pressure."

"Had me tell the class what I did last summer with the environmentally-conscious zillionaire shipping tycoon family. And when it came up we'd tried the Steyn rebreathers with them, she called me a curve wrecker."

Vega laughed. "That's not what spec admin Krol says."

"Ugh. And the real big bad is, on top of everyone already expecting me to be you or something... She requires us to disable capturing in the classroom. Note-taking the way the ancestors did it, or the highway. Burns different neural paths, or some sciencese thing like that."

"So. I had some of those old-school guys at Columbia. You can do it."

I groaned. "Pressure's one thing, but this is, like, crush depth."

"Mija," her voice nudged me, gentler. "Is everyone purely in competition there? Does she require you to disable working with other humans to make sure you got all the notes right?"

"Oh."

"See? No need to be all Oliver Junior about it. ...Okay, you have someone in mind?"

I thought for a few moments. Our cohort of twenty-five was dominated by Rajan Dessais and Lachlan Adies, with the odd Noemi Engel in the mix. None of them obviously my people.

There'd been one quietly focused young woman seated not far from me this afternoon, though, whom I wouldn't mind approaching. She looked maybe twenty, wasn't any more than my height, and sported skinny blue- and green-yarn-wrapped braids mixed throughout her long dark hair. In lieu of a portable screen, digital mat, or other device, she wrote her notes in an actual fat paper notebook; I'd noticed a delicate string of mantas tattooed diagonally across the back of her light brown right hand as it sped back and forth across the page.

"Yes. Okay."

"Looks fine in his swimming gear?" Vega pressed.

I let her hear my smile. "Not to worry, cabrona... adorable as she is, she's no competition for the Miami FC guys."

"'Pérate, there's Miami FC guys?"

"Oh, I mean, I thought that was a given. Me working my way through the whole team while I'm here. The first four were okay."

Vega laughed aloud. "Okay, mija. Good luck with your note-taking."

I worked up my nerve to talk to the girl with the manta tattoos at the next morning's diving session. After all, if smart people hadn't associated with me before, I wouldn't have most of my friends from at least this last year.

She sat with just her feet in the pool, eyes focused somewhere under the deep water, working on some breathing exercises. I did my best to read her first name off her badge: Karima Darzi.

Her light hazel eyes widened with her partial smile. "Oh. Hi. What's up, Arden?"

"I wanted to ask you a favor… You can say no, obviously."

"Oh." When she smiled fully, her tiny aquamarine nose piercing winked in the light. "Sure. Everyone here gets the friends and family discount. Just show up wearing anything UFE issue. Mom loves all you guys for, you know, saving the planet and stuff."

"Thank you… and her… though I don't know what that's for? The discount."

She laughed. "Sheereen-Amor. Her restaurant… No?"

"I'm sure I'll love her, too. And her restaurant. But no, I was… Looking for someone to compare seminar notes."

"Notes?" Karima blinked her enhanced cat-eye lashes. Lovely as they were, she had nothing on Ysmay.

"While I'm catching up on the material. And I get the sense I'm going to have some… knowledge gaps, coming in from the generalist track." I smiled crookedly. "Eh. Honestly, I'm just kind of shite at the whole classroom situation. If you could--even look at mine and let me know what to go back and research. I'm more than willing to pay you in… I don't know. Laundry. Errands. Dog-walking."

"Oh. Sadly, allergic to dogs." She laughed. "Um, yeah, I have no problem sharing mine, although they aren't digital…"

I gave her a conspiratorial single eyebrow raise. "Do you think photo captures of your notebook would be grounds for dismissal?"

Karima glanced over her shoulder. "You never know with her. But… no, of course, I don't think that violates the spirit of her crazy policy."

"Well, if it's okay with you, I'd appreciate it to no end. Just let me know what I can do in return."

"Sure," she said again. "Um, actually… How are you at this shit?" She gave another short laugh. "Sorry, is 'shite' how the classy people are saying it now?" As she spoke, she gestured with a head bend to the water, then to the rebreather pack beside her on the pool deck. "SCUBA's no problem, but this shite… I mean, I get it, lowest impact in small spaces, but. Ugh."

"This part comes easiest for me," I said. "I'd love to help you."

She grinned. "Well, then let's jump in, before she sees us on our butts and Ravenclaw and Gryffindor lose a hundred points each."

I had the odd but enjoyable sensation of having just met my summer camp buddy, as we both slipped into the water. She wasn't really shite at it, although she seemed to have a naturally limited lung capacity. In between sharing some breath control strategies I'd picked up along the journey, we learned a bit about one another. Unlike the buddies I'd jumped in with at the last camp, Karima was the age she appeared: only eighteen. Nonetheless, she had already completed her bachelor's degree with a marine bio-geosciences double major.

She dubbed her heritage "Persio-Rican:" three-quarters Irani-an-American, with a Puerto Rican grandfather on her mom's side, all of which boded exceptionally well for the mom's aforementioned restaurant. She'd recognized Dad's name as soon as she heard me in-troduced. She laughed to learn the non-famous half of my DNA was

Norwegian--the old truth made a particularly easy lie--and wondered which of us represented the odder combination. I was happy to let her think it was a draw.

Deep diving in the tank felt like far less pressure than lecture mornings at sea level. Because I'd joined the cohort late, today was diagnostic, with a series of tasks for me to try at will like a particularly fantastic version of the Montessori school where I'd started my less-than-illustrious academic career. Cameras, body sensors, and our rings tracked our performance. Dr. Shimizu would tailor my future assignments based on today's work. That meant leaving Karima behind by mutual agreement, hopefully just for the day. I still kept an eye out for her.

"Oh, damn," she said as she climbed out of the pool after me, and caught sight of the sparkly bits adorning my selkie feet. "Those are fantastic."

"Your style is too," I said, with a smile that felt suddenly different than it should look. Hopefully, she assumed I was rubbing the pool's saltwater from my eyes, rather than the stinging-sweet memory of falling so in love with someone so much too far away at this moment.

"You okay?" she murmured, not fooled.

I found a better smile. "Sorry. My boyfriend likes them too, and I happen to have left him in northernmost Scotland, so."

I cringed inwardly as soon as I'd said it; he was as far from a boy as he was beyond a friend. I'd have to come up with a better term.

"Mine's in Haifa," she answered, her façade of sober solidarity cracking within seconds. "Also he's a little old for me, and also he doesn't know I exist yet."

She flashed me up a news vid-image of a dazzling young guy in board shorts, dark beard, serious tan, and ball cap, thigh-deep in clear seawater, showing a stingray to a half-circle of rapt ten- or twelve-year-olds. Someone Pérez, I thought I read the caption. When in return I pulled up a favorite candid image Vega had sent me after the seal diving day, she grinned at my long-distance good fortune.

"Also you know, Mom has pastries for that," she suggested,

an encouraging hint of the smile lingering. "On a related note, lunch break is in twenty-five minutes."

I smiled readily, too. "I'm in."

Chapter 24

Stornaway

I still talked to my true love almost every day, strange as it was to rely so much on words. More nights than not, we left the ring connection open while I fell asleep. It messed with his normal bedtime, but he could no more resist a nice lie-in than other seal folk, and we both longed to stay together even if we weren't conscious the whole time. When he was within or below, though, he couldn't take his ring. And he was definitely spending more time in the North Sea than he had when I was around. All told, it was the furthest thing from enough for either of us. I wore Rosalind a lot, spritzing on a precious bit more at bedtime to ensure I'd dream about him.

The second week in July, just as Lachlan had once predicted, all my selkie folk took to the sea to catch up with Elis on his reconnaissance tour of the tiny islands off mainland Scotland's west coast. He'd given his research program director some explanation about gathering data toward his dissertation, not that his current studies had ever been tied to one place as tightly as mine. It helped a little, knowing I wasn't missing the fun in Shetland now.

Having my own kind of fun in Miami helped even more. I'd always enjoyed aspects of my work, but here there were things I passionately loved. Turned out, when Dr. Shimizu mentioned generalist multitasking as an advantage before heading toward a specialization, she'd had this particular job in mind: there wasn't just diving but policy, marine bio, even some marine geo I inwardly dedicated to Dad.

At the start of that second month, Dr. Shimizu added in student-led seminar afternoons. It would be intimidating when my turn came to lead. But as one of the most experienced cohort members, I found I could add a lot to the discussions, which regularly spilled over into shared lunches or dinners. As our dive workouts now were designed to target individual strengths and weaknesses, I didn't get to partner with Karima often, but we still warmed up together and I helped her in whatever other ways I could.

"Hey," I said lightly, slipping into the pool near her on a Wednesday morning in early August. "Thanks for the notes, for the eighty-ninth time."

"Any time," she wheezed.

"You okay? Thought you were just catching a breath here…"

Karima smiled partway. "Easier--said."

"Asthma?" I was only surprised I hadn't guessed sooner. "Sorry. Have you always had it?"

"Yeah. Not--great for a--diver."

"Yeah. But merge you and me into one person, with the brains and the lungs, we could take over the world. Or at least the ocean."

Making her laugh might not have been the best idea.

"Where's your inhaler?" I said. "Let me get it for you."

She granted my ring one-time access to her locker; I hopped out of the pool and made the quick walk there and back.

"Usually I'm not this symptomatic. Shite air quality this week," she said when she could breathe easier.

"Along with the two hundred percent humidity." She laughed as I fluffed my hair out even more huge than the weather had inflated it.

The gesture made my scalp itch, though, an incongruous annoyance I'd noticed lately. Maybe that was due to poor air quality as well.

"They never gave you meds for yours, too? The holes in your notes sometimes. Inattentive ADHD, right? Firuz takes injections for it..."

Her big-eyed beanpole brother, who bussed tables at Sheer-een-Amor, was fifteen or sixteen if I recalled. "I tried them when I was his age. I didn't feel like myself."

She nodded. "Anyway, there's worse things than a little day-dreaming."

"Especially when you have good people on your team to balance the space-cowgirl factor," I agreed, rather than elaborate on the actual size of my daydreams.

"Likewise with the can't-drag-my-round-ass-up-to-get-the-in-haler factor."

"Any time," I said. "Ready to jump back in yet?"

"A couple more minutes. You go ahead, though. Progress check today, remember. Don't let me mess yours up."

"If you're sure..." With a few stretches of my shoulders and spine, I slipped back into the water.

"Oh," she stopped me after all, as I hung from the pool's edge by four fingertips. "Didn't you say you'd been in Aberdeen this spring?"

I nodded.

"I've just been scanning news as I'm failing to oxygenate--the jerks trying to take refugee kids, were you there for that?"

I gripped the rubberized tiles a little tighter. "Yes."

"They found one of the guys. Still lurking around in Scotland... dumbass. Resisted arrest and not a problem to humanity anymore, it looks like."

"Good," I said with all my heart and gut. "Where in Scotland?"

"Someplace called Stornoway... you know it?"

"You're kidding..."

As much as I needed to focus and get back to my workout, I opened the story she rang to me. Gavin Fyfe, a doughy Aberdeen native, had been one of the names given up by the criminals arrested back in March, a collaborator with the larger international ring we'd already understood we'd encountered. I skimmed past the depressingly familiar statistics linking climate refugees and modern slavery. At least he'd been attempting to lie low this time, not threatening anyone else's freedom. And at least the accompanying photo of four young women who'd escaped the organization's grasp in Aberdeen, standing tall and sober-faced on a medieval bridge that had withstood the terrible surge up the River Don, didn't appear to include any more selkie lasses.

Fyfe had been shot in the shoulder, fleeing the UFPKs. A few centimeters too low, unfortunately for him; bullet fragments traveled to his lung and he'd died in surgery. Unfortunately for more than just him, actually, since now he could never tell the authorities anything more.

"So my agenda's wrong and we're having a spa day?" came a dry alto voice from behind me. "Great. I'll take the hot stone massage."

"We're not, Dr. Shimizu," Karima answered apologetically. "More like I forgot how to breathe again, so Arden offered to get my inhaler. But I'm pretty good now."

"Thanks," Shimizu said to me, her tone softer than before. But when she gestured with a head tilt toward the deep end, I obeyed immediately. Further news would have to wait. I linked to a feed of Dad's favorite work music, the lazily seductive Afro-Caribbean jazz of Yemayá, and got down to one of the best parts of my new job.

My appreciation for the diving facility extended to its bathrooms: plenty of unisex cubbies with self-sanitizing toilets and blissfully hot shower water. After the workout, I decided to ring Geir in Stornoway from the privacy of mine.

It had been a big news story there in the Hebrides, of course. Everyone in our family was fine, unaffected as far as he knew.

"Oh, because I sort of wondered if Berenys…"

"We've been ships passing in the night here lately…" He was quiet for a thoughtful moment or two. "But now that you mention it, Elis did say that this morning, Berenys came into the room I've been sharing with him here… when he's not sleeping someplace else… He was there this time; I was out with Bryn. She didn't say much, just helped herself to a bottle we've had on hand and knocked back a couple drams as though they'd been water. Ten-thirty, maybe eleven o'clock, he said. And she didn't want to talk about it and left as quick as she'd come. Both of them have been out and about with the locals quite a bit, so he and I figured this was her usual boy trouble… but now I'm wondering if she spotted someone she'd met in Aberdeen."

So was I.

"Not that anyone can divine what's going on in that one's head before she's ready to say."

"True." I took a big cleansing breath, exhaled the bad from the story. "And she's okay, I guess."

"I think so. And you, my jo? What are you getting up to?"

"Just been diving," I told him, then hesitated a second. "I'm in the shower."

"Oh," he said, with a delicious laugh I hadn't felt in ages too long.

"How about you guys?" I asked, giggling too.

"We've just checked into a bed and breakfast for the evening. The weather's been rubbish here, for summer. Twelve or thirteen degrees and pouring rain for two days straight."

I thought about it for a heartbeat or two more. "You in your room right now?"

"Yes, but we're going down to supper in about twenty minutes."

"Is Elis there?"

"What? No…"

He laughed again, lower, as I sent a pulse requesting a video connection. "Arden. Oh."

"I mean, tesoro, if I'm not getting home until September..."

"Ach, selkie lass," he breathed, as the connection picked up and I enjoyed the unprecedented achievement of making a finman blush from sixty-six hundred kilometers away.

When I emerged from the steamy cubicle, my cohort was gone, the pool's surface still, the echoing space quiet. I figured I'd slink out and grab a quick bite before the afternoon's session of taking notes until my head hurt, followed by a night of forgetting how to sleep, an excellent local coffee, a morning of getting some energy and sanity back in the saltwater, rinse, repeat.

Shimizu was still on one side of the pool deck, though, working on the usual freestanding screen displaying her ring data. She looked up with mild amusement.

"Not quite as fast in the shower as you are getting to depth, hmm," she remarked.

I failed to keep back a startled giggle. With any luck, maybe it looked like I was still flushed from the workout and the hot water. "I, uh, I'm a lot older than most of these guys. I need a head start on being able to get up and down stairs tomorrow. The sauna thing seems to help."

I felt marginally better when she laughed too. "Ring me in forty years and we'll compare notes about our encroaching mortality, yes? Anyway, Karima said to tell you some of the group are off to her mom's place for lunch."

"Thanks. Sounds amazing. You're not going?"

She smiled as she shook her head, powered off and started to roll up her portable work screen. "I know the budding crewmen need their space. Have the kuku sabzi for me. Oh, and if you haven't tried it yet, the rose and orange blossom ice cream is not of this world."

"Thanks, I do love a good fairytale treat. See you later, Dr. Shimizu."

"So was that how you respond under a little professorial pressure, or would you say it was a normal workout for you today?" she added when she was already a few steps behind me.

My cheeks burned differently as I turned back to meet her keen-edged gaze.

"I can push it harder next time. I'm, uh, not very good at judging what's normal," I said.

She smiled. "Well, either your sensors need recalibrating, or you're superhuman." Since she'd just tucked the screen away, she projected a pair of charts into the saltwater-scented air above her ring. "This one is respiration rates for everyone in the pool today. This is CO_2 tolerance. Spot the difference."

The bio-trackers were primarily a safety feature; it hadn't occurred to me that she might also use them for evaluative purposes. I hardly had to ask whose wavy line was solidly separated from the rest clustered pretty tightly together, well below on the first graph, well above the second.

I caught a breath, smiled as best I could. "I'm sure it's pilot error."

"Maybe, since they were way off on your diagnostic day too. Easy enough to figure out at the next check, if so." Her reassuring light laugh cut off a little too sharply. "Though just your previous record definitely puts you beyond any freedivers in this cohort."

Stomach twisting, I aimed for uncharted middle ground between the real truth and the one I could tell. "I do also think... I probably made some gains in Shetland that I haven't tested yet."

"I see." Her smile was as hair-raising as Brynja's had ever been. "Well, let's make it a point to push it harder, and test them."

All the fun of my shower time evaporated as I made my quick exit, and I suddenly didn't feel up to joining everyone for Persio-Rican lunch either. How had I not realized sooner how unprepared I was to keep the enormous secret I'd stumbled upon? Yet if I downplayed my strengths here, how would I manage to maintain my tenuous place in the program?

Not that I should follow Berenys' example in much of anything, I stopped for a Ron Collins, eventually adding a couple of juicy empanadas de picadillo to keep it company, at the place around the corner before heading back to work.

Chapter 25

Forest of Arden

Amid the seeming success of my newfound hyper caution, I let Dr. Shimizu arm-twist me into visiting Doña Maite and her husband a week later. At the funeral, she'd wanted my promise to get in touch if work ever brought me to Miami as I'd hoped. Between my star-crossed wedding and then, I hadn't seen her but once or twice. I'd never been to her current home, atop a glittering, state of the environmental art high-rise with an incredible view of the bay.

The jovial, smoothly bald man who answered at our knock still didn't look close to what I knew was his actual age of eighty-eight.

"Arden," he said with a broad grin. "Hi, sweetheart. It's great to see you."

"Hi, Mr. Grant."

"Jamar. Please."

So he'd always insisted, but now, no one was left to make me talk to him like I was still a child. Or to mutter unfair wicked stepfather references, with that tissue-thin veil of humor for politeness' sake.

"Okay. Jamar." I accepted his strong hug. "Thanks so much for inviting us."

"You bet. And Noa. My God. My beautiful María is gonna grumble something Spanish about why can't you have the grace to age a year or two, in all this time."

"Don't be ridiculous." She got her own bear hug, reaching up to pat him on the back like a brother-in-arms. "And please tell me that intoxicating smell is coming from in here, not some five-star place downstairs that happens to share your ventilation."

"She's making her famous seafood paella." He chuckled. "Gotta show she still has it all."

Well, since she certainly seemed to, she might as well flaunt it. I shook my head in admiration as Jamar ushered us into the airy apartment, all in shades of cloud and dune, with spotless windows from floor to high ceiling on every side. He and Shimizu took seats by the dazzling view, while I headed to find my grandmother.

Maite's experience in the shouldn't-really-exist club had been the surprise landfall of Tropical Storm Oliver when she and Santos Rivera were just seventeen. Only a few years before the treatments became mandatory for all public high school students, it hadn't slowed María Teresa Araujo Quintana down for a second. And she'd no more need-ed Santos to stick around than he'd been interested in staying; probably less. (I'd never met him while he was alive.)

She'd given their son her surname and, never missing a beat, gone on to Dean's list and honors, law school on a scholarship, all with him in tow. Superwoman. She'd achieved years of successful practice, eventually a judgeship from which she'd retired with acclaim ten years or so ago, around the last time Dad and I saw her together. And, of course, there was her fruitful marriage of fifty-plus years to Miami's most adorable real-estate developer.

Maite emerged from the kitchen in a swirl of silky caftan and her distinctive iris-benzoin sillage; that I'd never known the name of her signature perfume didn't mean I could ever forget it. I twitched smooth the open shoulder of the fluttery sea-toned georgette dress Berenys had helped me pick out over grid video (almost stylish enough for her, though I'd annoyed her by not planning to wear it out in public sans underthings). Standing straight in skin-color high-heeled sandals from the same shopping trip, I braced for the inevitable slow build-up of tension, keeping my hand lightly on the hilt of my diplomacy composite at all times.

"Hi, mi amor," she greeted me with an air kiss which I returned, her big glamorous pavé hoop cool against my cheek. "I'm so glad you called."

"Thank you. Me too. Can I help you in here?"

"No way. It's in the oven now, doing its thing. Let's go say hi to Noa. I'm ready to get off these old feet."

I laughed. "All right."

"So good to see you. I forgot," she said as she sifted a handful of my loose curls through her long, steady brown fingers. "Now you're not messing with it, you really have Maggie's hair."

"Dos partes luck of the Irish, una parte sabor latino, Dad always said," I agreed as we retraced my steps to the window-wall.

"He say how good she was to me when I needed her? Que Dios bendiga her crazy soul."

"Oh, he only had good things to say about her."

Her chestnut eyes, beautifully several shades lighter than the creased skin around them, went on studying my features. "And did you always have so much of her and Santos in the face, por Dios... More than Oli ever had."

Jamar, listening, raised silver-white brows but didn't comment.

"He was pretty lucky to look so much like his lovely mami," I smiled.

Despite her insistence that there was nothing left to do in the kitchen, after greeting Dr. Shimizu and chatting a few minutes she swirled away again. That left us to enjoy the start of a nice bottle of Pinot Noir, watching the correspondingly ruby Miami sunset get underway.

It was the most normal conversation, but I couldn't shake the oddness of hearing *drottenmín* Shimizu discuss anything to do with her age. Jamar had needed follow-up laser eye treatments, and was reluctantly giving up his beloved golf games because his grip just wasn't what it had been. Shimizu grumbled something about osteoporosis and degenerative disc disease, increasingly as challenging on dive days as on those she spent behind the lecture podium or her desk. That was the price anyone's bones, let alone diminutive Asian ones, paid for continuing to dive so intensively, so long past menopause.

"Well, I'm sure folk would say you've given more than enough years in service to your planet, Noa," Jamar said. "I'll introduce you to my country club buddies. Any time."

She gave me a little wink. "Retirement does seem to agree with you two, but I'm sticking to the shark method of survival. Never stop swimming."

Given Jamar's career history, he understood a lot more about my present job than I did yet myself, peppering me with interesting questions and commentary and plenty of stories of Shimizu's previous tenure here. I wished Dad could hear us.

Maite served her ridiculously good paella in the asymmetrical hollow of translucently fine, shallow white bowls set on a sparkling expanse of glass table. Somewhere around the second scoop, or the third glass, I realized with wistful relief that the expected tension would never materialize. It wasn't just the big new professional step up, putting me somewhere closer to their level. I started to see that hadn't ever been the problem. The catalyst that had always triggered the past cold and stiffness was permanently missing from the equation now.

I knew, even as I enjoyed hearing the good career and family news about my father's three younger half-siblings, it must have been excruciating for Maite's only real mistake to coexist with the offspring of her successful adult life. So thorny in his brilliance and difference, I doubted he had ever understood how ready Jamar and his children would have been to accept him if he could have bent their way a little.

Amid the happy stories of weddings and graduations, big anniversaries, and the first great-grandchild, Maite cocked the inevitable Caribbean grandmotherly brow and wondered if I was still single myself.

I smiled as I shook my head. They'd like him too if they ever got to meet.

Dr. Shimizu raised both brows too. "No one in your cohort, is it? Or else I'm slipping."

"No. When would we even have time for that? So I… it hasn't really come up in a professional context…"

I thought for a second, then pulled up my favorite photo, courtesy of Vega. "Here. This is my… Geir. And our Shetland."

His perfect profile was turned to the bright southwest and dark eyes focused in the distance, strong shoulders straight but relaxed, wetsuit unzipped as low as a shirt would be unbuttoned in Miami. Damn. With sunlit wave caps and rugged shore for a suitably stunning backdrop; and me at his side, the North Sea still beading off my hair, where I belonged.

"Ayyy, okay," Maite agreed with my unspoken opinion. "He kind of has that Santos Rivera look to him too, doesn't he? Is this finally a Latin boy?"

"A hundred percent Scottish," I laughed, shaking my head to think how much the old lady calling him a boy would be only a kid to him. "Pretty much the opposite of Latino, I guess. He works for Lachlan Adie," I told Shimizu as an aside.

"Woman, you bring up that bad high school boyfriend one more time," Jamar muttered at around the same moment, with a good-natured shake of his own shiny head.

"Ay, mi tesoro, por favor." She chuckled, preparing to sweep out to the kitchen with our empty bowls.

"Abuela, please let me do that," I said.

"No way. I'm not washing anything. I'll just soak it all and Rocío can get it when she comes in the morning."

Shimizu still got up with her, taking the empty wine bottle to the recycling and a couple of glasses in her other hand.

Jamar smiled fondly as he watched them go, but he shook his head again. "Oli is still on her mind all the time, of course, but you never hear her say Santos. Not in years."

"I hope that's not me bringing up the bad stuff by being here…"

He put a warm hand on the back of mine. "Honey. Just 'cause your dad made it tough for her to love him, doesn't mean she hasn't wanted you closer your whole life, you know?"

Home, my selkie heart whispered. How lovely, after so long and so far, to understand that--be it ever so complicated--there could even be more than one. I turned my palm up under Jamar Grant's kind hand to give it a grateful squeeze.

When I rang Geir on the day I thought was our four-month anniversary, I hoped for another virtual encounter. Half-dress being so much more provocative to his selkie eye than everyday nudity, I'd hidden lacy wisps Berenys would surely endorse beneath an innocuous beach dress, and let my hair down around my bare shoulders in all its tropical glory. His ring signal buzzed long enough I figured he was within our North Sea, and I wouldn't get him, but before I was quite ready to give up, I heard the ring going through.

"Mr. Craig's office, Elis speaking." His baritone voice was distinctively brighter, appealing as the top-shelf Scotch I'd sipped while viewing his photo in Inverness once. He had no trace of selkie accent.

I smiled despite my disappointment. "Oh. Hey."

When I found it quite early on, I'd almost taken Geir's ring for a classic wristwatch, sitting in an antique dish with some old coins on his dusted and polished dresser top. I'd chuckled aloud: he hadn't just been white lying to Jens Jespersen. His device was a relic from the days when they'd still had a square glass display screen instead of projection or a retinal interface, and charged via cable instead of kinetically with the wearer's movement. It could still interface with mine. I'd swiped Ysmay's contact ident (she being more likely than most fairytale creatures to possess a bit of modern tech, after all) and the one listed just as E K.

"At-sea day for him, I guess?" I asked E K now.

"Yep. So he's not around to object to you chatting with me for a few minutes."

"Why would he, anyway?"

"Well. I've been given reason to wait on the video connection…" he murmured, another smile in his smooth voice.

I laughed. "Ach. I promise I'm decent this time. Go ahead."

The connection with Geir's old device flickered on as reluctantly as usual, allowing Elis to get a good look. Dressed this afternoon in a chunky light brown fisherman's sweater about a century newer than Geir's favorite, he pushed sharp mirrored shades past his meticulous hairline as he received my image.

"Dear God." He gave me a slow selkie once-over before flashing a perfect smile. "Hello, Arden Araujo."

"Actually, since you're the marine bio expert for the species, maybe I can ask your advice."

"Hold on," he said as I focused the camera link on my hands and arms. "Does the old man know someone's given you jewelry to wear on a significant finger?"

I laughed, flashing my wide square zirconia on its sparkling skinny band back and forth. "Nah, it's, you know, like a No Trespassing sign. Beware of Dog. Just for when I'm out in the city… I picked it up for about twenty dollars after turning at least the tenth pushy miamense down. I swear some of them are worse than finmen."

"Is that a challenge?"

"It is not, Grandpa. Now, put on your science hat."

He chuckled. "If you insist, Junior."

I showed him the rough, reddened area that had appeared inside my elbow. Both arms and behind both my knees and ears looked and felt the same; my palms and heels were in constant danger of cracking, despite the Florida humidity. The hydrocortisone Vega had recommended only kept the symptoms at bay.

Not for the first time, I had the pleasure of seeing Elis transform into his brilliant professional self. He told me that although the twins enjoyed finite travel around the northern parts of the British Isles, he and Geir and Brynja had learned to limit their days within waters south of the Pentland Firth, even if it was still the North Sea. From the limited testing he'd managed, the minerals and salts of their birth latitudes were very specific in their composition and concentrations, and he theorized that selkies' well-being required their homes' particular recipe.

"Sure, for you guys, but I've been swimming all over the planet," I protested. "I've never had a problem."

"Until Geir cast his spell over you, so you'd never be happy unless you were near him." He shook his head, hair sleek as a crow's wing in the sunlight. "This is how it begins."

Smiling, I echoed his head shake. "Pretty sure Geir's a straight-up transfiguration guy."

Elis laughed softly. "But acute sensitivity can show up in just that way. Years spent in contact with something, you go away from it, and the next exposure triggers the reaction. Then, too, for you to go directly from anywhere as remote as Shetland to a huge city--I can only imagine the contaminants where you're working, the way that coastline has crept in the last century. Sorry, but it's no wonder you're having trouble."

"Well, shite," I said. "Makes it kind of hard to do my job."

He was always more handsome when he was completely in earnest. "I wish I could have my own lab and staff and funding. I'd bump your case to the top of the list."

"Of course you would."

"But until then…. I'd wash in purified water, even steam bathe if you can, flush out your eyes as well, and anti-inflammatory eye drops and barrier creams for your skin."

"Barriers," I grumbled.

He sounded more tenderly proud than Dad had ever been. "Yes, that's the balance we finfolk have to find. The more open you are to it all, the more vulnerable. No one pushed that particular envelope harder than your mother, by the way, which leads me to expect great things from you too."

I'd first spoken to Elis not long after we'd figured out my probable pedigree, sitting on Geir's bed although connecting via my ring. He'd made a point of telling me he'd known Nereiður better than anyone living in Shetland or even Orkney these days. (But no worries, he'd tried to assure me. Even if she hadn't been so far out of his league, he preferred to hunt on land, the same as she had.)

I breathed a short sigh. "So is there, like, a minimum number of times you have to bring her up in every conversation?"

He nodded, brows a bit raised although his voice remained calm and cool. "Not every conversation. Just the ones with you. And as many times as it takes for you to realize you have her to thank for the absolutely ridiculous depth you're achieving with people you barely know… and now, even with places. That it's not normal at all for selkies born into this day and age, let alone for someone with only one parent who was. Just that she came from so long ago. And she was…" He shook his head slightly. "Would have been spectacular, in any time. I know you see the side of her that took from others, and that's true… but in my experience, she offered as much as she demanded, and more."

I could only nod, the ingratitude wiped cleanly off my face.

"Right," he murmured.

"Right. Anything else, doc?"

He smiled. "Seek assignments closer to home, when you can."

"Ha. Thanks a million. Cheer me up and tell me you've found anyone interesting there."

He favored me with a rotten little smile. "Gorgeous natural blonde ornithologist, age forty-three, found my unexpectedly old soul quite interesting for a couple nights in Benbecula."

I made my best Dr. Shimizu face. "You know I'm asking about brunettes."

The smile mellowed into something more wistful. "None as yet. We're sure they're still here, though. At least a few. I don't know if you'll have met a lad called Ruadh?"

"Uh… Friend of the twins'. Yeah."

Elis nodded. "He came to us from out this way, and left others behind when he did. These ones are fairly nomadic, compared to our folk. Ruadh was born in one of the Northern Irish islands if I'm not mistaken. They'll be round here somewhere."

"So he's okay moving permanently from the Irish to the North Sea?"

"He's very much younger, remember."

"Thanks again, Nereiður," I sighed, equal parts honest frustration and knowing it would push Elis' buttons.

My alarm flashed in front of his smiling "See here, Junior..."

"Kidding. Ish. Hey, sorry, Elis, I've got my next seminar in half an hour."

"Okay. Tell the magnificent Dr. Shimizu hi from me."

"I will."

"And let her know, if she's ever up this way, I make a splendid tour guide for visiting scientists. After-hours companionship included at no extra charge."

"Sure will. And here, you can tell Geir about this for me." I flashed him a couple centimeters' worth of rose-gold lace near my armpit.

He bit his lower lip in a variation on his usual devilish smile-charming, if calculatedly so. "Ach. You and the old man, though, Arden, really?"

I conjured my inner Vega Hazan for just a moment of drama. "Oh, hell, yes."

After we'd rung off, I kept thinking about it. Even after a delicious seafood dinner and mojitos out with a couple of young crewmen, as I administered the do-it-myself purified water and barrier cream spa treatment. I could imagine worse things than putting the globetrotting life in my rearview. I'd seen Tierra del Fuego, and I could live without Namibia, especially if the Forest of Arden could ever be a long-term option instead.

Chapter 26

County Donegal

Geir didn't ring me back that night or the next morning: frustrating, although not uncommon for my selkie folk. I took the opportunity to stay connected with others closer to the North Sea than I could get right now. Noemi almost made my mouth water with live video captures, playing tourist before she moved on to her next assignment, across the planet in Vega's and my old stomping ground of Perth. She'd gone all the way up to Unst, where many coastal Viking sites had been lost to the tsunami, but a new one unearthed; inland there were still several fascinating digs and a seventeenth-century castle.

Stefek sent a wonderful capture of his own from twenty thousand feet, with the sky below him and the Belgian coastline above. (I flashed back in wonder to the moment, approaching Aberdeen Beach, when I'd fleetingly forgotten which side of the water's surface was my expected habitat.) He'd chosen a sample spec track option to please his airline pilot father, and liked it more than he'd expected so far. He was just flying triphibious hovers, but a new Francophone UFPK buddy had gotten clearance to take him up in her fighter craft.

Vega was living the good life, too, enjoying teaching as well as the challenging research environment. It had been a while since she'd been surrounded by people as smart as herself. She'd switched apartments, and gave me the quick video tour of her funky little kitchen and balcony, the dreary mist outside shooting a pang of longing through my belly. Turning the camera link on herself, she showed off the minuscule ringlets that had grown out enough for her to have them shaped into a soft fade, the ends lightened a shade or two on top, still dark on the sides. I took a turn; she praised my tan lines and saltwater highlights. We compared notes on the ethnic dishes we'd enjoyed since leaving Shetland. She persisted in asking about the delicious ethnic boy options in Miami, even knowing I'd disappoint her.

"I don't doubt you have some stories, though, ma." I laughed. "You and that sexy hair."

"Girl," she answered with a Brynja-worthy chuckle. "Para tu info, that's why you didn't get the bedroom tour. Gentleman caller, down for the count and definitely not within dress protocol."

I giggled. "Is he a doctor, too?"

"Researcher, not M.D., but yeah."

"Yeah? UF or native?"

"Local. Ish. A Scot, if you can believe that."

"Behold the power of the rolled Rs."

"Yeah, I guess that makes two of us.."

"Well, I'm glad it's good there."

The mischief faded from her eyes, but the shine remained. "You know, mija, I think I might love it. Early days, but I've been toying with letting the year run out here and applying to stay."

"Wow," I breathed. "Good for you, doc."

She flashed her usual flippant grin. "Stop by on your way back to Gary and the fam."

"I'm not kidding, then, put me on your calendar for the end of September."

Time was flying; I'd be heading that way before I knew it. Social time and work kept me beyond busy until Geir finally rang me back during the next morning's seminar--interrupting the Forest of Arden daydreams that kept interrupting a colleague's proposal on adding a wave farm off the Everglades coast.

I have missed You dearly and there is lovely News, dearest new Love.

Great sorry i cant call Will ring as soon as im out of work

That's quite all right. It will keep.

Meantime imagine the kiss im thinking of sending you right now

I am. Now and always.

I had every intention of ringing him back at lunchtime, but Shimizu nabbed me on the way out.

"Remind me, when's your turn in that hot seat and what are you telling us about?" she asked.

"Um. A week from Monday. Ecotoxicology studies in the reclaimed Keys areas."

"Right. I'd like to ask you to switch times with Keller."

"Sure, Dr. Shimizu, no worries. When is his?"

"It's, ah, at 1900." Her brows edged upward.

"Tonight?" I laughed as soon as the wry line of her mouth seemed to indicate that was an option.

"You'd think he might be ready since he's repeating most of this stuff from last year, but... The materials he presubmitted have underwhelmed me, to say the least. And I know you're better-versed on the topic than any of these kids. I'd rather not waste the seminar time if we can help it."

My eyebrows shot higher than hers. "What topic?"

She smiled. "The Steyn Minimalist Rebreather."

"Oh. I'm happy to talk about trying it but… I mean, I haven't studied the specs or any of that."

"That's okay. All he has are a bunch of nodes on their existing marketing. We'll use that, you can give him whatever you've got so far on ecotoxicology, surfer boy won't lose his spot this time either, Congresswoman Velázquez-Keller will keep up our funding, and so on."

She'd never said whose place in the program I'd almost taken, but if I'd had to guess, I could have.

"I'd really appreciate it," she pressed.

"As much as I'm usually against enabling underperforming blond surfer boy types…" I dared to shrug, earning a short laugh. "Of course. Okay."

For the next five hours, I holed up in a quiet work area to prepare. Dr. Shimizu sent me up a coffee and a big fresh medianoche from our place around the corner, which helped me focus as much as anything could. Still, I found my thoughts and memories slipping away to Lerwick Harbor and making Raj Dessai jealous… watching Ysmay's fairytale airlock technology work somewhere out in Scalloway Bay… the cracked mask we'd left under Out Skerries… Vega Hazan's smile as she tried the remaining one, playing with a baby seal off beautiful Eshaness. I'd share what I could with my cohort, but obviously had to leave the best stuff out.

When I finally thought I'd pulled together something worthy of the program, I checked the time, expecting to have to make a run for it. Only 1815. I tried ringing Geir back. I'd timed it as well as usual, managing to miss him again--but now that I'd started, I really wanted to hear his lovely News. On a whim, I tried the twins' shared ring next (the one registered to Ysmay, though Berenys nearly always answered it), instead of Lachlan's.

The video link came alive in a blur of motion, backlit by a periwinkle twilight sky. Crazy North Sea summer hours.

"Hey. I hope I'm not ringing you too late. Geir doesn't care what time I try to call, and then I—just didn't think."

"Och, I wasn't sleeping. No worries. Hi from County Donegal," Berenys answered, coming into focus with a familiar little toss of her head: off-center in the video frame, wind-tangled hair loose around her perfect face, with clouds tilting distinctively back and forth behind her. She was out on a boat.

"I guess he's within now? Or—below, if they have that there? He said there was news."

"Yes. He said to tell you sorry if he missed you, but… it was that important." She smiled. "Wait. Here… Have a look."

Her creative expertise didn't extend to camera handling. I fought near-nausea at the jostling shift from light to dim, as she went below the deck of a nice modern small craft. The camera link steadied, proving once and for all that Queen B was a wilder woman than even Vega Hazan as it showed the naked torso and three-quarter profile of the young man still asleep in a wildly unmade bunk.

If he was young. Despite the chestnut hue of the dark tousled hair, and the charming cinnamon-sugar freckles gilding his wiry sleek muscles and dreamy bone structure, the placement of the long-lashed closed eyes and the delicacy of the slightly-open pale lips made my own skin tingle in recognition.

"He's called Tadhg McNamara." She laughed under her breath. "As if he were an ordinary person. But as you can see…"

"I sure can. Is it just him? Or is that where they've all gone?" I asked, finding myself grinning, too.

"The latter, so it seems."

"How many?"

"Thirty-eight," she breathed, eyes appropriately round. "Between the Maghera caves and those who've been hiding in nearby towns."

Her quiet voice—or perhaps the thrill of recounting the discovery, as she sat on the bunk's edge with her hip against his leg—was enough to make her lover stir. She brushed the hair back from his reluctantly open hazel eyes, murmured to him in selkiese, showed him her ring display.

"Oh." His smiling brogue was slurred with sleep. "Good morning, Miami. Is it morning?"

"No." Berenys giggled.

"Hi, County Donegal." I chuckled too, warmly remembering the much cuter finboy who'd curled my toes with his softly rolled R, once upon a time when he called me California. "Look, if you guys are busy, don't let me keep you. I can get the details from Geir later."

"It's okay." Berenys laughed again, bending so they both went out of the frame. There was a little more whispering. In another moment, she was back on deck.

"So," I dared tease her. "Does it turn out it's really called shenanigans if he's Irish?"

I caught a Geir-ish hint of smile as the camera bounced around. But the video came to rest on her face again in time to show a less convincing next smile. "The Irish ones at least like different things. He's hardly older than you, though, so."

"Well... Surely he's not the only finman in town..."

The smile turned another shade cooler. "Not quite, but... It's no better proportions than at home, so of course, the few men likely worth knowing already have someone. Not that I couldn't steal one... but that's not very nice, even for me."

Long-distance selkie communication was so much clunkier than the low-tech, in-person kind. I was still trying to find words that wouldn't make things worse, when her eyes seemed to meet mine directly through the camera link.

"You know you needn't worry about Geir here, though. When your first husband was halfway round the world and surrounded by beautiful women, that was different. This one you can trust."

She watched me look like a fish trying to breathe air for a good ten seconds before she added a soft, smug "Oops."

The expression that finally bubbled through my tight teeth and lips was in her language, not either of mine. Although I'd never said it before, I could be pretty sure I'd gotten the meaning and the sound right by the way it smacked the bitchy look off her face. As soon as I'd seen that, I cut off the ring.

I needed to get to my presentation, but I couldn't go anywhere like this. I slipped out onto the floating walkway, stomach churning.

I didn't know how long I'd stood there listening to waves and gulls before my ring pulsed—not long enough for me to feel any calmer. Fortunately, I resisted the temptation to chuck it over the railing.

Dr s getting concerned youre not back, Karima had messaged me.

18:58. Shite. *On my way sorry*

I ran to the restroom first, splashed the cold sweat off my hot face, deliberately ignored my wild-eyed reflection and probably unprofessional hair, rushed upstairs.

It wasn't Berenys' emotional state, or even her childish way of acting it out, that threw me—I got all that. The small matter of selkie marriage vows I didn't recall anyone taking, though...

"Thank you for joining us," Dr. Shimizu greeted me when I tried to sneak in the back. "We're ready for you."

I felt her earlier indication of confidence in me slipping through my sweaty fingers as her black eyes poised, ready to dissect me for answers.

"I'm sorry," I murmured, even as I stood up straighter. "Family emergency."

The scalpel-stroke of her raised brow reminded me she knew I didn't have much in the way of family.

"I hope Judge Araujo's okay?"

"She's fine." I sighed. "This is the extended family with the rebreathers, actually."

"Wow," she answered, "those guys are awfully accident-prone."

Then she tilted her head toward the waiting podium.

Geir rang me back while we were still in the session: first a pulse requesting a voice connection, which I regretfully declined in mid meandering question from none other than Lennox Keller, who of all people ought to know this stuff already. I couldn't reply to the follow-up written message either, until I sat down with a weak-kneed little thud I hoped no one around me heard.

B told me what she said, and knows she had no Right. Sorry. Please Answer when you can.

I sighed. *Not mad tesoro just still at work*

He just pulsed affirmative, rather than bother me further.

The kids were off to get dinner after. Even though I was starving and I loved everything on the menu at Karima's mom's place, I couldn't join them. Instead, I grabbed a nutrition bar, refilled my water, and took a deep breath before reactivating my ring.

"She says you sound like an old Danish fisherman," Geir greeted me softly. "Well done."

I couldn't help laughing. "She did not say that."

"Shouldn't have said any of it. I'm sorry she did."

"Nah, you have nothing to apologize for."

"But," he said, unsmiling velvet gaze holding mine.

I'd never experienced such a desperate craving for anyone's touch. Not out of any romantic motivation; my inability to feel what he felt, know what he knew, galled me almost like lacking a limb must feel.

"Okay. But... When it's between two selkies, are there even wed-dings? Or is it just sort of a... done deal?"

He looked away for a long, quiet moment.

"You've known all this time that we old ones give ourselves completely, no other way. So no, between two of our kind... there's not much need for magic words."

His eyes shone as he raised them again to mine: without his characteristic mischief, without apology either. "But you don't come from where or when we do. I've had no such expectations. Go on calling this anything you like."

My heartbeat echoed through all my limbs. But the truth was, finding out the number on the gauge now made little difference. I'd been swimming at this depth for months. It was more than safe here; I knew I never wanted to leave. I'd even worn this silly zirconia to give people that exact impression.

He was right. I could call it whatever I liked. We both knew what it was.

As usual, we left the ring connection open while we fell asleep together on opposite sides of the Atlantic. I was more in than out when he breathed one last thing in my ear.

"Asleep?"

"Uh uh."

"I meant to say... I met a young fellow last night. He's always lived here, but his dad came here from Norway, only sixty years or so ago. And left other finfolk behind."

"Okay."

"So there's still likely someone there for you to find, my jo."

It wasn't so urgent now, not like before I knew she'd come from Orkney anyway, but I smiled to imagine he was right nonetheless.

"Cool," I murmured. "Do you think you guys will go over there too? Maybe after you check off all the boxes in Ireland?"

"I don't know… but if we do, consider yourself invited."

I didn't keep back a short sigh. "Okay."

"Meantime, dream about it." His soft tone of suggestion didn't make my body want to sleep at all, but my brain was tired enough to obey. "Maybe we'll find each other there."

"No way that works when you're thousands of kilometers apart."

"If it ever did, you'd be the one to make it happen."

At least, with his soft regular breaths in my ear the only time I really stirred, I got several refreshing hours' sleep trying. In the morning, my alarm interrupted the stately flight of a phoenix low over darkened Vaila Sound, trailing glittering sparks. I opened my eyes to see her fiery gold and orange reflected in the sky and water of morning on this side of the world.

My harried performance hadn't satisfied Dr. Shimizu. When I arrived for the day's dive workout, she pulled me aside without much explanation and turned me around to take a nearly three-hour exam in the other building. Facts, theory, problem-solving, and the like, it seemed like a variation on what I'd taken on arrival in Miami. Then again, that time had been a blur, and so was this. I could only do my best and cling to the hope that she wasn't reconsidering my disputed place in the cohort.

Upon submitting the test to her securely on-grid, I got a message back to meet her in her office at 1600 to discuss the results. Only then did I sigh with the relief of remembering Thursdays were independent research and study, not seminar afternoons.

Research and study weren't happening today. I went for a short swim on my own, had a big piece of rosewater-mango-mint tres leches and a glass of Chardonnay for lunch, then caught a fitful nap before the appointment.

"Hi, kiddo," Shimizu said without more than a glance up from the screen. "Give me a second to look this counter-proposal over for Kenneth. We're making headway."

"Of course." I leaned against the firmly cushioned back of my chair, watching the jewel-bright anthias, butterflyfish, and gobies gliding around her beautiful saltwater aquarium for two or three minutes.

"Sorry about that," she said eventually, sharp eyes extra big behind her blue-blocking work lenses as she looked up. "Are you all right?"

"Didn't get a lot of sleep. No worries."

She nodded. "I do seem to recall higher than average midnight oil consumption running in the family."

"Yep."

"Well, you know what they say. The flame that burns twice as bright burns half as long."

The thought took up my whole consciousness for a few seconds: the same amount of energy, burning out at different rates. Maybe that drew some selkie folk to humankind, the intensity of an unmanaged spark of life blazing away so many times hotter and faster than theirs. Bright and beautiful and dangerous. *Ardiente.* Dad had nicknamed me better than he knew.

I blinked at her a moment. "They say that?"

"I think Lao Tzu said that, actually."

Ardencita, echoed faint and smiling in my head.

"I always felt that way about Oliver," she went on, almost as if she'd heard him too. "After he'd started working in Kristiansand and caught the Storegga Slide II bug, particularly. I'm sorry to admit, it was pretty riveting."

"In the forest of the night," I murmured absently, sure that was what he'd say right now, if he'd burned slower. *William Blake, Ardencita.*

"Anyway. We digress."

I blinked again. "Sorry."

"Not at all. Listen, Arden, there's good news and bad news..."

My stomach squirmed around like I'd swallowed a couple of her pretty fish whole. "Okay?"

"I know I was vague about why I needed you to take the test this morning. I hope you'll allow me that, in the name of scientific accuracy. But here it is: Given the drive, talent, instincts, and leadership you've been showing, last night I went back through your files. Long story short, I hadn't considered the pretest you took when you got here, since you'd been placed already."

And now she realized I'd flunked it, I didn't guess aloud. Maybe I could sneak in a quick trip home before my next assignment. I wondered if I could manage to get Brussels or even London.

She smiled faintly. "Your scores were higher than plenty of young crewmen's at the end of the first year. Today's results put you squarely with the Year Two cohort, which is where I'd like to recommend placing you instead of wasting more of your time. It's infuriating to realize that if not for the stupid bureaucracy, Oliver could've seen you find your calling. Well. The bureaucracy and the distinct lack of love lost between Thierry and him, I suppose."

"Wait, did they know each... Oh, shoot--" I put on a cheesy French accent like I semi-remembered Dad doing. "Les Forces Unis, Division de Proctologie... Was that Dr. Farrah?"

"As usual, he wasn't wrong on the facts." She chuckled. "Thierry's quite an asshole."

I laughed, too, for a moment before sobering. "Even if he weren't, I'm grateful to have been here at the same time as you, instead."

"I agree." She gave me a wistful smile, setting fins and tails flipping around in my belly all over again. "Unfortunately, that's the bad news. Well. Fine for you, really, bittersweet for me. The day before yesterday, I got confirmation that the new full-time program head will start the week after next. I'd taken leave from the Academy for the semester already, all of us thinking it would take them longer to fill the position. So I asked around a little and as of early this morning, I've invited myself to jump in over in Stavanger, Norway to help with their building back. As much as I enjoy blowing stuff up and establishing a micro-reef, they have some very old buildings worth preserving. And it's good old Lars Aasland heading it up, who was the liaison with our MaGI people once upon a time in Kristiansand, so..."

Huge tears splashed over before I realized they were coming. She trailed off. The Vega in my head was not amused.

"Stavanger's, like, big oil country, right?" I tried to selkie-style explain them away. "Isn't the whole repeat Storegga Slide down to them? I..."

She gave me the samurai eye.

"No. Dr. Shimizu. Please, is there any way I could wait to start the second year with this same cohort, and go with you in the meantime--like as an intern or something? Generalist? I don't care..."

"What?" Now her smile was tender and bewildered. "I'm not being clear. You'll do just as well with Dr. Peretz. He's outstanding. Young, on fire, works almost as hard as you do. I'll give him an individual report on your plans and progress."

I wrestled with my breath for a moment. "No," I admitted. "It's just... if I could be doing anything like the same kind of work, closer to Shetland. I never would have left there, if that had been an option."

She smiled differently. "Is this to do with someone unnaturally gorgeous whom you don't usually mention in a professional context?"

I caught a few more tears on the side of my palm. "I miss the islands and the North Sea almost as much."

She chuckled, reached over the desk to pat the back of my hand with the ring I'd been wearing.

"I mean... I understand if it's not possible." I swallowed, not really dislodging the cherrystone-sized lump from my throat. "I love it here too. I just had to ask."

Chapter 27

Adventura

Shimizu didn't even need a wand; she just flexed her magical fingers. And Karima was so ecstatic at the chance to work with rockstar Yaron Peretz that she was willing to let her new diving coach leave for a few months, as long as I promised I'd see her next May at the latest. We made a bet as to the date of Lennox Keller bombing out of the program for good, and she vowed to keep me updated on everyone else I'd enjoyed getting to know there as well.

Geir's flight from Belfast landed in Stavanger a couple of hours before ours from Oslo, the last hop in our long journey. I found him as much by selkie sense as by his ring signal, though I made a show of following the latter for the sake of my traveling companion. We spotted him dozing in a waiting-area seat, Alasdair's cap down over his eyes, looking more like a worn-out unaccompanied minor than a powerful mythical beast.

"I see he has his bag there under his feet already," Shimizu said. "I'll get ours and meet you down by the pods, yes? Hopefully, that's far enough to walk off the damn transatlantic sitting still."

"Hey, Sleeping Beauty," I breathed, bending to wake him with a little kiss. In half a heartbeat he was fully alert, his strong arms warm around me. I found myself burying quiet tears against the sweet home scent of his neck and shoulder.

It wasn't just the weeks away from his Shetland waters, or how hard it was for him to fly, even the added stress of hoping his faked documentation was good enough for international travel. He didn't hide the rest from me either, the bleak gray grief I'd put him through this whole time. The color and warmth flooding back into his consciousness now, with his gentle hands and eyes and breath drinking in the texture, brightness, and perfume of my hair, only made his recent suffering more poignant.

"Sorry," I murmured.

He stroked my cheek dry, admiring my sun-deepened skin color. He hadn't been asking for an apology. The same hand caressed my hair, the side of my neck, then my newly toned shoulder, arm, and back, coming to rest on the curve from waist to hip. He was warmly illuminated with pride and wonder that I felt so different, more than just physically, after only a few months.

"Maybe it's how much I've learned…" He liked that thought. He liked that curve, too. I giggled under my breath. "Or… maybe just the Cuban food…"

He laughed. A couple kilos either way couldn't matter less to him compared to the rest.

"Anyway." He nudged my chin up with as much of a little kiss as either of us dared here or now. "Too bad I've missed the Cuban favorites, but let me treat you and your Dr. Shimizu to something Norwegian…"

From all I'd read, local cuisine seemed full of things a finman would enjoy, but Dr. Shimizu had more adventurous ideas. Geir had occasionally been to fun international restaurants in Edinburgh, but it was definitely his first time for a hole-in-the-wall Japanese noodle shop such as the one where they greeted Shimizu like a long-lost relative. We both wanted her expert recommendations.

"You know me." Anything she thought I'd love, no ingredient questions asked, was my standard order. She smiled, told the guys behind the counter something, then turned to ask what Geir wanted.

"I'm the boring one," he said, a hand on the small of my back radiating pride and the acute awareness of how long it had been since he'd gotten to touch what he'd always considered one of my best curves. "Anything that ever swam, nothing too spicy."

But the further impressions accompanying that light touch, those mildly-spoken words, tended toward wanting things far more spicy than boring. I shot him a panicked glare, softened by a smothered giggle; my only thought was a plea not to get up to selkie mischief in front of my boss.

"My kind of boring," Shimizu said with a smaller but no less pleased smile, unaware of the exchange.

With her eyes and ears off us to place the order, Geir poked me softly just below the hollow of my collarbone. "You know damn well who's the troublemaker here, Generalist," he breathed in my ear, keeping most of his laugh on the inside.

"So," she said to him as we sat back to await our noodles. "Grandmother's house in Miami didn't seem like the place to ask Arden about this, but--May I skip straight to the awkward personal questions?"

"Sure," Geir said, echoing my guilty laugh with an unfazed smile.

"Okay. What's the name of this North Sea population or ethnicity? Smaller stature, fair skin and dark hair, and--" she gestured a horizontal space--"with the eyes?"

My heart sped up. "What?" I laughed again. "You mean, like your average Japanese person?"

She gave a quick shake of her head, amused but dismissive. "You haven't noticed how completely this dashing gentleman could be your mother's younger brother? How much they look like each other, and no one else I've ever met?"

"Uh. Dad had no pictures of my mother," I stalled.

Her brows lifted briefly. "You never tried to look her up?"

I shook my head. "By the time it occurred to me, it seemed there was nothing to find." That was basically true. Now I guessed there'd be photos out there somewhere, but who knew what name she'd gone by at the time.

Muttering at Dad, Shimizu tapped some commands with her ring hand, and I held my breath. Tricky to track down a fairytale with modern tech, Lachlan had once pointed out; you could, though, if you knew just where to look.

Her bright eyes found mine again, fingers paused for a moment. "Or maybe I shouldn't assume you'd want to see one."

I took a delayed gulp of air. "No. I would."

At the end of a single nod, she kept her focus lowered, working on her image search.

"Colleagues may or may not have suggested a long-denied preference for Asians when he started upnoding pictures with your mother," she said lightly as she looked through older and older data.

"I didn't think he denied his preference for much of anybody," I muttered.

"Who says he did the denying." She smiled. "Shark, remember. Extremely poor survival rate in captivity." Geir chuckled just barely, under his breath.

So I wasn't the only one who hadn't been forthcoming about her love life. Good for her, though, if she'd averted a direct hit from the category-three or -four Oliver. Not everyone in the storm's path had been so fortunate.

"Anyway. Small and dark and North Sea, that's a Pictish type," Geir said steadily into the lull.

Shimizu still didn't look up. "The Picts weren't just in Scotland?" Her left brow angled sharper than the right as she projected what she'd found, semi-transparent for all three of us to see and manipulate if we wished. "Here. I think this was the one time that they were on-again while I was there to witness the beginning of the Araujo affinity for Pictish people first-hand."

She'd kept not just one image, but a series. It had been a formal event in what I supposed was Kristiansand, on a terrace open to the night sky, city lights behind them. Dad in immaculate black tie, not so much as a gray hair yet--within a few years of my current age.

Photography was so much more precise and objective than shared memories could be. She'd been as small as Brynja, especially tiny next to my tall father, even in her glittering high-heeled sandals. For this occasion, her dark hair had been streaked iridescent midnight blue, cut in a short sharp bob. Closer shots showed the spectacular length of her mascaraed lashes, the touch of silvery shadow to match her skimpy evening dress. When she flashed a model's sexy smile for the camera, her eyes were opaque. But when she laughed at something my father had said, they were as bright as her dress, so focused on him that the champagne flute tilted dangerously in her delicate hand. The desire to know whether she'd had a windchime giggle like Berenys' or a smoky wisp of a laugh like Ysmay's, or something else altogether, was a real physical ache.

I paused for an uncounted time on them slow dancing, her head against his chest, silver-lidded eyes sweetly closed. Her arms encircled his waist, his long hands rested around her bare shoulders. In thirty years, I'd never seen the same peace on my father's face as when he looked down at her.

"Who's this lovely lass?" Geir saved me from falling awkwardly apart, reaching a respectful fingertip into the projection to center and zoom in on another person in the photo.

I'd been too focused on Nereiður to notice the young Noa Shimizu: nearly as dazzling in her long blossom-embroidered sheath, cropped haircut showing off her eyes and the sparkling sweep of her earrings down her graceful neck.

"It was Dr. Lass, even a few hundred years ago when this was taken, thank you," she said, tart edge blunted by a faint sweet smile. She had no more immunity to finman wiles than the rest of us.

"Of course." He chuckled. "No offense intended."

"None taken, lovely lad."

She showed him another image of herself with my father--neither one quite as young, both still striking, a candid snap on the deck of a gorgeous yacht. She held a hazel-eyed, café-con-leche complected and wildly curly-headed toddler in organza and sequins, the lights of a different city behind them. Dad's gaze was far away. I smiled to recognize Miami's most adorable black Santa in the near background. Geir was the one fighting stinging eyes when the server arrived with our three steaming dishes.

Mine was milky pink, unidentifiable, not of this world; I finished every delightful drop. Geir continued charming the hell out of Shimizu with his game and smiling attempt to be taught chopstick use, although he ultimately went for a fork. He thought the richly marine-scented broth was the best invention since single malt. He wouldn't hear of me or her paying for the meal.

"I see now," she said under her breath, when he'd gotten up to take care of the check. "Why you'd drop everything and cross a couple oceans for this boy."

"Thanks." I smiled. "Hopefully it's as clear to you as it is to me how highly he thinks of you, as well."

She smiled, too. "And he may look like your mother, but he's not. If you don't mind my saying, she was--disquieting. I never really worried for Oli before he met her, like we all started to after."

"Yep," I murmured.

"But Geir is more like a river rock that fits in your hand just right... what a peaceful old soul, young as he is."

It wasn't too hard to smother a laugh with a slight sigh of admiration. "Obviously, I didn't know her, but you pretty much have him figured out over one bowl of noodles, doc."

Shimizu nodded once, then tapped her ring. "Quite coincidentally, it looks like I don't need you to come in tomorrow. I'll be busy getting set up with the local team."

The sky was still pretty light, and the locator showed my new address about a half hour away on foot. *Our* first new address. We set the pod full of our luggage to meet us there. Then we walked home hand in hand, enjoying our first sight, sound, and smell of the city as much as we had our first taste.

The pod was parked right outside our door, but I struggled to unlock the apartment with my ring: partly due to normal tech hiccups trying to access someplace new for the first time, mostly because of the troublesome kisses up the exposed back of my neck and the hands deliciously wandering elsewhere.

"Are you trying not to picture carrying me over the threshold?" I said with a giggle as I finally got the door open. "Or is this, like, reverse psychology, where you want me to know you know I don't want to see that?"

He chuckled too, arms tightening around my waist from behind. "Whichever."

I stepped inside. When I turned to face him and offered both hands, I definitely intended to invite him into the recurring Miami day-dream where he lifted me off my feet in the shower for as long as he liked instead.

"Modern girl," he acquiesced with a smile.

We took all the time we wanted giving each other the selkie na-turist grand tour of our little kitchen, sitting area, bath, and bed. We didn't have anywhere to be in the morning. Even better, now that we were both in a place with grocery and takeaway delivery drones, we had nowhere to be the whole next day, except together. (Oh, thank you, fairy godmother.)

It was Vega, not me, who attended a ball at the palace a few weeks later. Or near enough: when members of her Barts team were honored at a gala for their contributions to the tsunami relief effort, they brought her along to represent UFE. I sat up in bed late that evening when she rang me *Just drinks with friends downtown ya know*

I opened a knockout photo of the group, dressed to the nines: Vega in a side-slit deep plum halter gown encrusted in beads and sequins, with plush forbidden-fruit lips to match and a coordinating glass of wine.

Damnnnn, I rang her back.

Damn right

I dragged my eyes away from my beautiful friend to examine the rest of the image. *Scuse me is that Laurence Huang two people over from you?!*

YES Was handing out awards Hes a columbia med grad too We got to chat a bit Totally fine and normal friday evening stuff

I'd probably known, at some point, the First Gentleman of the US had attended Vega's alma mater some years before her. I couldn't imagine my evening-gowned picture with a world leader's spouse splashed all over the grid, but it suited her admirably.

Keep living the dream doc

Same to you mijita

My own work here wasn't exactly the dream, nothing like Miami had been and would be. Not that I'd complain--to have my North Sea and my true love back for this unexpected season was an absolute gift. The lack of real work for him was probably more maddening, but he kept our apartment spotless, hit the beach every day, and shopped for tiny treats and treasures for me rather than complain either. The closest I got to diving, most days, was the submerged foundations and flooded sublevels of our old buildings; it required taking a lot of tiny precise measurements, correspondingly meticulous record-keeping, and I couldn't lean on Karima.

She was hardly counting the days for my return, either. While she remained the gem of the cohort academically, Dr. Peretz wasn't satisfied with her diving progress and had assigned a serious regimen of additional physical therapy and training. She averaged five hours of sleep, six on a really good night. That was okay: if he'd asked, she would have spun straw to gold for him, or slain a hydra, or brought him down the moon. She put in daily extra study to be double sure she'd never fail to thrill him in written work, presentations, or discussions. Her future honoring at some glittering gala seemed inevitable to me.

Two more of my impressive sisterhood of saving the planet joined us soon, at the start of October. Both of them were giddy: Ysmay about her first flight in a big passenger jet, Berenys at the thought of exploring a city that seemed so huge and intense. Edinburgh was technically bigger, but not as dense or shiny, and so *Scottish*. Today was their birthday, they giggled to us in the pod; so to gild the lily, we took them for mid-afternoon cake and Champagne.

Ysmay wanted to unwind after that, at the flat they'd rented. Berenys had just begun to wind. We split up the party, Geir going with Ysmay, Berenys pulling me in her wake. Downtown Stavanger wouldn't know what hit it.

She insisted we go dancing, and was equally adamant that we dress the part. I was content to browse shops with her and see, but I couldn't have cared less about being seen. I slipped on my cute jeans and black top from Inverness, annoyed that I must have put the shirt in the dryer by mistake at some point in Miami, but I still thought it looked all right. Queen B was unmoved.

"Do you not understand, I need only say I want it on my birthday, and he won't care what you spend?" she pressed.

I sighed. Although I wasn't about to ask Lachlan to buy me anything, I guessed I could splurge a little. Around here, when I'd been out of uniform, I'd generally dressed down to match my favorite dinner companion, or been undressed entirely. But it wasn't just the money--after a packed half-day in and out of dive suits and uniforms, I was too tired to bother changing anymore.

Humoring her turned out to be worth it, just to witness her linguistic shapeshifting skills. She spoke mostly Norn, but as she interacted with the salesladies, she modified her words and phrases to sound more like theirs. They seemed to view her as a visitor from some more exotic part of Norway, which wasn't so far off. All the waters of the North Sea touched; it had no borders. Maybe my success at Ishtalian and other approximations sprang from a similar source.

She wanted to get our makeup done properly, and pedicures, a poignant bit of luxury since hers would be undone next time she went within her sealskin. I still agreed to the chance at being pampered. The salon workers expressed cute surprise at our matching selkie toes. When they heard she planned to go dancing, they asked if she knew their friends' club, and showed her captures. Smitten at first sight, she gave me her most irresistible "challenge accepted" smile.

The most beautiful thing I found in the boutique she picked next was a wonderful sweater tunic Brynja might wear, rich chestnut brown with copper and green and dark shiny threads worked in. Berenys sniffed and let me keep it in the basket, but it wasn't for tonight. She selected instead a floor-grazing black mesh duster, suited to someone who sang much better than I could. I sighed acquiescence with her superior skills, and let her accessorize me as well. For herself, she chose dresses so small and heels so high that Nereiður would have completely approved.

The crowd at the wild little hole in a downtown wall she'd chosen certainly approved, as well. Berenys moved like the creature of legend she was, glowing, weightless, and graceful, among people of every skin and hair color, expression and orientation, shape and size, style and origin, virtually all wanting a dance with the faerie queen. Not as if they were wrong.

I was happy to grab the seat that finally opened up at the corner of the long low-lit bar to one side, be the old working lady with my glass of soda water, and enjoy the prime people-watching. I caught B slipping in moves she'd learned from Vega and me, once upon a time in Shetland.

She came over for two pretty, pale pink free drinks. I set down the water, clinked my tall slim glass against hers.

"Happy sweet one-seventy-nine," I breathed, though by then we were into the early morning after her birthday.

She tossed her hair, laughing, and took her glass back out onto the dance floor.

Whatever it was tasted of fresh berries, and felt like aquavit. I sipped at it for a good long time, possibly annoying the selkie-sized server whose sky blue crew cut matched her bright eyes by switching back to soda afterward. She spoke to me in Norwegian. I answered in something North Sea enough that she seemed to accept it as no more unusual than the rest of what could be seen or heard here. Score.

I'd had my eyes off my charge long enough to make me nervous during the brief exchange. Someone else caught my eye before I could find her, though: a man, just walking off the crowded dance floor toward the bar, which meant my general direction. A long braid, so light it was almost cream-colored, snaked forward over his muscular slim shoulder. His unsmiling face was an even fairer white-ivory; the eyes languidly scanning the room were big and wide-set, but strikingly pale.

Before I fully formulated the pulse-quickening question to myself, he spotted me perched alone at my corner of the bar. The unsettling silvery eyes rested on my face a long moment before he started purposefully toward me. I couldn't imagine anyone noticing me when Berenys was in the spotlight.

Maybe at least he could be a hybrid like me and be able to tell us something about the finfolk side of his family. His features, beautiful almost to the point of androgyny, were too perfect for him to be anything else, except maybe a marble statue of some classical god. If he did turn out to be one of them, even in part, he was the first who didn't make me think for a second that he was too young to drink here.

As he came closer, I realized he was taller than any of our finmen, an average man's height where I'd come from. He just hadn't seemed that way while surrounded by young Nordic humans. He wore barely noticeable glasses, with no rims and no glare. That was something else new, unless you counted Elis' fashion choices.

He walked right up to the bar, taking his tidal-pool pale eyes off me only long enough to order another one of my pink cocktail and something in a smaller glass for himself. His voice was the farthest thing from androgynous, low as far-off thunder. I watched him pay the blue-haired faerie, who scanned his ring with wide eyes and an entranced hint of smile.

As he took the glasses, I noticed intricate tattoos circling his wrists. Not just fun doodles like Lachlan and Karima had. I glimpsed more blue ink at his open collar. Normally I didn't care for that more extensive turn-of-the-century look, but on him, I found them fascinating. Then again, his might well have been from the turn of some other century than ours.

He set both drinks down. Without a word, he reached one hand still cold from holding a glass to tilt my chin up so he could study my face. As intensely clear as any impression I'd ever had from Brynja, the consuming curiosity I provoked in him nearly flattened me back against the bar stool.

First Norwegian selkie contact or not, I looked him right in his wide light eyes and thought explicitly about Geir.

He lowered his gaze fractionally to one side with a quiet, deep laugh. When he lifted his eyes again the next moment, it was to assure me that his powerful response to the sight of me was not sexual at all. As he touched each of my features with cool, respectful fingertips, I saw the hairline, brows, eyes, cheekbones, and jaw of the Nereiður in his memory overlaid and lined up with mine.

I gulped, nodded unnecessarily, and thought an open-ended question toward him.

With his eyes still unwavering on mine, he took both my unresisting hands. My fingers tightened reflexively as, through him, I got to hear my mother's crystalline laughter for the first time, feel the warm silk of her skin.

She'd left someone else for him, desperate to experience the tall boy with the white hair. Geir wasn't nearly old enough to remember her with these luxuriant uncut dark chestnut tresses, this softness to her face and limbs, although the restless spirit already sparkled in her eyes and lent an edge to her every expression and movement.

No sooner had I begun to grasp all that she'd been to him then, than he shared with me some fragment of the utter emptiness that had followed. His adored first everything had stayed only a little while, as they reckoned time, until she'd left him without explanation. It had been a long time, even to him, before he dared offer to anyone else the shattered heart he'd had to sweep up and painstakingly reconfigure. Since then he'd found love in whatever form he could, over the years. From the way her image echoed in his memory, I thought I understood that had eventually included the occasional on again, off again between them, which did seem like her.

I was in his arms without another instant's thought: possibly even stupider than the way I'd fallen for Geir, who had hardly a dangerous bone in his body, but I could no more resist this man than he had once been able to resist my beastly-beautiful mother. He held me breathlessly close, laid his cheek against my hair, eventually pressed a gentle kiss to the spot where a tear fell on the crown of my head.

I considered that just maybe, if a tall, unusual boy much further down the list had been granted a selkie lifespan to get over her, things could have been clearer between us too.

"Sorry," I found myself telling him. "Both for misunderstanding your intentions a moment ago, and for… Her."

But he shook his pale head, smiling now, as we managed to let each other go. He answered in perfect British English, with just the faintest Nordic lilt. "One, I suppose you had every reason to think; the other is no fault of yours. Thank you for allowing me. My eyes are less reliable than my other senses; I could hardly believe them when I saw you. She didn't somehow make it all the way to America, though, did she?"

"I was born here," I answered, shaking my head, too. "Bergen. But raised in America, where my dad was from. I guess you can imagine why I didn't know her, or anything about who she was… who any of you are… until a few months ago."

His nod, his newly tender expression made me suspect he'd perceived a lot of that already, though I hadn't been aware of the exchange. He studied my features for a few moments more, but didn't pursue it. Selkie style, I allowed him to look, then to touch my hair with as reverent a hand as Geir ever had.

Nereiður had been lost to him, to anyone he knew, by the time he guessed I would have come on the scene. He'd heard of her death, not of my birth.

It occurred to me to wonder how long we'd stood there almost without words, what the blue-eyed bartender might think of our most unusual meeting.

Someone else wasn't pleased, anyway. I saw him being spun roughly around before I could register how small the intruding hand had been.

My defender was fairytale perfection, unbound raven hair waving down around her hips, fish-scale paillettes glinting on her minidress, lips and cheeks faintly flushed with indignation and dancing and the glass she still held. The shieldmaiden glare of displeasure ebbed as soon as she saw his face; a new expression, more difficult to define, flowed in slower underneath. Her embellished eyes widened to black pearls, and her petal lips fell slightly open. I noticed her pressing the fingertips of the left hand that had grabbed his shoulder against the base of the glass in her right, where ice cubes were still melting.

He drew a visible breath. "And you can only be one of Brynja and Kjaran's daughters," he said in their language, his quiet voice carrying under all the noise around us.

She stood motionless except for her hint of a nod, still taking in the impressive sight and the immense energy of him, and didn't touch the upturned hands he formally offered.

"I am Ióar of Sørreisa, the son of Hildr of Træna, the daughter of Hreidunn of Vega," he presented himself to her.

He watched her continuing to stare--while my own staring went unnoticed--long enough for me to get past the understanding of which name Nereiður must have pirated from his family history, and which one must sound borrowed from my own life just by astonishing coincidence, until I could remember where I'd heard his name approximated before. This was Brynja's elusive Norwegian counterpart: not Johan, as Lachlan had realized even then, but certainly the Fair in more than one sense of the word.

"Obviously. Only we didn't expect you'd be here. I'm Berenys," she answered him at last in whispery English. "Daughter of Brynja, daughter of Arinví, as you can already tell. From three tiny islands you wouldn't be able to tell apart."

He smiled and relaxed his hands to his sides. "Hi, Berenys. It's lovely to meet you. How are you finding my country?"

She smiled too, finally. "Much bigger than mine, so that's grand." She glanced around us. "This place is excellent."

"Is your sister here too?" Selkie twins were likely just a little less rare than selkie albinos, I imagined. He glanced a question my way, and added, "And--perhaps your brother?"

"Can't really go anywhere without Ysmay, can I. But--with this one, that's Bryn's little brother you mean, not ours," Berenys said with a tiny laugh or scoff, as if Ióar were not the first to make that mistake. "Arinví's fisher boy."

Ióar nodded as if he should have guessed right the first time. "He's the image of her."

"Geir, he's called."

Ióar's amazing eyes lingered fondly on my face again. "And Geir's beloved, daughter of my beloved, has a name also?"

"Arden Araujo of Monterey," I told him. "Daughter of Oliver of Aventura, son of Maite of Little Havana."

"Dr. Oliver..." he understood aloud, with a soft surprised laugh. "I see. Well met, Arden Araujo of Monterey."

Chapter 28

Cities Like Yours

Someone very young and rockstar-disheveled, waiting a few paces back for Berenys, lowered their chem-shadowed eyes at one neutral look from Ióar and melted away into the crowd.

For his part, our recent acquaintance seemed--improbably--not to have met any such new friends this evening. He was altogether alone in town right now, he told us as we walked up the quiet street toward the girls' flat.

Berenys kept her eyes straight ahead, tiny high-heeled shoes dangling balanced from two fingertips of her right hand.

"Brynja will be stunned we've met you. She supposed everyone here would be much further north, these days, if there was anyone left at all." Her low voice carried across the wet pavement; her faerie-light bare soles made no appreciable sound.

He shook his head. "I've four brothers and one little sister left, all in Bergen. I don't know of anyone else, anywhere in Scandinavia, anymore."

She did glance up at him then, and paused her small steps. "Wow."

"So I'm stunned I've met you, too," he said, matching her quiet tone as he held her gaze. Who knew how long since he'd seen a selkie woman he wouldn't refer to as a little sister, let alone one who was more Nereiður's heir than I'd ever be. For her part, I didn't think I'd imagined the slight tremble in her breath. I might as well still be in Miami for all they noticed.

"Are there still so many living in the British Isles?"

She held her head very straight. "Although we scarcely belong there either… You understand… sixty-four at last count. A few days ago. But they haven't gone all the way to the Isle of Man yet, so. Bryn hopes for a few more." She lowered her eyes and took a next step. "They're almost all my age or younger," she said to the glistening street in front of her pedicured selkie toes. "But. Twenty-five men and thirty-nine women who'll be stunned to meet you six as well, I'm sure. Well. You four, supposing your little sister must have spoken for one of you."

He didn't respond. We ended up walking the rest of the short way to the flat in the same shared, dazed quiet.

Ysmay, whose wide eyes peered around the door's edge before we could touch the knob, was a whole other story.

I'd never heard her have a complete conversation with anyone before. She'd apparently saved it all up for this guy. He effortlessly understood how dissimilar the identical sisters were, and seemed as delighted to talk to Ysmay as he had been not to say much of anything to Berenys. While the younger twin vanished for a lot longer than it would take to change clothes as she said she was doing, the older sister peppered him with questions in a whispery blend of English and Norn. Geir and I enjoyed the scene, sitting in the warm half-circle of each other's arms nearby. She wanted to know about lovers after Nereiður (selkies at first, earth girls more recently), and ensure there wasn't a current one; she examined with keen fascination his light eyes, his glasses, his tattooed wrists.

When he rolled his sleeves up for her, the tattoos were like some sort of ancient jewelry coming most of the way up to each elbow. I imagined the one around his neck would be like a matching collar. Ysmay finally lapsed into her usual quiet as her fingertips traced the swirling lines, the faded hue of well-loved denim; I considered how much upkeep there probably was, to maintain the designs at all on his ever-renewing skin. Different marine elements, kelp and shells and a sea fan, emerged from the complex patterns, now I viewed the design in more detail. His right arm had an octopus unfurling. It might have been cliché except that whoever had drawn them had done it all so exceptionally beautifully.

Geir knew the smile on Ióar's face because he'd worn it too, love and grief undimmed by the passage of time. But Ióar only answered Ysmay's unspoken remark, "One who couldn't resist drawing on all this blank white space."

Ysmay's tiny hand cradled the chiseled muscles of his forearm.

His eyes were tender, regarding her. "It wasn't meant to hurt me, but of course it did. Haven't you ever borne the same for love?... Then you know it was worth it so many times over, elskling."

I guessed she'd also asked by touch to examine what she'd spotted in his shirt pocket: he hesitated, fingers over his heart and whatever the object might be. But then, eyes still tide pool calm, he drew it out.

On his palm was a beautiful antique watch on a silvery chain with a few other things attached, like bits from long-lost charm brace-lets. I wouldn't have expected to see the only item close to the size of the watch: a faintly silvered, transparent disc small enough to fit even in Ysmay's palm. Though inactive, its enhanced negative charge still made it cling against her skin.

"You've got an immobilizer?" she said, her voice as neutral as his expression, but very soft.

The inevitable evil twin someone had developed within a few years of the tech that had saved Lachlan's life once upon a time below Out Skerries, they sure as hell weren't legal anywhere I'd been stationed before. I couldn't imagine peaceful and progressive Norway tolerated them either.

"I don't suppose I need to say the rest of the world isn't as safe as your beautiful little corner," he answered, matching her tone.

Rather to my surprise, Geir registered no real objection.

She shook her head without pulling her cautiously interested eyes away from the scary little object. "Can the--lightning strike me, or you, if I touch it wrong? Fry your own tech?"

He shook his head. "It's keyed to me, like a ring."

"Sounds like a great way to get yourself sent to jail for possession," I said quietly.

He picked up the device between his forefinger and thumb to hold it out in my direction, his features more like marble now than the heartbeat before. "If that's what you want."

"Of course I don't. I'm not law enforcement, anyway," I said, palm out. "Just, I know how it works."

He nodded. "It's worth being sure no one gets hurt unless they need to be."

I could only shrug. I no more wanted him to get caught with it than I wanted him ever to need to use it.

"Okay," Ysmay murmured, and moved on to the watch.

"Why haven't you had this repaired?" she demanded, after trying to wind it, then listening in vain for the whir of its gears.

He shook his head. "It belonged to my father. I've always feared they'd suppose I'd nicked it from some museum, and I'd lose it even if they didn't arrest me."

She didn't ask the next question in words; then again, I didn't need her to touch my hand to guess what she wanted.

"Ysmay," he said at first, with another little shake of his head. "It's very much older than you are. It's a treasure to me."

She held her ground, unblinking as the little cat she'd reminded me of before. Eventually, he unhooked it from the chain, pressed her child-sized fingers lightly around the case that nearly filled her open palm. Trust at first sight, or near enough.

Geir smiled, confident she'd do as she promised. The corners of her mouth turned up just barely in a satisfied little smile of her own as she slipped the watch into her pants pocket.

"Anyway, why shouldn't you have nice things?" Ysmay pressed. She touched his sleek gray jacket, hanging over the back of his chair. "I know what poor looks like. You're not."

"No, fortunately. But there's still a difference between an average working fellow and the kind of collector who'd own such a piece. Then, too, you know we don't want to invite questions, any of us."

She nodded, sober for half a second, before launching right back into too many questions herself. "Average work? What sort?"

He smiled a little. "Lately I've been writing."

Her eyes flashed suddenly round. Without another word she got up and padded away to the bedroom.

Ióar raised his winter-white brows eloquently, asking what offense he'd caused.

Geir chuckled. "Back in a moment, I expect."

She was--holding her sister's little notebook. Berenys, on her heels, protested in what could have been Norn or local slang. The gale-driven sleet sound of it required no translation, either way.

Ysmay put the notebook on the table. Ióar made no move to touch it.

Berenys fixed him with a glare frozen over just in a crackling thin layer at its surface, panic welling right below. Ysmay watched her steadily. I held my breath, and half wondered if Ióar was doing the same.

She had changed her clothes, after all. Now she wore her butterfly print kimono, just-washed hair clinging around shoulders, chest, and arms.

"What sort of writing?" she asked unsteadily, as if it hadn't been the other sister who'd posed the first half of the question.

He smiled so differently than the moment before. "Drab technical documents. Occasional ghostwriting.... suits me, no?"

"Suits us all." Her usual giggle was reduced to a smiling breath. "So your name's not really on your work..."

"Not always. And I've more than one name and ident to use when I need. Ivar Finn. Johan Vinter. Jarl Ness. As long as it's on the deposit into one of my accounts, whose assets from time to time are passed down on paper... or on-grid... to nonexistent heirs."

"Nice."

His smile shifted. "Well, obviously not." He briefly glanced my way. "But since outgrowing ways of life that limit one to anonymous dealings with boats and fish, I do what I must."

She wrapped slender arms around her waist, the sharp rising and falling of her slight chest scarcely masked by the dampened silk. "How did you learn? Well enough to make a living, I mean?"

"Ah. The one who taught me such things was a rare wise choice in love. Long ago." He surprised me by glancing once again at me. "It was a less wise choice and much longer ago, though, who first believed my thoughts were worth writing where other people could see them."

Berenys' white teeth worried at her lower lip. I wondered how much of her expression was in response to his words, as opposed to the silent communication undoubtedly flashing back and forth, fast as neurons firing, in the short space between her and Ysmay.

"If you believed my thoughts were worth other people seeing them... could you teach me such things, too?" she said at last.

He nodded, his eyes never leaving hers.

Berenys swallowed visibly. She came close enough to pick up the little book and hold it out.

"Then read it if you want. There's probably just us two in the whole world; we should be allowed to see each other's stuff. Just don't... You shouldn't... laugh at my handwriting, or any of the rest. We're not in cities like yours. We never got to go to school. If not for him--" she glanced at Geir--"getting his kids to teach him to read and write, once upon a time, there'd probably be no one literate on our side at all."

"It would be my great honor," he murmured as he accepted it.

She shrugged, but let his eyes hold hers for a few more heart-beats. "Okay. If you don't think it's complete rubbish, I've loads more where that came from. If you do... it would be nice of you to find some way to lie to me a little."

She turned, lightly as dancing, and brushed past Ysmay to leave the room again. Her twin, with an unrepentant little smirk, followed a few noiseless paces behind.

"Hey," I said to fill the staggering quiet that ensued. "I don't pretend tonight's about me, but you made me think--Nereiður. Do you know about her artwork?"

It took him a second too, but he found his smile. "Of course it's about you. It was your job that brought all four of you here. We're all inextricable from one another." His white hand drew familiar, wavy invisible patterns on the fabric of the sofa cushion. "Her artwork... Which period? Pressed flowers, embroidery, mosaic, spray paint, Sharpie and alcohol..."

"Mosaic," I whispered, dissolving around the edges.

"She thought she'd left them there anonymously," he said. "Same as she ever did. Gardens where she trespassed. Barn walls. Train carriages. Car parks."

"Sea caves. Make your mark without making your mark," I answered quietly. "Like you."

He nodded. "As I've said, she showed me the possibility."

"Was it meant to be the Northern Lights?" Geir asked. He was matter-of-humble-fact, not congratulating himself for guessing who'd created the beautiful glass graffiti.

Ióar looked up at him. "Always, even if it was within an image of something else. The North Sea, the mirrie dancers as she called them, or one reflected in the other."

My love responded with a faint, sweet smile.

"Why?" I couldn't help asking.

"A skeptic would say she had no real training, just artistic incli-nation," he said gently. "Anyone could do pretty wavy lines, colors that naturally flow together. But she once told someone too foolish to be skeptical, as far as she was concerned, that she loved the sky because it's even bigger than the ocean, bigger than the world itself. That she could never have too much of it." (*Sandra Cisneros, Ardencita*. My eyes stung suddenly.) "That islands and continents could do their best to separate water from water, but the sky had no borders at all."

Yet I ached, realizing her insatiable wanderlust had never taken her beyond these few small countries touching her North Sea; the shimmering sky she'd obsessively reproduced was the only one she'd known. Not the near-constant length of days near the sun-drenched equator. Not the Southern Cross, which I'd seen from three continents. I found myself wishing I could tell her how brilliantly it had glittered, like tiny mirrored mosaic tiles, over Tierra del Fuego.

Chapter 29

Neutral Space

I woke minutes before the next morning's alarm, to a panicked ring from Nereiður Junior.

awake? could i come see you please say Yes

I sat up. *Of course*, I rang her back. *Everything ok*

i rang has been reading my book all night… now says he urgently needs to speak to me

I had to blink a few times, clearing my sleepy eyes, to understand that *i* was not a pronoun but an initial.

so could he meet us at your place, Berenys added. *please Please*

I sighed. I'd been too tired to drag myself to yesterday's work-out. Missing again today wasn't a good choice, but this was a pretty extraordinary excuse. And I didn't have to understand why she felt that way, to know she needed to see him in a more neutral space. Likely she'd invited him and they were all on their way here already.

Of course OK, I answered, and slipped out of bed without waking Geir yet. Our apartment was already perfectly tidy, thanks to him. I brewed a pot of coffee with some of my precious stash from Miami, plus one of tea for my boring Scottish loves.

With a gratifying smile of pleasure at its fragrance, Ióar picked coffee.

"First off," he said when we'd been seated, each with our chosen cups, around the peninsula countertop that doubled as our table. "With your permission, I'd love to show some of these to Liv Ovesen, an editor of my acquaintance, who handles things less dull than my daily bread."

Berenys bit her lip, definitely not breathing.

Ysmay's quirk of brows and mouth was clearly *I told you so.*

"On one page you show you understand the rules perfectly, on the next you write between them like a jazz virtuoso," Ióar murmured.

"What could a selkie lass from the Northern damn Isles possibly know about jazz?"

He smiled slightly as he shook his head. "To think in all my long life, I've never seen our language written down. Until you."

"No, there's such thing. Old songs and such. Curiosities."

"Well, surely you're the first one bold enough to slant rhyme it with English when you wanted."

Her voice came out an even blend of whispering, laughter, and tears. "When I said lie to me, I meant let me down easy, not… You aren't serious."

He answered with the most deadly serious smile I'd ever seen.

"Well, how about her handwriting?" Ysmay said. Maybe to give Berenys a moment to master the tide rising against her long lashes.

Ióar smiled more fully in response, but without looking at Ysmay. "Quite small and challenging to read," he answered in the same steady low tone. "Exceptionally beautiful, for all that."

Perhaps rather than be an ungracious winner of the short but palpable staring contest, he opened Berenys' book to a page he'd marked with a scrap of embroidered ribbon. I sensed--as he tucked it carefully into a jacket pocket--that the trash-become-treasure belonged to the same family as Geir's hat, sweaters, and bedroom décor.

I'd vaguely imagined a diary, prose, but the graphite-darkened areas of these particular pages were nearly square, more like sonnets. Pencil sketches inhabited some of the white spaces between.

His white fingertip hovered over a man's aquiline profile and hooded dark eye. Not Rajan Dessai, but it could almost be his older brother.

"He has an old scar on the other side of his face, right here?" Ióar asked softly, touching one corner of his mouth and tracing a line down toward the jaw.

Berenys gave no answer beyond sucking in an audible breath.

"Only I can't remember where I saw him, that I'd know that about him."

"Oh, I--" She barely sighed. "Must've seen him on the grid somewhere. I like drawing from interesting photos."

She was a shite liar, even if he was too much of a gentleman to move his hand ten centimeters closer and prove it to himself.

"If they published it, what name would you use?" Ysmay bailed her sister out of the next moment of strained quiet.

Ióar smiled. "There's no need to change it yet, if ever. And your name is lovely."

"Och." Berenys tossed her hair around her shoulders as she shook her head with insistence. "No, I'd like one from this century, that people can pronounce. People other than Stéphane," she added, her eyes far away for a moment I doubted her new mentor appreciated. "He says some girls are still called that in French."

I flashed back to a day before Stefek had met her: early on, when he'd reminded me of the tech I could use to learn Norn. Her name was one of the terms I'd searched.

"Oh, wait. I know this one. Berenys means the same as Veronica. 'Bringer of victory.'"

Ióar smiled enough in earnest that she only met his clear bright eyes for a second or two.

She shrugged.

"What's mine?" Ysmay said, with a belated glance in my direction.

I couldn't remember, had to shake my head. "There was a thing, a legend, about the drowned city of Ys. Like the Atlantis story."

Ióar's smile shifted in the time it took to lower his gaze from one sister's face to the other. "If I'm not mistaken, Ysmay means the same as *elskling*."

Cities like theirs had excellent public transport, so no need for hovers. As soon as the weekend arrived, we five hopped the speed ferry to Bergen to meet the other five of Ióar's people. Ysmay craned her neck at the nearby bullet pod loop like a kid in a toy store, but even though they would have cut the trip time in half, neither of our old men was keen on traveling that way if they could avoid it. The view of a coastline new to all four of us visitors was worth the extra time, at any rate.

I overlaid grid imagery and information on the misty shore and skyline as we approached. Storegga itself was much closer to here than to Shetland--as responsibly as they'd tried to manage their rich natural resources, the oilfields where all this had started had been Norwegian, after all. Fortunately for them, the slide's momentum had taken the brunt of the tsunami west. They'd certainly dealt with worse than normal flooding, but I found myself far from grudging to see this beautiful coastal region basically intact.

As we stepped down through patchy fog onto the land where I'd been born, I hoped for the same tingling thrill I'd felt on landing that first time on Shetland. If it was there, though, the Friday evening energy of the relatively big city masked it.

"Maybe she didn't consider this home," Geir murmured his comment on my thoughts. "Maybe just somewhere she passed through."

I happened to catch Ióar's mist-gray eye as I nodded. He wasn't close enough to hear us, let alone for finfolk telepathy, but he gave me a gentle smile that said he was thinking of her, too.

Weak selkie belonging vibes or not, I still wanted more time to explore here than we had. The putative last Scandinavian finfolk lived not in the cool downtown, which to me looked like a more developed Stavanger, but in Fyllingsdallen, a southern borough we reached by light rail. (Ysmay had ridden regular trains before, and wasn't impressed.)

Ióar had told us his brothers and sister currently lived in two adjoining flats. The woman, Thyra, and Sindri, one of the young men, shared the place with his father, Síarr, where we'd been invited this evening. The other three, unrelated men (Halfdan and Kjeld, and Ióar when he was in town) lived upstairs.

Though we hadn't been talking in the stairwell, their door opened before we needed to knock. It was the next oldest one, Síarr, who stepped out to greet Ióar then meet each of us in turn. I saw how the elegant formal greeting Ióar had tried on Berenys was supposed to work. I didn't interject anything smart about California or Florida this time: simply Arden, *dotter av* Nereiður. Ióar quietly supplied her birthplace, Westray, and her mother's name, Eirun of Hamnavoe, now called Stromness. That pedigree earned me some very curious glances, which I couldn't help returning.

The Norwegian finmen were all taller than Geir or Hano, if none of them reached Ióar's height. Thyra was closer to the twins' size, and the only one with very dark hair, worn in a side-swept bob that brushed her angular collarbones. Everyone else's eyes and hair were varying lighter shades of ash brown and mink. Síarr and Halfdan kept theirs long enough to pull back. The other two had more ordinary short haircuts, surely chosen to blend in rather than displaying the flair of our one short-haired finman.

Their prodigal oldest brother had rung ahead and they had a nice late dinner waiting. Urban selkies had different dietary habits, I guessed, than Shetland hunter-gatherers. Still, even Ysmay partook politely of the light, creamy fish and potato soup, then much more eagerly of the cone-shaped waffle cookies filled with cloudberries and cream. I was apparently the only one whose belly was a little unsettled by the journey, so I passed on the after-dinner aquavit Geir and Berenys seemed to enjoy, still nibbling slowly on my lovely dessert.

Or maybe it wasn't the ferry-rail combo that had bent my digestion out of shape. Despite the fine meal, and their readiness to speak in a mix of excellent English and Norn for their guests' benefit, Bergen harbor had felt welcoming in comparison to this reception. The distant tone of their formal greeting never lifted. The four guys spoke coolly and without real smiles, not necessarily that unusual for selkies. Little sister Thyra, though, seemed to redirect her gray-hazel eyes a lot, rather than glare openly.

The tension wasn't that hard to figure out. Ióar had already made it pretty clear that they only tolerated, rather than accepting, his choice not to hide in plain sight with them in any time-honored way. He might be their eldest, but they didn't seem to regard him as Shetland folk respected Brynja. Nereiður would have presented a similar challenge if they'd known her personally. And her half-breed *ut land isk* American daughter, so conspicuous even without the recognizable uniform, obviously set off every warning light they had. I couldn't blame them when they'd just met me, only do my high-diplomacy-composite best.

As for the other two new women on the scene, little sister was within her rights to feel a bit threatened. I figured her for one of the younger generation, based on her normal pretty face compared to the two haunting fairytale dreams that had just shown up in her sleek blue-and-white home.

It wasn't only her husband who didn't seem swayed, though. The Norwegian guys might just seem courteous compared to our aggressive little Scots. Or perhaps they considered it damn unfair of Ióar to show up with two gorgeous new selkie lasses, only to have both focused one way or another on him and not the three other single men--who couldn't be him, but certainly weren't shabby. Whatever the reason, the opposite of chemistry was what I felt here.

That really wasn't like Berenys. Foolish as it was of me, I touched her arm to ask why.

Lightning rumbled in her dark eyes as she rolled them away in annoyance. She permitted my hand where it was just long enough to picture her tall Scalloway boy, then Ruadh, then Tadhg MacNamara. Filling the spaces in between the main images of her fleeting multisensory collage, there were needy big-eyed puppies.

So the young guys here hadn't been worth the trip it took to meet them. Plenty of girls across the pond would happily disagree with her assessment. Okay for her, too, as it only validated the singular magnificence of the elder one who'd brought her here. Not that I was about to press that inexplicably sore point right now. As a wise man had once said, for their kind, there was no rush.

For his part, it clearly pleased Geir to meet finmen he hadn't known for decades. I'd always thought of him as more of an introvert; I was glad to realize it hadn't been all bad times for him, while I'd been in Miami.

He was keen to compare notes with the Norwegian men about the high-tech Bergen shipyard. It sounded massive and complex compared to the modest Bressay site that had seemed such a modern wonder, to a guy who remembered when the vessels coming out of Bergen were wooden eela boats. They warmed to him more easily than to the rest of us, quick enough to keep refilling his after-dinner glass that I eventually pictured my fingers over it. Sighing a hint of a laugh, he agreed to slow down.

My head had drooped to his shoulder well before that point. I always found transport days wearying, but this one had particularly knocked me out. The ambiguous gray daylight wasn't helping.

Geir stroked my hair a couple of times while he waited for Halfdan to finish what he was saying, then paused the conversation to ask after sleeping arrangements. It was decided that Ióar would trade beds with Síarr for the night so he and the twins could stay here in the bigger flat, which had a spare bedroom. Geir and I would bunk upstairs with his three new buddies. That meant me conking out on our little inflatable mattress, while they stayed up till all hours swapping stories amid aquavit-fueled but selkie-quiet laughter.

Norwegian coastal weather being much like Scottish, our weekend plans to explore the city and its beautiful surrounding parks, mountains, and fjords were curtailed. I caught up on sleep while the guys got Geir in to see the shipyard. Kjeld recommended a place where we ate the best gravlax of my life. I did get to glimpse the hospital where I'd been abandoned, from inside a rain-streaked pod.

The sun peeked out mid-afternoon on Sunday as I approached the train station alone. I was happy for my selkie folk to stay together longer, but I had work in Stavanger in the morning.

Chapter 30

Loch Ness

I was worse than ever at sleeping on my own, now. Berenys rang me during the two hours I tossed and turned before finally slipping into weird dreamland. She was going with Ióar to set up an ident for her writing, if all went as he hoped. I wished her well.

Geir and I were together in the dream, diving in murky cold water where greenish shafts of sun pierced the gloom. We watched giant seahorses, as big as both my hands placed end to end, performing a solemn dance in and out of nature's spotlights. After a while, I noticed another animal: horse-headed too and of a similar size, but longer and more sinuous, silvery gray slinking in and out of the sunbeams' edges. In the dream, I remembered Dad saying they were called water kelpies. A tiny, gorgeous Loch Ness monster, was what it was.

It strayed from the fringes of the dance and approached me: not bashful like the Shetland baby seal, but insistent, snaking its head under my wrist and forearm, up close beside my breast. It swiftly undulated lithe tight circles around my ribs, waist, and hips. I held my arms away from my sides and didn't try to stroke the silky hide grazing my skin; it was surely too wild a thing for me to pet.

It paused, sleek head close to my sternum, as if listening to my pounding heartbeat; then it stared suddenly right up into my hopes and fears with wide-set black teardrop eyes.

I awoke gasping, as if I'd really been underwater the whole time. Waiting for the strange dream to recede, I could almost still feel the water kelpie writhing across my lower belly. The sensation quieted. I wiped the sheen of sweat off my face and sipped the water on my nightstand, only to have the bizarre kelpie-in-motion feeling return as the cool fluid reached my stomach.

Loch Ness.

I caught another painfully sharp breath.

It had been a scant twenty-four hours, not the prescribed seventy-two, from the peridot glint of my treatment injection to the fire-opal glow of aurora borealis over the firth. There was a possibility--just so remote I'd never connected the many dots that had appeared since then. Extreme emotions, extreme fatigue, both surely linked to my sleeping worse than ever and with spectacularly weird dreams, even for me. The bit of weight gain that I hadn't shifted, though Norwegian cuisine was leaner than Cuban. I laid a shaky hand on my belly. Even at the height of my competitive swimming and diving days, I'd had the cylindrical little waist of Doña Maite's youth, more than a flat abdominal wall. Had hers expanded this sneakily, once upon a time?

The kelpie did some magnificent somersaults for me as I tried to count backward. Since Inverness it had been five months of intense workouts and dives, late nights, moderate alcohol consumption alternating with immoderate use of caffeine… Basically only a couple rungs above Nereiður already.

I tried to talk my heart down out of my throat as I rang an automated pharmacy drone to deliver a test kit. No need to wake Geir before then, I reasoned. Not when it was so unlikely.

True, I'd experienced only one scant menstrual cycle since that night. But that wasn't new, particularly when I threw pretty green hormone-altering substances into the mix. The one before that would have been in Colombia, not that I could have said specifically when. Years before, various doctors had investigated why my cycles had never come into focus any better than the rest of me. Eventually, given my otherwise perfect health, we'd collectively shrugged and let the case grow cold. Since then I'd understood I probably wouldn't have children without medical intervention; I hadn't reached a phase of life where I'd seek them. Now I recognized it as one more selkie hybrid thing.

I turned a light on, sat at the counter to sanitize my fingertip then pierce it with the sterile lancet and watch the bright blood drop spread onto the prepared slide. It felt almost like helping someone else, rather than doing this for myself. Maybe because I'd been there when more than one friend over the years completed the same quick procedure, then scanned the slide with the med function on her ring. I remembered theirs taking a minute to verify. Not lighting up instantly emerald like mine, indicating the strength of the positive result.

I drew a big wobbly breath and let it out slowly. The invisible kelpie fluttered around again as I tried to ring Geir, although he didn't like to wear his ring to bed unless he'd been talking to me, and he'd never be up this early. Not that I could find words if he did pick up. When he didn't, I risked having to apologize for waking Ióar or the twins to get to him, but no response. Within or below, I guessed with another sigh. I so wanted to talk to my fairy madrina, Shimizu, maybe Brynja--but I couldn't, not before giving Geir the news.

He didn't ring back. I hoped I might drift off watching something on-grid like a normal person. I kept thinking about the half bottle of local dry Riesling in the fridge, previously one of my sleeping potions of choice. Finally, I dumped it down the kitchen sink, fighting stupid tears at its wasted fragrance, then recycled the bottle. Day one, at least a little better mom than Nereiður. I dug herbal tea out of the pantry cabinet and had that instead, along with too many imported dark chocolate ginger biscuits I'd found lurking nearby.

Too late, I wished I'd managed to put off the thought of my mother for longer. There wasn't any comfort there. Hurricane Oli hadn't picked up her slack especially well. Geir--who I had to figure for a pretty good dad compared to mine--couldn't even bother to answer an *urgent* pulse. I couldn't ensure Brynja's dream baby wouldn't turn out as insufficiently developed a human, let alone a selkie, as me. I went back for the rest of the packet of biscuits.

The dream that overtook me once I finally dozed off was so vivid, I thought it was some kind of movie I'd ended up choosing on the grid. I was walking under Shetland moonlight, with a sharp breeze making me draw my coat tighter. Geir was there, hand-in-hand on the beach with our child: a tiny faerie, wild brown curls flying in the sea air as her bare tiptoes danced in and out of the silvered waves' sparkling edges.

I heard the piteous yipping and howling before I saw the grayish puppy nearby, searching among the rocks and shells.

"Hey, bud." I crouched and offered a hand to sniff. It turned and looked up at me with light, feral eyes. It wasn't cute: it growled at my scent, weirdly knowing eyes narrowed.

Hadn't my friend said there were no wolves here? As if answering my thoughts, it gave a menacing low bark. Then it grabbed my wrist, needle-sharp teeth tugging at my arm.

I woke with a desperate gasp. My ring was pulsing insistently. 0708. I picked up the call in time.

"Hello?" Another fine sheen of cold sweat stood out all over my face. I rubbed at it with my open hand.

The friendly "Good morning" wasn't the voice I'd been anxious for, but one I was still grateful to hear.

"Hi, Dr. Shimizu." I failed to hold my voice steady.

"Are you okay?" she answered in an unusually gentle tone. "Coming down soon? It's almost ten after."

"Crap," I whispered. "I'm so sorry, I…"

"Arden. What's going on?"

All of a sudden, I was completely in tears and out of words.

She came upstairs. I just showed her the scan. She hugged me as if it were her own adored grandchild whose existence I'd discovered, and cried with me until we could both laugh as I recounted what I dared of the story. She rang Lars to postpone the meeting and made us both tea, and a sandwich for me while she was at it.

"Something in the water up here," she said as she handed me my steaming cup. "Can you believe you're the second one this week? Agnetha just told me on Tuesday she's expecting."

I paused, trying to think. "Do I know her?"

"Sorry. Lars' daughter. She's a marine engineer, working with the Norwegian preservation team, but maybe you wouldn't have met her yet. She's back in the office, analyzing the results you and I have been gathering. She was planning hers. Had been trying for over a year, actually, so they'd already changed up her assignment parameters…"

I blinked.

"Yes," Shimizu said. "Now that we know, I can't continue to authorize your diving. I may come from a long line of freediving women who didn't stop needing the money the abalone and sea urchins and pearls brought in, just because they were pregnant, and we all turned out fine, but that's the official rule we've unknowingly violated this whole time."

My face must have shown my unspoken concern: she shook her head and reassured me, "You'll have all the scans anyway. I know there won't be anything wrong, but if there were, we'd be able to take care of it."

All the scans. I felt the wind knocked out of me. In my day, finding a basic paternal match had been more DNA testing than most babies ever underwent, but the science had evolved greatly. Full scans were routine now, and surely precise enough to pick up on little details like the baby being only twenty-five percent human.

"Right. I guess all the tests and stuff are mandatory?" I said.

Her brows lifted. "You could decline them like any medical care, I suppose, but why? On top of the usual developmental things, although I'm sure all that will be perfect, if I can be candid... There are markers for so many mental health difficulties that no one had discovered how to track yet when your parents were babies, or even when you were. It's important to know if you're facing... any of that. Heal it before it hurts. Yes?"

I couldn't stop the emotional wave breaking over me, but I found myself standing steady in the foaming surf as it receded.

"Dr. Shimizu, they both made awful choices, but I'm not convinced anymore that they were driven by mental illness."

"What?"

"I know I've let you go on thinking that, but I'm pretty sure this baby has no markers for bipolar or whatever else... and completely sure there's no Pictish DNA, since Geir made that up."

Her startled expression transformed into a different little smile, and she folded her arms. "Okay. What kind of DNA don't you want identified?"

With one more quick pre-dive breath, I told her all of it, calm and fast.

"Son of a bitch," she said finally, rubbing a stray tear. "I've wondered what was going on a dozen times. The biotracker readings that weren't broken at all. Placing out of a year's training in under three months. But this? Fairytale marine bio? As much as I admire Oliver giving up all the glory out of respect for their desire to remain hidden... even if that meant depriving the scientific community... He could have trusted someone enough to tell them. He could have trusted me."

"But I don't think he knew." My eyes brimmed again too. "Well, who the hell knows what he knew. But if he did, he didn't trust me either."

"Honey," she said, softer, and with even bigger eyes. She shook her head, though, after only a moment. "No, I suspect he did."

"Well, if you're right, he picked a shite way to pass along the info…"

"Yes. Think about it, though. None of us understood him walking away from rockstar status at UCLA. But if he had such a powerful reason to raise you somewhere wilder…"

There was my beautiful old book, too. My Joan Baez song.

Could Nereiður have told him everything?

What if she hadn't, but he'd figured it out anyway? The timeline was more right for that than anything else. He'd published his big theory the year after I was born. Then had come the unending spiral of criticism and poorly chosen defensive maneuvers. I'd gone along with the world in thinking Dad's increasingly erratic and obsessive side studies into seemingly random sources, the literary monsters and faeries, the Irish grandmother's treasury of weird folklore, comparative mythology, phenomenology, all were symptoms of general dissociation from reality as everyone else knew it. But if he'd been doing his damnedest to investigate the reality I was living now, instead?

How much he must have doubted whatever he knew, or imagined he knew, in the aftermath of her loss and my arrival. Single working father was a tough enough job under good circumstances. What if, impaired as he'd become, he just hadn't ever pulled the data together enough to present them to me in a way befitting the standards he stubbornly maintained?

"Maybe," I answered with a sideways kind of laugh.

Shimizu nodded. "What was that he said about unbelievable truths?"

"'Because it is so unbelievable, the truth often resists being known,'" I murmured. "Kierkegaard, right?"

I sighed, still smiling. "Heraclitus, I think."

"Yet you just found each other," she said after a wondering pause. "Like it really was some kind of damn fairytale magic."

Then she smacked the flat of her hand on her slim thigh. "Now that we've got Clark Kent's glasses off, finally. Can you show me how he flies?"

"Wish I could, Miss Lane."

"Too bad... But still." She snorted with soft laughter. "They'd strip you of all your medals if they knew."

It hit me only then: I would have to tell my finfolk I'd spilled their secret to one *ut land isk* I trusted with my life. Geir might be justifiably concerned, but he wouldn't be mad. Brynja might; I hoped Lachlan would soothe her. You never knew with the twins. Ióar's guys would be the toughest nut to crack. Of all of them, one stood out whom I'd most wish for Shimizu to meet, study and befriend. I couldn't ring him yet, but he'd be delighted with my choice to confide in her.

I'd hardly begun describing him when the door handle rattled softly, followed by a quiet knock. I started to my feet, goosebumps standing all over my skin before I reached the door. If not for the wild emotional ride of the conversation he was interrupting, I'd have known sooner who was there.

"Guess I didn't need to worry I'd wake you," Geir said with the signature hint of a smile. "Dr. Shimizu, good morning."

She managed to keep a straight face as she greeted him, "Hi, kiddo."

I resisted throwing myself at him as immediately as usual, knowing words would be impossible for a moment once I did. During the unaccustomed pause, he set down a tasty-smelling paper bag on the counter where I'd done the test hours earlier.

I found a slight smile of my own. "So you got my ring?"

His eyes went wide for a second; then the little smile turned self-deprecating as he shook his head. "Oh. Sorry. That's why I had to knock, too. Someone warned me to buy a device from this decade before international travel, but I wasn't clever enough to listen to her," he said with a soft laugh. "I'll have to get a new one here, I guess. We got back late and saw you'd rung Ióar, only I didn't want to call then in case you'd actually got to sleep. But even before that, I--had the feeling you needed me. Weird dream on the local train back to his place. I took a bullet pod here."

"Thanks," I whispered. At least it hadn't been another helo. "I do."

I might not be able to show off the specific superpower Shimizu had requested, but I could demonstrate the laser vision. I buried my face against the sweet seawater scent of his neck and started to breathe out all of it together: my own weird dream, the waking realization, the test results, the pangs of uncertainty.

He turned my face back up to his with both gentle hands, taking great care not to impress anything on me yet. Nothing beyond the need to know first whether this was what I wanted, weighing down on him like thirty meters' depth. He was aware, of course, I'd tried to take the normal responsible modern girl steps to prevent it.

I didn't ever recall telling him about the minuscule brown African frog that appeared in my mind's eye, looking up at us from the summit of my finger with wide fae eyes dappled leaf green and muddy blue. It was the remembered thrill of knowing I'd helped do something so right, preserving this beautiful and valuable species we'd found, that would transmit itself to Geir with the memory.

If I hadn't been so sure giving this baby to the world outweighed the initial ambivalence of my banged-up little selkie heart, there wouldn't have been the need to trust my mentor with our precious truth.

The sharp acceleration of Geir's own tenacious heartbeat roused our tiny Loch Ness monster from the dark depths where she'd been resting, and he felt her fluttering for the first time.

"*Drøttenmín*," he sighed down the back of my neck. He turned his silky head to press one saltwater kiss to my unsteady lips, drawing me closer with all his strength before the intense shock of his pleasure, gratitude and adoration could buckle my knees out from under me. He looked me in the eyes a moment longer, which didn't really have the less overwhelming effect he intended.

"Thank you," he said to Dr. Shimizu as he reluctantly let me go. "For being here for Arden and the baby. For our people. If someone has to know, I'm glad it's you. I fully share Arden's trust in you. And Elis will jump at the chance to meet you in person."

"Holy shit," she murmured, wide eyes alight as they flashed from his to mine and back.

He smiled crookedly. "So please appreciate why I'm asking for the room."

She laughed and hugged him about as tight as he'd been holding me. "Fair enough, kiddo." I got one more fervent hug, too. "You'll see. We'll take amazing care of you three."

"Thanks for everything, doc… What time do you need me to come in?"

She ruffled my hair. "No, take the day. Give me time to figure out new plans. Maybe we'll go for noodles later."

It was sort of like that first morning in the Adies' cottage, almost too overcome for words but not yet ready for the shared emotions to drag us under. Now, as then, we focused on small details. It was breakfast sandwiches in the bag he'd brought, coffee for me, and tea for him. I shamelessly ate all of mine, even though Shimizu had fed me already. For once, I guessed I had an excuse.

"Can you believe it?"

He gave me a dazed smile. "I know. Another member of the 'shouldn't really exist' club. I guess she wants to be here that much."

"I guess. But--why are you saying it's a girl?"

"Why are you? She's already grown enough you can feel the spark of her life," he murmured. "Why wouldn't we be able to tell she's a girl?"

"Well--I only did the blood drop thing. I don't know if we should get the full scans…"

He was still smiling as he shook his head. "We don't need their tech to know this."

My next breath came out half laughter, half sighing.

He was quiet a moment. Then he took my head delicately between his hands again, focusing his dark-water eyes on mine with the finman volume cranked all the way up.

"Listen, my jo," he said. "When I told you I don't care what name we call this by, that was the truth."

He wasn't remembering that rough conversation, with one-third of us in Ireland and two-thirds in Miami, but instead a morning in Lerwick Harbor months earlier. Ysmay splashing Lachlan in unnecessary warning, me assuring them both *Never after*. I felt now the way Geir's heart had sunk then, to hear one so young say such a weighty thing so lightly.

"But for our daughter… Could you let me be the kind of dad I've always been before? Make what we already know clear to the rest of the world… documents at least, rings and everything if you'll go along with that much."

I sighed, but before I could summon an ambivalent shake of my head, my newborn self sprang to my mind unbidden. Those five weeks with no one calling me their own, without even a name, my beginnings had been the achingly wrong opposite of every good thing he asked and offered.

Eyes liquid bright, he didn't say anything more.

If I'd found the secret passage to this impossible place, already knew I was never going back… maybe it wasn't so crazy to make the rest of the journey his fairytale way.

"I draw the line at a fat wedding dress." I blinked my stinging eyes ineffectually.

"That's up to you." He laughed, soft and earnest. "Though I confess I won't have your back if you deny Vega the chance to sing 'How Long Has This Been Going On'."

It turned out not to be very hard to smile. "Okay."

"Okay." With one more kiss, he reached over the bag that had held our breakfast, fishing in his jacket pocket.

With a little thrill in spite of myself, I took what he held out on his open palm.

"Admittedly I'm rusty, but aren't you meant to lead with this?" I breathed, staring at the ring in its little black velvet box: a wide silvery band, encrusted with a micro-mosaic of tiny green, blue, and pale precious stones and mother-of-pearl in distinctive abstract wave shapes. I had no way to tell whether or when it had been made by her, for her, or in tribute to her art, but it did somehow seem to bear Nereiður's stamp.

"Ah, but you're an unusual challenge." He kissed the right place on my left ring finger.

I let him slide the real jewels onto the hand where I'd worn a cheap imitation. It fit me perfectly, wrapping the finger in the softest boreal glow almost up to the first knuckle.

"Where in the world did you get this?" I whispered.

He smiled tenderly. "Ióar gave it to me, in the hope of a moment like this… neither of us realizing it would be today. He doesn't know that it was ever hers, but it made him think of her when he saw it in a shop years ago, so… he's wanted you to have it since you met."

As the morning light played over and within the myriad small jewels, my eyes seemed to slip out of focus. A kind of impression I'd never encountered flooded gently through me: wordless, of course, but imageless too, even without emotions. For those few seconds I felt the tilted movement of my world, then a subtle shift in that tilt: a resetting of something greater than my small self, and longer dislocated.

Geir's breath escaped him in a slow, wondering sigh. A drop of hot coffee spilled onto his leg as the cup tilted nearly forgotten in my other hand, making him jump, and the moment faded.

"Damn." He smiled. "No one said it was a magic ring."

"Silly," I found myself saying. "Of course it is."

A bit later, I upnoded a capture from my ordinary ring showing my test results, and a photo of the magic ring as well. I sent them without further commentary to my fairy godmother.

"Oy, what the ajo, mi meshuggenita imposible," she greeted me within seconds. "I swear, this could only happen to you."

Unable to tell her in full how right she was, I just giggled.

"But there's laughing, which means we're happy, right?" She paused. "Gotta make sure Gary doesn't drop out of high school over it, though. You know. Get the family to step in and--"

"Y cállate. Yeah, you can spoil her and give her back any time."

"Yeah, so no worries if there's not a lot of family on your side to do the spoiling. You leave that up to me and maybe Tía Abuela Luisa," Vega went on. No need to interrupt her with the realization that nowadays there were great-grandparents I wouldn't have counted on before, great-aunts and a great-uncle and their families in Miami. "And no considering any other candidates for the madrina to my lil Arden Rae Junior."

"Oh, that goes without saying."

She cleared her throat a little. "Speaking of gifts. The big bad of all jewelry, huh."

"I know it's crazy," I said, softer.

But I heard her smile. "No crazier than I've come to expect from you, mija."

Chapter 31

Aberdeen

Two weeks or so further into the autumn, my non-magic ring pulsed as I left the worksite late one evening. Ready to apologize to Geir, I saw Ysmay's ident instead. I didn't figure for a second that the quiet sister was the one using the device, any more than she ever did.

Hi just leaving work How are you world traveler weird sisters just returned from fyllingsdallen, hoping to trip the light fantastic again--i'd rung to invite you but now realizing—the chosen one should be home with your feet up, and a prince to feed you soup. ysmay will do

Ask ioar? I couldn't help shooting back.

im so unsuited to dance with such a one, she replied.

My *You cant seriously think he was looking for someone like brynja in a place like that* got no further response, not that I expected any. As much as any sassy Latin step Berenys had picked up, this veering away from what might matter too much was a classic Hazan move. Then, too, I could only imagine my prodigal big sister's ambivalence at the new kid in town achieving Brynja's fondest wish for the selkie kingdom. I didn't push it; I didn't hear back from her, either.

Her suggestion of soup proved irresistible, anyway. Geir and I went for a late noodle dinner and a walk along the seaside promenade. Autumn's early nightfall made the area's blue-lit walkways that much more fun. A kilometer or so south, we paused to debate by an ice cream stand, not like me at all. Geir insisted I deserved my own cone, countering my hormone-heightened hope of not taking on too seal-like a shape before all was said and done.

I almost dropped what was left of the shared nut-brittle cone when my ring started pulsing wildly in a Morse code 999 pattern: signaling that someone's ring linked to mine had been violently broken. I'd only gotten two such alerts in my life before; the linked ring had been Dad's both times. Fighting visions of Vega getting mugged or Maite and Jamar in a fiery Dolphin Expressway podwreck, instead I found the twins' ident. I hadn't even known Berenys had opened such a link.

"Shit," I breathed, and quickly explained it to Geir. "I should have gone with her."

We both immediately tried to ring back, but nothing connected.

"It'll bring law enforcement automatically, right?"

"Yeah. I guess just figure out the breach of her majesty's secrecy later?" I sighed, already submitting a pod request.

He looked at me with the same rock-steady dark eyes as the day we'd pulled Lachlan to safety from far below Out Skerries. We'd need to do things off-grid if it came to that. My stomach constricted uncomfortably.

Ióar didn't answer my ring either, though. I left an *urgent* pulse.

"Maybe she busted it swinging from a chandelier," I said as lightly as I could.

"Probably." Geir put a reassuring hand on my arm, right before I felt another pulse.

I expected Ióar but it was Ysmay, who erupted into pyroclastic Norn. Nothing I said slowed or stopped her. I couldn't catch more than a word in twenty. I finally just projected her voice to let Geir respond.

His face stayed stoic as he listened, then began to talk under her, but there was big surf crashing on his inner shore. His mind's eye was on Berenys: not her image, but the stomach-dropping hint of a smoky memory fragment I understood was hers.

"You think they could have followed her here?"

He shook his head. "I think whoever it is, she spotted them skulking round Stornoway and sent in an alert that must have scattered them over in this direction. If I were their kind, I'd be headed well north of here." Anonymous on the edge of the world. I nodded, insides tangling in sea-serpentine knots.

"But they don't--have her, do they? She's safe?"

He shook his head. "She's hiding. I don't know about safe."

We found Ysmay outside the club where we'd first met Ióar. He hovered a few meters away, blending in among club-goers who'd emerged to ogle the developing police situation.

It startled me to see her in a micro skirt, faux lamb jacket, and shimmery heels from Berenys' shopping spree. She held the broken ring, which she'd somehow jury-rigged together to call us earlier, on her tiny unshaking palm for a local officer to scan it and ask her questions.

To watch this twin expertly dip her mythical lashes and charm the stolid Scandinavian dad taking her information scared me more than Brynja's moonlight smile ever had, but I was desperately grateful it did the trick. There weren't many follow-up questions, beyond the ones implied in longing backward glances as the cop walked away a bit dazed. He rejoined his colleagues with a soft chuckle; quiet laughs as the group got into their vehicle before speeding away.

"I've told them a faerie story about some bloke trying to steal the ring from me," she said, in my ear but loud enough for the men to hear--or in Ióar's case, near enough for him to perceive the truth whether he'd heard or not.

"You gave them his description?" Ióar quietly thundered.

Her liquid eyes lifted to his, a long silent moment before she shut them tight and pressed against his shoulder. In under thirty seconds, she turned, slipped off the luxe jacket, and handed it to me without anything close to eye contact. Then-- ignoring my "Ys, please wait"--she walked away with the consummate Berenys-like hair flip and straight spine, and nabbed an approaching pod as if she'd been doing it her whole life.

Ióar looked ready to take off without explanation, too, but he let me stop him with a hand on the tensed muscles of his upper arm. He touched my hand, showing me the nearby coffee shop where Berenys had planned to run after slipping out the club's back exit in the slight disguise of her sister's clothes and shoes. Ysmay was thoroughly done with the situation, headed straight back to their flat now she'd played her distasteful role.

"Okay, but she gave them whose description? Who is this guy?"

"Oh," Ióar murmured. "I thought it was just me she wouldn't tell."

Geir shook his head. "Beyond slips here or there, she's told no one but her sister anything."

Ióar recalled the sinking sensation her sketch had provoked, the man who looked like Rajan Dessai. I let my heart be dragged downward with his as, in response, I remembered how badly meeting Raj on the dance floor had spooked her.

"I don't know whether he's here, with the one who just tried to take her tonight," Ióar answered aloud. "But I have seen him before, and... so has she. Not just on the grid."

"In Aberdeen, yeah. And maybe Stornoway? But where the hell would you have seen him too? How do you know he has anything to do with--"

"In Bergen. Waiting to speak to the man who does our idents," he said, quietly but without any hint of apology. "Along with someone who, judging by what Ysmay has shown me, strongly resembles the man Berenys just got away from."

I saw him in Ióar's memory, bent close talking to the man who wasn't Raj. They were about the same height, but the new man had fairer coloring and a heavier build, with short, sandy hair lightened by a lot of gray for someone with a face as young as his.

"They spoke Russian together, or something with that sound," Ióar added. "I'd guess it's this man's first language, but the man she drew has some other accent."

"And no one's fool enough to suppose their purpose for being there was as honorable as yours," Geir said, quiet and steady as ever. "Okay. Ys… showed you more than what's happened just tonight, I think. Surely it's past time her family knew more as well."

Ióar nodded, his usually stony features pensive and sad for a few moments. Finally, he tilted his head toward a long, backless concrete bench a dozen or so paces away, near the water's edge. We followed, matching his purposeful quick walk.

We sat thigh to thigh to thigh, looking out at the city lights reflected on black water. What part of me wasn't swept away at once appreciated his diplomacy composite skills, far superior to my beloved queen's. I had no idea what the hell might have happened if I hadn't been sitting.

The experience he shared felt encased in a shatteringly thin but intense protective shell of his tenderness toward the new Nereiður Junior he longed to know. As that fine layer dissolved, we were immersed in a lossless duplicate of what he'd just learned: Seurat-like Ysmayvision, but the original impression she'd entrusted to him belonged to Berenys.

She remembered with intensity smoke and vapor from legal and illegal substances, the pungency of someone unwashed, stale beer and liquor. It felt like she'd done a few shots herself in the moments before. I understood why, in the same moment I realized why there were only narrow flashes of visual memories, a dim room with a dark ceiling and a few different-colored lights. She'd also been trying to keep her eyes shut. It took a heartbeat to sort out the other remembered sensations. I'd never experienced such a toxic mixture of revulsion and attraction, thrill and terror.

She'd gotten mixed up with them by being her dopamine junkie self, flirting with badder boys than were usually available in Orkney or Shetland. Then she'd gleaned, from a few rings overheard close together, their intentions for the girls in that so-called shelter.

She'd called the authorities from the toilets, then distracted the two men in that back room of the bar, the only sure way she knew how, until she'd heard the police entering the building. Then she'd fled, leaving her favorite sweater on the pool table where she'd been with the second man--whose face she'd drawn in her journal. Someone else's garment, carelessly thrown over an empty chair, had proven a double mercy: its hood concealed her face and hair as she slipped away through the mist to the honest safe place we offered. She'd pitched her ring into the river along the way, even better rendering herself untraceable.

She hadn't cared about our food, or the bed where she'd never closed her eyes; she'd only wanted a shower, and to be anonymous until she could board the ferry.

Geir reached across Ióar's legs to grab my hand. "It was down to you she got away as cleanly as she did."

I shook my head, my throat too tight for speech. Maybe, but here she was for what I'd begun doubting was only the second time.

"Can you--What influence have you got, here?" he was saying gently.

I had to swallow to get two small words out. "None, really."

"Could you see local police activity?"

I fought the tears, fished around the grid for a minute or two. UFPK presence in most of Scandinavia was pretty negligible at this point. It did turn out, though, any UF ident got me in far enough to see that the matter of Scottish national Ysmay North was under active investigation.

We hurried to the coffee shop; both men waited outside, equal parts hailing a pod and guarding the door.

Inside, Berenys slumped, all soft and bent lines against the straight Scandinavian design of a cheerful blue chair. I perched on its sturdy arm and touched a tendril of her hair escaping from beneath tonight's borrowed gray hoodie, this one child-sized. Her eyes lifted, extinguished embers that had smudged the pale skin beneath. I hadn't expected she'd be in this much physical pain, the sole impression I got from touching her. Managing a wry smile, she showed me the pink and swollen wrist where she'd been wearing the ring.

"Come on," I whispered. "Let's get you out of here."

By the time I went to the counter to cover the tea she'd probably planned to finfolk her way out of paying for, our pod was there. We set it for my place.

"The man whose face you drew in your book, you're sure he wasn't there tonight?" Ióar murmured like a distant black cloud, as soon as we started to move.

She shook her head, almost with impatience. "This was no one I'd seen before."

"I had, though."

She blinked a sudden, silent tear down each wan cheek.

"Elskling," he urged when she didn't answer. He reached to take her uninjured hand in his. Not to give her a mental shove, I understood, but to show her something more.

Berenys slipped free of his touch, rubbed both hands over her wet face, looked at me instead of him.

"The one I drew was--there in Aberdeen," she barely breathed, the darkness in her eyes so profound it stopped my breath. "I called the police and got away to you."

"Ysmay told us," I said quietly.

The pale lines of her mouth wavered but she nodded, and for once, went on meeting my gaze. "And before I got rid of my ring, I sent them that sketch. It wasn't enough to help them catch him, though, I guess."

"Well done, even so," Geir murmured.

"I didn't know the man tonight had any connection, but..." She sighed. "He was so lovely at first. Until I smelled whatever he'd put in the next drink... All I thought was, why does everyone want to lock me in a shipping container? But if they're working together--maybe he could've understood my part in Aberdeen?... I don't know."

"Or what if they know what selkies look like, who you are, and they were trying to--"

Her dismissive head shake was a precise echo of when I'd seen Brynja make the same gesture. "Trying to capture a fairytale creature? No. I don't think we've been anything more than bycatch in the nets they keep casting. But either way, he caught me in the alley at the back, trying to ring the police again." Berenys closed her eyes. "I broke the ring myself... to get away from him, and knowing the signal would reach the police and you."

I sighed. "The ring and your arm."

Berenys shook her head. "It's only twisted. And not my writing hand."

Laying his careful hand over the injured wrist, Geir answered her in the language of their birth. I didn't get every word, but he said *home* and *soon*. He was right: that was the safest, and the best and quickest way for Berenys to heal. When, inevitably, she evaded his touch, his hand found mine instead. His fierce grief and regret hit me harder than he'd wanted: she hadn't managed to keep back memories of bones broken before, no more by accident than this injury.

"He ran for it," she answered me as if Geir hadn't spoken. "Then I--Ys always has to talk to the police. The ident and proper work history, such as it is, are hers. If they checked a fingerprint or anything... You know we're not that identical."

Understatement of the decade. "She did okay," I said.

"Any more word on that yet?" Geir asked softly.

There wasn't; we headed to our flat to wait. Berenys slipped onto the balcony, her own fur jacket over her sister's sweatshirt against the mildly cool evening, rather than talk to us anymore. The guys found some unimportant conversation to pass the time. I felt suddenly ready to collapse on the couch, now the adrenaline had ebbed. It was almost two.

I jolted awake from an orca nightmare, safely curled between Geir's side and a heap of pillows, when my ring pulsed an alert from the police case. I blinked, weary eyes focusing too slowly. My brain, too, took time to understand the peaceful background noise wasn't rain outside but water running in the bathroom.

"Wait," I protested. "Shite. No."

Neither man asked aloud.

I projected the innocuous photo of someone stocky with a fair-colored buzz cut, clean-shaven, with deep-set light eyes and a relaxed smile. "They detained this--Dmytro Tataryn. But questioned him and found no reason to hold him."

Íoar sat up straight, flexing his ring hand. "Can you track him?"

I answered with a startled nod. "Required to remain available for further questioning. He can't leave Stavanger without express authorization."

"Trust me, that's not his name and he'll go wherever he likes." The glow in Íoar's eyes belied his low, even tone. The projected photo half reflected, half penetrated to the pink at the backs of his irises: fae and feral at once. I loved them all so much, it was easy to forget how much more than human they were.

"Unless," I said. The baby kicked me hard in the ribs.

He nodded, eyes flickering. "Will you come? Just to get closer to where he is. You'd never get out of the pod."

Geir stroked my hair. I didn't have to do this, but if I did, my rock wouldn't leave my side.

Ióar went into the bathroom, thundered a few Norn syllables over the sound of the shower. I didn't hear Berenys argue or see her emerge in the seconds before we left the apartment. It made such perfect sense for her to stay the hell inside, apparently even she'd been convinced. Easy to forget, too, this guy had been in charge here for centuries.

We followed the locator signal to the most ordinary street, nearing the outskirts of town. Another man waited there on a bench, as if for a slow-arriving pod of his own. Entering, then canceling a changed destination address, we misled the pod into looping the block, letting Ióar disembark slightly behind Tataryn, out of sight of either man.

Ióar made his purposeful, unhurried way toward the bench. He came close enough to speak to the man seated there and the one now stooped as if to talk to him. He lifted a seemingly friendly hand behind Tataryn's shoulders.

Tataryn jerked mid-reply, as with a violent seizure, and crumpled to the curb. Before his friend could respond with more than a startled exclamation, Ióar whipped his arm around to catch him in the middle of the chest; he dropped too, crumpled at weird angles over the arm of the bench.

With a glance to ensure he'd incapacitated them both, Ióar disappeared into an alley. I'd never wondered if they were as fast on land as they were in the water. I certainly had my answer about him now.

I could suddenly answer another question too, that I'd never dreamed of asking. Berenys wasn't the only one to have tangled herself up in such danger in the past. When it came to solving problems human justice failed to solve on behalf of his kind, I'd have bet his pocket watch--hell, Celeste Cameron's whole jewelry collection--that Ióar's first rodeo had taken place long before immobilizer technology could help him achieve his goals.

"Hijodeputa," I whispered. Geir silently agreed; we got out of the pod together.

I alerted Norwegian police before approaching, with a scant handful of passersby, to look at the two unconscious victims.

I showed my badge and people let me through, speaking sharp anxious Norwegian over my bent head. Tataryn had a nasty electrical burn to the back of his neck; the second man, a similar injury where the button placket of his shirt was singed through. I couldn't activate an emergency alert on either man's ring. They'd both been fried.

Fortunately, it hadn't been set high enough to stop a heart--and I should have known Ióar better than to fear that. Both men were breathing, if unevenly--no need to administer first aid. I just made sure no one woke too soon. Then again, no one got right up and walked away from that kind of pulse.

I didn't have to fake looking uneasy, scanning the fingerprints of Tataryn's splayed hand. The new Interpol/UFPK warnings (and other aliases) that flashed up for everyone to acknowledge with a ripple of concerned murmurs were real, as well.

All the enforcement officials reached us at about the same time. Several onlookers melted away at the sound of the sirens. No, I hadn't answered the alert before them. Dr. Shimizu's intern, totally unrelated, happened to be passing. I let them scan my information. No, I hadn't gotten a good look at the man with what I assumed was an immobilizer. Neither, to my gratitude, had anyone else willing to answer the question.

Soon they let me step back and breathe easier while they did their job. The second man's prints raised their own alert. The responders zip-tied their hands, loaded them into the police vehicle. By then, I was down to fumes.

Safe in another pod, my ring pulsed. With a started little jump, I activated it, expecting further communication from Ióar--but it was my UFE buddy Bahar Abdullah, who'd worked so hard with me in Aberdeen. *Hope all is well in Shetland Isles or next port of call Seen this? Thought of you*

He linked to a developing story about the apprehension of a Russian national suspect following tonight's sudden vigilante attack, the anonymous tip leading to a sting on a rented house where four young undocumented people had been held captive in a picturesque Norwegian town.

Aha There's two of them, came Abdullah's next message before I was halfway through the story. I refreshed.

Are you reading this Was either of these one of the Aberdeen assholes, Karima chimed in.

My heart plunged at the sight of the just-published photo captured by a surveillance drone.

NO, I might have said aloud as I sent the message. *And the second one is the damn good guy*

Exhausted or no, I was all for heading to the police station. Geir pretty quickly talked me down. Now that the perpetrator was finally in custody, he reminded me, Ióar himself wouldn't find his situation urgent enough to risk breaching selkie security with a story concocted too fast about why we would even know each other.

That wasn't to say Geir didn't want to help at all. One by one, sitting on our couch under Berenys' wide and red-rimmed watchful eyes, he rang everyone in Fyllingsdallen. After no more than ninety seconds of soft, urgent Norn syllables, Síarr abruptly ended the first call. Neither Sindri nor Thyra even answered. Kjeld did, and I heard

Halfdan come on the call with him. This conversation took longer, but I'd gotten the gist: same non-reply. The first three weren't willing to stick their necks out for their eldest. The other two wished to help, but the risk of exposing their own precarious identities was simply too great.

Weary rather than weeping, Berenys laid her silky head on my knees. As I caressed her damp hair, cheek, and temple, for the first time I felt her give up, slip below the surface with me, choose to be perceived directly as she remembered the hopes and goals she'd left in pieces along with a different ring, at the bottom of the mist-shrouded River Dee.

Born and raised far from my kind, she'd never convinced herself we could be irresistible for any but worthy reasons, never developed more than superficial defenses against us despite plenty of opportunities to learn the reality: throughout her long youth, her guileless generosity was met more and more with greed and perversion beyond her ability to comprehend. Now we'd broken the very foundations of the home her people had never minded sharing. In the aftermath of its wounding, we'd horrifically attempted to steal and sell the pleasure, fun, and love they'd only ever wanted to give away freely.

I had no answer, beyond deep shame and sorrow, as to why we'd always taken every good thing so devastatingly, irreparably far.

She raised dry eyes to find mine streaming. "Not you, my jo."

I scraped up a smile from the bottom of the barrel. She received it as if it had been a more appropriately regal gift.

"Who next?" Geir asked me. "Lachlan?"

"I think I have a better idea. Trust me?"

"You know we do."

Berenys' water-kelpie stare didn't waver, even as she felt me make the decision, but I felt her shift a safer distance away from my awareness. Fair enough. She'd been brave as hell today already.

"Mr. Adie, I'm sorry to call so early. Thanks for picking up."

"No worries. As I told Noa yesterday, though, I haven't got anything to report yet--"

The baby fluttered, perhaps enjoying his gruff voice.

"Oh. It's—not that, sir. Sorry to bother you two days in a row, but this isn't on behalf of Dr. Shimizu. It's—regarding a technical writer who's worked at your Bergen site."

"Is that where you are? Your ident shows—"

"No, we're back in Stavanger now. This is—" I took a big breath. "I don't know what name you like to call Elis and Brynja's people, sir, but several of them have been working there."

"What? How many is several?"

"Six…"

He sighed barely audibly. "Bloody hell."

"Yep. Strange as it feels to be the one to tell you."

He was silent a moment, followed by a scoff as quiet as his sigh.

"On Shetland, how many on the payroll?"

Geir held up a couple moving fingers. "One or two."

"Ach, well. Not as if I didn't wonder as soon as I saw your face, Arden. Too much like Elisabeth by half."

Geir smiled; I did too, in spite of everything. "Fair enough, sir."

"Aye. Fair enough."

The selkie bairn, waking bit by bit from her post-maternal-adrenaline nap, worked up to some pretty good kicks. Berenys' wide eyes leapt to my face. I didn't need her thrill of amazement to show itself as an external smile she couldn't have mustered. She laid a wondering hand along my belly, gasped her delight aloud when the next kick connected with her open palm.

"Okay, then," Adie was saying. "What have we got ourselves into in Norway?"

I directed him on-grid, sharing directly to his ident the news story about the attack and subsequent arrests.

"What, was this not shut down already? It's like—trying to slay the bloody hydra, these lot. Every few years, there's a new case in a different country. Seems like with all our progress and all our tech, someone ought to be able to stop it."

Maybe Dad would be proud that I knew how to answer. "Well, it took teamwork to slay the hydra, right? So… Norway with the sword this time, and Scotland right behind with a torch to make sure no more heads can grow back."

He chuckled briefly. "You sound like Lachlan, lass."

"Thanks."

"But you're calling about another mythical beast, right."

"Yes. Keep going until you see the name Ivar Finn?"

"Immobilizer pulse," Adie said, all hint of laughter gone from his voice.

"Yes, sir. I know the tech's illegal, but I assure you he only used it to stop the actual bad guys… which has to be exactly what the surveillance video shows. The thing is, you must know about the…. Sketchy idents."

Adie sighed softly. So much effort, over the years, not knowing about the idents or any of the rest.

"Albino?" he murmured. "That's new too."

"Very old, actually, but… Mr. Adie, you know it's not only the immobilizer," I said. "You know how they can't really get on the grid. None of his people there can help him without getting arrested too. I was hoping there'd be… uh, possibly the kind of magic someone like you could work in a situation like this, sir."

Another short pause. "Your father did this sort of thing for their people?"

I found myself momentarily caught up in wondering whether Dad ever would have had to bail Nereiður out. It wasn't honestly much of a stretch, but of course, I'd probably never know for sure. "Not that he ever told me, sir."

"Fair enough," he echoed me again, his tone surprisingly softer. "Right. What's this Ivar's real name?"

"Ióar of Sørreisa. Might be under, um, Jarl Ness or Johan Vinter."

"Okay. Let me ring some people on that side, and we'll see what we can do." There was a pause; I expected him to disconnect, but he didn't. "And Arden?"

"Mr. Adie?"

When he answered, I heard his smile. "It's Kenneth. Listen, there ought to be more than two warriors with swords and torches to kill this monster. We'll work on the Ivar Finn thing first, but then I'm going to make some more calls."

If I'd been Geir, or Ióar himself, I could have found the perfect turn of phrase to recognize this larger-than-life present-day fighter on the side of good for what he was without sounding horribly cliché. As it was, I just smiled too. "Thanks very much. Kenneth."

Chapter 32

Fair Isle

Thanks to my new fae-adjacent godfather's connections in the Stavanger government and elsewhere around the North Sea, the criminal whose real name was Dmitriev didn't walk free this time. When faced with the prospect of consequences appropriate to his gross abuse of his own species, in the hope of lessening his own penalty, Dmitriev (so we read) pretty quickly offered up the name of a kingpin in his shadowy business.

She hadn't seen his face on-grid before, but now Berenys' anonymously-submitted sketch appeared there beside the photo of a slippery human piece of excrement called Al-Otaibi. One of the ones pulling the strings had been there in Aberdeen, after all. Authorities hadn't located him yet, but I hoped it was only a matter of time, much as I wished he could know his evil organization had been torpedoed by someone he'd never perceive as anything more than a little girl.

Also thanks to Kenneth, Ióar went free in under twenty-four hours. He made immediate plans to head north, slip on a different ring and a different name. As soon as he was safe, Berenys made a quick exit too, flying solo back to Belfast the next day. Ysmay wavered for a few days beyond that before signing over the flat to a family friend who would be arriving in town shortly, then catching her own train to Bergen. Both sides of the North Sea breathed a collective sigh that we'd managed again not to blow our cover.

Berenys called me from Lachlan's ring the morning Ysmay departed.

"Hi," she said, the ring picking up seagull sounds nearby. "Are you working?"

"Yeah. Such as it is, with no diving."

"I won't keep you, then. I just--needed to say--I should have said--Ach." She sighed. "Okay... We both know you're right about him. Everything about him."

"Okay," I said, although uncertain where she might be taking this.

She drew a big breath, let it out in a shaky gust. "Even knowing it's a huge If. If he really were to fall in love with me…"

Her use of the hypothetical was dead wrong, but it seemed smarter to wait instead of correcting her poetic jazz-improv grammar.

"No one's said it because neither he nor anyone else wants it to become anything like a challenge, but he's surely older than Brynja."

In person, I'd have been sweating to avoid breathing out specific impressions. This way, I could just wait.

"What would I ever do, after him?" she blurted finally.

My eyes stung too. Words took their time coming, but the ones that did were the truth.

"That would be an obstacle for someone weak. You took down an international human trafficking ring with nothing but your fragile little body and a pencil."

She was quiet for a few moments. Then I heard one sharp sniff, and knew for sure she'd just tossed her hair back. "That was all I thought I should tell you. Oh, and that Elis is terribly keen to get there soon."

"We're keen to see him, too," I replied softly. No point pressing her further. I knew she'd only said this much to me because of the eight-hundred-and-some kilometers of North Sea and lovely green islands between us.

Elis insisted no one get him from the airport. Instead, he rang us the coordinates of a place he'd chosen, to meet and buy us dinner. I took a pod from Dr. Shimizu's office; Geir assured me there was no point going out of my way to meet him either, and he would enjoy the walk.

Our visitor arrived before me and waited outside the restaurant, looking straight off a different kind of runway. He offered a smooth, strong hand out of my transport, as from a fairytale coach or magic carpet. His speechlessness--at the hair I'd worn loose for Geir's pleasure, the tawny shoulder peeking from the loose neckline of the sweater Berenys didn't like--was contagious. I gave him my other hand too, stood there on the sidewalk as if I'd never heard any of the legends, and we just stared at each other.

Much as I recognized the source of Lachlan's imposing spirit, no ring conversation could have prepared me for the maglev launch that was Elis' energy signature. No one from Shetland had prepared me, either, for the fresh haircut and manicure, crisp white shirt beneath a beautiful ecoleather jacket whose subtle scent mingled with a touch of nice cologne, oud and sage and quiet musk. He was taller, maybe one seventy; I had to lift my face to meet his sparkling eyes. A few shades lighter than Geir's, they would have liked hours to decipher which of my features were Nereiður, which were Oliver. He couldn't find a smile.

"Oi," the most beloved soft voice snapped us both out of it. I felt the sharp tap on Elis' probably mythical backside almost as if it had happened to me. He flashed a much smaller boy's guilty grin.

Geir was already laughing. I took a few deep breaths as they embraced, trying to get my hot cheeks to fade. When I'd regained enough composure to risk meeting anyone's eyes, I found Geir touching Elis' hair. His sweet slight smile was an exact match for how he'd felt, remembering Alasdair.

We indulged the new arrival (one more eagerly than the other) by trying a tasting menu he'd spotted on the grid--samples of traditional Norwegian cuisine, twisted with international spices and tricks of molecular gastronomy. Me on a plate, if you thought about it, he noted with a suggestive smile; Geir just laughed again and shook his head. Elis was the first selkie I'd known to enjoy anything like harissa and preserved-lemon braised reindeer or smoked game bird with juniper berry-mirin glaze. I felt no need to taste any drinks paired with the men's meals, except the intense pre-dessert drop of spiced mead served in a clear bubble, no more than a centimeter across, that dissolved on my tongue.

He effortlessly caught the attention of the entire wait staff and, by my estimation, more than half our few dozen fellow diners. I got it if Berenys didn't want to date Mom's choice; it was scarcely to my benefit to protest if some finmen preferred earth girls, either. But it seemed like such a waste.

"Not bad for a feral boy from Fair Isle," he murmured to me with a little smile, sitting back in his chair after reducing our sophisticated server to a stammering girl just by leaning in for her to scan his ring, paying for dinner.

I laughed. "Really?"

"No," Geir said with a hint of smile.

"Alone in the world even younger than you were, Arden," Elis insisted. "Until the most beautiful lady, on a boat full of rich English travelers, spotted me coming up from a swim one evening. She'd thought there were no more selkies in Fair Isle, decades before that."

"How would she know there were selkies there at all?" I smiled, not fooled.

"Ach, did no one say?" His fingers twined around mine to show me the lady: impossibly slender in her wasp-waisted gown, parasol shading her alabaster skin, wide-set hazel eyes favoring him with an astonished smile. This long ago, her hair had been its natural brunette shade, twisted becomingly up at the nape of her delicate neck.

"Oh," I whispered.

He squeezed my hand lightly before letting go. "She thought she'd bring me to her friend Eoin Black, who'd made his way north some time before, but in those days he wasn't the fine role model Geir is." Elis smiled fondly. "Though if you're new to this story, perhaps that means our Mr. Craig won't have mentioned he taught me everything I know."

He watched what must have been quite an entertaining progression of emotions across my face.

"I hope you met the lovely former Mrs. Black?" His next smile was one hundred percent finman-manipulation-free, but his thought trailed off as someone behind me caught his eye. I turned to find the server watching him unabashedly: slim and athletic, long platinum hair, ten years on me, ten centimeters on him. His shapely right eyebrow and both corners of his perfect lips raised a few inviting millimeters each.

"On you go, then, lad," Geir startled me into another laugh, "show her how it's done properly."

"Don't forget we have Dr. Shimizu at nine," I said as Elis reached behind him for the nice jacket.

"Promise, darling," he murmured, with a smile that wasn't for me.

The server never looked away as Elis bid us good night, fair-skinned cheeks beginning to flush. He couldn't have breathed as many as ten magic words in her ear. As she held her ring next to his, he pressed a kiss against her fingers, held her gaze until she bent her head his way. The look of hypnotized bliss I must have worn the first time I'd kissed Geir suffused her pretty face, sunrise pink by the time the glass doors closed behind him.

I sighed, still laughing. "I guess I'll never get to see what you're capable of, will I?"

Geir smiled too, but only a little, as he shrugged. "Likely she'll never get to see what he's capable of, either."

Elis met me outside Dr. Shimizu's office building at 0855, fresh as a masculine daisy in a dark suit and seaglass-green tie. Next to him in my plain gray uniform, I felt suddenly drab and round as the mother seal I'd met on the other side of our North Sea.

"Hi, gorgeous." He smiled in greeting, touched my wet hair as we started inside. "Slipped your skin and headed under that pretty water this morning, did you?"

"Half right." I sighed, even as I smiled too. "I'm not allowed to dive right now—"

"That's rubbish…"

"But I still try to get in a workout most mornings."

"Well done, you. I got a nice one in too." He pressed the elevator button with an unrepentant half-smile.

But for Dr. Shimizu, who met us just outside the elevator doors, he had an impeccably correct handshake and a perfect echo of her usual hint of a bow. They launched into fluent marine biologese on the way to her office. My implacable mentor was no less susceptible than the random Norwegian lady. If anything, he'd saved his best moves for this morning.

The topic didn't shift to specifics of respiration rate, CO_2 tolerance, or other Pictish DNA permutation hypotheses until we'd closed her office door and seated ourselves around the amazing Gyokuro green tea she'd prepared. I did my sincere best to follow the intense technical conversation. But the vegetal scent rising from my small white cup, its contents' grassy hue, somehow transported my tired brain to New Orleans, a morning at the green-striped Café du Monde with Vega. I fleetingly yearned for a beignet. I struggled to remember the lyrics to "At Last," my then-favorite of her performance pieces from the nearby club, where smoke and humidity swirled in the stage light beams like steam in the sun now angling through the office window…

Elis' fingertip was tapping the back of my hand. "Earth to Arden," he teased, giving me a gentle smile when my eyes refocused. "Have you really not done the fetal scans?"

I shrugged. "You don't think it's way too risky?"

All humor evaporated from his expression. "I think it's too risky to skip them. You're at how many weeks?"

"Twenty-two, almost twenty-three."

He nodded. "The old man might not have said, but one challenge with a selkie bairn is always the timing. Seals have about a seven-month gestation, but delayed implantation such that the pregnancy can total a year. Humans, obviously not. The child of two selkie parents might be born at twenty-eight weeks or well past forty."

"How well past forty?" I groaned. "No, the old man definitely didn't say."

His brows drew together as he nodded. "We should ask him for the details, but I've got a feeling his children before followed their mothers' biology pretty closely in this regard. Only there's no guarantee yours will. I had one other daughter before Elisabeth, and they both came fully developed closer to the seven-month mark. Needless to say, you're quite a spanner in the works as well…"

I sighed. "Yep."

"I buried my first girl along with her mother," he pressed in a disarming soft tone. "And I find it less than likely that Elisabeth's death was the freak thing Kenneth has always let himself believe. The creation of you beautiful in-between beings, I think it's… complicated."

"Okay. Keeping the massive secret in an on-grid world is damn complicated too."

His smile quirked back to life. "Indeed. That's why we make it our business to know people who can create an ident centuries after someone was born, and rig it to stay at age twenty-two."

"Or one man with at least four names…"

"Or a bloke becoming his own grandson." Now we got the boyish grin again. "Both of whom long for such an opportunity to see what we're really made of. Please say you won't deny us."

"I want the scans too, but devil's advocate here," Dr. Shimizu said. "Arden's not the same as a regular citizen. Less privacy, more potential scrutiny."

"Then we ask the other grandson to pay for the absolute top of the line this time, my darling, and all shall be well."

She certainly must have been falling under his sway, because she didn't even tell him it was Dr. Darling.

My marine biology lingo competency score was somewhere on the level of my Ishtalian, but hacker jargon was complete Greek to me. As I understood the plan that evolved in the next day or so, there was a way to limit access to my results only to myself and Dr. Shimizu, bypassing the rest of UFE and the health network. She would downnode the original data, redact whatever she found as quickly as possible, then the hackers would release the block, hopefully before anyone noticed the anomaly. We'd figure out later how to proceed with care for the finbairn and me.

Getting into the secure system at the health facility required sleight-of-hand. That task fell to Elis, much better at our newer tech and armed to the perfect teeth with every finman wile in the arsenal. I remembered how little effort it had taken for him to access the restaurant server's data. He would accompany me to the appointment sporting an altered ident--that of my unborn child's father. Geir agreed to that part with definite reluctance, as well as some laughing but strongly-inflected Norn admonitions to his selkie son. It would be easy enough for him to attend follow-up appointments himself if we decided they were worth the added risk. Shetland finfolk all looked so conveniently alike.

Hi mystery colleague Dr S tells me you're also expecting (Congratulations) and are ready to get fetal DNA scans, Agnetha Aasland rang me the evening after we'd finalized our plan. *She thought maybe you'd go with me for moral support Mats wants to be kind but*

Agnetha and Mats had faced some kind of fertility challenges leading up to this, I remembered Dr. Shimizu telling me. There, but for the grace of strange fairytale destiny, went I.

Id be glad to mystery colleague, I rang her back. We synced our appointments for Friday morning, two days away.

The four of us met outside the medical building. Agnetha looked about forty, tall and still ballerina-slender at this stage, with feathery flaxen hair in a fetching pixie cut. Too clearly Elis' type; I gave him a pointed warning look when his energy revved at the sight of her. He laughed softly and slipped a pretend-husbandly arm around my shoulders. Mats, an engineer somewhere else, was also tall and blond, his temples and goatee going white enough to suggest he was some years older than she was. He seemed quietly cordial if a bit on the robotic side.

No sooner had Agnetha and I rung ourselves in for the appointment than my charming rogue of a fake spouse went to work on the next cute fair-haired female he saw. This time, though, it was according to plan. The voluptuous middle-aged strawberry blonde med tech warmed to him from the moment he leaned over her station as she checked us in. By the time we went to our separate cubicles to leave urine samples as directed, they were chatting away in friendly medicalese. Unlike Berenys, he stuck to his winningly-accented English.

She was answering his questions about images on a big work screen when I returned. Maybe blood flow to the placenta. We took the fancy medical chairs she indicated, side by side so Agnetha could grip my free hand. I didn't know if I could exert finfolk emotional influence over a regular person, outside of the romantic sphere where maybe I'd done so unknowingly my whole life… but it was worth a shot, so I breathed out whatever peace and calm I could summon. The one big intrauterine needle was the only unsettling part, and it didn't take that long. Meanwhile, the tech remained fully under the influence, on the perpetual verge of a blush, talking and laughing with Elis.

"So many As," she giggled, hesitating before rearranging a couple of the vials she was organizing into a slotted tray. "All right, we'll ring you both in about forty-eight hours to schedule your follow-ups. Oh. First thing Monday, rather."

I'd imagined more tests than this, actual abdominal scans; that must be part of the follow-up, I guessed. I held Elis' hand long enough to wonder whether he'd had a chance to interfere with my medical records as planned. He smiled tenderly into my eyes in equal parts mischief and affirmation.

"Okay so far?" I asked Agnetha as we headed out into the blustery day. Elis let me wear his nice ecoleather jacket against the chill.

She gave me a sheepish smile. "I suppose when all's said and done, this was the easy part."

"Well, call me if you want backup on Monday too, okay?"

I knew for sure that if I did come in for my follow-up, I would devoutly want the real Geir at my side. Maybe we'd dress him in Elis' jacket and shades, to be safest.

By the time I left work, I realized that in my preoccupied state, I'd left my own jacket in the prenatal clinic after taking it off to have blood drawn. I didn't feel like heading back across town in the dark and rain. Even if my gut was right and there was no next appointment, I could pick it up Monday morning, or one of my Geirs could collect it for me.

Chapter 33

The Great Edge

The rain continued unabated all weekend. Saturday, I slept away some of the waiting time curled against the contentment and soothing warmth of my favorite rock. We ordered takeaway and stuck close to home.

It was still dark (although this late in the year, and in this weather, that didn't give me much clue as to the hour) when we were jolted from bed Sunday by urgent pulses--both on my wrist and Geir's device, sitting on the bedside table.

I groaned. "Ajo, not again, B."

My eyes took a moment to focus on the steady flow of text coming at us from the other side of the sea.

appears ive got my own fairy godmother—shes called liv ovesen here have a look

She upnoded her letter from Liv, Ióar's acquisitions editor friend. *Striking... timely... uncanny,* I picked up as I scanned. And with the amount Liv was offering her to further develop and publish a first volume of selected poems, Berenys would be more than able to buy stylish outfits to go dancing in celebration, even pay for Champagne herself if she felt like it. Too bad she'd exiled herself back to the tiny British islands that made her so stir-crazy.

Still, we dared hope her wonderful news might be a sign that more of the same was on the way for us.

Since the weather remained inhospitable enough for me to want it back, my truthful and faithful Geir (rather than his expert liar of a temporary counterpart with the distinctly wandering eye) went with me before work Monday to retrieve my forgotten jacket from the clinic. The doors burst open as we reached them, forcing us both to take a fast half-step back. I knew the tall, slender patient who rushed past us, but her flooding eyes hadn't seen me at all.

I hadn't received a notification yet regarding a follow-up visit. Her being here already surely indicated something wrong with her results.

"Agnetha." Anxiety's sharp fingernails gripped me in the liver on her behalf. "Are you okay?"

She gasped a little as she turned, recognized me, speechlessly shook her head.

"Where's Mats?" I asked, gentler.

"Coming. He was trying to reschedule his meeting... they took me in early and I decided to get it over with. I just didn't think..." She kept shaking her head.

We made our way, weaving slightly, to an atrium bench. I sat close by and had her ring her partner again. Geir hovered near enough to support me, far enough not to crowd her. Patients and people in lab coats moved purposefully around us.

Mats answered immediately. Hearing only her side of the conversation put my emerging Norwegian skills to the test, but I understood enough to break out in a cold salt sweat.

I heard *pike*, girl. *Not ten but twenty-three* (weeks, I understood). That she'd modified her work long before then. I took her hand, let her grab it tight as she sobbed and told him *tvillinger*, twins, but now just the one. *Mosaicism*, I thought she said. The doctors' best guess was that the surviving twin had been the *genetisk normal* one, before absorbing the one that must not have been viable. DNA like nothing these doctors had ever seen.

She couldn't bear the thought of choosing to end a pregnancy she'd waited so long to achieve, but they had to face the possibility…

"Agnetha." I didn't even try for Norwegian. "No, listen. I think… those have to be my test results, not yours."

In my peripheral vision, Geir's dark head lifted suddenly to attention.

Agnetha gulped and blinked wide eyes at me. "What? Why would they…"

"You remember that tech," I managed to say. "So distracted. Agnetha Aasland and Arden Araujo at the same appointment, too many As to keep track of. Right?" As far as I could figure, she would have had to swap our pre-labeled empty vials completely for this to happen, drawing Agnetha's samples into the ones prepared for Araujo and mine into Aasland. All in a day's work for Elis Kyles, although he'd never meant to cause this level of disruption.

"And I know…" I gritted my teeth. It might be a mistake but I couldn't let this family suffer needlessly. "That's the right number of weeks for us. And there's--genetic abnormalities in my family tree…"

Geir was back at my side. "Does Agnetha need to hear the private family stuff?"

"Don't you get it? It's already done," I snapped, in sudden tears.

He put his steady hand on my shoulder, feeling like when I'd pulled a broken rebreather mask from beneath the micro-rubble of a geological formation that had taken millennia to grow.

"Okay, my jo," he whispered, trusting me now as he had then.

Aasland had murmured something to Mats and now was quiet, looking at me with big North Sea eyes.

"Let's get mine," I answered, steadier than I would have thought I could be. "Then we'll know for sure."

I rang Shimizu directly instead of furthering the clinic charade, and linked Agnetha into the call.

"Hey, mamacita," she greeted me, making me laugh in spite of everything.

"Hi, doc. I'm here with Aasland at the prenatal clinic. Her results are in. Have you had a look at anything?"

"I just saw the notification. But no peeking before the four of you, of course."

"Okay." I drew a sharp breath. "Mine first. Go."

There was a pause. "Oh," she said with a smile in her voice. "All the precautionary measures we talked about seem to have worked perfectly. It's not what you thought, though, hmm. Only ten weeks, four days? Maybe you'll name him after your father? Anyway, congratulations. Everything looks great."

"Not what I thought at all," I agreed. "Big fat waste of money on those precautionary measures. You know you kept me too busy to have anything to tell Geir about when I was in Florida and he was in Scotland during that time frame..."

Another, longer pause as Shimizu got Aasland's report. Then, finally, "No. No no no no. Shit. Arden, how could this happen? This is what her doctors gave her?"

"This is what the Scandinavian healthcare network can all see now. Yes," I whispered. My eyes were blurring but I noticed, through the glass doors, Mats hurrying out of a pod, still in his own lab coat.

Shimizu's voice took on the cool metallic edge I never liked having swung in my direction. "Agnetha, I imagine they've referred you to a number of specialists?"

"Yes?"

"You won't need to go. Your son is perfect. I'm so sorry for the stress. Whoever messed this up, I'll get them fired."

"He doesn't work for any of you. You can't fire him," I said with an involuntary laugh at the absurdity of the unfolding disaster.

"What?" Mats protested. "What is this, some kind of awful joke?"

"Is that Mats? He's there too? And Geir? Good." Shimizu breathed a short, purposeful sigh. "All of you stay there. I'm on my way."

I felt myself starting to erode under the rising tide, now I wasn't holding Agnetha up by myself. "You want to get in touch with the expert on my family's genetics, or should I?"

"I'm on it," she said, her voice steel-solid in answer to the tremble that had developed in mine.

The moments that followed were as strange as any jumbled selkie impression. Mats was a good sport, sitting on Aasland's other side while we waited. She and I clung together on the bench the way Geir and I had once held each other on a life raft riding aftershock surge. She tried to ask if I was all right. I had no words. But she'd find out soon, along with the rest of the world--unless we could somehow stop what was already in motion, irrevocable as the previous Storegga slides.

Shimizu arrived in a pod with Elis. They'd obviously made a plan on the way. She drew Agnetha and Mats aside. Geir took Agnetha's place, his strong embrace radiating calm and trust that permeated slowly. Elis startled me by kneeling at my feet, more beautifully in earnest than I'd ever seen him.

"I know I should apologize, but I can only thank you," he murmured. "Ripples spreading outward from the moment you landed in Scotland."

Even when he wasn't remotely trying to steal me out from under his old man, his sparkling eyes were so compelling I couldn't help but give him the little smile he wanted.

"You're welcome," I said when I found my voice.

His steady smile was a lot better than my lopsided one. "Okay. So we'll ring her majesty now, and I won't let her say off with your head, or anything of the sort."

We did. She didn't.

She cried for a few terribly quiet moments, this time intensely enough to dim her loveliness just a little, but she wasn't angry at anyone.

"We've had to retreat to the caves, only to have the seas start rising too high for us to stay. Then the tsunami. It's meant to be now," she said at last. "It's such a heavy thing, that this would come during my time as our eldest.

"Yet I've been sure it would, ever since we met." She cast her red-rimmed eyes upward at her prince, who smiled uncertainly in response. "You were born to speak for us, once we were ready to tell. And that you came to me when you did… it could only mean the time was near."

He blinked, ran a hand through the thick regrowth on top of his head. "Shite," he said under his breath. "My heart, I never thought…"

"It was for me to carry, not you," she breathed in reply. "Not before today."

He sighed as he shook his head, but his smitten smile wasn't far behind. "Okay, *drøttenmín.*"

"Then you do see it too."

"Everyone with eyes can see it too, my queen," Elis interrupted. I'd never seen him so aglow with pride.

His bright eyes darted in my direction. "And then there's this one," he said, softer.

"Oh, indeed." Brynja smiled through her tears. "Arden, love, if I've made you think it was only for the children you might have, that I wanted you with us…"

Lachlan shook his head again. "Everyone's always known it was far more than this."

Geir's sweet agreement lit up my blood vessels and nerve pathways like the seaside promenade. I just found a smile, and let them both make me cry a little.

Brynja met Elis' eyes straight on through the virtual connection.

"So. You know what to do there, and we'll begin preparing from here."

"Ach. The conversation with my dad's first, isn't it," Lachlan realized aloud.

Elis answered with a low chuckle. "Sorry, lad, I'd have wished to be there with you."

"Nah, I know." Lachlan smiled gamely. "You've worked toward this day a lot longer than I have. You do your part, and I'll do my best."

Elis went to ensure all the loose ends were tied up with the science and engineering team. The soon-to-be-recognized world leader and her spokesman set about their own critical business.

That left Mr. Peace and Love to take care of me and our little bombshell in utero, which was all he desired anyway. Shimizu wanted us well off the medical campus, just in case. So we took a pod to the sunlit sidewalk cafe Berenys had liked, both keenly aware we'd probably never sit there anonymously again. He got us a slice of almond-meringue-cream cake to share, with tea for him and a little cup of coffee for me.

He took on the more difficult of the next tasks, too: ringing Ióar and Ysmay first, then Berenys, in whispered Norn. I wanted to sit safe in the half-circle of his arm, to understand what was being said, but I had some surreal calls to make too.

Vega, who stepped out of a conference to say what she thought would be a quick hello, laughed and told me I shouldn't partake of whatever she guessed I was smoking or ingesting, not in my condition. She had to ring off before I could convince her I wasn't high or joking. Doña Maite couldn't make any better sense of it, not in either of the languages we shared. I was trying to figure out what I'd say to Stefek, who might prove a more likely believer, when Shimizu rang me back.

"Is everybody all right?"

"So far."

"Good. Listen, Kenneth and Lachlan rang Elis and me just now. We're all thinking the same thing. The walls have retinal implants and cochlear circuitry, yes? So let's get you out of Dodge. "

Geir agreed instantly.

"Okay, but to where? It's not like I can really get off-grid."

"So, two things. As to where, Kenneth has a place in mind. And for the how… I promise I'll fix this as soon as I can, but for right now, kiddo, you're terminated from UFE service."

Chapter 34

Off-Grid

As my immediate selkie family already knew, off-grid life wasn't so bad for friends of KXA. A yacht registered in the name of friends of friends of Kenneth spirited us north-northwest to a lightly and loyally-staffed research station, built like a small oil platform with plenty of room for hiding in plain sight and easy access to the ever less daylit sea. English was the lingua franca for the international team, nice for us both; there were even Americans based there, a mother and son team of glaciologists from Newark.

Between the length of the nights here and the bizarre luxury of no work, I slept as much as I wanted, albeit at odd hours. It might have been a weird destination for a romantic babymoon trip. But I'd been pulled up here with a top-level spec in that field, not just your regular run-of-the-mill services generalist, and made sure to take full advantage of his expertise.

An innocuous drone shipment of essentials from Bergen preceded the massive white seal and the little spotted gray one who joined us as soon as they could get there without a boat. His people followed, a few at a time. Fortunately, the place was big enough for them to continue keeping their space from him as well as from us.

Meanwhile, on-grid, Lachlan, Elis, and Shimizu decided which truths to reveal and how. Even as they told the rest of the world the biology and history side of things, they remained selkie-level coy regarding geography: our whereabouts, as well as those of the Northern Isles and Hebridean folk who'd gone to ground at the first whisper of the big news. They shared a secure node where anyone wondering about that mystery bit of their family's DNA could get in touch.

Not even in the aftermath of the tsunami itself had I seen the grid explode like this, consumed with one single story. Everywhere you looked, flickered bright and dark lines and bars representing the DNA of the newly-discovered semihuman species squirming nonstop around my uterus.

Between the lines surged maps of Norway, Shetland, and Orkney, resurfacing tsunami animations, photos of my mother in her silver cocktail dress, still-startling clips of Dad speaking fluent sciencese, and plenty of finfolk madness. "Is the Answer to Anti-Aging Found in North Sea Minerals?", "selkie eye" makeup tutorials next to lash enhancement ads, "Shapeshifter Sex Secrets Revealed" (my eyeballs sprinted away from that headline), "Nordic Diet and Cold-Water Workout Plan," and my favorite, "Oliver Araujo: Selkies Gave Me Storegga Slide II Theory (I Just Wrote It Down)."

Not that I believed so-called journalists had contacted my father beyond the grave, but I did wonder whether they'd stumbled onto a truth I'd also suspected for some time. Lachlan, when I'd brought it up with him, agreed right away.

Nereiður had been one of the oldest in the world by the time Dad knew her. The selkies we loved supernaturally understood their ocean home; how much more profoundly had it communicated itself to one such as her? All those years listening to the planet, perceiving the moods and movements of seabed and sea from both above and far below the surface. She must have had some sense of what was to come. Whether or not she'd told him how she knew, we could only suspect that had drawn her to Kristiansand, little realizing she'd find there the source of her hope and her destruction.

I didn't take most calls that came in, but a few I picked up right away.

"You will not guess who just rang," Vega greeted me.

"First Gentleman Huang."

"Ha. Jake Fontana."

"Who?"

"Still doesn't have the nerve to talk to you--"

"I wouldn't have anything to say if he tried."

"Even after I convinced him it's not all a huge prank and he's been with another species. I pointed out the obvious, that it's been a hell of a long time since you missed anything about him... beyond his mom's cannolis..."

"Well, all her cooking," I admitted. "But I have your mom now, and Yasmin Darzi, and Berenys, so."

"True. So I passed on some helpful information you gave me."

"You didn't let me tell you anything..."

"For instance. I explained that by the 'skills' you told me about, you meant centuries of experience in a body that looks and feels as young as yours."

I giggled. "Younger, as I recall you insisting. Although you weren't wrong about the hacked ident."

"And that by 'mind-reading,' you were, of course, referring to how the sensory telepathy works during the marital bliss times."

I just kept laughing.

"And you actually went to Miami. Mija, have you learned nothing at all from me? Damn." She laughed too, low and wondering. "But you found the way to your happily ever after, even so. With some thanks, weirdly enough, to what's-his-name, who's now crystal clear on why you don't miss him at all."

I'd been officially remarried for a while by then, had the surfer boy who'd never been much of a first husband chosen to check my ident. Since we'd gone that far, I'd ordered Geir a ring, too, though someone in our corner had to creatively reroute it from Stavanger to our current lack of address. He'd annoyingly had no opinion as to the style. Possibly because he'd already worn all the popular ones, still not a conversation he ever seemed to want to have with me. I chose a wide satin-finished platinum band to match the shape and color of mine. He was within when the insured drone arrived, so I wore it--weighty and cool on the second finger of my right hand--until I could slip it onto his finger. The same way he'd done for me, except that for no fraction of a breath did I wonder what his answer would be.

A couple weeks in, with the dust having not so much settled as started whirling slower, we received visitors. The deliberately un-flashy triphibious hover belonged to someone connected to Lars Aasland; it landed after dusk, better ensuring some of the most famous people in the world could join us without fanfare.

Lachlan looked great, tanned and strong, with a fierce bear hug to match. I'd had no idea how much I'd wanted to see him and Brynja again.

He waved a mock-stern finger at her before she could embrace me, too; laughing, she just laid a light selkie fetal scanner, palm and fingertips, against my belly. So Berenys had inherited the perfect radio-silence ability from her mother. I could only guess what my queen might perceive; her two perfect glittering tears of delight threatened to undo me nevertheless.

Elis offered Berenys a hand down onto the deck, the two of them arguing like an old married couple the whole time. He turned back for Dr. Shimizu, but she waved him off. She needed a moment between standing up after the long ride and getting down the few ladder-style steps. The pilot jumped out to offer assistance as well, a dark-skinned young guy in--

"Stefek," I shouted; they both grinned at having pulled off the surprise, her fatigue and discomfort falling momentarily away.

Geir laughed when he greeted us in startlingly correct Norn.

"Alien first contact, right?" my linguist buddy reminded me with a laugh of his own. "Although when you said your intentions for her were shocking, man, we had no idea…"

"Ha, yeah… Outdone myself, haven't I."

They went together to unload the hover; this was only a temporary stay, a place between, so no one had brought much.

"Damn," Elis murmured as we watched the VIPs meeting and greeting, in one of the more sober tones I'd ever heard from him. I followed his eyes to where Ióar had come up on the landing pad, his people ranged silently behind him. Brynja rushed to embrace and kiss him like an exceptionally long-lost brother, to exchange unhurried wet-eyed selkie stares and no words at all, as far as I could determine.

"I like the lad, too, but you won't really let him come between you and Moby-Dick, will you?" Elis said, his smile only showing in the quirk of one eyebrow.

Berenys narrowed eyes aglitter and lips pale with what might have been actual frost crystals. "Excuse me?"

"Great majestic bloke, frequently mistaken for an ugly duckling when he was but a wee finbairn? Surely you know the one."

Berenys turned her shoulder sharply toward me, away from him. "Please say there's enough space here I don't have to share a room with anyone," she muttered.

I didn't know where Ysmay had been sleeping anyway. As soon as I showed Berenys where to find out about her accommodations, she stalked off without another word.

Elis winked at me. "Obviously, young Stéphane is more Tinker-bell's type."

"Nice to see you're an equal-opportunity pain in the arse, Brynja junior."

"Touché," he chuckled, moving away too as Lachlan, at Brynja's side, motioned for him to meet Ióar and the other Norwegians.

Some natives took Berenys and Brynja for a restorative night swim while the rest of us gathered in a communal kitchen. Lachlan, in the absence of his usual competition, worked with his grandfather to create a more than acceptable vegetarian curry and rice from supplies on hand. Ióar and Halfdan ate with us, then gave us our space. Ysmay just had some of the Belgian sweets Stefek had brought, but she amused me by sticking around anyway. After handing off to Ióar a small gift-type bag I'd seen among the things Berenys brought off the hover, she camped out at a small table with none other than Stefek, their heads bent over something, once he'd polished off his meal. When we said we were heading off for a nightcap, she waved us away in irritation.

Elis and Dr. Shimizu took available rooms next to one another, sharing a balcony; he invited us out to enjoy the fantastic star-watching opportunity. I hoped for aurora borealis, though we hadn't seen any yet this season.

He produced from his luggage a bottle that provoked a smile from the old man, along with five coffee cups swiped from the kitchen. He poured a shot each in four and a scant teaspoon in the last one.

"Isle of Mull," he said as he distributed them. "Don't have it yet. There's a list of all we have to drink to." He gave Dr. Shimizu a sweet hint of smile, yielding the floor.

She nodded. "First, though it's only a promise at the moment, let me reiterate that I'm working on getting your job back in some worthwhile form." She clinked my cup. "I know you can't necessarily make it to Miami for a while. Anyway, your marine bio advocate over here is pretty strongly in favor of waiting until after finbaby and maternity leave and such."

Geir slipped his free arm around me. Usually so careful not to tell me what to do, this time he was unabashedly in Elis' camp.

I sighed. "Thanks."

She looked up at Lachlan, who raised his cup. "Second. Part of the urgency to run up here was for you to hear this before the media get it. Dad's been in a buying and selling and dealing frenzy whenever he's been off-camera. Not just rewilding the Bressay depot, but annexing to it. He's got nearly half the island for us. More to follow. To give selkies their own territory."

This time, Geir's thrill of satisfaction was in perfect sync with what I felt. "Damn," I breathed out both our reactions together. "He's amazing."

"A force to be reckoned with," Elis murmured in all sincerity.

"You've got the last one," Lachlan said with a smile of pleasure in their collective accomplishments. "Since you two wouldn't even say what it was."

"Right." Elis' sparkling eyes met Shimizu's bright gaze over the rims of their respective cups. "Best for last. We've finally had a look at your full DNA analysis, and… Nereiður 3.0 comes out around, at a minimum, seventy-eight percent finkid." He raised his dark brows and waited for me to do the math.

"Uh. I don't think so."

"Uh." Dr. Shimizu laughed softly. "We didn't think so, either, so we re-ran your results separately. They're quite consistent... Confirmed detection of pinniped skeletal remains in there with the guayaberas and the academic regalia, my dear."

Lachlan's excited laugh was louder. His "Damn me. That's bloody brilliant" pretty accurately vocalized Geir's response as well.

I stared at them, shaking my head. "I cleaned out his closets myself. And he always said guayaberas were for old guys…"

Elis, still chuckling, crossed his arms, bright eyes issuing the challenge. "Think."

One thing was for sure. If I'd become practically allergic to Biscayne Bay after a few months of North Sea, there was no possible way a selkie had made Cuban or Venezuelan waters home. It couldn't be that part of the...

"Oh. Damn. Magdalene Fairchild."

His eyes went round. "Fairchild? Really? From where?"

My pulse was dancing quite a merengue all of a sudden, too. Or, I supposed, a reel. "It has to have been her--I mean, you were there, you saw the ones with that chestnut coloring. County Donegal."

"Oh." His laugh looked and sounded an awful lot like one of relief. "Well. To Noa, to Kenneth, and to Magdalene Fairchild." He held up his coffee cup; we all toasted, and I readily downed my one incense-rich sip.

"This is Maite's Maggie we're talking about, yes? With the big heart and the red hair?" Dr. Shimizu guessed.

"Right. Dad's paternal grandmother," I said to Elis and Lachlan.

"And I'm thinking you've used the name Fairchild before?" Dr. Shimizu laughed, too.

Elis' laugh faded to a sly little grin. "From Fair Isle."

She shook her head, smiling.

"Any idea who the selkie parent was?" Lachlan said, eyes sapphire-bright.

"I mean, only in the folktale sense of the word... It was the scandal of her little town when she was born to a relatively wealthy young lady who would never name the man."

"'Little ken I my bairn's father, far less the land where he dwells in,'" Geir quoted with a mischievous smile.

"Oopsy daisy," Elis murmured. "Or... did she?"

Another laugh spilled out of me. "Ach, no, relax. Let's see. Her name was Ellen?--no, Eleanor Carroll. Fairchild was who she eventually married... and he adopted Maggie, who one day came to the US for med school..."

"Not all of med school. Her fellowship in hematology," Shimizu said. "But, ah, carry on…"

"In Boston, right? Where she met a dashing intern named Álvaro Rivera Ochoa, also born on a faraway island… Santos, the son they had not many years later, was my father's father." The troublesome Santos, if this was true, had been the same volatile man-finman mixture as Lachlan Adie. And Doña Maite saw it, even though she hadn't known what to call it. (Oh boy. I'd need to ring her back.)

Old stories. The tattered and stained selkie book, safe in storage in Monterey, appeared in my mind's eye. It was old enough to have been Maggie's. My father had said she'd always told the most amazing tall tales when he was a child; how could I have known to beg him for every detail he could possibly recall?

"She must have looked like the rest of us," I said. "Right? So if he had some inkling about her, then when he met my mom, don't you think…"

"Not to mention, I've never met anyone as perceptive as your mother, anywhere, any time. She could have picked up on his twelve or so percent. Whether she'd have brought it up with him is a whole other question."

"Ugh." Frustration spurred me from my seat to look over the railing at the glassy dark swells below. "Weren't we supposed to be freezing important people's brains by 2100, preserving their consciousness for posterity or whatever? Dammit. I wouldn't wake him up for long. I just need to ask him this one thing."

"Flying cars, too, right?" I didn't think I'd ever seen Dr. Shimizu look wistful, but it suited her so well I intuited she must feel that way far more often than she showed it.

"Which would you rather, that he did know and didn't see fit to tell you, or that he let himself be fooled like Blaine Maclachlan or Kenneth Adie?" Geir murmured. "Best just to own it now, and do with the knowledge whatever we want."

With another sigh, I turned to see the quiet reassurance on his face. Stupid hormones making my eyes sting.

"Isla knew the old tales, well enough to laugh when she found herself in one," Elis said. "And she was brave and clever, like you. We wondered, after I'd told her, whether she didn't have a few drops of the ancient salt in her own blood. I mean, if you do the maths, most Shetland families who've been there long enough must have a touch. Irresistible as we are." He gave me a sly wink. "Geir's handiwork alone, over the years…"

If there'd been any Scotch left in our cups, we'd both have spit it out for sure.

Dr. Shimizu chuckled. "You're a one-man rollercoaster, aren't you."

Elis managed a simultaneously cute and evil return laugh. "But it would help explain Elisabeth shifting when plenty of hybrid children couldn't," he said, after allowing us a moment to laugh along with him. "Maybe even explain why Isla never fell out of love with the arsehole wicked stepdad, you know?"

He watched me pondering. Then he put his smooth hand on the back of my arm.

Isla Russell's azure eyes laughed in his memory, luxuriant ginger-gold curls tossing in sea wind and sunlight, not much older than I was now. I blinked and she was white-haired, hands slowing, fragile on her harpstrings. Another blink, he and Lachlan scattered her ashes in Vaila Sound.

I didn't expect the next blink to show someone else's gray-streaked hair, sharp dark eyes, the hard-won satisfaction of provoking her smile. I wasn't sure he'd meant me to share it; he shook his head, realizing I had.

Noa Shimizu was not what quick flings were made of. It made sense if he wasn't willing to start what he had no desire to finish as fast as it would happen in her case, not this soon after Isla. I sighed, thinking only that I'd never reveal anything to her that he didn't wish.

He took his hand away and gave me a smile. "Such is life. How does it go? 'Everything flows, nothing stays.'"

For a fantastic beastie who'd gone undetected the first twenty weeks of her gestation, the baby had made up for lost time ever since. I'd swear she gained a hundred grams on a slow day. I constantly slathered her tight, itching chrysalis in Caribbean cocoa butter. Luisa Ramos and Mrs. Darzi recommended the same brand, replete with such fairytale-sounding ingredients as rosehips and dragon's blood extract. And I couldn't get through a night without at least one reprieve for my crowded bladder, then some kind of snack to keep the insatiable monster going until breakfast.

Lachlan, Brynja, and Dr. Shimizu didn't stay more than twenty-four hours, but Elis and Berenys did. Stefek had a long weekend off from his coursework to spend with us.

A few nights after our new arrivals settled into a routine more normal than mine, I lumbered into the deserted kitchen area closest to our room. A big bakery box, labeled in Sharpie FREE TO GOOD HOMES PLEASE ENJOY WHILE FRESH, drew my eyes and nose. Heaven bless Lacey Silverman's ex-mother-in-law in New Jersey, and her abiding concern that her thirty-something Ph.D. grandson be properly nourished up here near the Arctic Circle. The mostly empty box still contained a half dozen real bagels, and there was cream cheese in the fridge.

I shamelessly grabbed the one everything bagel left, thinking back to my eponymous adorable seal buddy in Monterey Bay as I sliced and spread and blissfully chewed. Who knew what she'd think of all this. Maybe, if my finbairn was the traveling kind, I'd take her to meet EB one day, reclaim her California USA roots. Mam's little girl seemed plenty happy with the current East Coast feeding options, as well.

In the quiet, I noticed the faint fast percussion of approaching barefoot steps. Geir walked that softly, but not normally at such speed. I turned to find Ysmay rushing in.

"Oh," she said with clear annoyance, and shook her head, already turning back.

"Who did you think you'd find at this hour?"

"Stéphane's not in his room," she said with a gusty sigh.

I blinked, waiting for words, checking the time while I waited. 0430. "Well, he's headed back to Brussels in a few hours. Maybe he needed--"

"Ach," she scoffed and tossed her head. She retrieved something from her pocket, dropped it into my hand without really touching me. "Just tell him his last idea worked."

Ióar's watch lay cool in my palm. I knew before lifting it that I'd hear it ticking away as if it hadn't lain dormant all those years.

"Wow. Why not tell him yourself?" I said, smiling.

"I've nothing to say to him," she huffed, topping her sister's teen drama queen tendencies with a single sentence. "Here." In a few economical movements, she slipped out of her tank and sweatpants, thrusting them toward me. "I'm having an at-sea day, if anyone bothers to ask."

She stalked off toward the interior deck where the selkie folk had been making their dives, either confident it was too early to run into Isaac Silverman and the other researchers, or not caring. The thing was, I reflected as I made a point of still enjoying the rest of the bagel, I couldn't agree with what I guessed she thought. The vibes she'd radiated loud and clear were agitated for sure, but not in the way she'd previously allowed me to understand she felt when Berenys was up to her usual. If Nereiður Junior had really decided to have her way with Stefek, Ysmay wouldn't have needed to search the station for him: she'd have known far too much about what he was doing, surely to include exactly where he was.

That led me to hypothesize, by the time I crept back to bed, that Queen B had been messing with some of us. Served Elis right, at least, all but daring her as he had. Ysmay and Ióar, on the other hand, hadn't earned this.

I lay awake so long I figured I'd just make coffee and see Stefek off myself, only to blink and find it late enough even Geir had gotten up before me.

Geir and I sat out on Elis' balcony again when Ysmay showed up well past dark; Ióar and Halfdan were still with us, while the rest had headed to bed. A thermal blanket, heavy with seawater from her skin and unwrung hair, trailed her like a cloak. Halfdan gave her a little smile and offered the last beer the guys had been keeping cold. She answered with the haughty hint of an upward nod, but the small white hand she extended from within her cloak opened toward me.

I leaned awkwardly onto one hip to fish what she wanted out of my pocket. I'd shown Geir but I hadn't told anyone else. Her expression softened once she held it, warm and ticking, in her palm. She never smiled, though, leaving that to Ióar when he understood what she'd pressed into his hand.

He murmured a string of delighted syllables of which I understood *dakk, elskling,* and *hjarta,* drawing her close to press a kiss to her salty forehead. With a sigh, she melted against him, face against his neck, little body nestling between his arm and side. As he stroked her hair, she extended her arm back toward Halfdan who chuckled quietly, opened the bottle, and placed it in her hand.

As the rest of us went back to chatting, she and Ióar shared the beer, with not another word between them. From the way his smile faded, I knew she was recalling the morning's events for him. But from the smile that remained to play about his beautiful features, I was pretty sure he'd come to the same conclusion I had; and that, like my own true love, he was willing to play the long game.

Chapter 35

Bressay

The good people of Shetland responded with characteristic generous pragmatism to the efforts of their most famous son, his son-in-law and grandson, and most of all to the superhuman neighbors whose identity they'd never fully known--now an officially recognized and protected species. All the rewilded areas of Bressay, Whalsay, Fetlar, and Unst were designated as Selkie territory as of November 15, 2097. The political situation would continue evolving, to say the least, but our family considered it a hopeful start.

By the time we made our way home ourselves, a few days after the official declaration, finfolk from south and west of us had begun converging on Shetland. Not everyone; some wanted their peace and freedom more than the uneasy beginnings offered in a land that should have been their own, but now surrounded by local and national police and UFPKs. The Norwegians came with us. Although half of them were pretty open in their ambivalence, connecting was selkie nature.

The twins were ready to get back to the beautiful gray house on the bluff, after months away; Berenys asked us to wait, though, as she got out of the hover. I would have expected Geir to feel the same, but it unsettled him deeply to see armed PKs at each door and a small craft hovering overhead. Neither of us went inside.

Berenys came back down the sandstone stairs with the sweet, lidded antique picnic basket, which she handed to Ióar as though it were laden with something quite a bit heavier than scones and strawberries. "For whenever," she murmured.

He nodded, eyes bright with a smile that didn't need to reach his other features.

Kjeld's light brown eyes, on the other hand, looked migraine-pinched. Síarr's weren't even open most of the time. We'd arrived via triphibious hover. Now that we were on the tranquil water they loved, though, I understood flying wasn't so great for these ones, either. We dropped them off, with Thyra and Sindri, to rest at the guest cottage they'd booked in Hamnavoe.

An armed PK met them at their door, too. My unease deepened as we watched Sindri stare the guy down several seconds longer than would have been comfortable. I hated to admit I saw his point. Were the guards here to keep their newly-discovered species safe from the rest of the world, as stated? Couldn't it be the other way round?

In any case, we five—Geir and me, Halfdan, Shimizu and Elis— with our unarmed escort, were apparently still free to move about the islands of our own volition. Stefek snuck us into May's little back room: fish and chips for old time's sake. Our hostess was solicitous of me and my selkie bairn, settling me with her mam's favorite ginger tea and extra biscuits I ended up feeding to Stefek and Geir.

I was amused, not bothered, she didn't seem to consider Geir off limits; never mind his impending fatherhood of another woman's child, let alone the fact her own lovely husband was working right outside the door. They'd been friends long before she met Niall or I met Geir, after all. Eventually, she just sat with us, flirting away in fluent selkiese like it was old times, even as she politely ogled our new guests. She refused to take our money.

Halfdan bent to kiss her hand in thanks before we slipped out the back to our waiting hover, breathing sweet nothings about her beautiful blue eyes. Shimizu, accustomed to Elis' antics as she was by this time, still muffled a laugh. If he hadn't already been my favorite of the younger Norwegian guys, that cute gesture would have done it.

Kenneth Adie's private triphibious met us at the former site of the KXA depot. This time of year, the island's striking green hadn't begun to regrow yet over the facility's bare footprint. It wouldn't take long, though, come spring. The removal efforts had been painstakingly thorough. Shimizu wore a particularly delighted smile as she waved up at the approaching hover.

I'd expected he would greet her first upon landing, or perhaps Brynja's imposing Norwegian counterpart, who'd arrived just before us. My heart beat halfway out of my chest with pleasure when he went immediately to Elis Kyles instead. I couldn't hear over the hover motor what they said, close to one another's ears, but there wasn't much need when we could all see the earnest, lasting embrace that followed.

My queen took my hand, as pleased as I was. Beyond Elis and Kenneth, I saw the rugged misty coastline overlaid three times upon itself: once with my own eyes, twice with hers. She associated no pain or disappointment with the memory of the thriving facility. Rather, she respected and even loved the titan who had developed this site; I didn't try to tease out what was her honoring his longstanding desire to protect her realm, what was affection for the man who'd fathered the prince her people needed at this appointed time. Whatever tension had existed between them in the past had been just a surface-level disturbance.

But there was a quiet thrill deeper than her love for any person, as she showed me what this place had been before KXA or any modern industry. Her vibrant memory even smelled and tasted like a cleaner, more intact version of itself, as distinct from our time as fresh-picked fruit was from imported. She felt immense gratitude for all the ways

Kenneth Adie sought a return to what he couldn't remember, but she could.

As she lifted shining eyes to mine, my inward horizon tilted, though physically I stayed stable. The morning the tsunami struck this place, on the other side of the world I'd had the fleeting dream or vision of an ark upon the rising waters. I hadn't ever stopped to think of it again, but Brynja caught that one bright bubble streaming back up into my consciousness now. She thought about the people in that old story, stepping down out of their craft as their own corrupt era's resulting hellish flood began to subside, onto a land as close as it would ever be again to what had existed in the beginning.

My queen's awareness delicately reached for my sense of the beautiful new hybrid creation growing inside me. This moment overflowed with so much of what she had sought. I was too far within us both to realize my knees were close to doing what tended to be a side effect of the selkie sensory overload that was my queen's particular specialty, but as usual, my rock was there to hold me steady.

"Have I not asked you, *drøttenmín*, to go easy on the *piri* lass?" he said with a laugh soft as antique suede.

"On the piri lass*es*," she agreed, with a thrill of hope so deep it really was best he was there to keep me upright.

Others had gathered with us, by the time I regained my focus. The remaining Norwegians were back from their rest break, along with some of our people and several Hebrideans I hadn't met yet. Geir motioned over two I didn't recognize at first. Both of them were taller, so probably younger. He put a hand lightly behind one man's shoulder. Looking closer, I noticed the lighter hair, the particularly gorgeous warmer mahogany hue of his big eyes, the delicacy of his chiseled features. I just hadn't been able to place him in jeans, work boots, knit hat, and plain navy parka. I hadn't seen him since he'd gotten safely free of the Out Skerries caverns.

"Kenneth, you asked if any others had worked here. Besides me, that's just these two of my brothers now. This is Holm Innes and Ruadh Doran."

"Mr. Adie," Ruadh smiled, shaking the boss' hand. The English I hadn't even known he spoke sounded as much Irish as Scottish. "I've just been a short-term hire now and again. Still, thanks for everything."

Adie smiled in reply. "My thanks to you, as well. Glad to know you."

Then Ruadh turned the adorable smile on me. "Thank you, too, Arden."

Speechless, I just smiled in response, and hoped to let the touch of our hands do the communicating. But it was hard to say what he might have gotten from me: I couldn't perceive much of him, beyond the undeniable gentle finman charm. His young daughter's diminished impression had almost been stronger.

Holm Innes greeted Kenneth Adie with a Norn accent as strong as I remembered Hano and Runa having. He made no move to shake my hand, and sure as hell didn't display any intent to be charming. Taken a bit aback, I realized I'd felt his ice-glazed granite stare before. He hadn't wanted *ut land isk* visitors anywhere near his Scalloway Islands home. He was no more a fan of having us on Bressay.

"Holm Innes the third, right?" Adie said thoughtfully. "Took over when your grandfather of the same name retired, one of the last ones to go who'd opened the site with us."

Holm showed the first hint of a chilly smile. "Something like that."

Down on the beach, the billionaire shipping tycoon politely averted his gaze while his son's wife and her daughters, along with Thyra, got into the water. But with Lachlan's arm around his shoulders, he watched unflinching as everyone else except Geir shifted to their seal shapes, a few at a time.

Photo drones buzzed overhead: the world was watching. Holm Innes spat a few choice North Sea sailor words and an accompanying gesture in their direction before diving in himself. Several small amphibious ones followed them under the surface.

Shimizu and Elis had been first into the pool (Vega's HOT DAMN NEKKID GRANDPA splashing before my right eye, making me giggle); they were already several meters down. She'd had the privilege of seeing him transform before, but still laughed "View of a lifetime" in my cochlear at this whole underwater spectacle.

I watched and listened for a while to Lachlan's capture, to the drone ones on-grid, projecting it for Geir. But after maybe five minutes, the virtual experience failed to hold my interest. I'd rather be here and now, with my true love, enjoying the quiet on a rare sunlit late morning this time of year. I disconnected from Shimizu and Lachlan; we turned the projection off and watched incredible numbers of birds wheeling above the nearby isle of Noss instead.

"There's one of the smaller caverns there, at the north end," Geir said. "Might be a tight fit for Kenneth but I'd be glad for him and Noa to see it."

"Speaking of a tight fit..." I sighed, a sudden hand to my lower belly. "Damn, Nessie... give it a rest, would you."

Geir tenderly listened in on my Braxton Hicks contraction with all his finman senses. "Practice one, right?"

"Yeah, no worries, tesoro. If she'd ever stop moving. I keep reading how normal babies, you're supposed to make sure they kick a certain number of times every hour or two."

He bent to kiss the side of my neck. "Sorry, but I don't think you'll be having any normal babies."

As if to agree, our selkie bairn demonstrated one of her impressive world-serpent writhing maneuvers. I groaned and waited for her to settle. Geir put his hand next to mine, breathing out his usual deep calm, sighing with sympathetic laughter.

"Truth is, all I want is to hold her and let you rest. So time it like a baby Kyles instead of a baby Craig if you like, little princess," he addressed the baby in an adoring murmur. "We've got your playground all ready."

Most of their kind took the scenic underwater route to the beautiful nearby island; with Lachlan, Kenneth and Shimizu, we climbed into the hover, canopy open, for the short ride across. The sun was already low over the calm surface ripples. Had my finman been a werewolf, the bold flashes glittering off that water would have been the aroma of a juicy rare steak.

"Don't stay just for me," I said, with a half-smile he was pretty quick to return. He put a hand on my belly, admonishing the kelpie to be good for Mam. Then with a short sweet kiss for me and a wave to the others, who continued deep in conversation about the Bressay site, he slipped out of his human skin and dove in to join his brothers and sisters. As usual, I wore his ring for safe-keeping.

The well-deserved *hot damn nekkid Gary* I would have expected didn't appear; perhaps Vega was absorbed in the feed from one of the drones, most of which were no longer watching the lack of activity on the hover deck.

I'd figured I would want to look in on the ongoing casts again myself, once my fellow passengers followed the finfolk below the water's gilded surface and I sat on the top rung of the stern ladder, trailing my feet in the cold swells, but the momentary quiet was too delicious. I'd so rarely had time to sit alone and breathe since the news had hit the grid. As I watched the wild birds' elaborate, unhurried aerial song and dance, drank sweet salt air, and rocked gently with the North Sea's motion, I even thought the baby grew calmer.

Until every hair on my skin suddenly lifted, my heartbeat shifted time signatures, and the water kelpie kicked nearly hard enough in response to crack a rib.

Adie's ring, then Lachlan's, pulsed 999. Without ever drawing another breath, I picked up Lachlan's cast.

Chapter 36

Isle of Noss

He couldn't hear me; I could make no sense of what I saw from his perspective. Madness. A predator's horrible teeth yawning wide, going for Lachlan's face. The dive knife I'd never seen anywhere but strapped to his thigh, flashing in his hand. Another sleek form torpedoing between, knocking Lachlan backward. Coils of angry dark bodies battling where soft-spoken brothers and sisters had been, until bright red swirled sickeningly into the pristine sea.

The first real contraction I'd ever had tore through my center and left me retching into the water. Lachlan's cast had cut off. As I sat frozen to the ladder rung, there was only hideous hybrid partial-awareness and the screaming of terns. Then the low throb of the first approaching triphibious hover.

The surface boiled with emerging finfolk. From just their dark wet hair and pale skin streaked with red, it was so hard to understand who'd been hurt.

Ióar's white head and shoulders stood out more clearly in the last slanting rays. He cradled a limp, bloodied form in his arms, a man with short hair—one of his brothers? Lachlan's back was to me, but it looked like he carried someone else. Another one of the Norwegian men--Halfdan, I thought--held a third injured man; the head lolling back from against his shoulder, with the longer black hair of one of ours, sent an aftershock shudder through me. My eyes strained for Geir, but I couldn't find him.

I caught half a razor-edged breath when Brynja surfaced unharmed. She refused for the hover to take her. Waiting for--No. No no no no. Shit.

I was fairly certain it was Elis who was pulled up into the hover. He appeared safe enough, but the person motionless in his strong arms, her bloodstained gray hair spilling backward into the water, was the only selkie-sized one who had needed to wear a wetsuit.

Before they sped southward, the second hover was there to take Lachlan, Brynja and two of the other three wounded--por Dios, let them only be wounded--somewhere to the northwest. Kenneth Adie got into the third hover. Thyra struggled to follow, bleeding and favoring one side. Ióar lifted the remaining victim to them but did not embark himself. The motor shifted lower as they waited on the surface. I searched the upturned faces again. Where the hell was Geir?

Ióar shot back under the water, fast as a seal though he remained in human shape. Clinging to the ladder, I lurched numbly aside to let him, dripping blood and saltwater, up on deck.

As on the night we'd met, I couldn't begin to find words. He let me lay my head against his chest, and held me close. He gently disagreed with my worry about his injuries: clear and shallow water compared to the icy, turbulent deep currents flooding most of his consciousness. He stroked my hair and didn't want to see me hurt, which only provoked a brutally contrasting happier memory that came out as something between a groan and a sob.

"Just tell me."

He sighed deeply, but showed me what I needed to know. In his memory, motivations and characters I could recognize drove the blurred seal forms.

An especially intrusive drone had bumped the back of Síarr's seal-form head. He'd spun it away in anger--not intending to strike Dr.

Shimizu between the shoulder blades, causing her to crumple horrify-ingly forward. There was a blur, Ysmay shifting into human shape to try to help her. Seal Elis charged to his dear friend's defense.

Sindri, and Holm at his shoulder, erupted like a seething un-dersea vent as the first sparks of conflict reached them. Finfolk who wanted the same thing, even if they'd never said as much, turned out to be capable of catching one another up in a waking nightmare as well as in an exquisite dream.

Seeing it unfold as Íoar had, I realized I should have understood without his help. Not every selkie heart was as resilient as the great one beating inside tiny Berenys. Holm, Sindri, Thyra and Síarr, and who knew how many others, would never forgive my kind. For Lachlan to pull a knife underwater was just the most recent in the series of wrongs they perceived he'd done to their world. They couldn't stand sharing their most secret place with the endlessly invasive, exploitative, destructive force that we *ut land isk* were.

The pitch-black depth of Íoar's sorrow overcame me. He didn't share his brothers' wrath against humankind; even if he had, he would have hated the unfairness of this consequence. I'd seen him protect Kenneth Adie. He'd been the only selkie easy to distinguish in the melee. In response, he felt an almost physical pang of not having done enough.

I brought to mind the unspeakable photo-negative aurora bore-alis spreading upward from the tangle of shifted shapes.

"Elskling." He sighed, giving me the truth in less-forceful words instead of sensory impressions. "They attacked Brynja and Lachlan for being the ones to betray our secret. Lachlan had his blade on him, to defend himself. The ones who shielded our queen were young Ruadh and your Geir."

If I'd had any control over my clenching fingers, I never would have chosen to rake Íoar's already wounded skin. Again, he dismissed my worry for him. I sobbed aloud, but the begging him for the truth without words.

"Arden, they're both gone from us. Along with my Sindri," he breathed, remembering having shifted to carry the younger man's beautiful lifeless form to the surface. Halfdan had borne Ruadh. The victim in Lachlan's arms, the one I'd been unable to see clearly… Oh, God, no. I screwed my eyes futilely shut against the sight in Ióar's memory.

He said more, but I couldn't even understand what language it might be. If Geir had been torn out of the world by this senseless brutality, how was I not even selkie enough to have felt him go? I cried like a child against Ióar's bloody shoulder, the deck beneath us suddenly tilting wildly. The last thing I felt was the breath knocked out of me, as I was thrown overboard into profound black pressure and cold.

Even before I managed to open my eyes to see the bright ceiling of an all-white room, I knew Ióar wasn't with me anymore. My original fairy godmother, eyes closed too in a chair at my side, was almost as welcome. I reached a hand toward her, which she squeezed in a firm warm grip.

"How the hell are you here?"

"Skin of my teeth and only for a few more hours," she murmured, red-rimmed eyes lifting. "You've had the team pretty freaked out, losing consciousness this long without a blow to the head. I tried suggesting it might be normal for selkies."

Not as if the human doctors should comprehend what I still couldn't. "Who else?"

She swallowed visibly. "Just you. They tell me Lachlan waited about an hour before he had to go. He and his father are getting ready to hold a press cast."

"Ióar?" I was still in the same clothes, awful amounts of his blood darkening on my clothes and caked in my hair.

"I think he's all right. He held you until the medics came, then the little queen sent him with about a dozen of their people in to the police."

"Dr. Shimizu?"

"Airlifted to Inverness. Grandpa went with her."

"Okay." Then she'd survived, too, and would be in good hands.

Vega kept meeting my gaze, but her tears spilled over before I could get the last name out.

"Geir?"

She shook her head.

There were too many things I hadn't learned. I'd thought there would be so much more time. "Did they say--I mean--" I dissolved. "Ancestral selkie burial ground? Where do I go?"

She smiled through more tears, and shook her head again. "Nowhere yet, okay? All I can tell you is that before Adie got his people out there to shoot down any drones that get close, Ióar took another boat west to deeper water and just dumped the one Norwegian dude, like the damn shark bait he was. Then headed for the police station. Wherever they lay their loved ones to rest, if they even do, Geir gets the honor but that guy doesn't."

I still wouldn't have wished for that. The fluttering tension in my diaphragm, as I attempted to control my breath, stirred the baby awake to coil and uncoil in her too-small space. A nearby monitor beeped. I took belated notice of the electrodes under my ruined sweater. Though UF had moved on, Scalloway had kept the temporary hospital facility where Vega had worked. That seemed to be where they'd brought us.

"You're both okay," she said, as I looked over at the lights on the screen with no ability whatsoever to parse their significance. "You were having contractions when they brought you in, but they didn't last, and otherwise you're weirdly fine." She sighed. "I mean, not… Baby's vitals are good. Your head scan and bloodwork came back normal. You're just in shock."

"Can I go, then?"

"Not my call, unfortunately. We can ask…"

But I caught at her hand before she got up, as the ring began pulsing around my other wrist. I needed her there at least until I knew what news there was.

It was Lachlan, getting ready to start the cast. Vega stayed in her chair and watched with me.

I hadn't realized that KXA, father and son, would be casting from Edinburgh, although it made sense. Part of Lachlan's effectiveness in his duty as our spokesman stemmed from having done a fair bit of it in telegenic regular sweaters and jeans or diving gear, but this was the kind of day both men wore flawlessly tailored suits.

"I have something I'd like to read first. Then hopefully go on a moment or two from there." Lachlan blinked a few times downward, adjusting his focus.

"'I am a being technologically enhanced to access and process information at the most advanced levels and fastest speeds in the history of my kind. I can connect as effortlessly to a research drone at the deepest points in the Pacific, as to the lighting and climate controls of my home. I can investigate, process, and send information to the far side of the world: influencing others without knowing their names, seeing their faces, touching their hands.

'But sometimes I think too much has been lost in the creation, the evolution, of our powerful cyborg race. Why should connecting to the Kermadec Trench become simple as breathing, while real bonds with those who should be closest prove increasingly, painfully elusive?'"

Lachlan looked into the camera, as if right at me. That I'd stopped reading his stuff before this came out didn't prevent me for a second from knowing who'd authored these words. I sent a quick pulse to let Lachlan know I was listening, saw him touch his ring wrist and smile faintly.

"That's a quote from the late Dr. Oliver Araujo, who was in the news early this year for predicting the Storegga Slide II, as well as more recently for his inter-species romance some decades ago." Lachlan didn't hide his sudden tears from the cameras, just blinked his blond lashes a few times. "One thing I can tell you, he'd have been spoiled forever."

"Ach," I breathed, in exact sync with the moment he paused to swallow a few times before his voice resumed obeying him. Vega squeezed my hand tighter, while Kenneth Adie laid his own strong hand on his son's unbowed shoulder.

"He was as right about this as he ever was about marine geology. We can only guess half of what he learned from the selkie who did connect with him on a level deeper than he'd ever dreamed, but we believe she showed him what was coming.

"He couldn't tell the world what I can: how vulnerable, how honest, how steadfast these people are in their integrity," Lachlan said, softer. "How they see below the surface and truly listen. What they understand, value, and love about this planet, without using any tech at all. How much more human they are than we ourselves have become.

"They deserve the North Sea more than we have in centuries. Still, they've only ever shared it, even tried to help us thrive here. Contributed to the founding of United Forces Environmental and changed the face of the North Sea shipping industry, even if both changes came too late. Warned us about the tsunami in the only way they could. When that came too late as well, they put themselves in the way of all manner of harm to help keep boats afloat, rescue those who'd otherwise drown or be trapped in damaged buildings. Humanity responded to the tsunami by trying to traffic some of the evacuees. Selkies risked themselves again to stop it.

"It's down to us they're on the edge of extinction. Maybe if we'd had the decency to keep our distance today, their current known population would not be under a hundred souls."

He cleared his throat and glanced up at Kenneth, who gave a supportive caress of his shoulder. "It is our continued hope that these people will be granted status as their own small sovereign nation or entity. As such, some things aren't for me to say. But--"

He looked directly into the camera again, sapphire eyes newly spilling over, and pulsed me back. "My queen and our people will stop at nothing that's within their power, nothing, to try to get back what was lost today.

"On their behalf, I'm asking the world. If you're one to send prayers or thoughts or positive energy, we'll have those. But no more damn drones, or any other physical intervention. We've all got to back the bloody hell off and let them heal."

Questions erupted from the press pool, but I was past hearing. The monitor abruptly went as loud and flashy as Berenys' nightclub in Stavanger. I couldn't remember how to breathe.

Think what my queen could do for someone in need of her, the Geir in my memory said softly. *Think of what it would cost*. Brynja hadn't been willing to risk the attempt to bring Runa or Hano back from death. She'd been saving her energy for such a moment as this: for Geir, she would stop at nothing.

They strapped an oxygen mask over my face, wouldn't let me leave the damn bed. Something about the baby's heart rate in response to my distress. I was beyond following the medicalese discussion, but I understood clearly enough that Dr. Hazan didn't take my side when I demanded they let me go north to wherever my people were gathered.

"Cafecito, according to what I heard your bouncer telling everyone just now, that baby of yours is about the most important person in the world," she said. "Whatever's going on up there, whatever help you think you could give them, you're the only one who can take care of her."

"Go to hell, hada madrina."

"I love you too, mi tesoro."

Sobbing all over again at her choice of phrase, I still argued with the medical staff who wanted to sedate me. They were not giving my daughter any unnecessary chem in utero. Vega wrangled me half an hour to show what I could do unmedicated.

I plucked off the irritating electrodes, opened the window to drink in cold salt air. Touching the water would have been a hundred times more effective, but this would have to do. I pretended Karima was by my side as I went through pre-dive breath exercises, slowing my heart and respiration. I tried to imagine myself in Ysmay's peaceful dreams, strong and free and weightless, exploring the quiet forests of our undersea kingdom.

That held the medics off a few more hours. Vega and I were almost done eating the thermos of soup May had sent up, when her alarm pulsed. She had to get back on a flight to London.

"Mira, I'm trying to get back up to you cuanto antes, pero your timing is pura shite," she said. "Be good for ma while I'm gone, okay?"

"I'll try."

But I threw my empty bowl at the nurse who found me pacing after she'd left, when she gently brought up the option of drugs again. She had the grace to offer me cookies instead, along with one more chance to do things my way.

By about two the next morning, I'd finally stopped climbing the walls and had mostly settled into the bed. I made the stupid mistake of going on-grid for a few moments.

"Unborn Selkie/Araujo Grandchild in Distress at Scalloway Hospital Following Noss Shetland Massacre," I read. When I got to the series of photo images taken in my room, I flung my ring against the wall. Next, I went for the monitor, whose base unit was plenty heavy enough to break the window, and whose screen shattered spectacularly all over the pavement below.

I was leaning out over the open sill, considering what wonderfully originally things my mother could have crafted with the million shiny dark shards, when I half-felt the laser injector at the base of my neck.

Chapter 37

Kermadec Trench

During the long drug-induced night, a tangle of venomous reptilian-crustacean hybrid creatures filled the harbor, plastic-based exoskeletons impenetrable and shiny. The UFPKs fought them back, but couldn't be everywhere at once. They crawled all over the outside of the hospital, scratching at windows and air vents. And I'd left myself completely vulnerable with the foolish monitor stunt. It was a matter of time before they swarmed through my broken window, clawing onto my bed, over my belly, and up to my face.

As I scrambled backward and a little way closer to waking reality, it wasn't an awful little monster, but a hand on my temple, stroking my hair back from my forehead. A selkie hand with the intent to soothe, not to make me squint my stinging eyes open--in the full sunlight of a different room whose windowpanes were intact, for now. The other little monster and I were connected to a new monitor.

"Sorry, darling," Elis whispered. "You were having a bad dream."

I blinked but couldn't clear my groggy vision. Effing chem. "You're not meant to be here, are you?"

I noticed his red, shadowed eyes. "I'm not needed anymore in Inverness," he told me softly.

"No." I dissolved into tears of my own.

"Arden... She never even regained consciousness. Her spinal cord was in pieces. No one would've wanted her to live like that. Least of all her."

"Tell me again how I'm the one who set all this in motion," I sobbed.

"Don't you dare say that again. Not ever."

I had no more words to answer him at all. I let myself be the one he lifted like a rag doll, my head dropping at once to his shoulder, and we cried for an uncounted time. It was quite a while before we shared anything but the grief with one another. He wanted me to know how deeply, almost maternally proud and expectant she'd sounded of me when I wasn't present during their conversations. I remembered for him a few times I'd caught her checking out his mythical rearview.

He groaned with appreciative laughter. "Thanks, lass." He wiped both hands over his face. "Ach. Let's remember her like that, shall we."

Richly as she deserved his smile and mine, both were short-lived. We remembered too much else of the last twenty-four hours.

"Do we know anything yet, about... what's happening with Brynja?"

Elis shook his head. "I came straight here. I've been talking to the doctors about letting you come home. Since I'm told you haven't exactly been a model patient, they want to get a few more scans and such, first."

"Not interested."

"Come on, my love. You don't want to go a thing like this alone."

"Screw you," I whispered fiercely. "I don't get to pick, do I."

I felt a partial pang of guilt as his eyes shone liquid brighter again than the moment before. He didn't fight back, though, except to lay a light hand on the back of my wrist. Remembering the bitter grief of losing both his daughters much too soon was his way of begging me not to risk myself, taking on this fraught state inherent in the creation of in-between beings without whatever help we could get.

I could only shake my head and impress his way how much I had no idea where to go from here.

He nodded. "Well, to start, let them make sure you're both okay right now. I promise I'll take you home afterward. Lachlan should be back by three or four, then I'll go lend whatever help I can for the old man. All right?"

I wrapped my arms around where my waist had been. The baby kicked like she was going for a depth record.

Elis stayed with me for the scans, this time the kind where we could visualize her on a big screen. They had a challenge keeping her image in focus, which made me chuckle despite everything: sometimes the heart or brain or whatever just blurred around, though it always came back. When she did hold still, it all looked miraculously normal, from her strong speedy heartbeat and full head of floating mermaid hair to my good amnio levels and unchanged cervix. I guessed I was glad my tiny jo had no clue that nothing was normal at all in our world, and might not really ever be.

"If you're right, though, about the timeline," I said as we exited the hospital hand in hand, ignoring photo drones. "I don't want her born amid all this."

"Me neither, Junior, but…"

But I realized I knew a superwoman who didn't require the hospital or any of its tech. She could help me do this stuff completely off-grid if need be. I rang Mairi Ross on the ride home, and she agreed to come round in the event I should need her. When I granted her permissions to view my med file, she chuckled knowingly and assured me it didn't look like anything was on in the short term, whatever my marine bio buddy who didn't have ovaries tried to tell me. In her expert opinion, there was plenty of time for my finsisters to complete their current urgent business and help me through the birth their way.

Elis insisted I put my feet up while he made a pretty decent spaghetti puttanesca, grumbling about how Berenys had been rearranging the kitchen. He served us each a bowl but only picked at his, watching the time.

"I'm sure he'll be here soon if you can't wait," I said.

"Nah, it's okay."

"I'd be there in a second if I could, and I've only known him a few months."

My *he* and *him* weren't the same person, but Elis nodded soberly. "If he got a vote, you know he'd have me take care of you and Nereiður the third right now, sweetheart."

"Oh, geez, I hope she's not." I managed a bit of a smile for him.

"Well. I'll go on record as hoping she is."

I twirled the last few noodles around the bottom of my bowl. Not until Elis was well on his way back below, and Lachlan dozing in Isla's velveteen chair, did my mind turn back to my mother. To the kind of dance Nereiður had thought she had to do to keep from losing herself over the consistent, and eventually permanent, distance and absence of my father. Too bad she'd failed, even so, to keep her beautiful mind or her selkie heart intact. Or ours.

"So we're not doing it that way," I whispered, laying a hand over my abdomen. "Okay? Whether we get him back or not."

She kicked my hand a few times, a baby high-five in affirmation. That was enough for me to wake Lachlan with a sudden storm of tears.

"Sorry," I sobbed, rubbing at my face with the back of one hand.

He shook his head and came to sit beside me on the all-weather sofa. It helped not having to explain my outburst in words.

He held me until I wore myself out, and could have drifted off against the strength of his chest and shoulder. It wasn't a two-person sleeping arrangement, though, not if one was of Viking proportions and the other was a half-selkie and a half.

"Look," he said. "No one involved will misunderstand if the three of us go lie down. It's probably our only prayer of getting any rest."

I nodded, and we helped one another up.

He laughed roughly. "And if I'm wrong, it'll be fun to see the wee man kick my arse, right?"

Laughing in response hurt, but it was better than not being able to laugh.

During the night I found myself staring down into a vertiginous black void where the pressure of the solitude all around was enough to pulverize every organ of my being. I woke, cool salt mist mingling with my cold sweat, barefoot on the dock beneath a starless sky.

My heart thudded to full alert. Little Miss Loch Ness wound around in her own dark place, though hers was all closeness and comfort. I rubbed at my face, wishing I could hug her back. The tall figure dangling his feet off the pier in the corner of my vision hadn't shown up this way very often, never since Cabo de la Vela, but I still took momentary solace.

He didn't look up as he spoke to me in his most melodic Miami Spanish, catching me off guard after all these weeks back on the North Sea's shores. Something about how death only existed when the dead were forgotten. How as long as I remembered him, he was still with me.

"Seriously?"

His beautiful wide-set eyes seemed to lift, waiting.

"Ugh. García Márquez."

"Isabel Allende, mi tesoro."

"Whoever. As either of them would tell you, you should've been here for this too, hijo de puta, and not just in recuerdo form. Both of you."

The truth was that Nereiður's absence, one of the constants of my life, had prepared me all along for saying goodbye to Dad so much too soon. I'd known Dr. Shimizu for a much shorter time; my heart and mind could cope with her loss, appalling as it was, accordingly. Geir and I had only founded the Shetland chapter of the shouldn't-really-exist club eight months ago. I should have been able to begin wrapping my thoughts and emotions around this, too, instead of having disturbing psychological episodes several layers deep.

The difference was that he'd been so much more willing than anyone else on Earth to give me every fiber of himself: every half-smile, every moment of strength, every surreally delicious touch, nearly every memory of his own pain or joy. Offering as much as he demanded, and so much more. I'd never had a tenth that much of my father. I'd certainly never had anything like the chance to share the same dream my mother was dreaming.

I couldn't see below the quiet ripples at this hour, and I'd just been trying to tell myself I should know better, but I stared anyway. Whose dream had I been in tonight?

I didn't know anything for sure. Maybe I never knew what the hell was real. I did know that at the possibility, my heartbeat wouldn't calm itself until I sat alone in Dad's vacated spot on the dock's edge, rolled up my pant legs, and put my feet with a sharp gasp into the frigid waters of our shared birthplace. No magic words needed, not that I could have found any, I tried with all my heart to call my true love back.

Eventually, I dragged myself up to the house, choosing Geir's bed over Lachlan's for my friend's sake this time, but didn't find my way back to sleep until dawn. Orca and earthquakes pursued me in my dreams, followed by *architeuthis krakenos* tentacles getting increasingly tight around my abdomen.

I woke in uncomfortable stages, like a hangover with none of the previous fun, to the realization that the monster to blame wasn't a big squid but a small kelpie.

"Knock it off, little miss." I got up to brew the critically necessary one small cup of coffee that was all I was advised to have these days. Usually, getting up and walking around would throw the Braxton Hicks contractions off their rhythm. Not this morning.

Lachlan was out again; he'd rung me that he'd be managing the post-fairytale narrative. In time, I needed to ring him back.

Uncle Alert Much as i hate to tell elis hes right Contractions about 2 hrs not stopping Does not feel like a drill So

I hadn't wanted to interrupt whatever he was doing, but he called me back immediately. "Arden. Hey. You're okay?"

"For now..."

"On my way. Did you call Mairi already?"

I sighed. "No."

"Look." He was trying to make his Viking voice more gentle, but that only ever worked particularly effectively when he was under Brynja's spell. "I wanted ours back in time too, but we can't really wait later than this."

"I know."

"You want me to ring her?"

"Yeah. Okay."

"Okay. I'll be there soon."

I ended the call, waited out another searing contraction. Then I rang Vega, just to see. She didn't respond. I hadn't really figured I'd get her, but she'd asked me to let her know when the time came.

I pulled on my coat and aqua boots and went out in the cold sunlight to walk at the water's edge, staying near the house. I paced back and forth a while. Even if it was ridiculous and stupid, I wished again that some part of my spark might spread outward through the sea, calling the ones I really wanted here. To call seals you had to be closer, almost within sight. But my selkie folk were infinitely more than seals, and I could think of no other way at least to try to tell them.

Near the end of one contraction, I felt a kind of pop, then a rush of hot waters down my leg into the cold water around my ankles. I gasped out loud.

I sent Lachlan an urgent pulse.

Almost there shes with me You ok?

Water just broke

Shite Hang on

Dont ride like an actual berserker

The next contraction pressed more fluid out--I hadn't considered that, but it felt wretched--and hurt with sickeningly greater clarity; the baby felt heavier.

I welcomed the low roar of Lachlan's bike. They parked by the house, would have gone inside if I hadn't yelled up to them. The nurse-midwife appeared to give Lachlan some instructions; he went in, while she came down to the edge of the sea.

"Hey, supergirl." She tilted her curly brown head. "Not planning a water birth, are we?"

I found a smile. "No. It's hard to be inside that house when it's empty."

"Okay. Well, your mate's there now, making you some tea. And we'll maybe get you in the shower, warm you up."

I nodded and allowed myself to be led up the steps amid gentle medical chatter. A new and improved pain made me pause maybe two-thirds of the way. I had to bend forward a little, couldn't answer the next routine question.

"Ooh," she said. "Pretty good one."

I took a second to catch my breath. "Yeah, so fun," I answered belatedly.

"Have you been timing them?"

I shrugged.

She had a hearty, friendly laugh. "Right. In the house. Let's check where you are first."

Where I was turned out to be four centimeters already. "Wow," she said. "Is that how fast all the selkie mams do this? Yesterday you looked nowhere near starting."

"No idea. Sort of planned on having them here to tell me…" I gritted my teeth. Not crying right now. Work to do.

"Okay, darling," Mairi said, softer. "If you still want that shower or the tea, let's do that for you. Might get wild in here soon, the way you're going."

We were lingering in the kitchen each with a cup, Lachlan and Mairi at the table, me pacing restlessly, when there was a quick knock and the front door opened. Knowing with every cell in my body that it wasn't him didn't stop my heart from turning a crooked somersault.

Seawater dripped from Elis' slicked-back hair onto Geir's old clothes he'd taken from the stash in the geo. Lachlan jumped to his feet.

"Any news?"

"None yet from us," Elis said as they embraced. "Looks like there is here, though."

Lachlan nodded, fighting disappointed, anxious tears. Elis gently rubbed away the one that fell.

"How'd you know to come, then?"

Elis smiled. "Just had a sense. You know I always feel you, lad."

I missed whatever else he said about their connection, gritting my teeth to keep from interrupting the conversation with the pain I couldn't keep inside me very well at this point.

"Hey," Elis said, waiting until I could answer him. "Forgot who was the star of this show for a second. You all right?"

I gave a little grunt as if I could get the discomfort to fade faster. "I'll be better when you get your own clothes on and put his back where you got them."

"Ach, my love, yes. He'll still need them and they'll be there when he does. I'll change right now." His smile was so gentle.

I drew a real, full breath and grabbed his wrist before he could walk away. "Elis. Sorry."

He shook his head, even nice enough to tease me a little. "You know perfectly well I'd never choose to wear this shite."

I managed the laugh he wanted. He squeezed my hand between both of his. I saw in his mind's eye a cavern floor, shallowly covered with clear seawater. A place for entering and exiting the undersea kingdom, here with a gradual sloped shape like a beach.

Geir was submerged, curled into a fetal position, bloodlessly pale. Like a sliver of moon, though I couldn't tell if he was waning or waxing. Brynja, within, was curved skin to skin around him. Her head rested on his ribs, above the water's surface. No one else was in the pool, but all along the water's edge were outstretched small steady white hands. Lending their own spark, awaiting the return to life of two so deeply beloved.

Something tingled at the very edges of the impression. "Is that--" I barely breathed, finding Elis' eyes.

"Damn, you're good, Junior." He nodded. "I thought I'd have to say. With my hand in the water, I can just sense him. He's not gone far, Arden. She won't let him."

I tried to fend off more tears, but they were fully armed and I was already at a disadvantage. They beat me down almost immediately. I sank into a chair, fought another beastly contraction starting already; between the intensity of the sobs and of the labor, I came close to vomiting my tea on the kitchen floor. Elis held my hand so I could keep hold of what he'd felt in that pool.

Over my head, the three of them were talking. She thought it was time I move to my bed and we wouldn't all fit, she hoped we weren't thinking of... Elis laughingly promised to give us a wide berth; he'd be here in case we needed help figuring out a selkie baby, as well as for his grandson. For his own part, Lachlan said he wouldn't interfere unless--

"No," I grated out. "Stay. You don't have to look."

He laughed a little, soothing me. "Okay. Regular selkie naturist now, hey?"

Mairi was still concerned there wasn't enough space in the small back bedroom.

"Mine, then," Lachlan said. "Whatever she bloody wants right now, do you understand?"

"Okay. Go put a clean sheet on for us. On top of what's there now. And bring us whatever towels you've got."

I reluctantly let go of Elis' hand, wiped tears and sweat off my face. "You're a good sport, signing on for this one," I said.

"Hey." She smiled encouragingly. "My fifteen minutes, right?" She glanced over her shoulder at Elis. "Maybe we can do the baby cast together."

"Funny girl," he murmured, but the smile he gave her as he walked away was not his real smile.

I didn't know how he coped in the short term, but I was fortunate to have my attention fully taken up. I was good at this phase of labor. It was just hard work, with a little bit of listening: services generalist stuff. I gratefully lost track of time; it still didn't seem very long before she was saying the baby had such lovely thick hair, we were progressing so well, soon there was the head born, next push would be the shoulders, which were the tricky wide bit--

Hijodeputa, no kidding--

The intense pressure was relieved, the warm, slippery little body sliding free.

"Dear God." Mairi gasped and pushed away from the bed. I slumped involuntarily backward the other way, from squatting to sitting. Her lamp fell with a metallic clatter, the only lit bulb in the room shattering. She pressed the child into Lachlan's arms; I heard her rushing from the room, then the tones if not the words of Elis hurrying to meet her in the hallway. What I didn't hear was my baby crying. It was dark and there was sweat in my eyes. I couldn't focus.

"Lachlan, what's wrong?"

Elis was at the bedroom door. "Can I?"

"Yeah," Lachlan answered roughly when I couldn't. He tugged a cover up to my waist.

I heard Elis come in, his whispered Norn acclamation. Out loud he said toward the door, "Lass, you've no prayer of doing that cast with me unless you get back in here and finish this."

Then he knelt near my feet. "Sweetest. You have any idea how well you've done?"

"Why isn't she crying? Is she okay?"

"More than okay. She's a dream, Arden."

He brought up some light on his ring so I'd be able to see her. Carefully, together, he and Lachlan propped me up on pillows, then laid my firstborn on my chest. A being the size of a human infant, but shaped like a baby seal. I answered them with an inarticulate little scream of shock.

She was heavy for her size, which I thought I'd known before now. Her wet, grayish-white pelt was sleek under my tentative hand. Her inscrutable black eyes peered at me. Once upon a time, Geir had told me it was a rare good omen for a child to be born within the seal shape. Now, I choked on tears and nausea.

"No," I said to both of them. "You take it."

"She'll shift," Elis tried to encourage me. "Just hold her."

"You hold her," I snapped.

"Mairi," Lachlan said fiercely, directing his voice away from me. "You know she still needs your help."

In the exhausted quiet that followed, Elis picked up the seal baby and crooned sweet adoring selkiese nothings to her. I leaned back into the pillows, closed my stinging eyes, thought of the two daughters he'd lost. Maybe, if Brynja couldn't return Geir to us, Elis would want this one. All I knew was that I wasn't ready for whatever she was.

I heard Mairi's voice outside, but not her words. It almost seemed another woman was there to answer. Her sister? Elis lifted his head, listening too. Soft footsteps came to the doorway.

"Mija, can you forgive your ma for missing your big recital?"

I couldn't believe I had tears left in me to spill over.

"Oh," Elis said with a new smile. "Good morning."

Vega rewarded him with the laugh the songstress kept for her most appreciative audiences. "Good morning to you, grandpa."

"Doc." I wept through my rough laughter at them both. "I guess you could still scrub in for the last number if you want."

She already had her gloves on, leaned over to hug me and stroke my sweaty hair back. "That's what poor Miss Mairi said. I hope it's okay I set her up at the bar out there. She's done."

"Me too," I whispered.

"I know, babe. You will be in a minute."

Vega ministered to me with cool, careful hands, taking care of the placenta and cord and fundal massage, assuring me I'd done perfect work, without even a tear. I turned my face to the wall the whole time and felt a sudden, unforeseen kinship to my own mother in a bed like this, once, on the far side of the North Sea. Except Nereiður, if I had to guess, must have managed it even further off-grid: so much more alone, maybe in hiding. I ached with gratitude, understanding now that she'd done what she thought she must to ensure it would be different for me.

My dear friend knew me too well to let the men pressure me into holding the little seal. She kicked them out, got me a glass of cool water, and lasered me in the thigh with some of the good stuff Geir and I had been on, the evening this all started. Then she stayed by my side, uncharacteristically quiet, until I was no longer aware of her.

Chapter 38

Challenger Deep

I didn't know how much later I awoke to the tiny cry I'd longed for. I guessed baby selkies would have the same underdeveloped vocal cords as the rest of them. I'd had no idea how heart-twistingly precious the resulting call would sound. How could I possibly have thought I didn't want her?

I started to go to her, but I wasn't even dressed to leave the bed. I cleared my throat and tried to decide whose name to call out.

Fortunately, someone already had the presence of mind to bring her to me. The thin thread of crying came down the hall, soft footsteps bringing her nearer.

"Hey, mamacita," Vega murmured from the doorway. "Is it visiting hours yet? Gary Junior won't stop asking."

I laughed; she sat on the bed and hugged me tight with her left arm a moment before she let me take my baby, who fussed at the way we were holding each other.

My peerie lass might be a shrimp, but as the scans had seemed to indicate, she was far from a scary micro-preemie. She was soft and round in all the places you'd wish for a newborn, with delicious flower-petal cheeks. The room was too dim to see her face clearly.

"What time is it?"

"About six. I guess I got here between midnight and one. Ooh, before I forget to tell you. I saw the best Northern Lights ever on the flight here, landing at that hour."

I closed my eyes, remembering.

When we brought the room lighting up, Tía Vega was right: she was Geir Junior, much fairer than me, all her features so delicate except for the eyes. Not that they were really open right now, but I still recognized with a sweet pang their great size and wide spacing even in such a tiny face. Geir's daughter was Arden Rae Junior as well, though. I stroked her feathery thick hair: not as dark as I'd thought, aglow with chestnut fire.

We tried to get Junior to nurse, which she hadn't figured out as well as shapeshifting yet. At least she was comforted enough to grow quiet in my arms after a few minutes. I held her, skin to velvety skin, caressed the lines of her back and her legs where they were scrunched up against my chest: all the way down to the smallest selkie toes I could imagine.

Seeing her loveliness made it so concrete to me. She was the last we would see of him, but he'd passed along all the best of himself before he left us. It must have been because of her presence, these last few days, the near-unshakable feeling he wasn't really gone.

I could almost see my way to where it was all right, or would be someday. As many times as Geir had loved and lost, he'd never been built for it like I was. I could find my way blindfolded around the aftermath of a love affair cut short; one strange child plus one under-equipped but hardworking parent was the only kind of family I'd ever known. This way, I'd never leave him like all the others. And though there weren't enough, I would give her every picture and story I had of her incredible dad. Even the green hoodie, maybe, when she was big enough.

Vega didn't ask why I needed a minute to let the tears spill over as I went on learning my child's face by heart. She just put her warm, strong arm around my shoulders again.

"So what do we really call this little beauty?"

I could only sigh-laugh-sob, and shake my head.

We hadn't agreed on a name. Geir's taste ran to the sweet and old-fashioned, ones you'd need when christening a fairytale princess. Fairytale she might be, but this was the kid of basically two career generalists. I preferred short, strong names, like his own, for her; maybe something unisex. Whatever he picked out of books or memories would make me laugh in dismay. My favorite suggestions provoked a little expression like he thought they tasted vaguely off, but didn't want to tell me to my face. Neither of us really cared to fight the other; every time, we'd push it off for another day. Then, too, we'd had a lot more pressing worries to occupy us.

Once, Berenys helpfully suggested Martini Olive Araujo. Geir watched my face for an anxious moment before realizing with obvious relief that a dismissive laugh would be quite appropriate. Uncle Elis earned laughs too, relatively sincere though he was in recommending Joan Baez Craig Junior, for her Scottish and Latina heritage and for our song. Ysmay advised, both twins now giggling in delightful two-part harmony, that we combine our names and call our daughter-to-be Air or Garden. Or combine the combinations, for Hydroponic Blossom Carajo.

We'd still had weeks, if not months to go, after all.

"You'll know when you see her face," Elis had said.

But seeing her face, all I knew was that I wanted more chances to argue about it.

"Coquito, I was thinking," Vega said softly. "To go with the chocolate caliente and the cafecito, right? Almost Christmas time. Creamy." She stroked the baby's cheek, then a little fluff of hair near her forehead that looked likely to grow into a curl. "Hint of spice. Someone disregarded the recipe and snuck more than a little extra special whisky in there, but por qué no?"

Surely he'd have loved it. "Closest thing she has to a name for now. Thanks, Titi."

Vega kissed my messy cheek.

"Did you see her shift?" I found it in me to ask eventually.

Vega nodded, wide mahogany eyes shining. "I was holding her. A couple hours in, probably. Cutest part was, she didn't even wake herself up. Like she figured out how in her baby dreams."

"So stupid of me to miss it," I sighed. "I don't know why I couldn't…"

She shook her head, reached out to rub my hand and the baby's head at the same time. "Damn, woman. I've known you a decade and all you ever do is bear up under everything life piles on you… if you didn't crumble a little, once in a while, how would we know you were real? You'll see it next time. And you know, you can take the girl out of UF if you want, but… You had put an excellent team in place. They've had her every second while mama and daddy couldn't."

"I don't know…"

She shook her head. "Uh uh. I got the update from those guys—" She gestured with a little backward nod toward the doorway. "We have the best team on that, too. So we're not sad. We're just waiting."

"Vega," I whispered. "No more fairytales."

But she just shook her head. "Also, if her teeny majesty can't get it done, I'll go on down and drag him by his pretty hair. Ya sabes que tengo considerable powers of persuasion y un triphibious hover with a piloto excelente at my disposal."

I smiled for her.

She patted my hand and the baby's back again. "You hungry?… Ha. What am I saying?"

I nodded, realizing I hadn't eaten since yesterday's early, distracted lunch.

"Well, I'll see what's in your kitchen, then. Since Lachlan K is getting some sleep in Gary's bed, after he ran your nurse home because the real doctora got here. I have a feeling we'll find grandpa asleep in his chair out there too, now that no one's talking his ear off."

Remembering Berenys' long-ago prediction regarding the two of them, I found another smile.

The next day, she reluctantly headed back to London, but promised a follow-up appointment the first moment she could. Stefek hoped to sneak north again too. I filled a lot of my time with video links to London, Brussels, and Miami.

Beyond the inevitable kindness of Vega herself and Tía Abuela Luisa, I hadn't really considered there would be gifts. But the first drones I'd been happy to see in a long while sweetly kept coming, and helped me get through the first hours of single parenthood. Amazing fair-trade African dark chocolates made by Stefek's mom's company. Gorgeous winter-white organic cotton baby clothes and blankets from Celeste (surely hand-chosen by Siobhan) were nearly too nice to use. A lavender-oil mist and coordinating petal-infused candle from Imani Ahmad, whom I'd only known a few weeks, but who kindly remembered my poor sleeping skills. Geir's adorable old farmwife girlfriend from up the way brought us lovely fresh sheep's-milk cheeses and a lacy crocheted afghan, magically my forever favorite blush pink. Mrs. Darzi express-droned an assortment of pastries that stung tears when I opened the package, with a baby-sized terrycloth mermaid tail beach cover-up from Karima tucked in along one side. Maite and Jamar blessed us with plans to open and generously fund a college savings account, as soon as Coquito had a real name--and the first ident ever issued to a newborn finbairn, to go with it.

Lachlan sent the most bittersweet gift of all: a contact forwarded from the on-grid private selkie hotline. An Alix Daniau in France, who had taken up genealogical research following her recent retirement, believed she'd traced her family back to a wartime romance between Josiane Bellerose and Sub-Lieutenant Alasdair Craig of the British Royal Navy. She was eager to have full DNA scans and help in the hunt for the inevitable other Craig descendants. I rang her a photo of her distant ancestor's newborn daughter, and gladly promised to keep in touch.

On the second afternoon, the Ross sisters came to check on us and brought a wonderfully uncomplicated dinner. Wiggly newborn Finley with the tiny disapproving old lady face had transformed into a china doll with a wild halo of fine blonde curls and a belly laugh even I couldn't resist. She kept us on our toes in the open living room and kitchen, none of which was remotely baby-proofed yet: crawling lightning-fast, pulling up on drawers and end tables and the bassinet. She was keenly interested in my own new infant, who didn't earn it just then. Martini Olive mostly slept while they were there, and didn't show off her shapeshifting talents again--probably to Mairi's relief, although she was back to brusquely friendly business today.

Emer looked amazing. There was someone new in her life and Finley's; she'd regained the sexy sparkle we'd had to intuit in her at our first meeting. Not that I could begin to look that idea in the face yet, for myself. There was really no such thing as what I'd want to find, anyway.

Mairi told me the baby's great sleeping skills would likely wear off in a few days; meantime, she wanted me to rest whenever Joan Junior rested. As evening turned to night, then morning, then a briefly-lit next day, I obeyed when I could. It helped to lie next to her sidecar bassinet and breathe in the simple peace she embodied, along with the sweet scent of her downy head.

We sat with Lachlan that evening, eating good leftovers and watching a stupid movie he'd projected. I was glad to go along with whatever distracted him, but British humor didn't always translate.

For the first time, my child cried and wouldn't settle: she didn't seem to want her own (second or third) dinner, or a diaper, or to be held in a different position. Uncle Lachlan took a shift walking around the house with her until I got sick of listening to her berating him. I zipped her up inside my coat and we went to pace on the dock under a cold mist.

Lachlan wouldn't have to hear me out here. I hummed and sang her the old song under my breath, accompanied by quiet waves, until at last she gave up and relaxed into sweet boneless baby sleep against my chest.

I was the one who stayed awake for hours, too afraid she'd perceived some sadness I couldn't sense.

I started awake sometime before dawn to a small firm hand on my arm. The deeply shadowed eyes and dull complexion belonged to Ysmay; over her physical face pulsated discordantly shaky layered images of Runa's in shadow, Brynja's like lightning, Berenys' perfect features weary but uplifted.

"Ajo, okay," I breathed, and sat dizzily up, rapidly accelerating heart first.

I let her hold my child while I got into my wetsuit as fast as my fumbling fingers would manage. Lachlan waited near the front door, already dressed.

"But," I stopped short. "The baby can't wear a dive suit…"

Ysmay smiled. "Whatever for?"

"But she's a *newborn*," I said, panicked.

Ysmay drew a breath. *"Trudu mjer."* Trust me.

She joined us in the hover since that was fastest, and so she could direct us. We went northwest this time, not south or east to the selkie places I'd seen before. It wasn't far. When we'd sped all the way to the coastline, Ysmay had Lachlan continue out over the bay to a smaller nearby island, veering westward along its shore.

"Papa Stour," Lachlan said. "We didn't get up here together before, did we? No selkies live here. They keep it for times like this."

"No, though I came up here playing tourist one time... Isle of Priests," I recalled.

He nodded. "May lived here as a girl. And this coastline was what made me want to go for marine geology instead of just hunting Nessie—"

"Ach, man, the now?" Ysmay said impatiently. I laughed in spite of everything.

He smiled, too. "Sorry."

"Another time," I said. Either way, Shetland was home now for me and little miss seventy-eight percent. We would explore this and every other corner.

We rode on a few minutes more in charged quiet, intense enough for me to wonder whether it was really manifesting itself as a tingle on my skin before Ysmay told Lachlan to cut the motor and drop anchor.

"Here, not further north?"

"Backdoor way, obviously," she said. "Foyer's full of guests already, isn't it."

She stashed her old sundress under a seat, slipped without a splash into the water. Then she looked up, holding her little white hands out for my baby.

"Shite," I said through gritted teeth.

"Come on," Lachlan breathed. "She was born to do this."

Ysmay's firm jaw and the set of her brows said she didn't appreciate me wasting precious time.

"If she doesn't shift for Ys," Lachlan said finally, "I'll stay up here with her."

He'd give up the only thing he wanted in the world right now, for the sake of Geir and the baby and me. Biting back a sob, I unwrapped her organic cotton layers, then let him take her--so small in his careful hands--and lay her steadily into the curve of Ysmay's elbow.

Ysmay scooped handfuls of seawater over her, as gently as any mother bathing an ordinary child. The tiny limbs flexed and stretched, musically splashing into the still early morning air. Her big dark eyes opened all the way. Then, easily as any of them, she glimmered back into the sweet shape she'd worn when we'd met, and flipped onto her belly with such agility that Ysmay had to make a quick dive to catch her. My heart lurched low, like a fist into my stomach.

As she resurfaced, the baby seal cradled safely in her arms as though she'd been a new puppy, Ysmay grinned like a ray of moonlight through the clouds. "See? Lovely selkie bairn," she said in a tone people usually reserved for her mother.

Lachlan laughed under his breath as he put a warm hand on my shoulder. "You, on the other hand, will use all the damn tech this go round."

Lachlan slipped the baby's things into the waterproof sack, sealed it, and clipped it to his belt. He rolled the diving sled into the water, made sure my rebreather mask was tight enough. Then he offered a hand down to my waiting carriage.

Ysmay led us, but the baby—a miraculously strong swimmer—didn't go in a straight line. Lachlan expertly steered the sled behind them. The vent we sought, masked by a waving curtain of kelp, wasn't very deep. The twisting tunnel up seemed endless, though, and so narrow we eventually had to deactivate the sled and leave it at one sharp bend. Fortunately, by then we were nearly there.

Ysmay waited, still nude on the narrow rock ledge of the smallest entry pool I'd seen yet, as my seal baby flopped around her. She picked the baby up when she saw us, though, deliberately holding the little head to her cheek and exhaling soft breaths down her back until she glimmered into her tiny human self again.

"You'll have to teach me how to do that," I murmured. Ysmay gave me one of her looks--she couldn't fathom how I didn't already know--but she nodded.

Lachlan was already out of the water, pausing only long enough to give us the bag with the baby's clothes. As Ysmay dressed herself and I quickly diapered the baby and wrapped her in her blanket, he headed away up a tunnel.

But when I started after him, Ysmay caught me by one shoulder. With eager urgency, she drew me down a smaller passage I understood must run roughly parallel to the one Lachlan could navigate. Here, even I had to duck my head, nor was there room for two selkie folk abreast.

At first, I took the random sparkles in my upper peripheral vision for a side effect of sleep deprivation, of diving too soon. But the more I tried to blink them away, the more there were.

Ysmay laughed, smoky and low like her mother's laugh. "Eyes up there."

In my headlamp beam glittered to life some of my own mother's best work. Here she'd chosen to adorn the cave ceiling, all in shades of green. Her mosaic tiles and bits of glass and shell ranged in size from the tiny squares of her holy water font to a few as big as my palm. For a few seconds, dazed with tears and estrogen, I thought she'd cemented a scattering to the floor as well--but those had fallen, presumably when the Out Skerries wind turbine toppled. The glory of this secret place was undiminished.

Hairs on the backs of my arms stood perpendicular to the underground aurora. It was more than the nearness to Nereiður, more than the startling charged air below what had long been considered a sacred place. This felt like standing in front of the gray house, knowing that Geir was about to open the door.

Chapter 39

Font

Berenys met us in the opening to the cavern where I'd seen Brynja and Geir in Elis' memory, her hands still dripping. She hugged Ysmay wordlessly, then me.

She'd barely slept, only enough to have strength to lend. Others rested at the cave's perimeter, as though they'd been taking shifts.

Gyða lifted haunted eyes from the water's edge. Berenys had just left her friend's side; I saw one of her little notebooks by Gyða's knee. The still face wavering beneath the clear seawater in Berenys' memory now was not Geir's; it was Ruadh, his striking mahogany eyes closed for the last time. I sighed my regret, my own eyes blurring.

Berenys had stayed with Gyða and Sefa somewhere else as they sought his spirit first, before coming to help here. I didn't begrudge them that for a second.

Berenys sighed now, in turn, and she shook her head, hair lank around her sagging shoulders for the first time since I'd known her. It hadn't taken long. Already, though they'd gathered to minister to him almost right after tragedy struck, there had been nothing left to find of his slight sweet energy. They'd just had to let him go.

"Sorry, B," I whispered.

She rubbed away a single tear as she nodded, her heart's eyes turning back toward Geir before I could finish the thought.

I kissed her cheek in gratitude, and let my focus follow hers.

We weren't a moment too soon; or maybe our queen had waited for this moment, instead. Lachlan hadn't had his hands in the water sixty seconds when Brynja stirred, flickered back and forth a few times before coming to rest in her human form. She drew an audible breath as she sat up, ivory pale and so thin I could count her ribs and vertebrae.

"*Drottenmín*," Lachlan greeted her, as much a quiet sob as a word. She turned and lifted bottomless black eyes to his face. The quiet chorus of her assembled people softly echoed the salute, although she seemed to notice only him. She rose, steadier than I expected, reaching twig-fine fingers for his hands. He stood to help her out of the pool, and she pressed into his desperately willing arms. The spiderweb thread of her voice consoled him as she calmed his ragged weeping with caresses and quiet kisses.

I bit my lips shut, watching for any tiny movement from Geir, but he remained perfectly still under the gentle clear ripples. From Berenys I learned I should wait, not touch him unless he came up from the water on his own as his sister had miraculously done. I couldn't semi-see the precious energy Brynja had sacrificed, the way Ysmay (via Berenys) could: the tantalizing hint of a swirling faint tracery brighter than the rippling surface, like the inner workings of a defibrillator or immobilizer disc. But I did understand that we dared not risk disturbing the charged water before its work was complete: touch him too soon and it might go to us, instead. So I gritted my teeth and continued to wait. I remembered, in time, to breathe.

"Come on, tesoro," I urged quietly. Berenys pulled me closer against her side, and trusted.

It was Brynja who answered me, stepping around the pool's edge to stand at my other side, now wearing Lachlan's rash guard like a dress. She pressed a wet, salty but warm kiss to my already twice-salty cheek. By touch, she asked to hold the best gift I could have brought her.

The baby was more asleep than awake against my chest, and who could blame her after her big swim, but she opened her eyes to behold her queen.

Brynja managed a low, sweet laugh even less expected than the first time I'd heard it. "My heart," she said to me. Then without asking, she removed and handed back the dry diaper while keeping the baby.

She took a few steps back into the pool and lowered the child into the water, keeping her hand on the little round belly. The baby soon donned her sealskin and flopped her adorably uncoordinated way straight to Geir: over his motionless feet and ankles, to poke her little seal nose into his face. If she was the best implement for channeling and transforming Geir's energies, I guessed the faerie queen would know.

My whispered giggle of pleasure and hope died into a breath-held sob that swelled sharply in my chest and throat the longer he still didn't respond. She squeaked softly at him a few times before settling with her head on his shoulder, nose above the surface.

I let my head drop to Berenys' slight shoulder too. Brynja, behind me, stroked the length of my hair. Some part of Berenys was readying for the worst after all, much as she tried to keep it from me. Not Brynja.

She tugged gently on a handful of my curls. "See," she commanded me in an urgent murmur, the moment before there was anything to see. I lifted my smeared and exhausted face in time to catch the first subtle flash, stark white to dark gray-brown. I'd never seen anyone linger so long between forms, flickering from one to the other and back like heat lightning beneath the water's disturbed surface. Finally, his spark came to rest in the seal form.

The baby nudged at his still face. They looked so perfect together, made for one another. If only he'd open his eyes and find her there. But he never moved, never lifted his head to breathe. The sob I'd held in my chest all this time trickled out as a desperate groan.

Until Ysmay, her hands in the water, turned to grin up at us. My heart dropped with a splash in my chest, then started to thud hard.

"Go," Brynja said, and someone was making a space for me to walk into the pool. I knelt beside the baby, leaned down to whisper close to his seal ear.

"Okay, cabrón. Snow White or whoever you want to be…"

As I pressed a kiss to his head, I wished with all my heart for his sleek black hair, his fine fair skin instead of the thick pelt under my hands. Eyes closed, I waited.

When he shifted at last, my lips were against his temple, my face under the water with his. His left hand moved, lacking strength but not purpose, to rest against my outer thigh. I felt the first glimmer of his smile when I tugged his magic ring off and replaced it on his finger.

When I lifted my head just far enough to catch an aching breath, his teardrop eyes were looking up at me, the little smile already lifting one corner of his pale lips. I had the dream-faint but unmistakable impression of another time he'd seen me through the water, blowing a sunlit kiss his way.

I groaned and sobbed and laughed together, reached down to put my arms under his and pull him up to me. His head was heavy on my shoulder, but his arms came up around me and he softly returned my kiss, against the side of my neck. He didn't want me to cry, hated knowing I'd needed to grieve.

Had there been a sweet pup somewhere in the thread his fumbling memory struggled to grasp? Or had he been dreaming of our unborn child? Such a beautiful little seal maiden, come to try to wake him before me…

"Nope," I said aloud. "Look."

His right hand went to the newly soft side of my waist, as he turned to his left and found the baby really there. A shock of adoration blazed through him at the sight; then the much softer glow of another memory, blurry with sweat and tears and centuries. The delicate doll's hands and arms lifting the remembered selkie bairn reminded me of Berenys'. It was Arinví's impression, passed on long since to share her thrill with the fisher boy who had also been born within.

Geir drew our child to him now, blissful tears spilling through the other saltwater beading on his face. She was light enough for him to lift without trouble, weak though he was yet. He held her to his chest, her little head tucked under his chin, her small rounded shape only partly covering the brutal scars across his chest and throat. Thanks to Brynja's enormous gift, they had not only knit together but faded to pale pink already. They made me shiver nonetheless. He didn't want her to shift right away, precious as she was to him like this, but in time he asked to see her other face and she was pretty quick to show him.

He felt a question, keenly enough that I understood he wanted her name.

My intended light answer tangled up in sharp sobs I hadn't seen coming. "I was still hoping to work that one out with you."

He could cradle our tiny daughter in one hand, while his other arm reached around me. He kissed my tear-stained cheek and sea-wet hair. I insisted he didn't get to die before me again. Next time was my turn. He laughed, soft and low in his throat, in answer and agreement.

"Frog prince," he whispered in my ear, as sweetly as if it had been another kind of embrace.

"What?" I looked up with another rough little chuckle of my own. Reflected ripples of light danced in his wet eyes as they met mine again.

He nodded. "Not Snow White. I'll be the frog prince, and this one is Aurora… Right?"

I wasn't too much of a wreck to laugh out loud. No sooner back from the dead than he was already flirting his way to what he wanted.

Yet... his top pick all along for our daughter's name would be the perfect way to honor her origin, this moment, and so much of what had gone between. "Aurora Craig it is," I agreed, shaking my head at him.

"Aurora Craig Araujo. Not Snow White either, but surely the fairest of them all."

"Yeah," I whispered, stroking a dark downy plume of her hair where it clung against his wet skin.

He bent his head to breathe in my ear again. "And we'll call the next one Jo."

The cloud-obscured sun, just now on the horizon, burnished the surface to dull copper as we emerged. Light snow fell around us. We all rode back together, some in rags and some in tags they'd stashed under a bulkhead, some in wetsuits, Elis laughingly wrapped up in just an emergency blanket so Geir could wear his own damn pants. Lachlan tucked another one around my little family, Aurora asleep on Geir's chest and me wonderingly awake against his shoulder. Brynja slept, too, cradled in the circle of Lachlan's arms. His eyes were also closed but I knew he was keeping his perceptions vigilantly wide open.

Ysmay, not Geir, hopped out to tie up the hover this morning. He didn't really like it. "Too bad for you, mister," I breathed in his ear. "You don't get to be the services generalist today."

To think I might have never felt his laugh against my skin again.

Cameras flashed from above us as Lachlan carried his exhausted queen to her bed, as the dead man walked up the steps on his own. For today, we let them look, even left the shutters open. I knew casts were going live when my ring began to light up like Christmas morning. I ignored it; except when I saw Vega's quick *TOLD YA SO*, and her locator showing Scalloway.

I invited her over at once. She, Elis, and Berenys pulled together a celebratory breakfast, arguing companionably in the kitchen the whole time. They even conjured some coquito with ingredients Vega swiped from her friend Will's place (no passionfruit, but somehow he had coconut milk). After she'd shared the lovely family meal and done a quick mother-and-baby checkup, she gave us our space, distributing heartfelt kisses and fond name-calling all around.

The rest of us lingered long enough, relishing one another's presence, that Brynja reemerged with a sleepy-eyed smile. She perched on Lachlan's lap, picked up a remaining piece of scone and jam from his plate, and leaned her head on his shoulder to eat it. Eyes falling sweetly closed, he kissed her forehead and ruffled her hair with one hand.

He opened his eyes again, wide and no longer smiling, to look at dozens of strands that had come away in his palm.

"Oh, my heart," she breathed, "it's okay."

The man who didn't even want someone else clearing the table or mooring the hovercraft couldn't bear to ask what price she'd paid for his return; neither could I.

She shook her regal head, shedding a few more strands. "First of all," she said, low and clear and more than a little scary as the old, deep-earth energy still radiated from her. "This was my decision to make, no one else's. And second." Now she spoke more quietly, and she looked into Lachlan's eyes. "I've kept enough for myself. For you. Yes, if it's like I remember, there will be some changes..." She touched his own temporarily short style, the corners of her mouth barely lifting. "But hair grows back."

His powerful chest slowly rose and fell with a deep breath, his gaze locked with hers. She smiled and kissed his tear-streaked face.

Just let them have the rest of his life together, I thought. Geir trembled.

Brynja turned to look at us. "I will say this one time," she stopped him, her clear voice authoritatively deep. "Even if somehow the worst were to happen, I would still have chosen the right way."

His eyes struggled up to find hers.

Maybe I never would grow accustomed to her astonishing laugh.

"No sooner do you finally begin to do what's required of you, than you try to leave us? I don't think so," she said, steady and low and smiling.

Her hand was gentler than her words as she reached to stroke Aurora's hair, where she lay contentedly in the crook of Geir's arm dressed in the mermaid tail coverup Ysmay had decided was the perfect party outfit.

"Okay," he managed to say quietly out loud, accepting his mission. "*Drøttenmín.*"

The armored spikes of Brynja's unspoiled lashes flicked a challenge toward the last guy standing.

Elis just smiled. "So get to work, golden boy," he deflected with ease. "You need us to clear the room, just say the word."

I giggled for him. No one was remotely ready for that yet, much as I treasured the chance to feel the inevitable temptation of my love's bright liquid eyes and the rest of him already.

Laughing, too, Geir kissed me for the benefit of our sweetly appreciative audience. *No rush*, we both remembered him assuring me once. That was Brynja's unimaginably great gift to us now.

"Ugh," Ysmay said when the embrace lingered beyond a few seconds, intentionally over-dramatic and provoking more laughter all around.

Elis smiled at her. "Where's a real gentleman when you need one, hey, Ys?"

"Sort of under self-imposed house arrest at the moment," she answered primly. "Hopefully not for long."

I happened to catch Berenys' unreadable, unsmiling eyes. They didn't hold mine.

"No, not for long," Brynja said. "We'll go today."

"I'll ring him today," Lachlan dared correct her gently, "and tell him we're coming soon."

Geir was unwilling to sleep that night, though the rest of us did. He sat on the bed at my side, the length of his leg pressed against my torso. When the baby stirred, I dragged myself awake too, rather than leave him a moment longer in the lonely state of alert that had seeped into my dreams.

Only later, once he gave in to exhaustion, could I really understand. It would linger for months in his nightmares like staring into the Challenger Deep, the abyss between, where even Brynja almost hadn't been able to find and keep hold of him. We would wake in a shared cold sweat, holding each other tighter than passion had ever compelled us. Letting Aurora sleep on his chest usually helped restore him to his accustomed slightly-smiling calm, but he didn't ever want to fall asleep with her there and risk contaminating her peaceful baby dreams.

Chapter 40

Tromsø

Though many of those staffing the hospital were once again UFPKs, the energy was completely different today than when Vega had worked here, or days ago when I'd been the patient. Ióar and his folk were isolated on one hallway, surrounded by armed guards.

At first, I couldn't place the tall, muscular peacekeeper who met us at the door. Her elegant little welcoming bow was twice touching: because it was so like Brynja's selkie gesture in reply, and for the resulting hundredth shock of missing Dr. Shimizu.

"Charlie from Atlanta, daughter of Chi-Mei from Shanghai," my queen greeted her.

"Lady Brynja," the PK responded. The cute accent and friendly grin reminded me where we'd met. Her brown eyes lifted to mine with the quickest wink. Maybe she remembered offering me potato chips in the cockpit of her helo, too.

"You're back," I said to Kuo with a wondering smile.

"And you're home." She smiled too, brows lifting.

Geir pressed my hand and agreed with his whole selkie heart.

Thyra was the only one who still required medical attention. Kuo escorted us to her door, opened it but remained standing outside. Two counterparts, much smaller but no less intimidating, greeted us. Brynja must have delegated what would have been her own role to two of the oldest women who had come here from the other islands when the news broke. They'd been on the craft to Bressay with us but I didn't remember their names. The shieldmaidens parted, heads bent, for Brynja.

Halfdan sat on one side of the bed where Thyra slept, with his back to us and a hand on her slight shoulder; on the other side, Kjeld's leaf-brown eyes lifted to us. Ióar turned from where he'd been looking out through the blinds at the tranquil bay gilded by late afternoon sun. He didn't smile.

Geir squeezed my hand tight and let it go. Without a word, Brynja had him enter the room first.

Ióar caught him in a hug precisely as fierce as he could withstand right now, the force of his pure gratitude blurring my eyes. When I managed to clear them, the Norwegians' leader was joining Halfdan and Kjeld, who had already knelt at the feet of our death-defying queen. Síarr, eyes rooted to the gleaming floor tiles, stayed where he'd sat half-hidden on the far side of Thyra's bed.

I didn't get all the words Ióar said, but their purpose was clear enough: deepest apology, unresisting surrender to whatever consequence she chose for the ones who had brought destruction to her shores.

She didn't answer in words, or even shake her head. Gesturing with only her fingertips, she asked them to stand.

Ióar pulled his shirt off over his head, let it fall at his heels. His hands stayed slightly lifted, palms forward in a gesture of surrender. There was an ugly gash from his left wrist up to his bicep, closed with numerous tape strips, and smaller punctures and cuts to his arms and torso. It didn't look like he'd had much selkie energy therapy to help them heal. I remembered Stavanger, when none of his people had been willing or able to bail him out. He was in an infinitely more challenging spot now.

Brynja spoke soberly, her voice a wisp of mist over the water. He nodded and lowered his eyes. Something about how she wished she could be the one.

Then she started speaking pairs of names. Elis went to wake Thyra with a particularly respectful and distant touch. Gyða and Kjeld sat together on the tiny sleeper couch beside the bed. Ysmay and Holm. Ailsa, from the Hebrides, with Halfdan. Muirgen, the oldest Irish one, with Síarr.

Geir made sure he wasn't required. Then he took the baby from me and retreated to the corridor. It wasn't only that she'd begun stirring in her sling and we didn't want her disrupting what needed to take place here. Still trusting Ióar was one thing, but he wasn't able to remain for more than a few aching heartbeats with the rest of them yet.

Brynja didn't say the last two names, just drew a line with her eyes from Berenys' face to Ióar.

"I can't," Berenys protested in her usual English.

"I can't," Brynja corrected her in the fiercest sotto voce. "You won't. Maybe you'd like to see what happens to Geir if we make him try."

As I looked around at the ones who had complied, I understood Berenys' reluctance. Each loyal subject silently embraced one suspected of breaking the peace of Brynja's undersea kingdom. Some still in undergarments, others bare to the waist like Ióar, no one had gone full-on naturist, but they needed skin to skin.

I watched Ysmay, delicate and small even in the arms of a finman. She stood there in one of her child-size tank tops and petted Holm Innes' hair as if he'd been a cat. He sighed out a slow breath and didn't resist her, though her eyes snapped open in a glare that was disapproving even for her.

Berenys' jaw tightened visibly but she, too, obeyed in her way.

"I wish you didn't have to go through all this," she said in English, whispery and low. "Of course you could never have betrayed us."

"I wish a lot of things could have been different," Ióar murmured. "I always will. But we can only go forward."

She echoed his rueful smile for a moment before unbuttoning her silky blouse with unsteady fingers. She didn't take it off, just left it open in the center for her heartbeat to sync with his. Then the judge wrapped her slender arms around the naked torso of the accused. He kept his arms near his sides, raised just enough for her to reach through. She took a sharp breath, laid her cheek against his chest and shoulder. Listening to his heart, his breath, his thoughts, memories, and intentions. He bent his head toward hers, but otherwise stood straight and still, eyes closed.

The movement in my peripheral vision was Halfdan, who seemed to have been cleared of any wrongdoing already. Shallower water, I guessed, quicker search. Still, it was nice to confirm that he was as unpolluted and bright throughout as his surface appeared. He smiled without rancor at Ailsa and picked up his shirt and jacket. She ruffled his hair as if he'd been a son.

My eyes fell upon Gyða, taking her time listening in on Kjeld's consciousness: a slower process that eventually involved a few whispered words from him, then tears, not on his part but on hers. They went on holding each other in stillness, cheek to cheek, quite a while after I would have guessed she'd confirmed he was one of the good guys too. At last, he pressed a kiss against her forehead. Her wet eyes, still grief-shadowed, lifted unhurriedly to hold his. Brynja's conservation agenda at first sight, perhaps. He nodded in answer to whatever she hadn't said, took his sweater, and walked over to join his brothers.

Ysmay came to stand at Gyða's side then, and placed a light hand upon the other woman's shoulder. More tears spilled over as she looked upward, not at Ysmay but somewhere more distant. She nodded.

I saw the defined moment when Berenys' trial of Ióar also became an embrace: when her hands moved comfortingly over the marble musculature of his back, he rested his cheek against her hair and his arms went around her.

"Where is forward?" she whispered in that way she had, as if minutes had not passed since he'd said it. "Will you go home now?"

She didn't see the careful smile that sent an ache shooting down my sternum, into my belly. "Do you mean you'd like me to go?"

Berenys slipped free as she hesitated. Saltwater trembled on her lashes, spilled down to spot the silk when she bent her head to button her blouse.

She spoke without looking up. "If I meant I'd like to be in Norway at least part of the time, and I'd want you there... What would you say?"

A magnificent magical creature such as himself didn't have to say a thing.

Just then Ysmay came to my side, her cool exterior belying a bundle of unsettled energies as soon as she bumped against me. Not only was she thoroughly done with Holm Innes, but she was not about to miss this moment.

She'd always been able to feel her twin, whether they were touching or not. Usually, Ysmay had confided to me before, she hated experiencing her sister's sensations of romantic desire. Not this time. When Berenys reached for just the fingertips of Ióar's outstretched hands, her thrill of fear and hope and tentative pleasure lit Ysmay from within like an electrical storm, surging over to me as Ysmay's little fingers tightened around my arm. He was thinking of her bravery in releasing her books of secrets to the world. While we'd been home awaiting Aurora and Geir, Ióar had been here: waiting too, reading and re-reading every wondrous page of the small volumes stacked in her basket.

"Oh," Berenys breathed, and broke contact again to reach inside her discarded jacket for the latest sequel. I recognized its lapis-blue marbled cover--the one she'd had with her while they were coaxing Geir back to this side of the world. She offered it unhesitatingly to Ióar, who answered with a honey-slow smile as he slipped the treasure into his own pocket.

"Your usual flawless timing. Liv rang me just this morning to see what you might have relating to recent events. She's far from the only one who'll never get enough of you."

Berenys let herself be drawn near enough again to steal that spellbinding smile with a hummingbird sip of a first kiss. He stroked her unbound hair a few times, his hands bright white against the black velvet strands he barely touched. Though he returned her kiss with the utmost delicacy, it was still enough to make her shiver and send a glittering tear spilling down the pale face she turned aside for a moment. Daring to sense so much of him had been challenge enough. Allowing him to begin to do the same in return was much scarier.

The hand that smoothed the tear away remained to cradle her cheek and the nape of her neck, encouraging her streaming eyes to meet his. Ysmay held her breath and gripped my arm with hope desperate enough to leave slight pink bruises I wouldn't notice until later.

Once upon a time, I'd found sharing one person's consciousness overwhelming; now, as Berenys began to let Ióar in at last, I found there was room in my mind and spirit for four of us. Awash in such a moment as this, Ysmay and I hardly existed: it felt like something akin to the first time Geir had let my hair down in Inverness, together with the morning he'd brought me the magic ring in Stavanger, to the tenth power. Offering as much as he demanded, and more.

Finally, Berenys let out her pent-up breath in a shaky sigh, laid her head against his chest in an echo of before, and let him hold her close. When he dared to bend his head lower, to brush a white-hot kiss against the pulse pounding just below the silken skin of her tight throat, I managed to pull my hand free from Ysmay's.

"Okay, since when are you into this?" I whispered with an un-accusing laugh under my breath, as her echo of her sister's emotions swelled stronger.

Ysmay giggled voicelessly, and grabbed my wrist again anyway. The tentative kiss in her slightly unnerved mental image was hypothetical, not a replay of this one, although they would have looked almost identical on the outside. Ysmay adored him so completely she'd even considered trying to be what he needed if Berenys wouldn't. But he was worthy of so much more than her reluctance; he perfectly embodied everything she'd wanted for her sister. Her wide eyes gleamed, remembering the morning he'd appeared in their flat: the eager spark flaring from herself to Berenys, the struggle ever since to convince her twin to muster the courage for this moment.

From the hallway, Aurora announced it was past time to wrap up the proceedings. Brynja, resting against Lachlan's shoulder, opened her eyes to give me a smile of the purest royal favor. She gestured to Halfdan, who was nearest the door.

While Geir and I placated the newly ravenous bairn, Brynja touched each of her surrogate judges to confirm what they had learned. Ysmay stood and went to her mother last; all it took to communicate everything was her little tapered fingertips smoothing away Brynja's weary grief.

Our queen closed her eyes for a few moments. "Gyða," she said in softly audible Norn. "You know already?"

Gyða whispered yes. Kjeld squeezed her hand, etched lines of regret aging him uncustomarily closer to his actual years.

I hadn't been watching Berenys when she turned away from Ióar. Now all three weird sisters trained their collective gaze on Holm Innes, intent as orca matriarchs leading the hunt.

Brynja raised the volume of her voice while the pitch remained low, authoritative. She was asking Gyða to name what she wanted from him in recompense.

Gyða sighed a gust of tears, but spoke to Holm directly. Her cadence was pure North Sea music, untouched by any hint of English. "Why Ruadh?" I understood clearly; and then, I thought, something like Why a lad who never hurt a single soul?

Holm's dark eyes and his jaw were stony as ever as he shook his head, but his voice sounded softer than I'd heard it before. I thought he said he'd known nothing at that moment, beyond the need to defend their only home. And—a stitch caught in my chest, like when I'd once found Seoras drowned in Lerwick Harbor—that he hadn't recognized Ruadh at the time.

Her focus lowered, her voice even quieter now. She was asking if he'd known her love for a selkie at all… Or if he'd supposed it was some common seal, caught in the dark and cold of what their human selves were doing to one another.

He bent his head too, and didn't answer.

"I know," she whispered. When she looked up again, her face was turned toward Brynja's. Asking only that he be gone from among their kind, that she and Sefa need never see his face again. He could do nothing to bring Ruadh back... not even her *drøttenmin* could have. But, she asked, let him find a woman somewhere far from here, if it might be, and give the world a new boy to replace the good man he'd taken from it.

Berenys shuddered with stifling a sob and Ysmay clenched her teeth visibly, but when Brynja solemnly nodded, no one argued.

Last, our queen reached for Geir's hand. Asking the question even I hadn't dared.

But he refused her touch. "Is there anything of me that you haven't seen, now?"

Brynja smiled just barely, despite the gravity of the moment.

"Then you know who. Just as you know he did what he thought he must, and you know I wouldn't have wanted his life to be forfeit as it was."

"Yes, my heart," she said, looking at all three of us. "Life, and not death, is our way."

Geir's nod mirrored the trust in her leadership that he felt within.

She nodded, too. "I can't speak for the authorities elsewhere in Scotland, or--" she glanced pointedly in Síarr's direction-- "for those in Japan. But for our kind... We can spare no one here; everyone may stay. Knowing we have seen your hearts." She lost her hint of smile. "Knowing that in the future, anyone of our kind who commits such violence against another will leave the lands that touch the North Sea forever."

Only then did she ask Íoar. "Brother. Do you agree?"

"My queen," Íoar murmured, bending his head in assent.

Síarr remained behind with Thyra when the rest of us left the hospital. I spent as little emotion as I could on the question of whether they would stay on Shetland, try to become part of the offered family. Heaven knew it would be a long time before I could find anything to say to either of them; or to Holm, who took off on his own as soon as we were out the doors. All I could honestly do was raise my child, keep up my life's other work, and hope in doing so to earn their trust.

Some twenty more had gathered outside in a thickening mist to greet us. Drones popped above, a few capturing what would become award-winning images of powerful small bodies, miraculous pale hands, and wide-set teardrop eyes, united and still in one silent embrace amid swirls of earthbound cloud. Standing near the center with Geir and Aurora, I thought no camera had yet been invented that could record the healing truly beginning here. Elis and his new team should make that a priority.

When I turned their way during the hover ride home, I glimpsed three beloved souls in particular still sitting close together, with no need to talk among themselves. Berenys' right fingertips intertwined with Ióar's left on the empty seat between them, their eyes only for one another, while Ysmay curled against his right shoulder, absurd lashes sweetly lowered. Hours later, when he hugged me goodbye after all who wanted had shared a quiet dinner, I noticed how fast the wounds on both his arms had faded from angry red to pale sunrise pink.

Lachlan, Brynja, and Elis went down to Inverness for Christmas. Geir and I stayed behind with her girls and our own. They'd be back in time for the winter fire festivals when our favorite Viking hybrid joined dozens more, parading in costume to throw their torches onto a replica ship, blazing defiance against the dark season. Both my parents, I thought, would have loved it.

By then, late January, the Shetland finfolk population swelled to a hundred and nineteen: minus four who'd been here, plus a steady trickle from the other islands as our new kingdom took shape. Several more began living openly in their current homes, including a very few happy surprises who contacted us from northernmost Norway. Some folk wanted to stay in their quiet caverns, at least for now. I had no idea where Thyra and Síarr took off for, and didn't care to know. Halfdan stayed, and took finding the right selkie bride very seriously, based on the pleasure and zeal with which he dove into the opportunity now that it presented itself. Kjeld, on the other hand, appeared to be biding his time.

Ióar was gone by then, though he'd stayed a while, too, renting a hovercraft and a little cottage not far up the Sandness coast. Although he never invited Berenys there, he came by most days to see her. I'd never forget his amazed pleasure the first time she cooked for him in her own proper kitchen. Other times, he'd taken her for boat rides, meals out, walks on the shore. Until one afternoon, when he advised her to wear something even prettier than usual so they could go to dinner at a picturesque spot he'd found.

They weren't back that night, or the next morning. With a knowing smirk, Ysmay told us the spot was a quiet inn, located in Tromsø. She'd rejoin them, there or wherever, just not yet.

She took Aurora off our hands as much as we let her. It was a delight just to be together without any of the stresses of the outgoing year and catch up on sleeping, and not sleeping, and show the baby her glorious namesake, and watch my tesoro regain his strength. Every day we'd swim with the seals, as well as whoever else might have come to visit. It wasn't too cold for any of us selkies, Geir and I in our suits, Ysmay and her friends and the baby within their sealskins.

Berenys rang me some days later,

not fool enough to suppose i matched you for valor…. but how do you bear these Old ones Knowing things? … yet all this time the treasure's hid with them

She included a candid photo of the gorgeous couple at a candlelit table, with a view of the sun low over the ocean, if they'd ever taken their eyes off one another. I was sure the inn was thrilled to host celebrities, but I wondered whether they knew this was a royal honeymoon: the "happily" page in the newly discovered fairytale where the black swan declared her love for the former ugly duckling. Not that I (or he, surely) expected her to be done causing trouble ever after, for him or anyone else--both of them being the complicated blends of beast and beauty they were. I still felt a surge of pride at having accomplished my part in the mission that had come to me once upon a dream.

Geir smiled too when he saw the photo, but he shook his head.

"You do know I was meant to sweep you off your feet like that, don't you?" he murmured, rolling his eyes toward me.

I laughed softly. "What you should be asking is why someone as fascinating as Ióar has to work that hard to win someone who's usually up for whatever… while you can get a woman who was pretty sure she was done with men forever to fall at your feet, just by tipping your cap her way."

He laughed too, and slipped his arms around my waist from behind, such that I could have immediately forgotten my own question. "I'll never ask that," he breathed just below my ear. "I know when I'm out of my depth."

I pressed my cheek against his. My own nature had swept me off my feet all my life. Smiling, I remembered him holding me up, rock-steady, once upon a time in a pool under Out Skerries. I would never want it any other way again.

Epilogue
Faerieland

When I eventually swept him off his feet instead, we had the magic words my dad would have liked, there being none for this in selkiese. My stylish Queen B consulted with the inimitable Siobhan to choose my simple silk and tulle gown, not white but my blush tint from Inverness. She and her prince didn't arrive together, although they seemed plenty on-again during our gathering. Her twin wove small honey-scented pink orchids into my unbound hair. The princess Aurora Noa Craig Araujo, near-universally known as Ro by then, was newly walking; she had a little dress to match mine, and a crown of pink baby's breath. We came down the aisle together, the glitter of mosaic eyes smiling solemnly from all sides of the chapel.

My gorgeous fairy godmother and maid of honor asked the family's opinions, not mine, on what to sing during the delicious pescatarian reception. They chose as wonderfully as she sang every piece. My groom got to share the Tchaikovsky waltz he'd missed hearing her sing the first time, dancing with both his pink-gowned lady loves together. He'd argued with the songstress over the good old Orkney folk tune, Vega rightly pointing out that it was a complete downer unsuitable for any party, let alone a wedding. But her deliberately quiet alto rendition transformed the simple folk melody into something even more beautiful, more entirely ours. This once, she didn't stop me from singing quietly along, either with that number or my Gershwin favorite, from my seat at our flower-strewn table with Ro on my lap.

Equally amazing was her bringing a date we already knew. The same karaoke night, when her handsome anthropologist-bartender served Champagne cocktails to her and the girlfriends he vaguely noticed, hadn't been the first time his rolled R had curled her toes. That hadn't even been the evening I'd stormed out of May's place, then assumed Anton's debatable charms had kept her out so late. She'd partly been trying to prove he didn't mean so much to her when she volunteered to leave Shetland, even as she left the bridge unburned (then well-traveled) by going no farther than London.

Our best man, who showed up impeccably stag, only claimed Vega had broken his selkie heart. The fact he hadn't brought a date meant no local woman's heart was safe, single or otherwise. He did contribute our unprecedented freedom to pick a location: by then he and his team had isolated enough of the precious North Sea minerals and salts they all required, that they could comfortably travel at least to other parts of Europe.

We chose Venice, taking a delightfully roundabout way there on a couple of family yachts. Other than its Scottish elder sister scattering of linked tiny islands, it was the most magical place I'd experienced. I wanted to show my frog prince the winter faerieland of swirling mists and blurred edges, knowing he might well live long enough for the rising seas to reclaim what was left of it. Elis even arm-twisted him into purchasing a most becoming new Italian suit.

He promised, if we gave him a few more years to work at it, he'd get us a dream Caribbean honeymoon, too. I smiled, a willing believer. The power of our collective dreams was no mere story.

Acknowledgments

Thanks, with my whole faerie heart, to

The watery-named family that raised me to love literal travel adventures as well as story-spelunking. You empowered me to explore as far as I could go, to map the caverns formed by godmother-earths who wrote before me, and to gather the sparkliest mosaic bits scattered over Europe, the Americas and beyond. You were, and are, my foundation.

Along with them, the family I've chosen, made, and found. George, Leo, Gem, first and foremost; but also my Hallway, and many who have created/storytold/participated in the song of the world with me. You spoke life to my dreams, boosted me to reach higher places, offered me a soft place to rage, figured out how to divert water that stood in my way, and helped me choose the most suitable glue.

All who've brought my earlier work to light, beginning once upon a time with another mosaic in an undersea cave. I've loved being found and featured in your travel guides—no matter how far off the beaten path my stuff was. (A note to readers: there's a linktree of these awesome organizations and zines on my "About the Author" page.)

Fantasy_Art_Z, whose intuition crystallized the story into one wondrous image, and Mariah Norris, who translated that into a brilliant cover. In the hands of the right artists, sometimes I really can't tell technology apart from magic.

Zinsy, my friend for a selkie's age and counting, the first to say these thoughts had been worth writing where other people could see them, and my tireless sounding board, indulger of my megalomaniacal daydreams, and fellow ogler of potential selkie lads ever since. Your recharging efforts have helped my rebreather scrubber cartridge last an astonishing seven years.

Last but not least, all the fabulously supportive people I've met at Shadow Spark Publishing, for whom my reckless disregard for genre boundaries was (finally!) an asset rather than a liability. Especially Dan Fitzgerald: bro, I don't get how you jury-rigged your headlamp into that small searchlight/spotlight situation, but thank you for declaring in so many ways that this story really should be in the world.

Ashley Anglin

The first real novel Ashley Bevilacqua Anglin read, age 6ish, was The Lion, The Witch, and the Wardrobe. Never looking back, she's still hanging out with valiant female protagonists at the intersection of contemporary fantasy, climate fiction, and the spiritual. Her passion for storytelling led her to a Ph.D. in Comparative Literature and Linguistics. Her short stories and poetry have appeared in Panthology, also from Shadow Spark; in Everything Change, Vol. I (as runner-up in ASU Imagination and Climate Futures Initiative's Climate Fiction Short Story Contest); and online in Miniskirt, Minison, Full Mood, and Tree and Stone magazines.

Ashley lives with her Jamerican family in Virginia, where she is a long-time community college professor of Italian and Spanish. You can find her on Twitter @dalyashleydrH2o, and her previous work (including other glimpses of the Undiscovered world) at https://linktr.ee/ashleyb.anglin

www.ingramcontent.com/pod-product-compliance
Lightning Source LLC
Chambersburg PA
CBHW011217190726
48287CB00008B/2649